PART OF YOUR WORLD

A TWISTED TALE

LIZ BRASWELL

Disney PRESS

Los Angeles • New York

*A special thank-you to organizations who help
save creatures under and around the sea, like the
Mass Audubon's Wellfleet Bay Wildlife Sanctuary.*

Printed in the United States of America
First Hardcover Edition, September 2018
3 5 7 9 10 8 6 4 2
FAC-020093-18330
Library of Congress Control Number: 2018931464
ISBN 978-1-368-01381-9

Visit disneybooks.com

SUSTAINABLE FORESTRY INITIATIVE
Certified Sourcing
www.sfiprogram.org
SFI-00993

THIS LABEL APPLIES TO TEXT STOCK

To Elizabeth (the) Schaefer, who started off the series as one of my editors, and continues on as a good friend.

This book is for everyone who helps protect Ariel's ocean—which includes *you*, whenever you eat sustainable seafood and skip the straw!

—*L.B.*

Prologue

In the foothills of the Ibrian Mountains . . .

Cahe Vehswo was in the field repairing a wooden fence. It was less to keep the wolves out than to keep the stupid sheep *in*, where the only slightly smarter child-shepherds could watch them.

It was a beautiful day, almost sparkling. The pines weren't yet brittle from late summer heat and the deciduous trees were in full glory, their dark green leaves crackling in the wind. The mountains were dressed in midseason blooms and tinkly little waterfalls. The clouds in the sky were ridiculously puffy.

The only off note in nature's symphony was a strange stink when the wind came up from the southern lowlands: burning animal fat, or garbage, or rot.

Everyone in the hamlet was out doing chores in such forgiving weather; rebuilding grapevine trellises, chopping wood, cleaning out the cheese barrels. No one was quarreling—yet—and life on their remote hillside seemed good.

Then Cahe saw something unlikely coming up the old road, the King's Road. It was a phalanx of soldiers, marching in a surprisingly solid and orderly fashion considering how far they were from whatever capital they had come. With their plumes, their buttons that shone like tiny golden suns, and their surprisingly clean jackets, there was almost a parade-like air around them. If not for their grim, haughty looks and the strange flag they flew.

An order was cried; the men stopped. The captain, resplendent in a bright blue cap and jacket, rode up to Cahe along with his one other mounted soldier, who carried their flag.

"Peasant," he called out—somewhat rudely, Cahe thought. "Is this the township of Serria?"

"No," the farmer started to say, then remembered long-forgotten rules for dealing with people who had shiny buttons, big hats—and guns. "Begging your pardon, sir, but that's farther along, on the other side of Devil's Pass. People call this Adam's Rock."

"No matter," the captain said. "We claim this village and its surrounding lands in the name of Tirulia!"

He cried out the last bit, but the words bounced and drifted and faded into nothing against the giant mountains beyond, the dusty fields below, the occasional olive tree, the uninterested cow. Villagers stopped their work and drifted over to see what was going on.

"Begging your pardon again, sir," Cahe said politely. "But we're considered part of—and pay our taxes to—Alamber."

"*Whatever your situation was before,* you are now citizens of Tirulia, and pay homage to Prince Eric and Princess Vanessa."

"Well, I don't know how the king of Alamber will take it."

"That is no concern of yours," the captain said frostily. "Soon the king of Alamber will just be a memory, and all Alamber a mere province in the great Tirulian empire."

"You *say* Tirulia," Cahe mused, leaning on the fence to make his statement sound casual. "We know it. We buy their salted cod and trade our cheese with them. Their girls like to wear aprons with braided ties. Perde, son of Javer, sought his fortune down south on a fishing ship and wound up marrying a local girl there."

"Fascinating," the captain said, removing one hand from his tight grip on the reins to fix his mustache. "And what is the point of all this?"

Cahe pointed at the banner that flapped in the breeze. "That is not the flag of Tirulia."

In place of the sun and sea and ship on a field of blue that was familiar even to these isolated people, there was a stark white background on which a black-tentacled octopus with no eyes gibbered menacingly. It looked almost alive, ready to grab whatever came too close.

"Princess Vanessa thought it was time to . . . update the sigil of house Tirulia," the captain said, a little defensively. "We still represent Tirulia and the interests of Prince Eric, acting for his father, the king, and his mother, the queen."

"I see." Another villager started to speak up, but Cahe put a hand on his arm to stop him. "Well, what can we do, then? You have guns. We have them, too—to hunt with— but they are put away until the boars come down from the oak forests again. So . . . as long as the right tax man comes around and we don't wind up paying twice, sure. We're part of Tirulia now, as you say."

The captain blinked. He narrowed his eyes at Cahe, expecting a trick. The farmer regarded him mildly back.

"You have chosen a wise course, peasant," the captain finally said. *"All hail Tirulia."*

The folk of Adam's Rock murmured a ragtag and unenthusiastic response: *all hail Tirulia.*

"We shall be back through this way again after we

subdue Serria. Prepare your finest quarters for us after our triumph over them and all of Alamber!"

And with that the captain shouted something unintelligible and militaristic and trotted off, the flag bearer quickly catching up.

As soon as they were out of earshot, Cahe shook his head wearily.

"Call a meeting," he sighed. "Pass the word around . . . we need to gather the girls and send them off into the hills for mushroom gathering or whatever—for several weeks. All the military-aged boys should go into the wilds with the sheep. Or to hunt. Also, everyone should probably bury whatever gold or valuables they have someplace they won't be found."

"But why did you just give in to him?" the man next to Cahe demanded. "We could have sent word to Alamber. If we'd just told the soldiers no, we wouldn't have to do *any* of this, acting like cowards and sending our children away into safety. . . ."

"I did it because I could smell the wind. Can't you?" Cahe answered, nodding toward the south.

Just beyond the next ridge, where the Veralean Mountains began to smooth out toward the lowlands, a column of smoke rose. It was wider and more turbulent than what would come from a bonfire, black and ashy and ugly as sin.

"Garhaggio?" someone asked incredulously. It did indeed look like the smoke was coming from there. From the volume and blackness there could have only been scorched earth and embers where that village had been just the day before.

"I bet *they* told the captain no," Cahe said.

"Such causeless destruction!" a woman lamented. "What terrible people this Prince Eric and Princess Vanessa must be!"

Eric

Eric woke up.

He was having that dream again.

It came to him at the strangest times—when reviewing the menu for a formal dinner with Chef Louis, for instance, or listening to the castle treasurers discuss the ups and downs of dealing with international bankers. Or when his beautiful princess went on and on about her little intrigues.

All right: it was when he was bored and tired. If a room was stuffy and he was sleepy and could barely keep his eyes open.

Or right before he fell asleep properly, in bed—that moment between still being awake and deep in dreams. The same split-second when he often heard angelic choirs singing unimaginably beautiful hymns. He could only listen, too frozen in half-sleep to jump up and quickly scribble it down before he forgot.

But sometimes, instead of the choirs, he had this:

That he was not Prince Eric wed to Vanessa, the beautiful princess. That there had been some terrible mistake. That there was another girl, a beautiful girl with no voice, who could sing.

No—

There was a beautiful girl who could sing, who somehow lost her voice forever on the terrible day when Eric fell asleep. He had been dreaming ever since.

There were mermaids in this other world.

He had known one. Her father was a god. Eric's princess was an evil witch. And Eric had touched greatness but been tricked, and now here he was, dreaming. . . .

He looked down suddenly, in a panic. His arms were crossed on his desk over pages of musical notation, supporting his dozing head. Had he spilled any ink? Had he blurred any notes? A rest could be turned into a tie if the ink smeared that way . . . and that would ruin everything. . . .

He held the papers up to the moonlight. There was a little smudging, there, right where the chorus was supposed to come in with a D major triad. But it wasn't so bad.

His eyes drifted from the pages to the moon, which

shone clearly through his unglazed window. A bright star kept it company. A faint breeze blew, causing the thick leaves of the trees below to make shoe-like clacking noises against the castle wall. It carried with it whatever scents it had picked up on its way from the sea: sandalwood, sand, oranges, dust. Dry things, stuff of the land.

Eric looked back at his music, tried to recapture the sound and feel of the ocean that had played in his head before waking, aquamarine and sweet.

Then he dipped his pen in ink and began to scribble madly, refusing to rest until the sun came up.

Scuttle

It seemed as if all of Tirulia were crowded into the amphitheatre. Every seat was filled, from the velvet-cushioned couches of the nobles up front to the high, unshaded stone benches in the far back. More people spilled out into the streets beyond. No one was going to miss the first performance of a new opera by their beloved Mad Prince Eric.

It was like a festival day; everyone wore whatever colorful thing and sparkly gem they had. Castle guards stood in polished boots along the aisles, making sure no fights broke out among the spectators. Vendors walked among the crowds both inside and out selling the bubbly, cold white wine Tirulia was known for along with savory little treats: bread topped with triangles of cheese and olive oil, paper cones filled with crispy fried baby squid, sticks threaded with honey-preserved chestnuts that glittered in the sunlight.

It would all have made a fabulous mosaic of movement and colors and dazzle from above.

And it did for a certain old seagull named Scuttle, who was quite enjoying the view.

He and a few of his great-grandgulls (sent along to watch him) perched on the rail above the highest, cheapest seats in the theatre. While the younger ones kept their sharp eyes alert for dropped morsels, ready to dive down at the tiniest crumb of bread, Scuttle contented himself with just watching the pomp and muttering to himself. Only one great-grandgull remained by his side, trying to understand what he saw in the human spectacle below.

The costumes were lavish, the orchestra full, the sets cunningly painted to look more than real: when a prince produced a play, wealth showed.

And when that prince came out to take his seat in the royal box, arm in arm with his beautiful princess, the crowd went mad, howling and cheering for their royal artist. Sometimes called the Dreamer Prince and even the Melancholic Prince for his faraway looks and tendency toward wistfulness, Eric looked momentarily cheered by this expression of love from his kingdom, and waved back with the beginnings of a real smile.

Vanessa gave one of her grins, inscrutable and slightly

disturbing, and pulled him along to sit down. With her other hand she stroked the large nautilus necklace she always wore—a strangely plain and natural-looking ornament for the extravagant princess.

The orchestra tuned, and began.

La Sirenetta, a Musical Fantasy in Three Acts

In a magical kingdom by the sea, a sad and handsome prince *[tenor]* longs for someone to share his music and his life. While he and his friends celebrate his twenty-first birthday on a decorated yacht, a terrible storm arises. The prince is thrown over the railing of his ship and is almost drowned but for the intercession of a young and beautiful mermaid, who has the voice of an angel *[first soprano]*.

Upon recovering, the prince declares he will marry no one but the beautiful girl who rescued him.

Then a *different* beautiful girl appears *[same first soprano, different costume]*, who, although she has the shining red hair of the mermaid who saved him, is *mute*! So she cannot be his one true love. And yet, as they spend their days together, he slowly falls for her.

But then a rival comes onto the scene. A handsome woman *[contralto]* serenades the prince with the same song the little mermaid once sang and casts a spell over him, causing him to forget the pretty girl with no voice.

[Note: The contralto is a large, full-busted singer, a favorite of the audience. She gets a standing ovation when she appears, smiling slyly.]

Hypnotized, the prince arranges for the two of them to be wed immediately.

In an aside, the princess-to-be admits to the audience that she is actually a powerful sea witch. She desires revenge on the mermaid, whose father, the King of the Sea, cast the witch out of his kingdom years before. By failing to marry the prince herself, the mermaid will have neglected to uphold her end of a bargain, and the sea witch will keep her voice forever.

The sun *[baritone]* then sings about the tragedy of mortal life, which he has to witness every day among the humans below him on earth. He also sings about the peaceful happiness of the immortal mermaids, and how love makes one foolish—but exalted. He drifts across the stage, and, with a clever bit of scenic machinery, begins to "set" as the ballet troupe comes out for an interlude before the finale: the wedding scene.

The prince and the false princess come out dressed

splendidly and singing a duet—but the prince's words are about love, and the princess's are about conquest. The mute girl looks sadly on.

Then, just as the prince and princess are about to recite their final vows, Triton, King of the Sea *[bass]*, resplendent in green and gold armor, appears with a crash of drums. He and the sea witch sing back and forth, trading insults. Finally he raises his trident to attack . . . and the sea witch points to his youngest, favorite daughter, the now-mute human standing sadly in the corner. With her other hand, she shakes a large painted prop contract.

Defeated, Triton gives in. He trades his life for the little mermaid. The sea witch casts a terrible spell, and with a puff of theatrical smoke the King of the Sea is turned into an ugly little sea polyp, which the sea witch holds triumphantly aloft.

[As a puppet manipulated by the contralto, it even moves a little, which draws a gasp from the audience.]

Triton's daughter turns back into a mermaid and jumps sadly into the sea. The prince and the false princess are married. The false princess croons triumphantly to the little polyp that was once Triton, and talks about how she will keep him forever in a vase in her room.

The moon *[mezzo-soprano]* comes out and sings an ethereal, haunting version of the sun's aria. But hers is about the inevitability and sadness of love, and questions what makes a happy ending. For if the little mermaid had stayed at home and remained a mermaid for all her days, ignorant of love, would that really have been better?

Scuttle

The crowd went mad. If the subject matter of the opera seemed a little fantastic, if the end a little gloomy, if the orchestration maybe just a *tad* simplistic compared to works by more professional, starving musicians—well, it mattered not. Never before had the amphitheatre been witness to such a display of clapping, screaming, stomping of feet, and whistling. So many roses were thrown at *La Sirenetta* and the sea witch that they were in danger of suffering puncture wounds from the thorns.

Everyone was already clamoring for an encore performance.

"Perhaps we should," Prince Eric said. "A free performance—for all of the town! At the end of summer, on St. Madalberta's Day!"

The cheers grew even louder.

Nobles seated closest to the royal box made a show of appropriately classy, restrained enthusiasm—while keeping their eyes on the prince and princess. Only a fool would have failed to notice certain similarities between the sea witch and Prince Eric's beautiful wife, Vanessa. That night in the great stone mansions, over tiny cups of chocolate and crystal glasses of brandy, there would be much discussion of the thousand possible shades of meaning behind the words in the lyrics.

But the brown-haired princess was grinning and laughing throatily.

"Eric," she purred, "that was positively *naughty*. And *wonderful*. Where do you *get* such *imaginative* ideas?"

She coquettishly took his hand like they were newlyweds and walked out proudly with him into the crowd, beaming as if she were also the mother of a very talented and precocious boy. Her two manservants trailed behind them, looking back and forth at the crowd with suspicious smiles, seemingly ready to kill at a moment's notice should it be required.

Nothing was required; everyone was joyous.

Among the hundreds of people and creatures that were audience to this spectacle, only one was flummoxed by it.

Scuttle stood stock-still, an unusual pastime for him. Two *very important things* had been revealed in the play. And while he was as scatterbrained as a seagull generally is

18

(perhaps more so), the wisdom of his long years made him stop and try to focus on those things in his muzzy mind, to remember them, to pay attention to his quieter thoughts.

"*PRINCE ERIC REMEMBERS WHAT HAPPENED!*" he suddenly cried out.

That was the first thing, and it was easy.

"Even with the whammy laid on him!"

Scuttle had been there when the land-walking mermaid had failed to win Eric's heart, the sun had gone down, and he had married Vanessa instead. Scuttle had seen the mighty fight break out between ancient powers, so poorly captured in the paints and papier-mâché below. He had seen the ocean swell and waves rent in twain by the power of Triton. He had watched as the King of the Sea traded his life for his daughter's and the sea witch, Ursula, destroyed him. The red-haired girl became a mermaid once more and swam sadly away, voiceless forever. Ursula-as-Vanessa remained married to Eric and now ruled the kingdom by the sea with little or no useful input from her hypnotized hubby.

"Yup, check and check," Scuttle murmured. "And somehow my boy Eric knows this. But how?"

And what was that other thing?

That important thing?

The . . . *almost-as-important* thing?

Or was it actually *more* important?

"*Waves rent in twain by the power of Triton,*" Scuttle

repeated to himself aloud because he enjoyed the sound of his voice and the big, epic words. His great-grandgulls rolled their eyes at each other and flew off. All but one, who sat watching him curiously.

"And the King of the Sea traded his life for his daughter's, and Ursula destroyed him. THAT'S IT!"

Scuttle squawked, jumping up into the air in excitement. He beat his wings and the few lingering spectators covered themselves with their arms in disgust, fearing what the bird would do next.

"KING TRITON IS STILL ALIVE!"

"I'm sorry?" his remaining great-grandgull asked politely.

"Don't you get it?" Scuttle turned to her and pointed at the stage. "If everything else in that show was true, then Ursula still has Triton as her *prisoner*! He's *not dead*! C'mon, Jonathan! We got to go do some investor-gating of this possibility!"

"My name is Jona, Great-Grandfather," the younger gull corrected gently.

He didn't seem to hear.

With a purpose he hadn't felt since his time with the mermaid Ariel, Scuttle beat new life into his tired old wings and headed for the castle, his great-grandgull gliding silently behind.

———

When the king and queen of Tirulia decided that the time had come for each of their children to assume the roles and habits of adulthood—and, more importantly, to move out of the main palace—Prince Eric quite unsurprisingly chose a small castle on the very edge of the sea.

The giant blocks that made its outer walls were sandstone, light in color and far more evocative of the beach than the granite and grey stone with which other ancient fortresses were built. A welcome addition by Eric's grandfather featured a walkway out to a viewing deck, supported by graceful arches in the manner of a Roman aqueduct. The two highest tiled towers cleverly recalled architecture of more eastern cities; a third was topped by a pergola covered with grapes and fragrant jasmine. The great formal dining room, another modern addition, was finished in the latest fashion with floor-to-ceiling windows.

In fact, all the public and fancy rooms—every single bedroom in the castle, except for the lowliest servants' quarters—had a view of the sea.

This was of great interest to the humans who lived in the castle, the villagers who bragged about their castle, and the Bretlandian visitors taking the Grand Tour who stopped to sketch the castle.

But the windows were of *especial* interest to the flying and scurrying members of the kingdom.

It was well known to all the local seagulls where the kitchens were, of course. Their windows were the most important. Boiled seashells, some with tidbits still stuck on; avalanches of crumbs that had gone stale; meat that had been left out too long; fruit that had rotted . . . All of it got dumped unceremoniously out the windows and into a hidden section of the lagoon. Hidden to humans, that is.

It was also well known that Countess Gertrude, a cousin of Eric's, was much enamored with anything that flew and could be counted on to stand at her window for hours, enticing gulls, doves, sparrows, and even sparrow hawks to land on her hand for a treat.

The Ibrian ambassador, Iase, paranoid and terrified of poison, was constantly tossing whatever he was served out the closest window.

Anything that got dumped out of Princess Vanessa's window, however, was known to be actually bad for you: sharp, and often *really* poisoned.

After a moment's precipitous scrabbling, Scuttle managed to perch himself on the lintel of this last unglazed window, his great-grandgull just beside him.

"Huh. Nice digs," he said, looking around with interest. Then he settled himself in to wait.

Seagulls might be a little scattered and unable to focus— sometimes greedy, and borderline psychotic if it came to fighting over a real prize—but the one thing they *could* do was wait. For hours if they had to: for the tide to go out, for the fishing ships to come back in, for the wind to change, for the pesky humans to leave their middens to those who so rightfully deserved to plunder them for treats.

Jona cocked her head once, observing a chambermaid dumping a chamber pot out the side of the castle, into the sea.

"And humans complain about *our* habits," she muttered.

"Shhh!" Scuttle said, keeping his beak closed.

Eventually their patience was rewarded. Vanessa came sashaying in, leaving her two manservants outside.

"I'll see you boys later," she purred. They bowed in unison, almost identical twins in matching uniforms that had costlier jackets and prettier feathered caps than other castle staff.

The princess began to disrobe, pulling off her gloves, her mantle, and the wide hat that topped her dark hair. This was brown velvet with golden medallions around the crown and the plumes of rare foreign birds in the band . . . and she still left it carelessly on her bed. She quietly hummed one of the arias from the opera, one of the *mermaid's* arias, and then opened her mouth wider and belted it out, knocking the seagulls back a little with the force of her musicality.

It did not sound like when Ariel used to sing.

Oh, it was the mermaid's voice all right, and the tune was dead-on. But it was too loud, and the words had no soul, and the notes didn't flow from one to the other harmoniously. It was as if a talented but untrained child with no life experience to speak of had suddenly been commanded to sing a piece about a woman dying of consumption who had lost her only love.

Scuttle tried not to wince. Seagulls of course had no innate musical abilities themselves—as other birds loved to taunt—but the song still sounded blasphemous in Ariel's voice.

Vanessa laughed, purred, and made other noises with her throat Ariel never would have. "Did you enjoy that, mighty sea king? The little song from a lovesick mermaid?"

"I don't see a mighty sea king," the great-grandgull whispered to Scuttle. *"Maybe she's mad."*

Scuttle had no response. He frowned and ducked and peered back and forth into every corner of the room that he could glimpse from the window. But there was nothing, not even a small aquarium, that might hold a polyp.

Vanessa paused in front of the overwhelming collection of bottles and trinkets on her vanity: musky perfumes in tiny glass ampoules, exotic oils in jars carved in pink stone, enough boar-bristled brushes to keep an army of princesses looking their best. The one thing she didn't have—which Scuttle would not have realized—was a maidservant performing these ablutions *for* her. She made a kissy-face into the mirror and then moved on, disappearing from view into her closet. It looked like she was holding something, but it was hard to be sure.

The two birds strained and leaned forward, trying to follow her movements.

"I'm so sorry you missed such a wonderful opera, Kingy," she called from the darkness. After a moment she came back out wearing a bright pink silk robe. Now they could see that she carried a bottle half hidden in her voluminous sleeve. "But I think Eric may put it on again, one more time. Not that you'll get to see it then, either. Such a shame! It was so *imaginative*. It was all about a little mermaid, and how she loses her prince to a nasty old sea witch. The *hussy*."

She paused . . . and then cracked up, her delicate mouth opening wider and wider and wider, billows of distinctly non-Ariel laughter coming out.

She turned to hold the glass bottle up to regard it in the light coming from the gull-decorated window . . . and the gulls gasped.

It was a narrow glass cylinder, like that which a scientist or a physic might use when doing experiments. On top was a piece of muslin held on with gobs of wax. Inside was filled with water . . . and one of the most horrible things Scuttle and Jona had ever seen.

A dark green mass, gelatinous, with a vaguely plant-like shape filled most of the bottle. One knobby end kept it rooted on the bottom of the glass. Toward its "head" were things that looked like tentacles but floated uselessly in the tiny space; these were topped with a pair of yellow eyes. A hideous cartoon of a mouth hung slackly beneath. In a final bit of terrible mockery two slimy appendages flowed down the sides of its mouth, aping the sea king's once foam-white mustache and beard.

The great-grandgull turned her head to avoid gagging.

"It's him!" Scuttle cried—at the last second covering his words with a squawk, remembering that the sea witch could understand the languages of all beasts, same as Ariel.

Vanessa spun quickly and suspiciously.

Jona thought fast. She pecked at her grandfather—realistically, as if she were trying to steal a morsel from him.

Scuttle squawked.

"What the . . ."

"*NO IT'S MY FISHY!*" Jona screamed. She widened her eyes at him, *willing* him to understand.

Her great-grandfather just stared at her for a moment.

Then he relaxed.

"What? Oh yeah, right," he said, giving her a big wink. "No—my—great-grandgull—that—is—my—fish!"

They both fell off the ledge, away into the air, wheeling and squawking like perfectly normal seagulls.

Vanessa ran to the window but relaxed when she saw just a pair of birds, fighting in midair over some nasty piece of something-or-other. With a snarl and a flounce she turned back inside.

"That was some pretty smart thinking back there," Scuttle said, giving his great-grandgull a salute.

"What now?" she asked.

"Now? We go find *Ariel.*"

Atlantica

Far, far below the wine-dark waves upon which wooden boats floated like toys lay a different sort of kingdom.

Coral reefs were scattered like forests across the landscape, lit in dappled sunlight that had to travel a long and slow liquid passage to reach them. Long ribbons of kelp filled in for their Dry World tree equivalents. These bent and dipped gracefully in the slightest aquatic breezes, and were soft to the touch—yet tough as leather, sometimes with sharp edges. Fingerlike tips reached for the sun, photosynthesizing just like their landlocked brethren.

There were mountains in this deep land, too, and canyons. Just as rivers drained the surrounding countryside and flowed downhill in the Dry World, so too different temperatures of water flowed together, creating drifts and eddies. Fissures in the earth erupted with boiling water that blasted out of the hellish depths below—too hot for everyone except the tiny creatures whose entire existence depended on the energy from those vents, instead of on the vague yellow thing so far above.

And everywhere, just as there were animals on land, were the animals of the sea.

The tiniest fish made the largest schools—herring, anchovies, and baby mackerel sparkling and cavorting in the light like a million diamonds. They twirled into whirlpools and flowed over the sandy floor like one large, unlikely animal.

Slightly larger fish came in a rainbow, red and yellow and blue and orange and purple and green and particolored like clowns: dragonets and blennies and gobies and combers.

Hake, shad, char, whiting, cod, flounder, and mullet made the solid middle class.

The biggest loners, groupers and oarfish and dogfish and the major sharks and tuna that all grew to a large, ripe old age did so because they had figured out how to avoid human boats, nets, lines, and bait. The black-eyed predators were well aware they were top of the food chain only down deep, and somewhere beyond the surface there were things even more hungry and frightening than they.

Rounding out the population were the famous un-fish of the ocean: the octopus, flexing and swirling the ends of her tentacles; delicate jellyfish like fairies; lobsters and sea stars; urchins and nudibranchs . . . the funny, caterpillar-like creatures that flowed over the ocean floor wearing all kinds of colors and appendages.

All of these creatures woke, slept, played, swam about, and lived their whole lives under the sea, unconcerned with what went on above them.

But there were other animals in this land, strange ones, who spoke both sky and sea. Seals and dolphins and turtles and the rare fin whale would come down to hunt or talk for a bit and then vanish to that strange membrane that separated the ocean from everything else. Of course they were loved—but perhaps not quite entirely trusted.

The strangest creatures of all lived in a city they built themselves, a kingdom in the depths.

Here no roofs separated the inhabitants from the water above or around them; creatures who could move in any direction had no love of constraint. All was open, airy—or perhaps *oceany*—and built for pleasure and the whimsy of the architect. Delicate fences led visitors into the *idea* of another place. Archways, not doors, opened into other rooms, some of which were above one another. Stairs were unnecessary. Columns, thin and delicate as stalactites in an undiscovered cave, supported "roads" that soared around halls and were decorated with graceful spires. Everything glowed white from marble or pale pink and orange from coral, or glimmered iridescently like the inside of a shell.

All this beauty was the result of many thousands of years of art, peace, and patience—and little to no contact with the rest of the world. If Atlantica was an unimaginable, dreamy splendor to the few humans who had gazed upon it before drowning, it was also unchanged by the centuries; magnificently, eternally the same.

The creatures who built and ruled this underwater world were long-lived and content, with nothing but time and aesthetics on their minds, governed by kings and queens of the same bent.

Or so it had once been.

Now Atlantica was ruled by a queen who had seen another world, and been betrayed by it, and who would live with the consequences—forever.

Ariel

The usual crowd gathered on the throne dais: merfolk of every hue, several dolphins who occasionally flipped up to the surface for a breath, a solitary oarfish, a thin group of sculpin. Primarily the occupants were mer, for the queen was holding court on the Ritual of the June Tide, one of the most important and solemn ordinances of the Sevarene Rites.

And she sorely wished she were anywhere else.

Kings and queens had to address crowds—that was part of the job. Most of the ceremonial aspects could be dealt with by just swimming someplace, looking regal, nodding seriously, and smiling at babies. But when the occasion called for a speech . . .

. . . and you couldn't speak . . .

. . .

Annio was chosen to be the acting priest of the Ritual, so it will be he, and not Laiae, who draws from the Well of Hades.

She said this with her hands, carefully spelling out the priests' names alphabetically in the old runes.

Sebastian and Flounder and Threll, the little seahorse messenger, were placed around the outside edges of the crowd, interpreting what she said aloud. They and Ariel's sisters were the only ones who had bothered to learn the ancient, signed version of the mer language—but only the fish and crab and seahorse volunteered to translate.

None of them shouted loud enough—not the way her father had—so not everyone could hear if only one of them spoke for her.

(The one time they had tried to use a conch to amplify Flounder's voice had just been a disaster. He had sounded *ridiculous*.)

In a perfect world, her sisters would be the ones doing it. Those who grew up with her and had similar voices could speak more easily for her—and since they were princesses themselves, everyone was more likely to listen.

But it was too much like work.

And the one thing her sisters tended to avoid—more than the advances of unwanted suitors—was work.

And so Ariel signed, and the interpreters interpreted, and various parts of the crowds listened to different voices trying to speak for her, and their attention was on the *interpreters,* and their questions were directed to *them,* and it was all a mess.

"Which Annio? The elder?"

"Was my child in the running, my darling Ferestia?"

"But at what hour?"

Her only recourse when everyone started talking at once was to blow loudly on the golden conch she wore around her neck as a symbol of office. She felt more like a silly ship's captain than a queen.

I will send out tablets with the details, posted in the usual public locations, she signed wearily. *That is all.*

After her helpers spoke and everyone thought about it for a moment—it was like waiting for the thunder after lightning, watching the meaning of her words sink in seconds later—the crowd made murmurs both negative and positive, and began to disperse.

Ariel sat back in her throne, leaning tiredly on one elbow, unconsciously assuming the exact position her father always had at the end of an exhausting day. Threll darted from one lingering mer to the next, making sure everyone understood and felt like she or he had been heard. He was a good little messenger, and had proven surprisingly useful in his new role. Flounder was in the back, having a low conversation with a fish she didn't recognize.

Sebastian came scuttling over to her, kicking himself up through the water to sit on her armrest.

"Ah, the Saga at the end of the Rites will be *outstanding* this year," he declared, parading back and forth in front of Ariel, claws gesticulating in the air. "So much talent. So much enthusiasm! Nothing could make it better. The sardines are in sync, the trumpet fish are terrific. Everything is perfect. Well, there is *one* thing that could make it better, of course . . . if only you had your lovely voice."

Ariel raised an eyebrow at Sebastian. Even if she had her voice, she doubted very much if she could have said anything that would have successfully interrupted his monologue. She shifted uncomfortably in her throne. The little crab didn't notice. Although he *could* expertly interpret her signs, read her lips, and decipher her moods—it was only when he was paying strict attention.

"Ahh, what a loss that was for de world. . . ." He put a claw on her shoulder and finally noticed her scowl. "Er, of course, in return, we received the best, most excellent *queen* in de world."

The best, most excellent queen in the world tapped her trident, idly considering turning him into a sea cucumber for a few minutes to think about what he had said.

But he was only echoing something Ariel thought about all the time, herself: whether or not she was any sort of decent queen. Since she never should have been queen to begin with.

When she had returned to her sisters five years before, voiceless and deep in despair over what had happened to her, she'd fully expected banishment, punishment—at the very least, severe chastisement. Instead her family did something utterly unexpected: they made her ruler over all of Atlantica. There was no precedent for this; as the youngest child of the mer-king it would normally have taken the deaths of all six older sisters before the crown came to her.

"You're responsible for the murder of our father," they had said. "It's only right that you take on his burdens."

Privately Ariel wondered if it was less punishment for *her* than a relief for *them*. None of her sisters wanted the job. As royal princesses they could sing and play all day, dress up in fancy shells, wear crowns, oversee dances and parades and balls . . . and never actually have to do any real work. These days she often watched her sisters laughing and singing and wondered at the gulf that had grown between them. Here she was, the youngest, some would say the prettiest— at one time perhaps most *thoughtless* of the lot—and now she sat on a throne, envying them.

The merfolk adored their queen despite her silence and melancholic air. Or perhaps *because* of it. Mer poets and musicians wrote odes and epics to the tragedy of her existence, the romance that had almost caused a kingdom's downfall.

She did not enjoy these.

She did not enjoy the attention of the mermen, either. Once upon a time, as a younger, more innocent thing, she had never even noticed boys. Mer boys, at least.

Now she was *forced* to notice them, to keep an eye on them, to be aware of what ulterior motives they had: to wed the queen, maybe to become king.

Ha, she thought bitterly. *If only they knew what a pain it is to rule.*

She hadn't been even a tide-cycle into her new office before she had begun to understand her father's temper and moods. He had been a firm leader who rarely smiled, presenting the perfect image of an old god: stony-faced, bearded, permanent. Prone to glowering and frowning. She and her sisters always teased him, trying to win smiles from him, trying to get him to steal an hour from his duties to play with them. Mostly they had to content themselves with his presence at official functions, banquets, and performances like the one Ariel had skipped—the one that had started the whole thing.

She wished she could tell him she understood. Being a ruler was *hard*. It made one frown, turn pensive, grumpy.

It should have been an easy job; the merfolk and their allies were the happiest, most carefree peoples in the world.

Well, until a tribe of branzinos moved a little too close to the viewing garden of a royal cousin.

Or the shark-magister insisted on expanding his people's hunting rights all the way to Greydeep Canyon.

Or, far more importantly, a reef suddenly turned white and died for no apparent cause. Or the diamondback terrapins couldn't make it to their favorite nesting place because there were houses there now. Or the humans had managed to catch—and eat—an entire delegation from the northern seas. Or the number of fishing vessels was getting too large to ignore, to relegate to the unwritten and ancient Dry World–Sea World laws of yore.

Yet despite these much more pressing concerns, cousin Yerena still complained about the branzinos and her garden and "their ugly faces."

It made Ariel irritable just thinking about it.

Besides general grumpiness, there was another more serious similarity between the king and his daughter. Any joy Triton had taken in life, even with his daughters, was constantly shadowed by sorrow over his dead wife.

Any respite Ariel took in her new life was constantly shadowed by her sorrow and *guilt* over her dead father.

And so she ruled, firmly and well, but silently and with much melancholy.

She cleared her throat, one of the few noises she could still make, and was leaning forward to give the little crab a piece of her mind when Flounder came swimming up.

Her old friend was larger and happily fatter than when they had first set out to the surface years ago. He had a medallion around his neck to show rank; the imprint of the trident meant he was in the innermost ring of the royal circle. But unlike the adorable little helper fish and servant seahorses, he didn't turn his chest into the light or waggle to make the golden disk extra obvious. He remained, despite the years and accumulated wisdom, likable, down-to-sea-floor Flounder.

"My Queen!"

He swooped in front of her, ignoring Sebastian, and gave the low bow that was required of all but Ariel usually tried to stop—at least from him and Sebastian.

Ariel cocked her head at him: *go on.*

"I've just had some strange—really, really strange—news from a plaice, who heard it from a turtle, who heard it from a dolphin. . . . Wait, I *think* it was the plaice from the turtle. There might have been another messenger in between. A bluefish, maybe?"

He felt Ariel's impatience before she even displayed it.

"There is a seagull on the surface who claims to have news for your ears only."

Ariel's eyes widened.

She signed carefully, spelling out the name.

Is it Scuttle?

"No, My Queen," Flounder said, trying not to show his own disappointment. "It was hard to make out through all of the . . . parties involved, but I believe it is a younger one, and a female."

Ariel practically wilted.

Seagulls were useless. Scuttle was a rare bird. Scattered but goodhearted, prone to flights of exaggeration, but a true friend. It should have been *him* coming to visit.

For several years after the day she lost her father, Ariel had tried to return to the land to see Eric and to take revenge on Ursula. But the wily sea witch had used her now very prosaic powers as a *human* princess to set guards all along the coast—officially, in "case of an enemy kingdom attack, or pirates." In some cases, close to the castle, guards were literally stationed *in* the water, up to their calves.

With Scuttle's help Ariel had tried to evade the guards, sneaking in while the gull whipped up a distraction. But it was never enough, and the men were all on high alert for strange, witchy red-haired girls.

After a while, and after much insistence from Sebastian and her sisters, Ariel gave up and returned to her life under the sea permanently. At the very least she could respect the memory of her father by devoting herself to her duties as queen. She had vowed to forget the Dry World forever.

Even Scuttle.

"But . . . it's a seagull. So doesn't that mean Scuttle *has* to be involved somehow?" Flounder pointed out, trying to cheer her up. "It would be really, really bizarre if some random gull came to talk to you. But I didn't double-check on the origin of the story. I didn't want to break your ban on going to the surface."

Ariel swished her tail thoughtfully.

"Don't even think about it," Sebastian growled. "I know what you're thinking. It's just a silly seabird. Don't even consider it, young lady."

Ariel raised an eyebrow at him incredulously. *Young lady?* In the years that had passed since the duel with the sea witch, she had aged. Not dramatically, but far more than a mostly immortal mermaid should have. There was something about her eyes—they were deeper, wiser, and wearier than when she was a young mer who had never been on dry land. Her cheeks weren't quite as plump anymore; the angles of her face were more pronounced. Sometimes she wondered if she looked like her mother . . . aside from her own unreliable memories, the only physical evidence of the former queen was a statue in the castle of her and Triton dancing together. But it was all pale milky marble, no colors at all. *Dead.*

Ariel's hair no longer flowed behind her as it once had; handmaidens and decorator crabs kept it braided and coiffed, snug and businesslike under the great golden crown that sat on her temples, like the gods wore. Small gold and aquamarine earrings sparkled regally but didn't tinkle; they were quite understated and professional. Her only real nod to youth was the golden ring in the upper part of her left ear.

"Young lady," indeed.

She didn't even have to sign, *You cannot talk to me that way anymore, little crab. I am queen now.*

Sebastian sighed, sounding old in his exasperation. "I'm sorry for speaking out of turn. I can't help it. Nothing good comes out of you going up there . . . *nothing ever has.* I just . . . I just don't want to see you hurt or disappointed again."

Ariel gave him the tiniest smile and tapped him once on the back fondly. Sometimes it was hard to remember that much of Sebastian's attitude was only for show. Underneath, he really did have—what he thought were—her best interests at heart.

But she was a grown-up now, and queen, and her best interests were none of his business. She turned to sign to the little seahorse who floated silently at attention, fins quivering, waiting for orders.

Threll, please tell the Queen's Council that I will be taking this afternoon off. Flounder will be accompanying me. Sebastian is nominally in charge until I return, though no votes or decisions are to be made in my absence.

"Yes, Your Majesty." The little seahorse bowed and zoomed off into the water.

"My Queen, as thrilled as I am . . ." Sebastian began.

But Ariel was already turned upward, and kicking hard to the surface.

Ariel

Mermaid queens didn't often have a reason to move quickly. There were no wars to direct, no assassination attempts to evade, no crowds of clamoring admirers to avoid among the merfolk. In fact, slowness and calm were expected of royalty.

So Ariel found herself thoroughly enjoying the exercise as she beat her tail against the water—even as it winded her a little. She missed dashing through shipwrecks with Flounder, fleeing sharks, trying to scoot back home before curfew. She loved the feel of her powerful muscles, the way the current cut around her when she twisted her shoulders to go faster.

She hadn't been this far up in years and gulped as the

pressure of the deep faded. She clicked her ears, readying them for the change of environment. Colors faded and transformed around her from the dark, heady slate of the ocean bottom to the soothing azure of the middle depths and finally lightening to the electric, magical periwinkle that heralded the burst into daylight.

She hadn't planned to break through the surface triumphantly. She wouldn't give it that power. Her plan was to take it slow and rise like a whale. Casually, unperturbed, like *Ooh, here I am.*

But somehow her tail kicked in twice as hard the last few feet, and she exploded into the warm sunlit air like she had been drowning.

She gulped again and *tasted* the breeze—dry in her mouth; salt and pine and far-distant *fires* and a thousand alien scents . . .

A small gull sat riding the waves, regarding her curiously.

Ariel composed herself, remembering who she was. Trying not to delight in the way the water streamed down her neck; how it dried from her hair, lightening it. Flounder whirled around her body anxiously before popping up beside her.

She signed: *I am told you have a message for me.*

But before Flounder could translate, before she could stop herself, Ariel signed again:

Do you know Scuttle? Where is he? Why isn't Scuttle here?

"Queen Ariel was told you have a message for her," the fish told the gull solemnly. "However, she was expecting her old friend Scuttle. He is the only bird she has ever been close to."

"You are correct to assume it was he who sent me out here. Great-Grandfather Scuttle couldn't make it this far," the seagull answered. "How are you breathing?"

It took Ariel a moment to fully register the second part of what the bird had said.

What?

She didn't even have to sign it.

The seagull cocked her head at the mermaid and stared at her, unblinking. "You went from under the water to above water with no trouble at all. Since you live underwater all the time, I assume it's not that you can just hold your breath forever—like if you were a magical whale, say. And you have no gills like a salamander. So how are you breathing?"

"You do not address the queen of Atlantica that way," Flounder chastised. Ariel was impressed by how grown-up he sounded, unruffled by the weird conversation.

"Pardon," the seagull said immediately, dipping her head.

Ariel twirled her trident casually, letting the water fly from it in a hundred sparkling droplets. Although the

merfolk accepted her lineage and rights to the crown immediately, there had still been a definite period of adjustment
while they still thought of her as the pretty, carefree baby
girl of Triton. Some spoke to her far too patronizingly, some
spoke to her far too familiarly. And *some* folk of non-mer
persuasion (sharks, mainly) had needed several displays of
her anger before they acknowledged her authority.

But she didn't think that was what was going on with
this odd little seagull. There was no *judgment* in the bird's
expression. Just fascination. She had probably never seen a
mermaid before. Ariel could have been a sea slug or a demon
and the gull would have asked the same question.

What is your name? Ariel asked.

"Jona," the bird said with a little bow after Flounder had
translated. "But . . . if you talk to my great-grandfather at
all, he may refer to me—incorrectly—as Jonathan. Jonathan
Livingston. He's a little confused sometimes."

Ariel smiled, thinking that sounded exactly like Scuttle.

"Why don't you tell the queen everything, starting from
the beginning, Jona?" Flounder suggested.

So the gull told the tale of watching the opera with her
great-grandfather, and her great-grandfather's reaction to it.
She told of their flight to the castle and spying on Vanessa,
and the revelation of the existence of Triton. She told it succinctly and perfectly: no unwanted description, dialogue,
or personal observation. Ariel wasn't sure how exactly she

could have been descended from the absentminded Scuttle. *Maybe an egg got misplaced from another nest.*

Ariel's mind whirled, in shock from the news.

Her father was alive!

. . . Probably?

Good queens did not react immediately to new information, especially if they didn't already have some inkling of what it brought. Snap decisions were rash and led to disaster. Ariel had learned this the hard way. Not having a voice was an advantage here: she could compose herself while working out how to say what she needed to.

You have really seen my father? Alive?

"I saw a . . ." Jona struggled for the right word. ". . . thing in a bottle that the princess spoke to like it was Triton, King of the Sea. And Great-Grandfather says the . . . thing . . . bore a more than passing resemblance to the entity he once was."

Ariel remembered all too clearly what that "thing" looked like. It did indeed sound like her father.

"Great-Grandfather thought you would be up to another adventure," the gull added, almost timidly. "And I am to let you know that he's in, to rescue your father."

How would we rescue him? Her hands shook a little as she signed. *Impossible . . . the guards . . .*

"While I am not directly familiar with the situation as

it previously stood, Great-Grandfather told me to tell you that the number of soldiers on the beach has been greatly reduced since the two of you last tried to reach Eric. He is not the best at counting," Jona added neutrally, "but when we were there to see if your father was still alive, I saw no more than eight. None of them were in the water, and most looked like they were barely paying attention."

Eight? There had been dozens the last time she tried. And they marched, resolutely, up and down the sands, eyes on the sea. But that was years ago . . . After Ariel stopped trying, maybe Ursula figured she had given up forever. Maybe the sea witch had turned her attentions elsewhere and let security lapse.

Ariel signed.

"I will take these matters into consideration," Flounder translated, "and will either return here myself in three days or send a messenger in my place."

"Understood," the seagull said with a bow.

"Understood, My Queen," Flounder corrected politely.

"Are you?" the gull asked curiously. "*My* Queen? How does that work with the Law of the Worlds—that of the Dry World and the World Under the Sea?"

Ariel found herself almost rolling her eyes and making that wide, sighing smile she used to with Flounder.

But the little gull had looked at her, at *her*, while she

signed. Not at her hands, or Flounder as he had spoken. There was a friendly heart under Jona's direct and inappropriate questions.

Ariel just shook her head and dove back under the water, tossing a sign over her shoulder as she went.

"The Queen says you may call her Ariel," Flounder said. Also, under his breath: "You have *no idea* what an honor that is."

On the way back down Ariel's silence was deeper than usual; it practically echoed into the quiet sea, filling the water around them.

"What are you going to do?" Flounder asked, trying not to sound as anxious as his old self. "We *have* to save Triton. Don't we? But can we?"

Ariel stopped suddenly in the water, thinking. Her tail swished back and forth as she held steady in a tiny current that rippled her fins and tendrils of hair.

Do we even know it's actually true?

Flounder's eyes widened. "But she said . . . I don't know, Ariel. She seemed like a pretty honest—if weird—bird. And Scuttle!"

It's been years. *Why would Ursula keep him around, alive?*

"No idea. So she can talk at him? All the time? She loves that kind of thing. But if he *is* alive, isn't that great news? Don't we need to *do* something?" Flounder was practically begging, swishing back and forth in the water in desperation.

I don't know. . . . I want to believe it's true. It's too much to take in. I'm going to go . . . think for a while.

Alone, she added.

Flounder didn't need to ask where.

"Sebastian won't like that," he sighed.

Then he tried not to giggle at the very unqueenly thing she signed.

"I'll tell him you've gone to consult some elders or something," he said, waving a fin. "Be safe."

He needn't have suggested that as he swam off; with the trident, Ariel could kill an army or call up a storm that would destroy half the sea. But it was hard to let old habits die. And it was harder still to care for a powerful queen, whose only vulnerabilities were ones you couldn't see.

Ariel

Drifting slowly now, Ariel wound her way through the kingdom to the outskirts of Atlantica.

A few fish stopped to bow and she acknowledged them with a nod of her head. No merfolk were around to bother her. As a rule, most didn't like lonely, dusty corners of the ocean where rocks thrived more than coral.

Eventually she came to the hidden grotto where her collection of things once was. Millions of years ago it had probably vented hot water and lava that provided sustenance for tube worms, which resulted in a perfect, cylindrical series of shelves for Ariel to display her finds on. Then her father had blasted it back to its mineral components. *Which tiny creatures will use again, completing the circle.*

Fine sand, the aquatic equivalent of dust, covered everything in an impressively thick layer. A couple of seaweeds had managed to anchor onto the rubble here and there, and anemones sprouted from the more protected corners.

Ariel looked around at the old destruction her furious father had wrought. She had hated him so much. And then he had . . . traded his life for hers.

And now he was . . . alive?

She could hardly let herself believe it. The cries and sobs she couldn't make aloud turned inward into her heart, in spasms of pain.

If he really was alive, Ursula had probably been torturing him all these years. She was not kind to her prisoners.

Or it could be a trap, a complicated setup to lure Ariel back so Ursula could finish her for good. A strange move to make half a decade after the mermaid had obviously given up, but the sea witch *was* strange. . . .

And all Ariel had was the word of a gull she didn't even know.

Although . . . despite the short amount of time she had spent with the bird . . . there was something unquestionably honest about her. The queen had a feeling that if pressed, Jona couldn't lie or exaggerate to save her own life. And despite Scuttle's tendency to misrepresent or fabricate or even believe his own lies, he never really meant it. If he thought there was a chance that Triton was alive, he would do anything in his power to help Ariel save him.

I should do it properly, she thought, hands tightening into fists. She should advance on the human castle with a mer army, and summon the power of the seas, and dash Ursula to bits on the rocks, and drown all those who opposed her, and sweep in and save her father; and he would be king again, and she would have a father again. . . .

. . . and she wouldn't.

She would never enlist soldiers sworn to protect the mer kingdom to help with a mistake *she* had made. She would never endanger a castle of innocent people just to get back the person *she* was responsible for losing.

Fate was giving her a second chance.

She would take it, but by herself.

She would right the wrongs she had committed on her own.

She would—her heart leapt despite her doubts—find and rescue her father, ask his forgiveness, and return the king to his people. Everyone would be ecstatic, her sisters most of all! And she would redeem herself. She might even be a hero. And they would all live happily ever after, under the sea.

But to do this, she would need to return to the Dry World.

She picked up a roundish thing from the ground and shook the sand off. It was the top of an old ceramic jar, once painted bright blue and gold. The humans had so many jars. And amphorae. And vases. And vessels. And kegs. And tankards. So many . . . things . . . to put other . . . *things* in. Merfolk rarely had a necessity to store anything beyond the occasional rare and fancy comestible, like the sweet golden-wine they used to trade for when she was a child. Merfolk ate when they were hungry, almost never had the need to drink anything, and rarely had a reason to store food for the future.

She dropped the lid and sighed, drifting over to the rock she used to perch on while admiring her collection. *Things*, so many *things*. Things she never found out the proper use for in her short time on land. Because she had been too busy mooning over Eric.

In some ways, that was the part of the seagull's story that bothered her the most. She could not believe the reaction her traitor heart had when the bird mentioned his name.

Eric.

Eric *remembered* something?

He wrote an *opera* about it? About *her*?

It wasn't just the flattery of it, though. If Eric remembered enough to compose music about it . . . would he remember her, too? A little?

She remembered *him* far too often.

Despite the fact that her life had been ruined because of her pursuit of Eric, when she closed her eyes to go to sleep, her last thoughts were often still of him.

Or when a perfectly handsome, reasonably amusing (and mostly *immortal*—not an irrelevant point) merman tried to win her affections, and all she could think about was how his hair might look when it was dry. Would it bounce, like Eric's?

An *opera*. What were his arias like? What did he write for her to sing?

She smiled, the irony of it not lost on her: she had run away from a concert to pursue a human, and he had written songs for her now that she could no longer sing.

She ran her finger along the sand on a nearby shelf, writing the name *Eric* in runes.

Maybe, just maybe, along the way to save her father, she could pay him a visit.

For old time's sake.

Sebastian

"NONONONONONONONO!"

Sebastian scuttled back and forth along one of the balustrades that demarcated the edge of the throne dais. It had been grown, as many of the mer objects were, from coral, the original inhabitants coaxed to move on once their job was done.

The crab's toes made little *tickticktick* noises as he self-righteously walked one way and then back the other, claws gnarled in the ready position, not even once regarding his audience.

She sighed. While it was, of course, not unforeseeable that the little crab would respond this way, waiting through his tantrum was not the most efficient use of her time.

As a girl, she would have swum off. As a girl with a voice, she might have argued.

As a mute queen, she could do neither.

She lifted up the trident and struck the ocean floor with it twice. Not to raise any magic—just to get his attention. To *remind* him of who she was.

The little crab stopped mid-rant. She raised her eyebrows at him: *Really, Sebastian?*

"Nothing good will come of it," he said, a little sheepishly. "Nothing from the surface ever does."

My father may be alive, she signed. *That is reason enough to try.*

At this the little crab wavered. He clicked slowly along the railing until he was close enough to put a claw on her arm. "Ariel, I miss him, too . . . but you could be just chasing a ghost."

"Give up, Sebastian," Flounder suggested. "She's already made her decision."

"I think you're encouraging her in this!" Sebastian snapped, aiming an accusing claw at the fish.

Flounder rolled his eyes.

He's not encouraging, he's helping, Ariel said.

"I could help you *more,*" Sebastian wheedled. "*I* can go on land for short periods of time."

You're needed down here, to act as my representative. And distraction.

"I am *not* going to get in front of a crowd of merfolk and . . . *similar ocean dwellers* to tell them that their *queen* has left them to go off on some ridiculous mission by herself! You want to leave, *you* have to be brave enough to tell them."

A single sign: *No.*

She rested a gentle hand on her throat, letting that action speak for itself.

Sebastian wilted. "All right, go. No one has ever been able to stop you from doing anything you wanted anyway—even when it costs you dearly."

For a moment, Ariel felt her old self surface, the urge to grin and plant a kiss on the little crab's back. He was right. She *did* have a habit of swimming in where angels feared to tread. No one could dissuade her once her mind was fixed. And it *had* cost her dearly.

What could it cost her this time?

"Please tell your sisters, at least," Sebastian said with a weary sigh, dropping off the edge and scooting himself along the ocean floor toward the throne. With some quick kicks and sidewise crabby swimming he landed neatly on the armrest, the proper place for his official position as the queen's deputy. "I cannot *imagine* dealing with them right now."

Ariel nodded, and then gave him a second nod, eyes lowered: *thank you.*

And then she swam off so she wouldn't have to see the looks he and Flounder exchanged.

Her sisters were in the Grotto of Delights, swimming about, well, *delightedly*; attaching little anemones to their hair, fluffing up seaweed fascinators, rummaging through giant seashells of jewels, pearls, and snails. Ariel could barely remember the time before her mother was killed but she was fairly certain that her sisters had been less frantic in their pursuit of pleasure then. Now they drowned their grief in safe, silly things that required little thought and provided constant distraction.

She ran her hand through a shell bowl absently, letting the trinkets slide through her fingers. Mostly they weren't cut or polished the way a human jeweler would treat them: they sparkled here and there out of a chunk of brownish rock. A single crystal might shine like the weapon of a god— but be topped by the lumpy bit where it had been prized out of a geode.

Ariel regarded the stones with fascination. Of course they were beautiful. Yet she still found the bits and baubles from the human world, *made* by humans, far more alluring. *Why?* Why couldn't she be content with the treasures of the sea the way the ocean had made them? What was wrong with them that they had to be altered, or put on something else, or framed, or forced in a bunch onto a necklace, in perfect, unnatural symmetry?

"Oh! Are you coming to the Neap Tide Frolic after all?"

Alana swirled around Ariel, her deep magenta tail almost touching her sister's. Her black hair was styled in intricate ringlets that were caught in a bright red piece of coral, its tiny branches and spines separating the curls into tentacles. The effect was amazing—and not a little terrifying.

Looking around, Ariel realized that her royal sisters were done up more than usual. Once again she had forgotten one of the endless parties, dances, fetes, celebrations, and cyclical observations that made up most of the merpeople's lives.

No, I'm afraid it slipped my mind, she signed.

"Oh, too bad," Alana said, making a perfunctory sad face before swooshing away. The sisters had come to expect her absence and no longer even showed disappointment when she declined.

It hurt a little, Ariel realized.

Attina saw her and came over. Despite their extreme difference in age, she was the one Ariel felt closest to. Even if her big sister didn't fully understand the urge to seek out a human prince, or to explore the Dry World, or to collect odd bits of human relics, she always treated her little sister as gently as she could—despite how gruff she sounded.

"What's happening?" she asked, swishing her orange tail back and forth. Her hair wasn't done yet; it was obvious she was devoting all her time to helping the younger sisters with theirs. The only slightly frumpy brown bun was locked in place by sea urchin spikes. "You look . . . *concerned*. All royal and concerned."

Ariel allowed herself a small smile.

I'm going away for a few days.

"Royal vacation! Aww yeah! You could use it, clearly. I've been saying for ages now you need to relax and kick back for a bit. Haven't I been saying that? Your skin looks terrible. I'm so glad you—oh. *Not* a royal vacation, I can see that now."

Attina said all these things quickly, one after another: revelation, opinion, realization. When people could speak aloud, Ariel had realized long ago, they spent words like they were free, wasting them with nonsense.

Her sister frowned. "Where are you going?"

Ariel didn't make a complicated sign. She just used her index finger and pointed. *Up.*

"What?" Attina wrinkled her nose, confused.

Ariel waited for the meaning to sink in.

"Oh, *no*." Her sister shook her head, eyes wide. "You *cannot* be serious."

Ariel nodded.

"No. Nope. No, you don't," Attina said, crossing her arms. "Not again. We lost Dad when you did that last time. You're not doing it again."

The other sisters felt the tension in the water and swam silently up, watching—*hiding*—behind the oldest.

Attina—Ariel didn't spell out the sign; she moved her hand to suggest the robes of a goddess, the sign for Athena, for whom her sister was named. There was an implication of regalness and wisdom; Ariel was appealing to her oldest sister for her best values. *Attina, he may still be alive. That is why I am going.*

Several of her sisters gasped. Tails lashed.

"Nuh-uh," Attina said firmly.

Then she whispered: "Really?"

There's a chance. Someone I trust saw *him, as Ursula's prisoner.*

"Huh," Attina said, crossing her arms again. "Huh."

"Let her go," said Adella, swinging her ponytails.

"She *needs* to go," Andrina, the one closest to Ariel in age, whispered.

"You should go now!" Arista urged, tossing blond hair out of her face. "Get Daddy back!"

Alana and Aquata were silent, looking at their leader, Attina.

"Can't you send someone . . ." *Else,* the oldest sister

was going to say. But she shook her head. "No, I guess you can't."

I have to do this, Ariel agreed.

"You sure this isn't just a chance to see your little human prince again?" Alana asked flatly.

Ariel felt her face redden. Her left hand clenched around the trident, her right hand clenched in the water, around nothing, around everything—she could throw foam into her sister's face and it would become a poisonous, spiky urchin, or a handful of sharp sand, or a thousand little scale mites.

Attina made her lips go all squooshy the way she often did, like a puffer fish before it puffed. She raised a hand to silence Alana. *Not now.*

Ariel reflected, for a moment, how much communication was in sign, even for those who could speak.

"Fine. Good luck. I hope you bring Father back," Attina said, perfunctorily. "You can go."

Ariel could feel the twists in the water: the oldest sister, who had tried to take over as mother when their real mother died, and never succeeded in that role. The other sisters, who liked the idea of power and ruling and strength and crowns—for someone else. They all just wanted everything the way it had been when Ariel was one of them, when they were all the same.

But Ariel had never really been the same.

I don't need your permission, she signed. *I was merely letting you know.*

"Well!" Attina said, raising her eyebrows.

You made me queen.

"Yes . . . I suppose we did."

The five other girls flowed and slipped into the currents, their fins flickering sinuously into the depths. Attina swooped and followed behind. "I really hope you do find him," she called over her shoulder.

No one's going to volunteer to come along? Ariel signed, half ironically; with her back turned, there was no way her sister could have known she was saying anything.

She watched them all go back to exactly what they'd been doing before: fixing their hair, gossiping, swirling around each other in a scene that used to delight their father.

Don't you ever get bored with your lives? she signed, even though no one would see it.

Aren't you even a little bit curious?

She mouthed these words, trying to will a sound to come forth. This one time.

Nothing but water flowed out.

It's been over one hundred years since Mother died!

No one saw her. Her hands, useless for communicating, gripped the trident tightly.

She swam off, unheard, unseen.

Ariel

This time she would be prepared. She took a bag, the kind artists used to carry their tools, and packed the few things she thought she would need. Carefully kept clothing, rescued from a trunk sunk when its ship capsized. Waterlogged but not worn. It had been so long since she had been up on land that it took a while before she remembered how to put together a complete outfit. *Dress* and *apron* and *under-skirt* . . . The number of layers of clothing humans wore was insane. Would anyone even notice if she forgot an undershirt or underpants?

Also she had to remember to bring money—every kind of coin, just in case. Last time Eric had paid for everything. This time, should need arise, she would have to provide it for herself.

Then Ariel settled herself into the vanity and shooed away the decorator crabs, a little impatient with their crowding presence and constant need to help. She could remove the crown herself, and would not be taking off the golden conch. She shrugged out of the heavy mantle that hung heavily from her shoulders and gave her an older, more regal appearance. It was immediately whisked away by two mackerel who would clean it and hang it properly on a reef to stay wrinkle- and anemone-free.

She pursed her lips and blew on her golden shell—low, not enough to arouse alarm. Flounder came swimming out of the depths, where he had been waiting, giving her some privacy.

She flowed her hand across her body, like a tide: *It's time.*

Flounder nodded and swam next to her. Together they rose.

They moved almost as one unit, his body bending back and forth in the middle, her tail pumping up and down in almost precisely the same rhythm. After a few minutes he ventured:

"It's just like old times, isn't it?"

Ariel turned and gave him a smile: so rare, these days. She had been thinking the exact same thing.

When her head broke the surface this time it was less revelatory but still exhilarating. The little gull was almost exactly where they had left her.

Ariel realized she didn't have a sign for *gull.*

"Great," the bird said. "I was really hoping you would come back."

Ariel blinked. *What a weird, banal thing to say.*

"Yes, well, and here we are," Flounder said, a little flippantly. "And by the way—this is a *secret* mission. No one should know about how the queen is leaving her kingdom to pursue matters on land . . . especially matters involving her father. *Especially* with the sea witch Ursula involved."

Jona stared at him.

"Kingdom? Or queendom?"

"What?" Flounder asked, exasperated.

"The mer are ruled by a queen. Shouldn't it be *queen-dom?*"

"No, that's—well, I guess so. Maybe. Does it matter?"

"It does if you're the queen," the bird pointed out.

Ariel had to hide her smile; she would have laughed, if she had the voice for it.

"I will fly ahead and find Great-Grandfather," the gull said, correctly guessing that her new friends were losing patience, "so we can prepare a diversion for the few guards left at the shore. We should arrange a signal so I know when you're ready to emerge onto dry land."

Flounder watched Ariel's signs carefully and then translated. "A fleet of no fewer than . . . thirty-seven flying fish will arc out of the water at the same time, heading west."

"All right, I will look for thirty-seven of the silver, flying, hard-to-catch, rather bony, but oh! very tasty fish, flying to the sunset."

"What's that in gull?" Flounder asked, translating Ariel's curiosity.

The bird squawked once, loudly.

It sounded like every other squawk.

Then she took off into the high air without another question or sound.

Ariel jerked her head and she and Flounder dove back under the water. They kept fairly close to the surface, skimming just below it.

She could sense the approach of land—taste when the waters changed, feel when currents turned cool or warm—but it didn't hurt to keep an eye on the shore now and then, and an ear out for boats. The slap of oars could be heard for leagues. Her father had told tales about armored seafarers in days long past, whose trireme ships had three banks of rowers to ply the waters—you could hear them clear down to Atlantica, he'd say. Any louder and they would disrupt the songs of the half-people—the dolphins and whales who used their voices to navigate the waters.

Even before her father had enacted the ban on going to the surface, it was rare that a boat would encounter a mer. If the captain kept to the old ways, he would either carefully steer away or throw her a tribute: fruit of the land, the apples and grapes merfolk treasured more than treasure. In return the mermaid might present him with fruit of the sea—gems, or a comb from her hair.

But there was always the chance of an unscrupulous crew, and nets, and the potential prize of a mermaid wife or trophy to present the king.

(Considering some of the nets that merfolk had found and freed their underwater brethren from, it was quite understandable that Triton believed humans might eat *any-thing* they found in the sea—including merfolk.)

Interested and curious sea creatures passed Ariel and Flounder, bowing when they thought to, staring when they didn't. Even without her crown, the queen was well known by her red hair and her friend's constant presence. It was a good thing she had warned Sebastian not to mention her mission; gossip swam faster than tuna.

She stuck her head out of the water and was delighted to discover that she had kept their direction true. They were at the entrance of the Bay of Tirulia, just beyond where spits of land on either side had been extended with boulders by the Dry Worlders to keep their ships safe. Inside these two arms the sea grew flat. On the southern side of the bay, the land was rocky and grey like southern islands where octopuses played and olives occasionally fell and floated on gentle waves. For a very brief stretch, in the middle of the shore near the castle, the rocks gave way to beach. North of that were tidal flats where the sea became land more slowly, gradually invaded by grass and rich brown tuffets of mud where all sorts of baby sea life began: mussels, clams, oysters, crabs, eels, and even some fish. Beyond that were the marshes proper, brackish water that mixed with a river that went, Eric had once claimed, all the way to the mountains.

And between the mermaid and the shore were the ships.

Small fishing boats with bright blue eyes painted on their prows to ward off bad luck. Fast and sleek whalers. Tiny coracles for children and beachcombers, for puttering around the marshes and low tides, for teasing out the eggs, shrimp, shellfish, and tastier seaweed eaten by the poor but prized by the rich.

Towering over all of these were mighty ocean-faring tall ships, giant white sails unfurled, ready to cross the open water and come home again laden with spices and gold, chocolate and perfumes, fine silks and sparkling salts.

Ariel regarded these last vessels with a twinge of jealousy. They carried their human riders farther away than she had ever been, to places she had only heard of in legend. They probably sailed right over the heads of the Hyperboreans, without even realizing it. It seemed unfair somehow.

Then she noticed one tiny boat—no more than a rowboat, really—that floated apart from the rest. It was by itself and farthest out, right at the edge of the bay, closest to her.

A person sat hunched over in the prow of the boat,

gazing gloomily out to sea. Ariel frowned, squinting to see better. She was tempted to paint over the blurry details with her imagination: a patch-eyed pirate or stump-legged old sea captain, chewing on a pipe stem, dreaming of his glory days and looking out for a storm that would never come.

But there was something about him . . . his hair was a little too glossy and black. And though he sat bent over, the curved angles of his back seemed still sleek with the muscle, sinew, and fat of youth. His hand reached up to pull his coat tighter in a strangely familiar gesture—

Ariel gulped. If she had a voice she might have yelped.

It was Eric.

Without a splash she sank beneath the waves: soundlessly, immediately, eerily—like any sea creature that didn't want to be seen. No drama, no excited tail thwap.

She hovered just below the surface, blinking slowly, heart pounding.

"Ariel . . . ?" Flounder asked, nervous at her behavior.

She looked at him, chagrined. She made the sign, spelling out the runes:

Eric.

"WHAT?"

She held up a finger, translatable into any language: *one moment.*

Keeping her motions small and efficient, she swam

closer to the boat, around the back, and silently poked her head above the water. There were, of course, sharp-eyed sea widows and captains, girls on the shore hoping to see something great and boys who wanted a prize for spotting a whale or its ambergris. But on the whole, humans were oblivious to the quiet world around them. She counted on that, and the sailor's eyes on the horizon, to keep her invisible.

It was indeed Eric.

His eyes were still the same dreamy sky blue—or sea blue, right before the sea becomes the sky. But they no longer looked prone to crinkling up in smiles of confused delight. Now they stayed wide, focused on things she couldn't see, miles and hours and worlds away from the bay.

His face was thinner, his appearance paler than that of a man who liked spending his days on a boat should have been. Still too healthy to be *haggard*, but not carefree.

His hair was much longer, caught back in a loose ponytail.

Although he had a worn, salt-faded cape over his shoulders, Ariel could see the trappings of rank beneath it: a crisp white shirt, several golden medallions, an unbuttoned but very fine and tight waistcoat. Below a fancy, wide belt of almost military lines he sported an *incredibly* well-tailored pair of trousers that obviously did not give as much freedom of movement as the old Eric would have liked. His boots were worn and seemed like an afterthought, like the cape, thrown on at the last moment. For disguise, or to protect the better clothes.

He kept staring across the ocean as if waiting for something. The tiny boat was anchored, Ariel realized. As if he had been there, or expected to be there, for a while.

"It's so nice out here, isn't it, Max?" he murmured. "It's so quiet. You can almost hear . . . Almost hear . . ."

Ariel's eyes widened. She saw the tuft of an old furry ear lift up above the side of the boat.

Hesitantly Eric pulled something out of his pocket. At first Ariel thought it would be a pipe—it seemed appropriate for someone of Eric's current age and station. But as he placed it to his lips she realized that it was a tiny instrument. Smaller than the recorder he used to carry around with him, and fatter. More like an ocarina, the instrument humans used to play in the days they still talked to animals and merfolk.

He took a breath and waited for a moment.

Then he played a few notes. Quietly and slowly.

Ariel's heart nearly stopped.

It was the song she had sung after she rescued him, the song that had burst unbidden out of her heart as he lay there, unconscious. It described the beauty of the sea and the land and the mortality of humans and the wonder of life. It had poured out of her like life itself.

Hearing it again was the sweetest pain she had ever experienced. Far deeper even than having her tail split in twain for legs. It coursed through her whole body, hurt and recognition and pleasure all at once.

He played only the first dozen notes, then trailed off. *Listening.*

Waiting.

Ariel opened her mouth, willed the notes to come out. She closed her eyes and tried to squeeze them from her heart, from her lungs. Didn't love break all spells? What was the good of it otherwise? *Please, please, Old Gods. Let me sing . . . just this once. . . .*

But all was silent.

"Mmrl?"

Max's little questioning noise caused Eric to blink, and Ariel to curse.

"No, I know I didn't use it in the opera," Eric said as if he were answering a much more coherent question from the dog. "I know, it would have been perfect. But it didn't seem right somehow. . . . I needed to save it for . . . for . . ."

He blinked suddenly and smiled at himself.

"That sounds ridiculous, doesn't it, Max?" He grinned and scruffled the dog's ears. Ariel dipped lower into the water, melting at his smile. Still! When he smiled it was like the whole world was smiling, his lips pulled the sky like a rainbow, the sun danced in laughter. She felt utterly helpless and stupid. Queen of the Sea! Brought to her fins by one silly smile.

Eric sighed. "Thanks for joining me on these little expeditions, Max. I know they wear you out. But out here, it's almost like I'm . . . clearheaded. Or slipping deeper, into another dream. One or the other. They're the same. Oh, I don't know."

He sighed, clenching his hand around the ocarina in frustration. For a moment Ariel thought he was going to hurl it into the sea, as he had his recorder so many years before. But he brought it to his lips and played the dozen notes again, letting them die into the breeze.

Ariel didn't try to finish the tune this time. Tears leaked out of the sides of her eyes and trickled down her cheeks, joining the briny sea.

Finally Eric put his ocarina away. "Come on, let's head back before the missus decides we've been out on our walkies too long." He pulled the anchor and took up the oars, expertly turning the little boat around with no wake and little effort.

As the prow swung out closer to Ariel, Max began to shuffle to his feet.

"Mmmrrl?"

He tried to look over the side of the boat, sensing that something was off.

Ariel dipped low into the water. She doubted the dog could see very well now, much less through the matted locks over his eyes. He put his nose to the air, sniffing . . . but Eric was rowing away, back toward shore.

Ariel watched them go, the old dog and his master on the tiny, tiny boat—the man who once commanded a ship as large as a castle and the heart of the sea king's daughter.

Ariel

Flounder stuck his head up out of the water next to her.

"That sure was Eric," the fish said. "Wow, he looked so different."

Ariel signed absently: *I'm sure he'd say the same about you.*

"Hey," Flounder said a little shyly, a little proudly, swaying back and forth in the water to admire his own belly. "I have an official position in the castle now. I *have* to keep up my weight!"

Ariel smiled.

But these were all just words meant to diffuse the tension and emotional weight of the moment. They didn't mean anything. Flounder was really asking if she was all right, and saying that he was there for her.

So little actual communication was represented by words that were said aloud, she had realized upon losing her voice. Often the real meaning lay underneath and unspoken.

Sometimes people forgot that she wasn't deaf as well as mute, and then the conversations got really interesting.

They scooted together just below the surface. The water turned and began to stink of organic matter, tar, things alien to the ocean. While the overall smell was a little much for a mer, human activity and refuse often meant extra food for the fish who dared to live so close to the shore. Covering every stony and wooden surface underwater were razor-sharp barnacles; ebon black bouquets of mussels; clusters of soft purple velvety tube worms, all mouth and utterly harmless. Crabs braver and less artistically inclined than Sebastian endlessly clambered up and down piers and ship-wrecks. Sometimes one would wave to her and then drop to the ocean floor, unable to hang on with one claw, and tire-lessly begin the climb again.

The way to the castle was a bit of an obstacle course between the trawling nets that scooped up everything on the floor of the bay, regardless of its edibility, and the raw sewage that leaked out of giant pipes hanging over the water. They had to swim a broad way around the marsh: water bil-lowing out from a drainage creek was an unhealthy bright yellow. The seepage blossomed and flowed into the sea as pretty as an octopus's ink, but it burned Ariel's scales. What were the humans *doing* up there?

When they made it to the blessedly cleaner waters near the castle (built a bit removed from the commercial center of town, specifically to avoid the bad airs and plagues), Ariel spun through the currents like an otter, shaking out her hair and ruffling her scales free of filth. Then she and Flounder popped to the surface and looked around.

There were exactly eight guards posted along the beach and at the entrance of the lagoon where she had once saved Eric. Easily a third as many as the last time she had tried to approach the castle. One was trimming his nails with a small knife; another had his boots off so he could rest his feet in the sand. Not a single man was taking his job seriously.

And why should they? The foreign princess of the castle had ordered soldiers to guard the beach against the incursion of . . . an unspecified pelagic threat. Possibly a mermaid. Who on earth *would* take that seriously?

Maybe . . . maybe this really will work this time.

A squawk drew Ariel's attention skyward. Seemingly innocent, a half dozen shining white seagulls soared picturesquely above the beach. Well, one had greyish underwings and a grey tuft of unlikely feathers sprouting on his head. Another, smaller than the others, trailed the grey one—Scuttle and Jona.

They were ready, waiting for the signal.

"On it," Flounder said, gliding off.

Ariel waited in the water while he sought out a flying fish and conveyed her orders. Just a few moments later she felt the shimmering vibration of the school swimming in unison, above and below the water, where worlds collided.

They were beautiful. Silver and winged, they took to the air as easily as they sped through the water, like the material world meant nothing to them: space, objects, water, air, time, light—they were all the same. They made the noise of a thousand large locusts or of the strange crackles before lightning strikes.

A couple of the guards looked up curiously.

And then the gulls attacked.

Ariel had to turn away, remembering that what they did was for her and that she should be grateful. She hadn't been quite sure what to expect when Jona had suggested a distraction; she figured it would involve eyes and soft human parts and clawing and maybe the dropping of sharp shells on their scalps. What they chose to do was far less violent but devastatingly more effective.

In any case, it made Flounder almost choke in laughter.

The guards ran. At first crazily, back and forth, around and around, trying to escape the stinking, terrible hailstorm. The smarter ones immediately made for the shelter of the castle and the cliffs.

"Go!" Flounder said, recovering himself.

With a few quick leaps Ariel porpoised herself into much shallower water. Using all her strength she forced herself upright so she was standing on her tail. Then she waved the trident and became a human.

That was it.

That was *all*.

Her father could have done it years ago. Long before all the terrible things began.

Before she had even met Eric.

He could have turned her into a human for a day, or several days, and let her explore life on land until she tired of it, or became scared, or grew lonely, or missed him.

Once she had met Eric, Triton could have saved her the trouble of selling her voice and her life—and then *his* life—for the chance to fall in love with the boy. She would have been able to walk on her own two legs, and say things with her own voice, like "I'm the mermaid who saved you. Yep, I know that song, because I wrote it. Let me sing it for you."

And she could have sung. And they could have fallen in love.

She and her father could have worked out a deal like the Old Gods: Proserpine and Hades and Ceres. She could spend some of her days on land, the rest of her life in the sea. And then everyone would have been—well, if not deliriously happy, then at least satisfied that it was the best they could all work out.

But . . . the slightly older Ariel added . . . *who knows what really would have happened?* The trident's power rose and fell with the sea and the moon. She could have stayed human for only a few days a month; a week, maybe two at best. Would that have been enough to sustain a relationship?

Would it have turned out that human princes were just as boring as merprinces?

Ariel dismissed the old familiar thoughts and focused on the matter at hand. She scooped the human clothes out of her bag and dragged them on as best she could. They were thick and coarse, and her now-human skin was tenderer than the scales of a mermaid tail. The shoes, crusted with old barnacles she had to scrape off, would have to wait until they had dried out on land for a while. She shook the trident and it changed, shrinking. Its surface glittered even more golden, as though the metal became more refined the more tightly together it was pushed. Finally it was in the palm of her hand and shaped like a comb. Countless tines replaced the initial three, each with a tiny spike on its tip that minutely replicated the barbs. She admired it for half a moment and then slipped it into her hair, above her right ear, wedging it in place among her intricate braids.

Keeping one eye out for the guards and her hands close

to the ground in case she slipped, Ariel clumsily made her way through the shallows to a sheltered part of the lagoon. It was like the first walk of a baby sea turtle in reverse: tentative claws in the sand, a burst of warmth from the sun on her face after incubating in the earth for so long. The dragging, terrified walk to the water. The land and sky full of danger and death, the ocean full of safety and warmth. All this was the same; she was just doing it backward.

It was hard thinking things and keeping track of her feet at the same time. Sand *felt*. Pressure on the skin of her feet *felt*. The breeze kept whipping away her breaths in little gasps. Salt, which surrounded her normally, dried in white patches on her skin and stung her lips like acid.

She stumbled, pitching forward.

With the will of a queen, she forced, she *ordered* her left foot out to stop the fall. Tail muscles recently converted to thighs screamed at the strangeness of the motions.

She paused, taking a breath, knowing her body would recover. It wasn't as if she were walking on iron blades that cut deep into her soles with every step—though that's what it felt like for a moment. This was beach sand, always described by humans as soft and inviting. If she fell, it wouldn't be the end of the world.

The noise of gulls and guards drifted on the wind to her.

"Stupid bird . . ."

"Get offa me!"

"RUN!"

But as she rounded the edge of the escarpment that began the sheltered area, everything shut off like a spell: the wind, the sting of the wind on her face, the noise of the guards, the constant *feel* of the air pushing against her skin. Without realizing it consciously, Ariel wound up in the lagoon with the rounded rock that stuck out of the sea where she had first brought Eric, where the water was warm and slow and shallow.

And it was silent.

Ariel slumped down into the sand and let out a sigh that was almost a sob. She took several deep breaths now that she didn't have to fight the breeze for them. She closed her eyes and tilted her head toward the sun. Years ago her desire to win Eric had been so strong that she had forgotten all the other reasons she wanted to walk on the land: to feel the sand and the warmth of Helios directly on her skin.

It was just as amazing as she had always imagined it.

But Ariel was spending too much time caught between sea and land in the little lagoon. She was there to find her father, not enjoy herself.

"I followed your footprints," came a voice from above.

Ariel turned and watched the seagull execute a delicate landing on the stone with such precise control her feet touched the surface just as she slowed to a stop.

"Think of that," Jona said. "I followed a *mermaid's*

footprints in the sand. That should be part of an epic poem. Or a book. Or something."

Ariel raised an eyebrow at the gull.

"It's something that shouldn't exist," the gull went on, explaining helpfully.

Ariel rolled her eyes. *I get it. I'm not stupid.*

Flounder popped his head out of the water. "Wow, that was amazing. It went right according to plan!"

Scuttle landed heavily on the stone next to his great-grandgull, more like a bomb of feathers than a professional flier.

"You bet your gills it did!" Scuttle crowed. "You shoulda seen them. They ran like we were the plague! Like we were terrifying multiarmed giants! Like we were—"

"Gulls making a mess everywhere," Flounder finished.

"Well, you say potato," Scuttle sniffed.

If you're all done, Ariel signed, *I think I have a castle to get to.*

"The queen thinks it's time to go," Flounder said.

"Phase two, I gotcha," Scuttle said, winking.

"You'll . . . you'll keep an eye on her, right?" Flounder asked softly.

"Aw, you bet we will," Scuttle promised. "She's like family. We'll watch over her like hawks. No, not like hawks. They're too snooty. Like albatrosses. No, they're so *difficult*. Like . . . lions!"

"We'll make sure one of us has an eye on her at all times," Jona translated.

"But right now"—the old gull wheezed a little—"I may take a breather, you know? These bones ache more than they used to. The kid here can take care of things for a bit. I'd trust her with my life."

In answer, Ariel scruffed him under the chin and kissed him on the beak.

She then turned to both gulls and bowed, clasping her hands together.

Thank you both for everything.

Scuttle tried to imitate the gesture. It came off as far less impressive, but was twice as endearing. Jona cocked her head and regarded him with a glittering right eye: if Ariel had to guess, she would have said that the younger bird was smiling, perhaps fondly, at her great-grandfather.

"Good luck. We'll be up above," the gull said, and waited for just the right wind to sweep her like a kite up into the sky, slowly and methodically. Scuttle flapped hard and took off like a shot.

"Be careful. *Please*, Ariel," Flounder begged, sounding like the old Flounder.

Ariel gave him a smile.

Then she made her way to the castle.

Ariel

She decided to avoid the stone staircase that led directly from the beach into the castle; that was for the enjoyment of the prince and his household only. She remembered joyfully racing down its steps to the sunset beach, then belatedly noticing maids and footmen carefully skirting the edge and going around to the back of the complex.

She followed her memory, circling around the north side of the castle. Right before the wet, compact sand petered out into a lush estuary, the well-trodden path of the commoners who worked in the castle became visible. Hidden from the amazing views and picturesque scenery of the bay, scullery maids scoured out pots with rags and the bristly stalks of local horsetail plants. Housekeepers beat carpets draped on the stunted, hearty little bushes and pines that lived too close to the salt water that was life to the sea and poison to the land. Scullery maids and boys dumped baskets of garbage onto a growing midden.

Right there.

In the middle of the rich, clean water that fed and drained the shellfish nursery, where seashore birds made their nests, where eels and elvers and minnows made their lives.

Ew.

There was no formal sign for that.

Ariel wrinkled her nose and turned away.

As she passed more servants and messengers and peddlers and couriers, she wondered if anyone would recognize the mute girl from years before. She hadn't aged the way humans did. Her face did look different, but was it different enough? Her hair was tightly bound against her head. She wasn't wearing the pretty blue dress with its fitted bodice and was definitely missing the giant, floppy, pretty-as-a-picture bow the maid Carlotta had put in her hair.

Was she imagining it, or were people looking sideways at her? Were they trying to take her in without seeming to stare? Did they notice her? Was she just being paranoid?

She didn't have a plan if someone stopped her. She had nothing more to go on than *sneak into the castle and find her father.* Either she had enough confidence as queen that she felt she could deal with whatever was thrown at her, or she literally had no way to plan for the unexpected and so didn't. *Probably the latter,* she thought with a sigh. Still the same old Ariel, swimming in where sharks feared to paddle.

On the other hand, I could always return to the other plan—calling up the waves to more forcibly rescue Father. . . .

She held her breath at the main gate, but none of the guards looked at her twice.

None of the guards.

She looked around, suddenly realizing what should have been obvious if she hadn't been so nervous: there were many, many more guards than when she had last been there. *Here,* in the castle, not at the beach where they once were. And not just guards, either; there were real soldiers patrolling the halls. Men and boys in keen military dress, shined boots, shined buttons, sabers hanging from their sides and caps cockily perched on their heads.

There were other people, too. Richly clad men and women walked in slow, carefully paced pairs and trios, talking in low voices, checking fancy pocket watches, smiling to other pairs and trios they passed with smiles that disappeared immediately after. Men in poufy shirts with questionable expressions, dour and shifty. Women in bustles and long-flowing gowns that trailed behind them like jellyfish tendrils, looking at each other shyly from behind fans or boldly from under giant hats.

Someone almost crashed into Ariel, pushing a small wagon with an open trunk loaded up on it. Laid carefully over sawdust and packing on the top were—*guns*. She remembered seeing the castle guards carry them, present them, occasionally shoot them. Muskets with cruel bayonets, shining and black and freshly oiled.

While she was staring, Ariel was knocked from behind by a self-important man with florid cheeks and weak eyes. He strode past her without apologizing and was followed by a servant carrying what looked very much like a small chest of gold.

What is going on here?

Tirulia was a sleepy little kingdom, and this seaside castle was the unofficial capital of its most carefree, bucolic quarter. Eric had no real duties. His parents were still alive and actively ruling—at least they had been the last time she was here. He had no particular desire to take over as king. He had a real desire to sail. He was young, he was enthusiastic, he loved music and the sea and wind in his hair. Everything that she loved, too, but flipped to its Dry World version.

This castle no longer felt like him. It felt . . . foreign.

Confused, Ariel tried to reorient herself and keep walking, undistracted by what was apparently the new normal.

When a washerwoman walked by, unable to see directly in front of her because of the pile of freshly dried linens blossoming like an anemone out of the basket she carried, Ariel swiped a couple from the top. She carried them in front of her as importantly as if they were a chest of gold, and no one even glanced at her.

I'm becoming as tricky as a human. So quickly! She thought with light irony as she marched into the next room . . .

. . . and then immediately hid behind a cabinet.

Standing there stiffly, giving a footman the sort of quiet, gentle-but-severe dressing down that could be done only by the Bretlanders, was Grimsby—Eric's manservant and closest confidant.

Much like a mermaid, he hadn't aged at all since the last time she had seen him. But perhaps that was because he had already been old when they first met and didn't have that many more changes to make before his final transmogrification. His light blue eyes did seem a little wearier—also like her own.

He finished with the footman, sending him off red-faced and chagrined, then headed with slow, solid steps down the hall. The energy of this new castle swirled around him; servants, visiting nobles' servants, the visiting nobles themselves, the men and women with the money . . . and though he was a true Bretlandian butler who rarely let his feelings show, Ariel watched him trying *not* to disapprove of it all with his clear and tired eyes. He moved like a shepherd of comb jellies, trying to urge them through a foreign school of quick-swimming minnows, neither affected nor scared by them, only vaguely concerned.

Ariel found herself holding the skirts of her dress tightly, almost like a timid girl.

She wished she could go to him. In his own way, Grimsby had been extraordinarily kind to her in her short time on land. Gently guiding when she did the wrong thing, leading silently by example rather than chastising aloud.

She wanted to grab him, to pull him aside and find out what was wrong. Why did he seem upset? What had changed? Did it have to do with all the activity in the castle?

But . . . even if she did manage to get him alone . . . they couldn't talk.

She couldn't talk.

And she highly doubted he could understand a sign language based on an ancient and, to him, foreign language.

She watched Grimsby go, his exit immediately camouflaged by skirts and jackets, scurrying and bustling, and felt something tighten within her. They could have meant something to each other, had things worked out differently.

She took a deep breath, willing the knot in her heart to go away.

The Queen of the Sea had a mission. She had come to find her father. Anything else she would deal with later, if at all. For now, she had to figure out where her father was being kept.

Think logically, she reminded herself. The gulls had told her that they'd seen Ursula getting dressed, primping, while talking with Triton. With a feeling of nausea she faced the obvious: as Vanessa, the sea witch was married to Eric. The two would either be sharing the same room or adjoining apartments in the royal tower. Ariel knew where that was.

She straightened up, held her linens out, and marched forward, trying to set her face into the blank stare of a maid. It was easier than it would have been the first time she had come on land, when she had no cause to do anything aside from stare around with wide eyes, drinking in the strange world and its goings-on. She had never even considered trying to blend in before; there *was* no strange or different in the world of the mer. It never occurred to her that people would notice or not like her if she stuck out and acted odd.

She brushed aside this slow-moving slipper shell of a thought to another corner of her mind, and wondered if there was a possibility of catching another glimpse of Eric.

The stairs were a little tricky—"up" was a strange movement for her still-new legs and feet—and she made it as far as the first hallway before she was discovered.

"Hey, you! Who are you? You're not supposed to be upstairs!"

It wasn't one of the now-multitudinous soldiers; it was a rather pretty but shark-eyed maid. Ariel didn't react; she just stood there, unsure what to do. She couldn't even make up an excuse for being there—or at least make it be understood.

The maid grabbed a passing guard. He didn't seem to have any interest in either one of them and tried to continue his rounds, but the maid sort of *shook* him at Ariel.

"*Hey!* She's not supposed to be up here. She could be a spy!"

The guard grunted in displeasure but started toward Ariel.

The Queen of the Sea dropped her laundry and ran.

Ariel wondered vaguely how her new legs would react to this new situation.

Just fine, apparently.

She ducked between footmen, dodged through couples, threw herself around corners. There was a second stairway she remembered, toward the back of the residency tower, which the chambermaids used. The one she probably should have chosen to begin with. She put a hand out to the sandstone wall to steady herself as she began her first descent with new legs. The firmness and familiarity of the rock gave her courage. She urged her feet down the steps like ceremonial dolphins pulling her golden chariot in a circuit race.

"Halt!" came a voice from behind her—along with the sound of polished boots striking stone.

Ariel panicked and practically fell onto the landing. She wasted a moment trying to decide whether to continue down another narrow flight to the sub-basement where the wine cellars were, along with another exit to the outside. But that was probably what the soldiers expected her to do.

She plunged ahead instead, toward where she remembered the grand ballroom was.

There was less chaos here, and fewer people. But just as Ariel thought she had escaped the last of them, she saw someone looming, blocking her escape at the end of the painted hall.

Carlotta.

The friendly maid who had tried to show Ariel the proper way to bathe. Who had taken it upon herself to pick out an outfit for the mermaid and show her how to dress nicely. With the floppy bow. Who hadn't been upset when Ariel made a fool of herself using human things the wrong way—who had only found it delightful, and a wonderful curative for the often moody prince.

Carlotta's black hair was still thick though shot through with grey, and in its usual bun—and not under the bright red kerchief Ariel remembered. Her bodice and new little hat were starched white cotton, pure and strict. But the strangely formal uniform upset Ariel less than the look in Carlotta's eyes when she saw the mermaid bolting toward her.

Surprise.

Realization.

Suspicion.

Their moment of glowering silence was interrupted by voices down the hall:

"Where did she go?"

"Did you see her?"

"You check downstairs, I'll check this floor."

They would be upon her in a moment.

Carlotta reached out and threw open a small door: a broom closet, its edges cleverly concealed in the overly ornate golden moldings.

She raised an eyebrow at Ariel.

The mermaid decided, for no reason she could logically explain beyond the past kindness shown her, to trust the scowling woman.

She dove in, trying not to wince as the door was slammed behind her. A cloud of dust rose from the brooms and rags and other cleaning implements. A distinct odor of mold and dry rot assailed her nose.

She tried not to sneeze, holding her face and nose with both hands, pressing her palms into her cheeks.

Queen of the Sea, she thought. *Look at me now.*

Voices outside the closet, muffled but loud:

"Carlotta—have you seen a maid? She wasn't authorized to be upstairs, and . . ."

"Oh, you don't mean the pale one, about yea high, skinny as a bean?" Carlotta sounded exasperated and very, very believable.

"Yes, with the blue skirts . . ."

"Blast that girl. She's new. Not gifted with much besides her girlish figure, I don't mind saying. You know, up here."

Ariel frowned despite knowing it was a lie. She could practically see Carlotta tapping her head in illustration.

"I told her the wash was for Lord Francese's *manservant*, not the lord himself. And then she disappeared. Should have known."

"There is a problem of security in the castle, Carlotta. The spies . . ."

"If that girl's a spy, I'm the pope," Carlotta snorted. "She's just a pretty dumb thing from the country. I'll give her a good talking to when I find her and lock her in her room without supper."

At this, the guard laughed. "You've never withheld a meal from anyone—or anything—in your life. You'll probably scold her and then force five rolls on her to fatten her up. But you've got to talk to her. Princess Vanessa . . ."

"Say no more. It will be resolved, or she will go."

"Thank you, Carlotta. I'll inform my men."

Ariel waited for the clicking footsteps to fade, then waited some more.

Just when she thought it might be safe to open the door a crack, it was thrown wide open. A serious, annoyed-looking Carlotta filled the entire frame and blocked most of the light.

"Come with me," she ordered, in a tone she had never used on Ariel before.

The Queen of the Sea meekly obeyed.

They went through the ballroom, over the beautiful inlaid floor covered in meaningless brown and golden curlicues. Ariel wondered what it would be like to glide over the slippery polished boards, music swirling around her. She had only danced with Eric once, on a cobbled plaza to an amateur violinist, but even that had been incredible.

The ceiling was a frescoed masterpiece: a sky with little fluffy clouds at the edges, winged putti peeping out among them. Giant glazed windows let in sea light, sparkling off the water as well as from the sky. Circling very deliberately was a single white gull, who managed to keep her head pointed at the castle wherever she was in her revolutions. *Jona.*

Carlotta hurried on through the great room into a white corridor at the end and pulled Ariel into a small space lined with benches and tables. It looked like a staging area for servants to plate hors d'oeuvres and wine before bringing them out to hot and thirsty dancers, very much like at the palace in Atlantica—but this one had a ceiling, and the tables were all at one level. Under the sea, you could swim to whatever height you needed. *How limited humans are. . . .*

But she didn't have time to ponder such things. Carlotta stood in front of her, arms crossed.

"It's you!"

Ariel nodded and shrugged. *Well, obviously.*

"Where have you *been*?" Carlotta demanded. "Where did you go?"

The mermaid winced. How could she explain?

"Eric loved you. You two would have been so happy together . . ." the maid continued accusingly. Ariel wondered if she had been spying on them any of the times they almost kissed. "And then you just . . . disappeared! And he married that horrible, horrible Vanessa, and now she's ruining the kingdom and he's . . . he's not the prince he was. Not the boy he was. That boy's gone. Where did *you* go?"

Merfolk and humans and fish and *all* those who spoke seemed to be the same: they wasted language, throwing out words like chum, hoping some of them would land accurately and truthfully convey what they were thinking or feeling. Ariel paused, carefully weighing and measuring the other woman's words while she figured out how to answer.

Eric married Vanessa. This was an objective fact; Ariel had seen that happen.

Vanessa is ruining the kingdom. Interesting! So the changes in the castle were probably due to her.

Eric is not the boy he was. Also interesting, and terrifying. He was still under the spell Ursula cast to put him under her power. That would certainly explain the haunted, hunted look on Eric's face when she had seen him earlier. He probably knew *something* was wrong, but not precisely what.

Ariel pursed her lips. Then she mimed a formal walk, hands together.

She drew her hand gracefully down her hair, indicating a veil.

She put her hands together again: flowers.

Vanessa marrying Eric.

"The wedding, yes, yes, the wedding. They got married," Carlotta said, impatiently.

Ariel tapped her head, pointed at the maid.

"I remember it! What do you mean? *Think* about it? It was just the wedding on the yacht. Beautiful. Hideous. At the same time. There was nothing . . ."

Ariel shook her head. She tapped her head harder. She rotated her other hand: *Come on, there's more.*

"What are you trying to say . . . ? They were married, and Max ruined the lovely cake, and oh . . ." Carlotta's vision went cloudy; she stopped focusing on the girl before her. "He ruined the cake because . . . he was scared. There was a storm. No, the sky was clear. No—but there was lightning.

Lightning . . . from . . . a man in the water. A man with a beard, and a crown, naked . . . like Neptune himself . . ."

Carlotta frowned, rubbing her head.

"What is this nonsense? Why is it coming to me now, clear as day? Clear as a picture: the man in the sea wasn't drowning. He was throwing lightning. And Vanessa . . . he and she were . . . *fighting*? They were fighting like . . . titans, from the old stories. There was magic. All around. Dangerous and violent. And then you—and then he . . . And then you and the naked man were gone. Both gone. But Vanessa stayed. . . ."

She sat down heavily on a stool. Her skirts puffed up around her, almost as if in sympathy. "I . . . haven't thought about that in years. I know I've thought it before, or dreamed it before. I haven't wanted to. It's like it *hurts* to remember. I couldn't remember."

She looked up at Ariel.

"Some funny business about Vanessa, isn't there?" she ventured. "That man—he was your father, wasn't he? He really was Neptune—or someone out of the Old Testament. A patriarch. He wasn't evil—I never felt that for a moment. And then you disappearing . . . into the sea. Eric acting strange and moony around Vanessa. She isn't . . . she isn't a good . . . person, is she?"

Ariel shook her head very slowly. *No.*

"She isn't like . . . us, is she?"

No.

"And what does that make you, then?"

Ariel hesitated. Would knowing the truth put Carlotta in danger? She already knew half of the truth. The *main* truth. That Vanessa was not a good person. That there had been a battle. And all the strange and terrible things that had happened on her prince's wedding day. So how would knowing this little extra bit make a difference, really?

Ariel looked around the room, searching for the answer. She didn't have a sign for it.

Finally she put her hands together and moved them sinuously forward, cutting the air like water.

Carlotta stared at her, mouth open like a gaping fish's.

Then she shook her head.

"You know what? Forget I asked. I don't think my tired old brain could deal with it right now anyway. The important thing is that Vanessa *is* bad, really bad, which is fairly obvious if you just see what she's doing. . . ."

While pleased that Carlotta had come to the same conclusion she had, Ariel was intrigued by this news. She reached out and tapped the maid's shoulder and shrugged obviously. *What* is *she doing?*

"Well, she has us at war with our neighbors. Look at Garhaggio," Carlotta said with a snort, throwing her arm out at the window as if the village were right there, visible. "Never had a problem with them before—never had much to do with them at all aside from occasionally getting their nice cheese in. It *is* a nice cheese, though. I love it, the fancy white rind. They say it's the mountain spring water."

Ariel tried not to look impatient.

". . . I'm just a senior house maid, I know!" Carlotta said, seeing her face. "I don't know about politics and wars and international policy. All I know is that Garhaggio was burned to the ground. By *us*. By Tirulia! So no more cheese. And there is a conscription for able-bodied boys here. So, I suppose, we can burn down more cheese-making villages that won't bend the knee to Tirulia. And yet we're friends with *Ibria* now? We've been on uneasy terms with them for over two hundred years!

"Strange, sneaky-looking men and women roam the castle, and they all have Vanessa's ear. And yet the princess also thinks everyone is after her. So everyone thinks everyone *else* is a spy and hopes for a reward by turning his neighbor in. Vanessa is turning the kingdom upside down, and no one trusts anyone else, and we're nearly at war with everyone around us.

"And you're back," Carlotta finished with conviction.

Ariel looked at her sideways. She couldn't figure out where the maid's look of satisfaction came from as Carlotta resolutely crossed her arms and nodded like she understood.

The Queen of the Sea started to tilt her head. *Yes. I'm back. And . . . ?*

"And you're here to set everything right, aren't you?"

The mermaid blinked her large aquamarine eyes.

"With Vanessa and Eric and all. You're going to make things like they were," Carlotta said, somehow perfectly mixing the utter belief of a five-year-old with the stern voice of an adult who knew Ariel would *do the right thing*. "You're going to defeat her, or make Eric fall in love with you, or something. Maybe you'll make him forget that you *and* Vanessa ever existed. . . . I don't know or care about the details, although you did seem like a nice enough girl at one time."

Ariel put her hands up and started to shake her head.

"Don't you start with that," Carlotta said, putting her hand up. "I may not be a scholar or a wisewoman, but it wasn't until *after you showed up* the first time that all of this happened. Whatever your role, you had some hand in this, in the destruction of Tirulia and our way of life—and *Eric*."

Ariel's queenliness faltered for a moment at his name. Everything else was just supposition, theory, people who had nothing to do with her. But Eric, that sad, aging sailor on his lonely boat . . .

Carlotta was right. He was an utterly defeated man.

And despite Ariel's mix of bitterness and wistfulness about the realm of humans and her misadventures in the Dry World, *none of what happened afterward would have happened at all without her interference.*

Not that she would take *any* blame for the chaos Ursula had wrought: the Queen of the Sea would not be held responsible for the evil sea witch's doings. But the truth was that Ursula would not be there, causing havoc, if it weren't for Ariel.

The world, both wet and dry, spun for a moment as Ariel thought about this. Although the humans had complete dominance on the planet, although they controlled all land and nature and everything around them, *she*, a little mermaid, had introduced a foreign element that threatened to utterly destroy the kingdom of Tirulia. Like a single pathogen infecting a coral reef. She wondered how far it would spread if she simply . . . found her father and left. Would Ursula stop with this one kingdom, or would her mad quest for power and glory continue until she took over all human lands?

Ariel's plan was to find her father, restore the trident to him, and leave.

Perhaps her plans had to be amended somehow.

She nodded slightly.

Carlotta sighed. "Thank you."

Somehow the maid intuited the squall that had just risen and dispersed in Ariel's mind, and seen through her large eyes to a calm decision made underneath.

"And now, were you trying to sneak in the castle for the reasons of this mission?"

Ariel nodded, again, feeling somehow foolish.

Carlotta laughed.

"And did you think doing it in the dress of a long-drowned princess, a visitor to Davy Jones's locker, would somehow fool us?"

Ariel looked down at her outfit. She now saw the worn shades of blue that striped and stippled the garment in uneven strengths. The strangely frayed hems, threads dried in all positions, used to the freedom of the sea and not to hanging in proper ragged fringes, straight down. The circles and whorls of salt she had thought sparkled so prettily under the sun. Her shoes, decorated with dead barnacles, which had a sad elegance about them.

"You're seeing it now," the maid said with a sigh. "And your *hair*, of course."

Ariel put a hand to her locks in surprise. Her hair, while healthy, thick, and long, was hardly an unusual color. There were merfolk families who had tresses the blue of waves, the green of gems, the purple of poisonous mollusks.

Once again Carlotta read her correctly.

"Maybe red is normal for . . . wherever you're from," she said quickly, skipping over any thoughts that she didn't want to acknowledge, "but here it's very, very distinctive. The people up north sometimes have it . . . and right now, everyone is suspicious of northerners. Come with me and we'll get you dressed up right, with a headcloth to cover your hair. And then you can save us all. Is it a deal?"

Ariel nodded, and Carlotta nodded, and no more words were needed.

Ariel

There were fairy tales—known even to those who starred in those fairy tales—about human girls who worked for mer-witches or mermaids in return for their help. The mermaids in the story would be so charmed by the good little girls that they not only help but also bedeck them in gems and pearls, and brush their hair with jeweled combs, and let them choose whatever gowns they desire out of a treasure trove of goods that were lost at sea.

This is a very strange, upside-down version of that story, Ariel decided.

Carlotta searched for the plainest, oldest, most unre-markable shift she could manage, a maroonish thing that was more bag than dress. It acquired a little shape once a suitably stained apron with braided ties had been fitted around Ariel's waist. They didn't even bother with stockings, just a pair of ugly boot-like slippers. The final touch was a rusty grey headscarf the maid expertly knotted at the nape of Ariel's neck and pulled down close around her braids, making sure it stayed there with a strip of dishrag she tied at the back of her head, above her ears.

Like a crown.

"All right, that'll do, though maybe you'll want to smear a little bit of dust on your cheeks," Carlotta said, eyeing her professionally.

Ariel looked down at her outfit. When she had been in the Dry World the first time they had outfitted her with a pretty little dress that the maid had thought was appropriate for a beautiful girl of no readily apparent station: she could have been a student or a modest princess. The mermaid tried not to smile, amused at the difference.

Then she thanked the woman the only way she could, managing it awkwardly without the supportive, thick feel of the water around her: she bent at the waist and bowed her head, giving Carlotta the respect that normally only another member of royalty received.

"Hmm," the maid said, suddenly a little unnerved. She made as if to curtsy, then patted down her hair. "Something's different about you, girl. You're not the same little strip of a thing who came dancing into our castle, making our prince smile. . . . You've changed. Somehow. I don't know how, exactly."

Neither do I, Ariel thought back.

Now she could search for her father properly. In her new outfit Ariel felt invisible, like she was wearing a magic cloak that allowed her to go anywhere unseen. Carlotta had given her a tray with some random food scraps on it—heels of bread, a goblet, some small fruit knives—that made it seem like she could have been on her way from anywhere in the castle. For a moment Ariel wondered if there *were* any spies from the north, or anywhere else, posing as servants. Apparently it was quite easy to go unnoticed if you dressed the part, kept your head down, and acted servile.

The one time a guard stopped her, Ariel just gestured the tray at him. That was enough: he grabbed a heel of the bread, leered at her, and ushered her on.

Ariel had to fight the urge not to gag. Was he really eating what he *knew* were someone else's scraps? Did these "advanced" humans, with their machines and fires and carriages with wheels, know nothing about the spread of diseases? Surely there was a land equivalent of the unseen, tiny sick-fishes that surrounded and lived in those who were ill. . . .

Thinking about this kept her from growing nervous as she approached the main royal apartments.

Two girls passed her, swearing and gossiping.

"Not me. I *love* how many baths she takes. It means I get a half watch to myself practically every night. . . ."

"Sure, but is it worth it overall? My aunt is paying *twice* as much tax this season as she did last . . . while our princess bathes in expensive oils and burns through wood in the middle of summer!"

"But she doesn't bathe in the oils *or* hot water. That's the strange thing. Her baths are always cold and usually with mineral salt."

"Whatever! She's stealing from the poor of this kingdom to finance her stupid army and her stupid baths!"

"Shhhh! Keep your voice down!"

Ariel chanced a look at the girls as they passed, trying to guess their ages. Would she have been friends with them if she were human? Or was she, despite her looks, already too old? Did losing your voice and the love of your life and having to run a kingdom change you in ways more dramatic than mere years?

From the moist air that hit her a moment later it was obvious that Ursula was in the middle of one of her fancy baths right then. *Good.* It gave Ariel time to search the bedrooms.

She knocked tentatively on the royal couple's apartment door. The way a servant might, or a nervous ex-lover.

No answer.

Disappointed and relieved, Ariel pushed the door open with her back and shoulders the way she had seen other servants do, so she didn't need to use her tray-encumbered hands. And once she was in . . .

She sighed in relief.

She had never been in Eric's room; humans had very odd notions of appropriate behavior. But if she had to guess, this was still Eric's room—and *only* Eric's room. No girly or princess-y things at all.

There was a bookshelf stuffed with maps and scrolls and folios of music. There was a drum from a foreign land. There was a portrait of the prince and a much younger Max, all smiles and sunlight. There were piles of arcane metal apparatus; tubes with thick glass lenses, pyramids with pendulums hanging from the apex of delicate golden crosspieces, things that were almost recognizable as rulers. There were several toy—*model*—ships.

There was a soft, puffy pillow on the floor that was obviously for the dog, but there was dog hair all over the foot of the bed.

There was a heavy desk under a small window, buried under endless sheets of music paper, inkwells, pens.

There wasn't a single hint of anyone besides Eric in the room. Nothing of a tentacled sea witch with questionable taste in decor, nor of a human princess with human-princess belongings. There was nothing soft, brightly colored, pastel, glittery, flowery—no random scarf tossed over the back of the bed, no velvet or silk shoe kicked halfway under it. Nothing that wasn't shipshape, masculine, and Eric-y.

Ariel wanted to stay and poke through things, try to get a glimpse of the boy she had loved. But her time was limited.

There was a doorway that connected his bedroom to an adjacent one. She tiptoed in. This was Vanessa's room.

The royal couple was living side by side. Not together. *Not together.*

Ariel didn't really want to unpack her feelings around this, but she couldn't help picking at them, like taking a stick and seeing what was in a crevasse of dead coral. Surely she hadn't hoped for Eric to stay . . . single? After all these years? To remain as he was in her memory?

Surely she couldn't *blame* him for having any feelings for Vanessa. The witch had cast a mighty spell on him. It wouldn't be his fault if he did everything she said, fawned over her, slept in the same room as she.

None of these logical thoughts explained away the joy that she felt. Somehow Eric had managed to keep a portion of himself separate from his beglamoured wife; somehow he knew something wasn't quite right.

Ariel allowed herself one tiny, triumphant pull of her lips into the ghost of a smile, then stepped into what was very obviously Vanessa's domestic demesne.

There was a ridiculous bed shaped like a scallop, or maybe a deep-sea clam. The ridges were wide and deep but far too precise and symmetrical for either creature. Its plaster shell was open, so the bed was in what would have been the bottom half of the mollusk; the top half stood upright as a decorative backdrop hung with golden lanterns and convenient little shelves for knickknacks. The whole thing was upholstered in purple silk the color of a deadly Portuguese man-o'-war.

The rest of the room, crowded by the bed though it was, was further filled with mismatched and disturbing treasures. There were statues of twisted and tortured heroes, their faces distorted in agony. Covering one entire wall was a painting of squiggly, squirming humans in some sort of fiery cavern. There was pain on their faces but glee on the visage of the one who was tormenting them—he was red and bearded and had a trident like Triton's.

Triton himself didn't appear to be anywhere obvious in the room. Ariel moved farther in, picking up and putting down the disgusting little pieces of bric-a-brac. Among all the horror was an ironically delicate vanity covered in mother-of-pearl—and, intriguingly, all manner of exquisite little glass bottles. Scents from the east, oils from the west, attar of roses, nut butter, extract of myrrh, sandalwood decoctions, jasmine hydrosols . . . Everything to make someone smell exquisite.

Or to mask whatever it was she really smelled like, Ariel thought wryly.

Or were the oils and butters for more medicinal reasons—for the cecaelia's skin? Ariel found herself looking at her own hands, rubbing them over each other lightly. Last time she had only been in the Dry World for a few days. Was it—literally—drying? Was it difficult, or painful, for creatures from the sea to remain for months battered by void and air, despite their magic?

Ariel shivered. Magic didn't make everything simpler. Crossing the thresholds of worlds was no minor thing.

But none of the bottles looked like it contained a polyp.

Father? she asked silently. *Where are you?*

Footsteps rang in the hallway outside.

Frozen, Ariel waited for them to pass.

But they didn't. They came *in* . . . to Eric's apartment.

The mermaid looked around. If whoever came in knew that Vanessa didn't like heels of bread or drink wine at that time of day . . . the jig was up.

The intruder continued to pad around maddeningly. There were accompanying sounds of things being lifted, patted, folded. A maid, straightening or cleaning . . . Ursula's room would be next.

What should she *do*?

What would she do if she were the old Ariel and a shark were hunting her?

Without a second thought, the Queen of the Sea folded herself down as small as possible and hunkered down under the vanity.

Less than a second later the maid came into the doorway.

Ariel saw padded cloth house shoes and closed her eyes, willing invisibility.

As if the person standing there knew Ariel's position and were bent on drawing out her torture as long as possible, she *continued* to just stand there: neither leaving the doorway, nor entering Vanessa's room.

Ariel felt the strange sensation of sweat popping out on the back of her neck. It was thoroughly unpleasant, and tickled besides. She had to fight down an urge to scratch, or move, or stretch. *I am a queen,* she told herself as the itch became maddening. *I am not ruled by my body.*

"Max!" the maid called out. Ariel could just see her skirts move as she put her hands on her hips. "Max, where are you? Dinnertime! C'mon, you silly thing. You can't have gotten far. . . ."

There was no impatience in her voice, only love for the old dog.

But Ariel was so angry with the servant's existence she wanted to turn her into a sea cucumber. *Just for a few minutes.*

"Well, I know you wouldn't want to be in *here*, the *princess's* room," the maid said, her final words heavy with meaning. She spun and left, going all the way back out to the hallway. *"Maaaax . . ."*

Ariel breathed a heavy sigh of relief. She unfolded herself carefully, avoiding hitting her head on the ornate edge of the vanity.

Whew! That was ridiculously, painfully close.

She proceeded into the dressing room, where Vanessa kept her ridiculous assortment of clothes: bright-colored gowns with tiny, corseted waists and laced bodices that dove deep to expose vast amounts of décolletage. Wraps and shawls and jackets and hats with jewels and goldwork and more often than not the feathers—and sometimes the entire body—of some poor, exotic, and thoroughly dead bird.

She felt the silk of one long pale-rose sleeve. It was expert workmanship and utterly beautiful and thoroughly disgusting that such labor had been wasted on the evil woman. In a fairy tale, Ursula would be the wicked, lazy girl who wound up with dried seaweed and empty shells. *And maybe shrimp crawling out of her throat.*

She noticed something funny about a button on the sleeve just as she was about to let it drop: it was etched like scrimshaw, with lines so fine and thin they must have been made by a master—or a creature of magic.

The design was of an octopus.

Not a friendly one, like many that Ariel knew; this was elongated and sinister, with strangely evil eyes.

Ariel's own eyes darted around the room like a barracuda distracted by sparkly things. It was immediately clear, once she knew what to look for, that every piece of clothing and accessory had the octopus sigil somewhere on it: the diamond brooch on a collar, the buckle on a belt, a hidden embroidery on the more traditional Tirulian dresses.

Whatever her motivations were in staying among the humans she'd married into, Ursula had not forgotten her origins or her true self.

But there was nothing in the closet that could have been her hidden father; not a bottle or a jar or even a repurposed shoe. Maybe there was a hidden panel somewhere, or maybe the sea witch kept him locked up in a real dungeon, downstairs.

And then, along with a current of moist, soapy air . . .

. . . came a voice . . .

Her voice.

In the trailing end of a song.

". . . up on the land, where my lover walks. But I can only pine from the foamy waves. . . ."

Her voice.

She hadn't heard her own voice in years.

The day when Ursula first took her payment, it had felt like Ariel's very soul had been sucked out of her body. The young, silly merthing she was then hadn't even realized it. Like a ghost she went on with her quest, her desires, intent on her prize, not even realizing she was already dead to the world.

Okay, perhaps it wasn't quite that dramatic, Queen Ariel corrected herself gently.

But seeing Vanessa wed Eric, and her father killed, and realizing she would never get either man—or her voice— back . . . a part of her *had* truly died that day.

And now that witch was using her voice to sing in the bath.

Ariel wouldn't let the rage that was coursing through her veins control her. She *wouldn't.* She was a queen, and queens didn't lose control. Not for sweat, not for rage.

It was no easy task; like sweat, this kind of anger was a new experience.

She had been sad. She had been melancholy. She had cursed her fate as a voiceless monarch, railing against her lot quietly. Once in a while she had a burst of temper when she wanted to be heard and no one would listen, when people were shouting over her and ignoring her hands, as if because she had no voice she had nothing to say.

This was like nothing she had experienced before. It was like lava, burning through her skin and threatening to consume her whole.

Without thinking she moved toward the direction of the sound.

"*. . . heartless witch of the sea . . . ha ha! . . . heartless, heartless indeed, ensorcelling me . . .*"

The air grew moister, but not with the accompanying clouds of steam one expected from a luxuriously royal bath.

"*Oh, let him see me for who I am, for without a voice, my face alone must speak for me . . .*"

This was a pretty, wistful aria, but Vanessa let the last note quaver just a little too long, seeing how long she could keep the vibrato going. Then she broke into a peal of laughter that, despite being in Ariel's voice, sounded nothing like the mermaid.

Ariel pushed the far door open a crack. Some previous king or queen had designed the royal bath to look as dramatic as possible, almost like a stage, perhaps so he or she could soak while members of state gathered around asking for decisions. There was even a sort of viewing balcony or mezzanine that the hall led to, above the bath; this held a few cabinets to store bath-related bric-a-brac and a privacy screen for robing and disrobing—although despite the plentiful storage, Vanessa's morning clothes were thrown carelessly over a chair. Wide and ostentatious spiral stairs led down to the bathtub itself.

"*If I could dance with him but once, I know he would love*

me. . . . One waltz in the sand; I would be free. . . . I don't know, it's really not so great. Not much to write home about. The sand, I mean. It gets positively everywhere and feels nasty in your foldy bits."

When Vanessa stopped singing and lapsed into her own editorial comments, the cognitive dissonance was almost overwhelming. Ariel's voice was higher than the sea witch's and lacked the burrs and tremolos the cecaelia was fond of throwing in when she was being dramatic. Yet still the tone and nuance was all Ursula.

Ariel edged silently out onto the mezzanine and peeped over the side.

Vanessa was clearly enjoying the bath. Her brown hair flowed around her in slippery wet ringlets that very much brought to mind the arms and legs of a squid. Great quantities of bubbles and foam towered over the top of the tub and spilled out onto the floor, slowly dripping down like the slimy egg sac of a moon snail.

Vanessa was splashing and talking to herself and playing in the bath almost like a child. Ariel remembered, with heat, when *she* had been in that bath, and was introduced to the wonders of foam that wasn't the just the leavings of dead merfolk. The whole experience had been marvelous and strange. Imagine the humans, kings of the Dry World, keeping bubbles of water around to bathe and play in. There was no equivalent under the sea; no one made "air pools" for fun and cleanliness.

For just a moment—so quickly that Ariel could have dismissed it as a shadow or a trick of the light and bubbles if she didn't know better—a tentacle snaked out of the water, then quickly back in, like it had forgotten itself for a moment.

Unthinking, Ariel reached for the comb hidden in her hair. True, the trident's power wouldn't work on dry land. But she didn't need its power. With barely a thought to nudge it in the right direction, the comb melted into fluid gold and reformed into something with heft: a three-pronged dagger, deadly and sharp.

If she had been human born and raised, she would have attempted to hurl it into the witch's heart. She had a perfect view and the advantage of height.

But she had been raised in a watery world where friction was a constant enemy. Except for the strongest, no one ever *threw* things across or up; stones slowed down and sank almost immediately.

Ariel crouched down, preparing to sneak and then run, driving the dagger into the witch's flesh with her own hands.

She lifted one delicate foot. . . .

"What's that?" Ursula suddenly demanded.

The mermaid froze.

"Did you hear . . . ? Was that a . . ."

Ariel put her back flat to the cabinet that was right behind her, sucking in her stomach and trying to shrink.

There was splashing, frantic. It sounded like far too many appendages or people were in the water for it all to be one person.

"No one is supposed to interrupt my baths!" Ursula shouted.

Ariel could tell by the change in pitch that the sea witch was standing up now, possibly on six of her legs.

The mermaid tried to slide along the cabinet toward the dressing room door, but the revolting carved-ivory handles and drawer pulls kept tangling in her ugly dress. One particular thread pulled tightly across her legs until she couldn't move.

Ariel gritted her teeth and forced her hip slowly out—and the string popped with a heart-wrenching *twang*.

She stopped breathing.

"Vareet! Vareet!" Ursula called out. "What is that? Go investigate!"

What if she just got up and ran? Would Ursula be able to see who it was? Would they send the guards after her? Would she be able to make it out in time?

Ariel worked muscles that were still new to her, stretching and bending her foot, trying to silently move her thighs so she could crab-walk to the door.

"Maaaaaaax . . ." came a lilting voice from the distance. The same infuriating maid from before.

"Ugh," Ursula swore, strangely echoing her own feelings. "If that stupid dog comes in here I'm having it muzzled. And *Max*, too."

There were more splashing and sloshing noises; the sea witch was settling back down into the water. Ariel could once again hear her own voice, muttering and grumbling to herself. A pail of water was poured, a tap turned, the tub refilled.

Relief and disappointment and continued fear competed like braids in a lock of hair hanging from Ariel's soul. She fell back against one of the cabinets. *What am I doing?* She was nothing like the warrior merfolk some of her ancestors and relatives were. She never cared enough to train for the Mer-games and win the golden crown of sea heather. Cousin Lara, with her mighty spear, was better made for this sort of thing.

Ariel was here to find her father. And so far, she had failed. She had been utterly distracted.

She should go back and thoroughly search Vanessa's room while she had a chance. If ancient plays, poems, and songs taught nothing else, it was always one of these two repeating themes: one, don't ever fool around with a god's wife or husband, and two, revenge always leads to sorrow. And while she had never been the most diligent student as a princess, she loved a good story.

She dipped her hand and the dagger turned into a comb once more. She set it carefully back in her hair.

How much more time did she have to search the bedroom? Had that interruption lengthened or shortened Vanessa's bath ritual?

Ariel risked another peep to see if she could tell.

Ursula appeared to be lounging carelessly in her bath again, full-on Vanessa, no tentacles in sight.

The mermaid could now see that standing close to the tub was a little maid waiting in attendance, maybe eight years old. Though her body faced the bath and Vanessa, she kept her eyes directed out at the sea, through the windows. She hugged a giant fluffy towel tight, ready for the moment Ursula decided it was time to get out.

She was biting her lip.

It was obvious she knew something about Ursula's true nature—how could she not, as bath attendant? She must have seen things even more terrible than tentacles. . . .

Ariel said a silent prayer for the poor girl and prepared to tiptoe back.

But just as she reached the door, something glittery caught her eye from the frumpy pile of Vanessa's hastily cast-off clothes.

She gulped, for once glad she didn't have a voice to vocalize whatever it was that came up from her heart.

The nautilus.

Ursula's totem of power, the necklace she wore everywhere. *The token that held Ariel's voice.*

Barely able to believe it was true, Ariel ducked down and crawled over to the chair.

With a gesture that was less "regally acquiring what was rightfully hers" and more like the crazed swipe for a sea bean by a starving mer, she snatched up the nautilus and held it to her chest. Dazed and in shock from her find, of *having it in her hand*, she rose and stumbled back to the door.

The little maid spotted her.

Ariel's mouth went dry and her heart sank.

She stared at the girl, and the girl watched Ariel with large, hollow eyes.

Realizing how strangely ironic it was, Ariel put a finger to her lips.

Please.

The little girl glanced over at Vanessa in her bath.

"*My dark and villainous plans, how they unfurl*—no, wait. Was that how it went? I can't remember . . ." Ursula sang and muttered to herself, heedless of her maid.

Please!

Ariel threw the word through her eyes, across the space between her and the little girl, praying for her sympathy.

The little girl gave the faintest nod.

Ariel put her hands together as best she could, clutching the nautilus, and bowed her head.

Thank you. If ever I find a way to repay you, I swear I shall.

Not that the little girl would ever know, but the gods would.

Ariel crept to the door . . . and then bolted out of the castle.

Ariel

She pounded through the castle as fast as she could, new heels hitting the stony floors with surprising force. Faces were a blur as she sprinted to the exit.

"Woof?" came from somewhere near the ground at one point.

Max! Your dinner is ready! she thought, and mentally promised to pet him later, if there was a later. She risked looking up to see if Eric was there with him—but he wasn't.

As soon as her feet touched sand she redoubled her pace, making for the hidden lagoon. Several guards looked after her curiously, but not too curiously; she was behaving like a scorned lover or someone who had been in a fight with a friend. In a castle full of enemies and noble spies, a scampering maid drew little interest from people with better things to do.

The hot sun hit her back like a reproving shove. At that moment she hated everything about being human. The long skirts of her dress tangled in her new legs and chafed her skin. Her stupid boots were clumsy in the sand, like she was stepping into holes and pulling her feet out of sucking, grabby mud.

But soon she was in the blessedly quiet cove where the wind was still and the noises of humans and their activities far off and easily forgotten. She sank down onto the sand like she would have as a mermaid: tail folded under her, leaning to the side a little, one hip up, the other down. The instinct to flip her fin impatiently went nowhere; the thought traveled down her spine and stopped where her legs split.

She opened her tightly cupped hands and looked at what lay in her palm.

The nautilus shell was exquisite, brown and white and perfectly striped. The math that lay like a dazzling creation spell over all who lived in the sea showed clearly in the spiral, each cell as great as the sum of the two previous sections. Everything in the ocean was a thing of beauty and numbers, even in death.

Mermaids could live for a long time, but their bodies became foam that dissipated into nothing when they died.

The poor little mollusk who lived in this shell had a very short life, but his shell could last for centuries.

Ariel sighed and brushed her fingers over it, feeling strangely melancholy despite the triumph she literally held in her hands. Years of being mute could be swept away in a second. Years of frustration, years of silent crying, years of anger.

And then what?

If she destroyed it, what would it change?

Ursula would immediately know she was back. That she had been in the castle, practically under the sea witch's nose.

And then what would happen to Ariel's search for her father? This was more complicated than a simple diversion; this could set everything back and make her whole task harder.

Queen Ariel held the nautilus and considered thoughtfully.

But the little mermaid didn't think. She acted.

Before she realized fully what she was doing Ariel had smashed the nautilus on a sharply faceted rock.

It didn't break like a normal shell. It shattered like a human vessel. Shards flew in all directions equally, unhampered by gravity or luck.

Ariel pitched forward.

She choked, no longer breathing the air of the Dry World. Her arms flailed up like a puppet's. Her torso whipped back and forth, pummeled by unseen forces. Something flew into her mouth, up her nose, and suffused her entire body with a heat that threatened to burn. It rushed into her lungs and expanded, expelling whatever breath she had left, pushing blood to her extremities, pushing everything out that wasn't *it*, leaving room for nothing else.

Ariel collapsed.

It was over.

It was like the thing, whatever it was, had been absorbed by her body and had now dissipated into her blood and flesh.

She took a breath. Her heart started beating again.

She hadn't been aware it had stopped.

She coughed. A few grains of sand came out.

And then she sang.

Eric

His hands were raised, trying to draw more out of the violins with his left while holding back the percussion with his right.

He fumbled.

It was like a pile of books had fallen from a high shelf onto his head, and, having broken his skull, somehow managed to directly impart their contents into his brain.

It was like a sibling had snuck up behind him, and, thinking he was prepared—expecting him to get out of the way—whacked him with a wooden baton. The *crack* on the pate was twice as painful as it should have been, the simple blow compounded by shock that a sister would strike so hard. Feelings and pain were utterly mixed.

It was like he were suddenly afflicted by a grievous, mortal fit of the body: as if his heart or kidney or some other important organ had seized up and failed.

He experienced the wonder of taking a first breath after the terrible pain receded with a clearheaded, deep relief that presaged either death or recovery.

Eric blinked at the orchestra and singers before him. Instruments faltered. A hundred pairs of eyes looked back at him expectantly.

He saw, as if for the first time, the plain yet comely smile of the second soprano, the brown mole on the likeable brow of the basso profundo, the L-shaped smudge on the copper timpani. A veil had been drawn away.

He was Prince Eric, and he was conducting a practice session for an opera.

Not sailing a pleasure ship or playing his recorder to himself, or, more appropriately, running this part of his parents' kingdom, which was his duty, his chore, his right.

Something was very, very wrong.

He gulped.

But the people before him waited on his very fingertips. For now *they* were his kingdom. They needed their prince.

He would deal with personal revelations later.

And so he conducted, and when the soprano sang he winced, and tried not to think of another singer with hair as bright as fire and eyes like the sea.

Ursula

Vanessa stood in the tub slowly drying herself, starting with her face. She always left the lower half of her body in the water as long as possible.

She sang quietly, luxuriating in the gradual process. The one thing the humans did right—at least the *princesses* did—was take the proper time and care in making themselves presentable to the world.

Her little maid stood attentively nearby.

"Mmm, something-something, and I shall be Queen of the Sea, mm-hmm . . . keeRACK!"

Suddenly the princess heaved violently. It felt like her uvula had been pulled violently out through her lips. Like her mouth had been turned inside out. Like the meat and blood of her lungs were following close by.

She coughed, certain that blood was going to spray out. But there was nothing on the piles and piles of white, sweet-smelling bubbles that filled the tub. No scarlet spittle, no physical proof of the massive change within her.

"My *voice*," she said, the words coming out in a low-pitched growl. The tenor of a much older, much larger, much . . . *different* woman.

"*MY VOICE!*" she screeched, pretty red lips squared and askew. She clenched her hands into fists, shaking with rage.

Her maid looked concerned, obviously unsure what had caused this outburst. She waited nervously for orders.

Vanessa, princess of Tirulia, clawed her way out of the tub and stalked up the steps, white foam trailing off her like smoke. Naked and not cold. Vareet, unnoticed, hurried after her with another towel. The princess dug desperately through the pile of clothes she had taken off so carelessly before and threw them every which way in her panic.

"*Where is my necklace?!*"

But of course it was gone.

She spun to focus her wrath on the tiny maid, who tried to hide behind the giant towel she still held at the ready. Not that her mistress hadn't lost her temper before, of course; she had *many* times, when no one else was present. But this time seemed particularly bad. Vanessa's teeth bit into her bottom lip; she didn't even notice the tiny droplets of dark blood that welled up. Her cheeks sucked in under high cheekbones until her face looked like a skull. Her eyes were wild and the whites seemed almost yellow, and sickly.

"*WHERE IS MY NECKLACE?*" the princess demanded again, tapping her chest to indicate it where it used to hang.

Vareet shook her head, terrified.

"*BAH!*"

Vanessa drew her hand back. For a moment it seemed like she really would strike the girl. But the sea witch wasn't dumb; the maid had been within her sight at all times. She had nothing to do with the missing nautilus shell or its obvious destruction.

It could have been a simple sneak thief, of course. It could have been some sort of accident. But it wasn't. It was . . .

"The *hussy*," Ursula growled, rolling the words out.

She paused her rant, savoring the sounds. Her stolen voice had been fun to play with, worked wonders on others, and caused pain for the one from whom it was ripped. That was more than enough. But . . . she rather enjoyed hearing her real voice again. It was a voice with depth, with command. With character and *substance*. It was so *her*. Not at all like that bubbling, perfect-pitched, whiny little merthing.

"The hussy is *back*," she repeated.

Vareet took one timid step backward, obviously torn between terror at this strange change in her mistress—and fear of her mistress herself.

"She was in here, somehow, and stole my necklace, and destroyed it."

Vanessa looked around, at the door to her changing room that led to her bedroom . . . but there was no evidence of anything out of place.

"This is a problem," she said, fingering her throat. "A disturbing development I need to deal with immediately— and *permanently*.

"*GUARDS!*"

Ariel

She sang.

Wordless hymns of the sea: immediate, extemporized passages about waves and sunlight and tides and the constant, beautiful pressure of water on everything. The glory of seaweed slowly swaying, the delicious feeling that foretold a storm in the Dry World and turbulence below.

The music came out of her without pause, driven by years of observing, seeing, listening, enjoying, experiencing the world and unable to express it. The wonder and sadness of being alive. The joy of being a mermaid; the pain of being the only one like herself—the only mermaid who had been mortal, temporarily, and then lost everything.

When she finally stopped, her eyes were closed and her

hands rested on her human lap, and she felt the dry, human sun and imagined wet things.

She opened her eyes.

The silence was now deafening in the lagoon.

She had the voice of the gods, some had said. The sort of voice that could lure landlubbers to sea and sailors to their deaths, a voice that could launch a thousand ships. She had the voice of the wind and the storm and the crash of the waves and the ancient speech of the whale. She had the voice of the moon as it glided serenely across the sky and the stars as they danced behind. She had the voice of the wind between the stars that mortals never heard, that rushed and blew and ushered in the beginning and end of time.

She sat for a moment quietly, remembering how it sounded but enjoying the silence.

The songs were from the old Ariel. Perhaps the new Ariel, too.

She coughed and tried again, cocking her head and effecting a stern look.

"Just *do* it, Flounder; I need the tax audits by the third tide so we have something to present to the council.

"Sebastian, I don't care about the gala or its details. I'm sure it's all fine in your very capable claws.

"And with the cutting of this ribbon, I hereby declare the Temple of Physical Arts open to all!"

Ariel smiled, then threw back her head and laughed—but it was brittle.

She picked up a shard of the nautilus and sighed.

Her voice had been such an important part of her life before. The merfolk celebrated her for it. Her father excused her occasionally questionable behavior because of it. Eric loved the girl who rescued him, because of her singing. . . .

But . . .

. . . she'd never really enjoyed singing for anyone else. In fact, she hated audiences. She sang because she liked to sing. She just . . . *felt* . . . something, and had to sing it. If she were happy, or sad, or angry . . . she would go off by herself and sing to the coral, sing to the seaweed, sing to an audience of sea snails or tube worms (who listened, but never commented). Most of her mergirlhood had been spent swimming around, exploring, singing to herself. Making up little stories in her head and then putting them into song.

Ruefully she remembered the concert that Sebastian had so carefully planned, which she had missed, which her dad had punished her for, which led him to set the little crab on her case, and so on. . . .

She hadn't been deliberately disobedient. She just . . . forgot.

Sometimes people thought she was a snob because of the way she acted. But she wasn't *trying* to be a diva—she was just a young mer whose head was full of fantasies.

And by taking away her voice, Ursula had stolen what Ariel treasured most: the only way she knew how to express those stories.

Without spoken language—and no knowledge of signs, back then—she wasn't able to tell Eric what had happened to her or how she loved him. She wasn't able to tell her father not to trade places with her. She wasn't able to rule her kingdom without the help of a fleet of people to interpret and speak for her.

She had lost a means of communicating her desires, her commands, her wishes, her needs, her thoughts.

"How do you feel?"

Ariel looked up, suddenly aware of the gull who was perched quietly on a nearby rock, watching her with a curious, beady eye.

"*Jona,*" Ariel said, relishing the sound of the name. "How long have you been sitting there?"

"I spotted you the moment you came out of the castle. But it looked like you needed a moment to yourself. I was going to interrupt if you kept on with that singing."

"*That* singing? Why?" Ariel asked archly. Her hands signed as she spoke, too used to the process.

"Well, you were getting a little loud."

The mermaid blinked at the gull.

Then she began to laugh.

She laughed so hard she began to have trouble breathing. Great, pealing gulps of laughter and air: it felt *good* to laugh and have it actually come out, not just be a silent recognition of something mildly amusing.

"I . . . beg your pardon?" Jona said, a trifle offended.

"Oh . . . it's just . . ." She breathed deep, trying to control herself, not wanting to. "I was *just* sitting here thinking about singing, and how much everyone loved to hear me sing, and how I was celebrated for my voice, and how someone fell in love with me for my voice, and you . . ." She lost it for a moment again.

Jona turned her head back and forth, trying to get a good look at the mermaid with one eye, then the other. "I mean, well, it was . . . nice. I just meant that you were going to call over the guards."

" 'Nice'? You've heard better?" Ariel asked, half-joking, half-curious.

Jona opened her beak for a moment, closed it, choosing her words carefully now that it was obvious she had offended. "Your singing is extraordinary; it is epic; it has something in common with the very forces of nature, like the wind and the sea itself.

"If you were to ask me how I felt about it personally, however, I would say I prefer the cries of my own kind, or the mindless trill of a sandpiper, or the sad call of a plover. They're more accessible."

Ariel put her hand to her face to stop the next peal of laughter. She snorted instead.

"What?" the bird asked, confused.

"I like you, Jona," she said, scruffing the bird under her neck. The gull closed her eyes and leaned into it.

"ARIEL! You're SINGING!"

An explosion of grey and white feathers landed on the beach next to them. As soon as he recovered himself, Scuttle threw his wings around her in a gull-y embrace.

"I am," she said, stroking his head.

"Oh, it's *so good* to hear you," Scuttle said with a sigh. "It does my old heart . . . It's just the best."

Ariel smiled. There was something specifically beautiful about what he had said: *It's so good to hear you.* He didn't say anything about her singing, just that it was good to hear her voice. He was genuinely pleased just that she had her voice back—whatever she chose to do with it.

This is a friend.

And . . . wait a second . . . she didn't have to just think these thoughts anymore.

"Scuttle," she said aloud. "It does *my* heart good to talk to you."

"You're so queenly now, listen to you. So noble and

regal and genteel and all. So does this change the Big Plan?" Scuttle asked, elbowing her with his wing and giving a conspiratorial wink. "You're still gonna look for your father, right?"

"Of course. But now . . . I've effectively . . . alerted . . . Ursula to my presence. I'm a fool. I should have waited before destroying Ursula's necklace."

She shook her head and sighed, picking up the leather band that had held the nautilus. Now a golden bail and a bit of shell were all that was left. For reasons she couldn't put into words—either aloud or in her head—she wrapped the strap around itself twice and slipped it onto her wrist. Maybe it would remind her to not be so rash in the future.

"I dunno, Ariel," Scuttle said. "What else would you have done? Left it there? Your *voice*? That would take the will of a mountain or something. You couldn't just leave it there with Ursula. *No* one could have."

"No, I don't . . . suppose I could have. I don't know."

"Did you manage to look around at all?" Jona asked. "Maybe get a hint of where she might be hiding him?"

"Only a little. He's probably in her bedroom . . . or *was* in her bedroom. I didn't see any bottle or anything immediately like what you described when I was there, and now that she knows I'm back she'll probably hide him someplace else. At least I have an ally in the castle. Maybe even two!

There's a little maid who didn't reveal me to Ursula—and also Carlotta, who was so nice to me the last time I was human. She's aware that *something* happened the day Eric and Vanessa were wed. She also told me that a lot has happened as a result of that day. Ramifications—bad ones—for people besides me and my father."

"Oh yeah? With Ursula as Vanessa, running the kingdom?" Scuttle asked. "I mean, you hear things as a bird, you know. But it's hard to tell when humans are happy or unhappy. Especially when you're just trying to pick through their garbage."

"What I don't understand is why Ursula would stay. Married to Eric, I mean. And *here*." She indicated all the Dry World with her hands. "What does she want? I thought her only desire was to beat me and get revenge on my father. She did that. This isn't her home. . . ."

Scuttle shrugged. "I don't know, Ariel. She's evil, right? Who knows why she does anything? To make more evil, maybe? Or maybe she just likes it here. Whatever is going on in her crazy head, we gotta take her down, that's what we gotta do. We'll eighty-six her, get your dad back, get the prince, and everyone lives happily ever after."

"I don't know about *all* of that," Ariel said with a smile. "I don't think I can be responsible for *everyone's* happily ever after." *Even my own. Get the prince?* It was an intriguing thought, but one for later. *Duty first.* ". . . I think it would be difficult to, um, 'eighty-six' a princess and a sea witch, especially now that I've lost the element of surprise. Let's focus on getting my father back, and then see what else we can do afterward."

"You don't want the prince anymore?" Jona asked curiously.

Ariel looked at her in surprise. Had the bird read her mind? "Excuse me?"

"The character of you really seemed to pine after the character of him in Eric's opera, *La Sirenetta*," Jona said with a shrug. "And Great-Grandfather always told the story of the two of you, and you *gave your voice away to win him.* . . ."

"It was a long time ago. I was young, he was handsome and exotic. I don't think—in reality—there's much of a possibility of a long-term relationship between a mermaid and a human."

It was so much easier to speak quickly first and then decide later if it was truth or lies. She was already losing the thoughtfulness that came with being silent. Ariel scolded herself mentally.

"Better ease off," Scuttle said to his great-grandgull in what he probably thought was a helpful whisper. "She seems a little touchy. Still an open wound."

Ariel took a deep breath and stood up. "Well, I don't think I can go back to the castle right now. Everyone saw me rush out."

"What will you do?" Jona asked.

"While I'm waiting for things to die down a bit, I'll go see for myself what mess Ursula's rule over Tirulia has created. If Carlotta is right, it makes my task even more urgent. I can't have humans dying because of a princess I—however inadvertently—gave them. I need to go to town, where the people are, and listen to what they are saying."

"Absotively," Scuttle said. "Having a sea witch for a princess has got to have some bad, you know, reiterations."

"*Repercussions*, I think you mean, Great-Grandfather," Jona corrected politely. She stretched her wings. "I should go alert Flounder of your status change—regarding your voice."

"Thank you, Jona," Ariel said warmly. "Please tell him to meet me in this cove four tides from now for an update. And make sure he *fully understands* not to tell anyone else at all yet."

"Anyone?" Scuttle asked, surprised. "Not even old crabby-claws?"

"*Especially* not Sebastian. Not yet. I already feel bad enough getting my voice back—and not my father. I can't bear the thought of explaining that to him right now. Also, if everyone knows that I can talk again, it's just more pressure—to get me back, to have me stay and rule. It would be hard to escape and look for Father a second time."

"But you wouldn't be telling everyone, just Sebastian," Scuttle pointed out.

"Once Sebastian knows, the entire kingdom will hear about it within hours," Ariel said with a wan smile. "He's as bad as a guppy with gossip."

Eric

He made his way back from rehearsal to the castle with the uncomfortable feeling that he was hiding something.

It was not unlike the time he had caught his first really sizable branzino. The old fishermen on the docks had cheered when the eight-year-old princeling ran home as fast as his little legs could carry him, holding his prize aloft.

But then, realizing he had a catch of serious merit, Eric was suddenly convinced that his mother and father, the king and queen, would yell at him for such plebeian pursuits and forbid him from cooking and eating the dinner he had gotten for himself like a real man.

He hid the fish under his shirt.

The branzino (known commonly as the wolf fish) had extra-sharp fins and spines and scales, all of which cut into the boy's flesh as it struggled.

Little Eric arrived at the castle desperate and bleeding. He went straight to the kitchens, where he collapsed into a puddle of tears, cursing his own weakness.

(The king and queen, as any parent could guess, were delighted with the skill and determination their son had shown. They gave Eric a really solid lecture on the importance of knowing what common people did to earn their dinner, for he would be ruling a kingdom of fisherfolk someday. Then the cook oversaw the bandaged, once-again cheerful Eric as he fried up the fish himself. It was presented to the royal family on a golden platter, and everyone lived happily ever after that day.)

This was *also* not unlike the time when, as a young teen, he had fallen in love with a stray puppy that did not at all fit the royal image of a hunting hound. This, too, he stuffed under his shirt and carried home. Guilty and tortured, he snuck Max into his bed and fed him the best bits of purloined steak from dinner.

He was of course found out.

"It's not a Sarenna imperial wolf mastiff," his father had said with a sigh. "We kings of Tirulia have always had those. For *centuries*."

"At least it's not a fish this time," the queen had pointed out lightly.

But little Eric and older Eric and even now oldest Eric never had a *truly* terrible secret. Those two were the worst ones he could come up with when trying to compare what he felt now to something similar in his life.

What was it, exactly, he was hiding this time? It wasn't tangible, like a fish or a puppy.

Clarity?

Was that a terrible secret? Why did he feel the need to hide it?

He tried to mimic the way he usually walked home, but all the Erics—little, older, and present Eric—were terrible liars. It was just one of the many reasons the prince refused to be in his own shows, even in a bit part. He knew his limits.

He looked up quickly, guiltily, askance, expecting things to appear different. More colorful. More detailed. More truthful. More meaningful.

But all the houses he passed looked the same; the flowers and plants were the same colors as the day before.

Yep, that grain storehouse is still the same. Same dry rot around the windows, same moldering timbers. . . .

Wait a moment, that looks really bad. I'll bet it smells terrible up close. Isn't that where we keep the surplus grain?

In case of blight or disaster? Good heavens, is it leaking?
*That could ruin everything. Why is that being allowed? I'd
better look into that. . . .*

*Oh, look, it's that girl from the market who sells the sea
beans. What's she doing here? I used to know her mother. . . .
What was her name?* Lucretia.

*My word—look at that enormous guarded wagon driving
up to the castle, with so many soldiers around it! What on
earth are they delivering? I want to say . . . munitions? Yes!
That's it.*

*Wait—munitions? But why? I can't quite . . . Why do we
need . . . ? This is all so bizarre.*

Then it hit him.

There hadn't been a *physical* change to himself or his
sight; the veil or whatever it was, the charm, had been lifted
from *in*side his head. It was like an old net, full of slime
and dead shellfish and falling apart and utterly useless, had
enshrouded his brain, and had just now been extracted by
some clever doctor. He could think for the first time in years.
He could react to the things around him. Generate opinions. Hold on to thoughts. *He* had changed, not his eyes.

That was reassuring, and having figured that out made
him feel a bit better and more in control. He strode confi-
dently into the castle. Grimsby was waiting just inside and
in one fluid, habituated movement helped the prince spin

out of his academic robe and into a very neatly tailored day jacket, dove grey with long tails.

"Thanks, Grims," Eric said, continuing on to the lesser luncheon room and fluffing up his cravat. All he *wanted* to do was grab his old manservant—out of sight of the guards—and grill him about the past. He was the only one in the castle Eric could trust. But that would look odd, and until he got the lay of the land, he preferred to play along like still-bespelled Eric.

Princess Vanessa was already seated at the delicate golden table where they would dine together after meeting with the Metalworkers' Guild. Thank goodness he didn't have to greet her and take her arm and lead her in. He had very, very mixed feelings right now, but all the ones around her induced nausea.

"Good afternoon, Princess," Eric said politely. She extended a gloved hand and he perfunctorily kissed the back of it, extending his lips so that only the furthest, tippiest bit, the part that often got chapped at sea, barely brushed the smooth fabric.

He noticed—and was unsure if this was the result of his new state of being—her dress: she wore an unusually demure pale blue day dress with less bustle than usual and understated lace ruffs at the wrists. Also a giant woolly muffler wrapped around her neck and shoulders. Oh, it matched, of course; it was a beautiful, expensive shade of blue and was fringed with the sort of exotic imported feathers that had long skinny shafts and little bouncing dots of color at the top that flashed in gold and iridescence. They obscured most of Vanessa's face.

More luck, Eric thought.

"Bit of a nasty cold," she whispered huskily. One delicate gloved hand went to her throat.

"I'm so sorry," he said, settling down into his own seat. Parched from the dry air in the practice hall, he picked up a carafe and began to pour himself a glass of *cava*.

Then he stopped. Did he really want to be foggy headed? At all? After this . . . awakening?

He reached for the crystal decanter of water instead.

Vanessa watched him silently.

The suited and dour captains of the Metalworkers' Guild stood before them, the symbol of their station gleaming here and there on their persons: silvery cane handles, the shining tips of their boots, simple rings, sashes with obscure buckles on them.

"If we may, Your Highness . . ." A short and stocky man stepped forward. He had a luxurious, well-trimmed beard, and if it weren't for his modern tricorn hat, he would have looked exactly like a character out of one of Eric's fairy tale books, one of the fair folk who actually dug the precious metals out of deep mines. "We don't want to delay your lunch any further."

"Very considerate," Vanessa hissed. Without her normal, lilting tone, it sounded exactly as snarky and sarcastic as she probably meant. The man's bushy eyebrows shot up, but of course he said nothing about it.

"T-to put it plainly," he stuttered, "we . . . of course . . . support any and all military actions as planned and carried out by you, of course. . . . It does keep us busy, after all. All the musket barrels . . . and mechanisms . . . and cannons . . . No shortage of work!"

Eric frowned. How much *work* did Tirulia's metalworkers have, precisely, involved in the crafts of war? The only reason there were fortifications in the city at all were because Roman governors and then medieval kings had liked the surroundings for their vacations by the sea.

"The problem is *supplies*. Your . . . strategies have unfortunately angered some of our trading partners. And the pass in the north is now unsafe for shipping, especially cargo that could be seen as military."

"I thought our mountains had some of the finest mines in the world," Vanessa whispered, asking the question before Eric could pose it himself. His father had first shown him the location of the mines and quarries on a parchment map when he was a lad. The ink in which mountains were sketched, in little upside-down vees, was a dull black for iron and metallic orange for copper. That had fascinated young Eric—although he had wanted to put a dragon in there as well.

"What, Your Highness?" the man said, leaning closer.

"I'm sorry, your voice . . ."

"*MINES*," she croaked. "FINE MINES. WITH COPPER."

"Absolutely, Princess," the man said. His eyes had darted briefly, questioningly, to the prince before resettling on her.

Eric started to feel relief at this close call of being noticed, then realized something: *no one paid attention to him anymore.* No one had in years. And that "relief" that he now seemed to be accustomed to? What was that? Wasn't he crown prince? *Shouldn't* he be dealing with the head of the guild and all his boring business himself? That was his duty!

The man was still talking.

". . . And if we didn't have to make bronze or pewter, or things out of tin, we would be set. Steel has its uses, but there are other things to be made besides weapons, and those other things need other metals."

"What things are those?" Vanessa hissed. Maybe if she were speaking normally, with her large eyes and eyelashes aimed at the men, it would have come out as *Teach me—I'm an innocent young girl who relishes your older-man wisdom.* But there was a strange cognitive disconnect because of the husky whisper: almost like she was a much older woman poorly play-acting the role of young ingénue.

While Eric was pondering this, he also was puzzled by *what* she said. *What things are made of* metal? Didn't she have eyes? Didn't she live in the castle and use the objects within it?

"Well . . . Your Highness . . ." the man said awkwardly, looking around for support. "Most people in the kingdom, even wealthy folks like myself, tend not to eat off golden spoons and forks." He indicated the royal couple's place setting with a tip of his head. "Or burn candles in silver candelabra. Pewter, bronze, and tin make all the tools and useful things for the rest of us—they have for thousands of years. And since we don't have tin in our mountains, we must trade for it. And we can't right now."

"Well, then," Vanessa whispered thoughtfully. "We must go to the place it is found and take it for ourselves."

The man blinked at her. *"Bretland?"*

She looked at him slyly out the corner of her eyes, gauging his reaction. Eric watched her tawdry performance, horrified and yet fascinated.

"You want us to . . . invade the *Allied Kingdoms of Bretland?*" the man asked again.

"Never say never," the princess purred.

"Excuse me? I'm sorry, I couldn't hear Your Highness."

"I *said*, 'Never say never.'"

"Beg pardon?"

Eric wanted to leap up and announce that this ridiculous meeting was over. That Vanessa should not even *suggest* the—incredibly stupid, unheard-of—idea of military aggression against one of the world's greatest powers to a civilian, much less without discussing it with him first.

But . . .

While he wasn't a *very* skilled chess player, his mother had told him that the most important thing in gamesmanship was this: you could never be completely sure of other person, so never make a move until you were sure of *yourself.*

And he wasn't. Not yet. Not until he had some time to think and figure things out.

"I think this merits more discussion," he said aloud. Which was perhaps more than he had said in a while, but so wishy-washy no one could accuse him of acting forthrightly with thought and opinion. Vanessa did shoot him a quick sidelong glance, but that was all. "Your concerns about tin and, I assume, aluminum, will be taken into consideration. Thank you for your time, gentlemen."

The group of men, somewhat startled at the prince's words, all nodded and made quick bows both to him and then the princess, and shuffled out. The head of the guild gave Eric one last, appraising look before following.

Eric steeled himself for a tense and obnoxious lunch with his princess . . .

. . . but once again, the prince was saved.

"My dear, I'm afraid I must off to bed now with this nasty cold. One must take care of illnesses before they grow serious," Vanessa hissed, indicating her throat. "So sorry to leave you alone."

"That's quite all right. I pray you feel better," Eric said, trying not to joyfully reach for a leg of quail before finishing his sentence.

He was nothing if not courteous.

Ursula

Good, little Eric swallowed the whole "cold" thing.

She strode down the hall to her bedroom, Vareet and her manservants trailing like eddies in the wake of a very large ship. Her mind raced. *This* was what it was like to be a queen. *Er, princess.* This was what it was like to actually rule and wield power and make decisions and get things done. Real monarchs didn't shy away from their problems; they dealt with them head-on and then either beat them into submission or used them to further their own objectives.

Every stumbling block is a stepping-stone.

She laughed to herself, remembering the first time she had heard that saying, from one of the especially sycophantic Tirulian nobles. At the time she had no idea what it meant. Because obviously if there was a *stumbling block* in the ocean, you just swam over it.

She checked out herself askance in one of the large gilt-framed mirrors that lined the eastern hallway. Getting her gait just right was one of the hardest things about being on land. Imperial, regal—yet simpering and attractive. She wished in retrospect she had chosen a slightly older, more imposing human body. But of course twits like the prince needed something young and pretty to fall for. Absolutely no respect for or appreciation of maturity and wisdom. And pulchritude.

But honestly, she didn't have that many bodies to choose from. This sad sack of a human with gorgeous brown hair that the sea witch now wore had wanted to be one with the ocean . . . and Ursula had been only too glad to give her what she wished.

The transformation was a fairly permanent one, its origins invisible to all but the wearer. She had been wise to keep that body's essence around for all those years. Some might have said she had a tendency to hoard, but Ursula knew everything had a use eventually. For an emergency, or as the Dry Worlders said in their ridiculous way, "a rainy day."

Vanessa adjusted her muffler. It was uncomfortable and itchy and made her sweat and possibly break out. Human skin was so temperamental, exposed to naked air—too moist, too dry, far too parched, pimples and rashes and exfoliation . . . was this true with all Dry World creatures? Or just mortal ones?

Ursula, focus.

She went into her bedroom and headed directly to the vanity, where she pulled off the ridiculous muffler and threw it to the floor. Vareet dashed over and immediately picked it up, shaking it out and dusting it. The sea witch coughed and touched her neck lightly, dabbing it with a silk powder puff. Then she leered into the mirror. For a moment she could almost see her true self. She grinned, delighted with her remembered appearance.

"Good to see you, old girl," she purred in her real voice, enjoying every syllable. "So tell me. *Where is the little hussy now?* Did she crawl back to the sea, or is she hanging around, hoping for a chance to reunite with Prince Dum-Dum?"

Anyone watching would have just seen a reflection of Vanessa, checking her teeth, running a hand through the top of her hair.

The transformation and accompanying charm and memory spells were some of the biggest, most interesting cantrips she had ever cast. She had done her sorcerous best in the three days Ariel pranced about on land. There was a lot there to be proud of. Still, it was a bit hasty and thrown together, and now its weakness showed, especially the mass-forgetting bit.

And was Eric regaining his will? He had acted a little odd at lunch, but sometimes it was hard to tell with humans. *Especially dumb ones.*

But if the day of the wedding began to grow clearer in the memories of those who had witnessed it . . . well, Ursula knew enough about mer and human behavior to know that it would amount to nothing. Mermaids? Witches? Sea gods? There was an opera about it already, for heaven's sake. People who saw the show would confuse that with reality, and people who hadn't actually been on the boat would think anyone who said otherwise was mad. No, Ursula wasn't worried about the staff, the servants, the peasants, the nobles, the riffraff.

Only Eric and Ariel.

A quick tempest of a rage crossed her face, deranging it for a moment into a hideous snarl of lips and eyes and teeth.

Eric and Ariel. Whether apart or together, they were determined to screw up her life.

The game had begun! Or . . . continued from years before. Ariel had made the first move, and it was a doozy.

Well, she would put an end to that. Now it was *her* move.

"*FLOTSAM! JETSAM!*" she snarled.

Both servants were in front of her less than a tailslap later. Upon seeing them Vareet quickly betook herself to the closet—perhaps on the pretext of hanging up the muffler—and peeped out timidly. *Ridiculous little idiot.*

Speaking of hiding, she would have to do something about old Kingy now. He wasn't safe from theft anymore . . .

. . . and maybe it was finally time to do *that thing* with him. The thing she had kept him around for, all these years, besides the fun of gloating. Just in case. Maybe it was time to set certain *other* plans in motion. Being a princess was fun. But there were greater stakes to play for. . . .

"I want this castle put on high alert," Ursula snapped. "I want a meeting with a captain of the guard—I want watches doubled, tripled. I want *everyone* to know about a certain red-haired enemy of the state. I want a reward put out for a sighting and another for capture. I want dozens of men on the beach again, men in front of every low window, and for every maid to be told exactly what she looks like."

"Absolutely, Ursula," Flotsam said with a grin.

"About time, Ursula," Jetsam said with a sneer.

Vareet said nothing.

The bright bit of beach outside her window caught Ursula's attention. A slow smile spread over her face.

"And," she said slowly, "I think . . . a warning . . . might be in order. . . ."

Ariel

She watched the two birds fly off. She knew that one of them—or another winged friend—would remain silently near her at all times, above her, keeping an eye on things.

What a strange ability to have in this two-dimensional land! To be able to break the barrier of *height*, to ascend and descend at will above their fellow Dry World creatures. Yet even for seagulls it was an effort. If they didn't keep gliding or flapping, they fell.

I need to keep gliding and flapping, Ariel thought as she picked out the path to town, *or I'll fall, too.* Right now she was neither a creature wholly of the sea or the land. She should be ruling the waves. She should have been married to Eric, ruling the little kingdom. She should have been swimming free in the ocean, singing and playing with her friends and dreaming. But here she was instead, doing none of those things.

The town rose over the next crest, and so did her heart at the sight. Houses and shops as pretty as a scene out of a play. Tiny dark temples filled with smoke and clingings and clangings and noise and laughter and shouts. *Life.* The quick, speedy movements of a people who ferociously enjoyed their short time under the sun.

Ariel stepped quickly past the first great pier that stuck out into the bay: fishing ships were unloading net after net of catch, and she really didn't want to witness that. By ancient law the rules for the World Under the Sea and those for the Dry World were different—but that didn't mean she had to witness the more distasteful aspects of their differences.

And speaking of differences, the changes in Tirulia from the last time she had been there were immediately apparent.

Three guards—no, *soldiers*—stood in a boyish cluster at the front of the docks, puffing their chests out, smoking, and bragging to a trio of girls who seemed so familiar Ariel could almost see them swishing their tails while flirting. They were rosy-cheeked with blushes as the boys regaled them with tales of their exploits.

"... they put up quite the fight, let me tell you. But that didn't stop Andral and me from gettin' them all out. . . ."

". . . aye, we torched the place good. Not a barn left standing . . ."

". . . orders. Got the chief of the village myself, I did. . . ."

"See what I got? Pretty, ain't it? It was just lying out, practically *begging* to be took. . . ."

Put up a fight? *Torched* the place? For Tirulia? Seizing people in the mountains, burning villages to the ground? Looting?

As Ariel looked around she noticed even more soldiers wandering among the crowd. Some had an extra medal on their lapels, some had bandages where their hands once were. New recruits wore their uniforms with an air of cockiness, finding every excuse to touch their caps when a lady looked their way. One scratched the back of his head with the muzzle of his gun.

Ariel shuddered. Eric had taken her to see a ten-gun salute at the castle; it was a tradition that honored Tirulia's connection with the sea and the old sea gods they used to worship. An explosion of modern fire and gunpowder was thought to be pleasing to the occasionally warlike Neptune.

But the gunshots were utterly terrifying, especially because they didn't come from the clouds or the waves or the sky or the rocks, the proper places for thunder.

Ariel had thrown herself to the ground under a cannon and covered her ears until Eric had taken her into his arms and told her it was all right. That had almost made it all worth it.

And here was a man scratching his head with a gun. There were men with guns all over the market. Carlotta had spoken truly—this was not the same peaceful and sleepy seaside town it was half a decade before.

The place wasn't completely transformed, however. Past the soldiers was the usual line of stands and carts displaying vegetables, fruits, cheese, dried meat. Customers haggled over prices while eyeing great stalks of leafy things.

There was also an amazing scent of fresh-baked . . . *something.*

Baking wasn't a thing under the sea. When Ariel lived at the castle with Eric she had tried breads, cakes, pies, rolls, and sweets, and found them all mystifying (though delicious). They were like nothing she had ever eaten before and sometimes came to her plate still warm, which was also an odd way to eat food. Eric had bought her twelve different kinds of pie at a fancy shop in town and laughed as she had a bite of each, swooning.

That was the old Ariel. The one who dove right into town life and interacted a little too closely with a puppet show, poking at things in shops that were for display only, dancing to music that was probably just for listening to. Now she stood back and watched. Was this the result of age, and experience, and time? Or of not having a voice for so long? Had quiet observation just become a habit?

Maybe this would provide an excuse for her to gather more information.

Observation is all well and good, but only if it leads to a thoughtful plan of action!

She followed the delicious aroma until she came to a small bakery. In front of it a young man with red hair—not half as bright as Ariel's—was setting out savory pies.

She pulled out her little satchel and went through the things in there: gems, pearls, coins, bits of mismatched and sea-changed jewelry that could be useful. Two coins looked like the same kind she had seen other people use; with those in her palm she cautiously approached the stand. She felt like she moved slower than when she was younger, as if the water on the Dry World had become heavier and thicker.

"Excuse me," she said, and it was still strange to hear her voice. The man looked up from his pies to give Ariel his full attention. There was a streak of flour in his red hair and a tired but pleasant smile in his eyes. So much plainer than Eric . . . *but still, so much more interesting than a merman!*

"How much are the . . ." She fought for the right word to speak aloud, which had no equivalent underwater. "That?" she pointed.

"Onion and cheese pie's a *real*," the man said.

Ariel held out her coins.

The man looked at her, raised an eyebrow, then carefully chose a single green coin.

Ariel tried to memorize it: the size, the color, the smell. *One* real. *Made of the metal that tastes like blood.*

The baker, still mystified but too polite to say anything, picked out a good-looking pie and handed it to her.

"Thank you," Ariel said, trying to make her words sound normal.

Then she bit into the pie.

It was all those tastes she remembered from before. Fatty, doughy flour crust. *Cheese.* Spices and flavors that spoke of foreign Dry World places. And, she supposed, the overwhelming taste of *onion.* Green, and not unlike certain seaweeds. But stronger.

The baker just watched her as she chewed and enjoyed.

Ariel stopped. Didn't people eat the things they paid for?

She looked around and saw that no one else was gulping down their treats immediately. There went the old Ariel again. *Impulsive.*

"Ah, this is wonderful," she said quickly, sounding interested; as if she were eating it only to compare with other pies she had in the past. "Very unusual."

"It's my pickled *calçots*," the baker said triumphantly. "It is the wrong time of year for those—so I preserve them in the early spring, when they are harvested. A special treat, for an . . . unusual lady. I haven't seen you around the market. You must not be from Tirulia?"

"No, I'm from . . . farther south."

"The *ocean*, then?"

She began to choke—possibly on an onion. Or calçot.

But before she could come up with a suitable reply the baker was already talking again. "One of the islands, or the continent of Alkabua, I suppose."

"Oh, but I've been here before," she said smoothly, as if he were right in his guesses and therefore it didn't merit more discussion. "Tirulia has changed a bit since the last time I visited. There seem to be a lot more soldiers."

"Oh, aye." The baker's look soured. "Prince Eric—or should I say, Princess Vanessa—is much more hungry for war than the king and queen ever were. Of course there's always been the fight over water rights or passes through the mountains or a particularly fine hillside for vineyards. . . . But this is a whole new cursed thing, and it's bad business, I don't mind saying."

"Why are you so against what the princess is doing? Specifically, I mean?"

The baker looked at her as if she were mad. "War is *war*. Fighting and death and more food for the soldiers and less for everyone else. Twenty-three Tirulian boys are dead and buried already. And still more boys flock to join the insanity, lured with promises of pretty uniforms and gold for their families. Have they been coming around and spending their new pennies on pies for their sweethearts? Certainly! Win for me! But rather less of a win for their dead comrades."

"Oh . . ." Ariel began, unsure what to say.

"And that won't be the end of it, I'll bet you *reales* to sweet buns, sister. There are already shortages because the trade routes are getting cut off. And we will lose more than our fair share of soldier boys, families, mothers, fathers, babies when the other countries decide to hit us back."

Ariel studied the baker: what was his age, really? He seemed young, but spoke with a strange authority on the subject. Like a mermaid suddenly made queen.

"You seem to know a lot about war," she ventured.

"My parents moved here from up north, where those kingdoms are always fighting. Kings and queens and princes and princesses like a giant bloody game of chess where no one cares about the pawns.

"*I* got out. I was nine. My oldest brother didn't. Enjoy your pie—and treasure peace, while it lasts. You won't miss it until it's gone."

And with that, the pie maker turned his back on her.

Ariel was a little flummoxed. She was queen; no one ever

turned his, her, or its back on her. To someone who couldn't speak aloud, that was the most effective—and devastating— way to end a conversation with her.

Then she remembered her voice.

"Your pie was delicious. I will think over your words. Have a nice day."

The pie maker waved over his shoulder: not upset, just busy. He was speaking his mind to a customer who would listen and held nothing against her.

Ariel wandered away with mixed feelings. On the one hand, everything the baker said was troubling.

On the other hand, she was exploring a whole new world—successfully—*by herself.* She was getting to observe a completely different way of life, and it wasn't just about breathing air; it was how families and people worked, and how food was made, and customs and actions and habits, and it was all *fascinating.*

Of course she knew that a ruler's actions had an effect on the people—but up until now, she had thought only of the *direct* effect. She wouldn't send merguards to storm Eric's castle, for instance, because she didn't want to put their lives at risk. But . . . would she have thought of how sending soldiers into battle might impact bakers, down the line? Was this something her father understood, and which had tempered his own decisions?

Father.

She hadn't forgotten her quest; she had just become distracted for a moment.

She ate her pie and made her way back through town, heading once again toward the beach. She passed the cart with the puppet show she had rudely interrupted years ago; sitting in the back was the man who made the puppets, carefully painting a lush set of eyelashes onto one of his manikins. *Fascinating.*

Of course merfolk had plays and costumes and costume balls, and dolls and temple figurines that boys and girls played with, making them "talk." But nothing was as rehearsed and polished as what the human did. Why didn't the mer have *that* art? Were the two peoples so different?

For there were obvious similarities between them that could not be denied. The tendency toward ridiculous monuments that commemorated unlikely events, for instance. The mer had a mural the size of a reef illustrating the division of the two worlds, embedded with gems and bright coral that hurt the eyes to look at. The Tirulians had an ugly fountain in the square where she and Eric had once danced. Neptune was carved into the face of the bowl, along with some utterly unrealistic dolphins. The Tirulians believed that the sea god had a fight with Minerva over who would be the patron god of Tirulia, and that he had won by creating this font of undrinkable salt water that was somehow channeled up from the sea.

(All wrong, as the mute Ariel couldn't explain to Eric at the time. Neptune had *lost* the fight, because he'd made a useless salt spring while Minerva/Athena had made the olive tree. Oh, and it took place in *Athens*, because, well—Athena.)

Besides monumental art and kings and queens, humans were very recognizably similar to mer in their normal, everyday lives. The women over there, heads bent together, were obviously gossiping. The men over there, heads bent together, were obviously discussing something they thought was *very important* and that they had great influence over—but which, of course, was also just gossip. A mother breastfed her baby, a beautiful fat-faced thing with the cutest feet.

How many other races were there on Gaia, more similar than different? Who would get along if just introduced properly? All they needed was a voice: the right voice, an understanding voice, a voice of reason that spoke everyone's language.

Ariel felt she had something there, the wisp of an idea, when something caught her eye and distracted her. Like a flash of sunlight that somehow manages to make its way, unobstructed and successful, to the seafloor and sparkles on a glistening white structure there.

Apples.

A tower of them. Bright red, red like blood, red like precious coral. Shining in the light. Some were half-green, which was both disappointing and yet more entrancing: did they *taste* different?

She would buy enough for all her sisters. Wouldn't that be a treat! Several for herself now, and a sack to present upon her return.

Not even realizing she was salivating, Ariel approached. The vendor was old enough to be a great-granny, but large and strong-limbed, and her black eyes sparkled, full of intelligence and interest in the world around her.

"I would like those, please," Ariel said, pointing to the apples.

" 'Those'? Which ones?"

"All of them, please."

The woman laughed. "All of 'em? That's a pretty penny, girl. I'm expecting that poncy little buyer from the castle over here in a moment—I'm going to haggle her up good. What could *you* offer me?"

Wordlessly Ariel pulled out her little satchel again and poured its contents into her hand. This time she let the pearls and gems spill out with the golden coins: surely treasure enough to buy all the fruit.

The old woman's eyes widened.

"I'll take this," she said, choosing a gold coin, "and

this," she said, choosing a pearl. Then she took her large hand and closed up Ariel's hand with the rest of the things. "And you just put that away. I'll get you a sack."

The woman rummaged around her stand and managed to fish out a dirty but sturdy burlap bag. With a sweep of her arm she guided the apples into the sack like a magician; not a single one spilled. She shook them down and then tied it with a piece of twine.

"Don't know how useful it will be, underwater, but it should hold for a while," the woman said.

"Thank you, I . . . what?"

"It's a marvel. . . . Your kind *do* like fruit of the land."

"I haven't the foggiest notion what you are talking about," Ariel said with great dignity.

"Those coins haven't been used in two hundred years," the woman said, nodding her chin at Ariel's satchel. "And those pearls and gems didn't come from no stronghold, no stolen purse. By the smell of 'em, they came straight from Davy Jones's locker."

"I . . . found . . . a chest . . . when I was walking . . . on the beach . . . and . . ."

As queen and as girl, as someone who could sing like the gods and someone who had been mute as a stone, one thing about Ariel had never changed: she was a terrible liar. Most of the time it didn't even occur to her to lie.

Which, now that she thought about it, would have made things a *lot* easier with her dad.

"Oh, a treasure chest found on a beach, like a pirate left it there," the old woman said, nodding seriously. "To be sure."

Ariel tried to think of something else.

The old woman leaned forward.

"Your secret's safe with me, seachild. I would give you all my apples in return for a favor someday instead, if I didn't need the money."

"What would you ask for?" Ariel asked, too intrigued to bother pretending further.

"I'd ask . . . well, if no emergency popped up to use it on, like 'I wish for someone to save my grandgirl from drowning' or something, well . . ." The old woman looked faintly embarrassed. "I'd ask to see *you*, in your true form, swimmin' out to sea. If I could see that, I'd know *all* the tales were true, all the good ones and bad ones. That there is more to the world than I see with my old brown eyes every day, and I'd die a happy woman, knowing there was magic."

Ariel was silent, overcome by the woman's words. The mermaid had probably been a little girl at the same time as this old woman. And the woman would die, happy or not, many hundreds of years before the Queen of the Sea had to begin contemplating her own mortality.

Ariel put her hands on the woman's and squeezed them.

"There is magic," she said softly. "There is always magic. Even if you can't see it."

The old woman looked at her for a long moment. Then she laughed. "Ah well, ye already paid, so no favor's necessary. But it sure would be nice to see you anyway—I've never inked a mermaid from real life! And I do them all the time. . . . Used to, leastways . . ."

"Inked?" Ariel asked curiously. "Are you an artist?"

"An artist of the skin. Argent the Inker, at your service!" She pushed up her sleeves and showed Ariel her arms. They were dark and freckled with even darker spots, scars, and other spots of varying shades without a name or purpose. But in the places where the skin hadn't aged or stretched or sagged so much were some of the most incredible pictures Ariel had ever seen.

A ship with its sails billowed, a fat-cheeked cloud puffing wind to speed it along. A single wave, curled and cresting with foam flying off, so full of life and movement Ariel almost felt it on her cheeks. A fish caught midjump— honestly, in an unlikely contrapposto of tailfin and lips, but still—seemed to glitter in the light.

Everything was a single shade of dark blue; Ariel's mind filled in the color without her even realizing it. The fineness of the lines was almost unimaginable from such a mortal creature; all the pictures were as detailed and delicate as scrimshaw.

On skin.

"I've never seen anything like this," Ariel breathed. Of course sailors drowned, and sometimes their bloated bodies sank to the bottom of the sea before scavengers tore them up. Often they had tattoos: blurry, dark images of anchors and hearts and words like *Mom*. Nothing that bore any resemblance to what she saw now.

"I was quite famous, before my eyes started to go," the woman said proudly. "Sailors—captains—people from all over the world would come to see me, them that could afford it. As far away as Kikunari! Oh, I did some amazing things . . . an entire circus for a girl in Lesser Gaulica . . . Ah, well. Now I'm selling apples to make ends meet. At least I have my little house and orchard by the sea. And my own teeth. There's them as have far less."

"What a fascinating story," Ariel breathed. She could already hear the song in her head: something about an artist in a shack by the ocean, whose pictures came alive off her arms and kept her company . . . Porpoises that dove into the waves, gulls that flew off her skin and into the air and . . .

. . . and squawked?

Ariel jumped. A real gull had broken her reveries: it

had landed on a roof nearby and was flapping its wings and making noises at her. *Jona.*

"I must go," she said, throwing the sack of fruit over her shoulder as gracefully as she could. Things in this world were *heavy.* "But I will see you again."

"I pray you do," the woman said softly.

The mermaid smiled to herself as she walked away, wondering when the woman would find the satchel of gems and coins that she had left on the stand where the apples had been.

Eric

He gnawed on his quail leg contemplatively, thinking about the strange meeting with the metalworkers, and of misty fantasy mountains, and of how much simpler life would be if he were a sailor, or a metalworker, or a real prince who went out and found dragons.

Suddenly he leapt up and strode out of the room, feeling something akin to panic.

The halls were filled with strange people. He didn't remember it being like this before . . . before he was married. Some looked at him—*the prince*—suspiciously. Men in dark breeches and boots barely gave him a passing glance and whispered behind gloved hands. Representatives from eastern districts walked with broad steps and wore more traditional garb, loose shirts and broad leather belts. These gave the prince a nod at least. Women with waists so tiny and tight it was hard to see how they could breathe minced along in skirts too wide to easily fit through doors.

"Who *are* all these people?" Eric asked, more confused than ever. "When did they all start showing up in my castle?"

But of course, it all started when *everything* that was bad had started . . .

". . . the night of my wedding." He paused, consciously directing his thoughts to that day. He replayed memories that were so dusty and unused they sprang up clear and glossy, unmarred by use or the merciful editing of time. Each moment played like . . . a play.

There really was *a mermaid. And a mer—uh, man?* La Sirenetta *was all real?*

A pair of soldiers walked by, and didn't even bother to salute the prince.

Am I mad? Eric wondered, feeling like a ghost as real life played on around him.

"Excuse me, I need your signature here, Your Highness." A stalk-thin man held out a small board with a paper neatly tacked to it, and a quill. *He at least sees me,* Eric thought dryly. "The dynamite from Druvest. I hate to bother you, but the vendor must get back on the next boat. . . ."

"Dynamite? The . . . explode-y stuff?" Eric winced at how stupid he sounded. But he couldn't think of any other way of asking.

"Yes, Your Highness. It's part of the new munitions order. Much more exciting than the bill for oats from Bretland I signed in your name last week, if I may say so. All new technology! What a world we live in."

"Yes, what a world," Eric repeated darkly. "No, I will not sign this now. I need to review our accounts first. No more orders for anything military without my review."

The man started to protest but saw the look in Eric's eyes. He chose instead to bow and back away. "Yes, Your Highness."

Eric sighed. He had read about dynamite, of course, and the idea *was* exciting—like firecrackers but bigger.

Much, much bigger.

And without the pretty colored sparkles.

When had Eric agreed to such an order?

Why did he know that those two who hurried by him now, the ones in red jackets from Eseron, were there to discuss a potential alliance, allowing Tirulia to trade up through the northwest in case their land grab directly north failed?

For how many years had he been under the spell? Five? Six?

Air. He needed air. Sweet sea air.

The prince stumbled through the halls, desperately trying to undo his buttons, trying not to knock into anyone. *Every*one. He ripped off the jacket and threw himself onto the first balcony he could find.

The sunshine and brisk, stinging breeze from the ocean had an immediately salutary effect. He took big gulps, leaning against the railing. When he closed his eyes he could imagine he was on a ship, surrounded by the water and gulls and a sail snapping in the wind.

When he opened his eyes he could see the gulls and the sea . . . but all that snapped were the banners flying above his castle.

And these banners no longer sported the beautiful Tirulian sailing ship that Eric had loved since infancy; now they were imprinted with a terrible, grasping octopus thing.

While his wi—*the princess* had been ordering munitions and seizing land and preparing invasions and changing their flag and who knows what else, he had done . . . what? *Nothing.* He hadn't put up a fight at all when Vanessa took over the day-to-day tasks of ruling. He had merely . . . grown bored, hanging around the castle with no responsibilities. And his ocean jaunts were strictly limited now; Vanessa didn't like him risking his life at sea. Or, perhaps, venturing out of the radius of the spell or hypnosis or whatever it was.

So he had begun to try his hand at real composition. Little movements, tiny concertos, even a ballad here and there. And all of Tirulia loved it—all of Tirulia encouraged him, even Vanessa. And thus he found a role and a purpose again: the Mad Prince, glamoured and dreamy, who wrote music while his wife ruled.

He found himself looking at funny spots in the sea, brown and black just under the water. Seals? Or mermaids?

He thought about Ariel. *Really* thought about her, for the first time in years. With the added insight of clear memory: the old ocean god hurling lightning, Vanessa hurling insults and waving a contract. The polyp. The sad, voiceless mermaid swimming away.

If Eric had just listened to his heart and not someone else's singing, none of this would have happened.

He *had* fallen in love with the voiceless red-haired girl. He was just too stupid and obstinate to recognize it. He loved everything about her. Her smile, the way she moved, the way she took delight in everything around her. She was impulsive, unmannered, willing to get dirty, a little strange, and extremely hands-on. *And* beautiful. So different from all the princesses and ladies his parents had introduced him to.

If he had just married her, he would be . . . married to that girl. Who was a mermaid.

He blinked at the thought. *Imagine that!* He, Eric, who always loved the sea, could have married a child of the sea.

Would she have stayed human? Would she have eventually returned to the water, leaving him heartbroken? That happened in a lot of fairy tales. Sometimes after having a child.

Would their children have tails?

And what about his father-in-law? Imagine having *him* in the family, a mighty king of the sea!

He could have had all the adventure a prince could ever want just by staying home. . . .

His thoughts slowly turned course, souring a little.

But if Ariel was a mermaid, what was *Vanessa?* Pretty and ostensibly human . . . But then again, Ariel had looked just like a human, too.

Eric couldn't remember Vanessa looking any different. His princess had just appeared, walking on the beach. And then she met Eric . . . and sang . . . and married him . . . and then . . . all was grey.

He was like a fairy tale creature come out of a long sleep to find everything changed, moved on without him—despite being awake the whole time.

The door to the balcony opened but Eric didn't bother looking around: he knew from the way it was carefully, precisely manipulated that it was Grimsby.

"Master Eric, are you feeling all right?" he asked, his tone absolutely neutral.

"Grimsby, what is that ship they are building there?" Eric asked, pointing toward town. The dry docks, which he often liked to watch from his spyglass if he couldn't get down there himself, were a strange mass of activity, like ants where you don't expect them. It was the peak of summer fishing; all energies should have been bent on catching summer flounder. Only after they been dried and salted properly, only after the autumnal equinox and harvest festival, should the town go back to the business of repairing nets and building ships . . . before the winter flounder and cod fishing seasons began.

"That is the *Octoria*, the first of three warships commissioned for the glory of Tirulia." Grimsby said it delicately, as if he had wished to clear his throat before answering but didn't get the chance. He busied himself with pulling out his pipe and preparing the bowl, possibly to give his hands something to do.

"I approved this?"

"You signed the order, Prince Eric, but I believe it was Princess Vanessa and her advisers who originated the plan and wrote up the decree." The butler frowned at his pipe, then went to tap it on the balcony and empty the old ash out into the water.

"Don't," Eric said distractedly, putting a hand out to stop him. "People live down there, you know."

Grimsby's eyes widened in concern, but he decanted the pipe onto the balcony floor instead, sweeping the ash into a corner with his foot.

"It's for the invasion of the north?" Eric asked, nodding at the warship.

"An alliance with Ibria requires that Tirulia provide the sea power, Your Highness."

Both men were silent for a moment. Eric stared out to sea; Grimsby looked at Eric, his pipe forgotten in his hand.

"She is going to bring us to war with the whole continent before this is over," the prince swore.

"Oh, I hardly think so, sir," the butler replied mildly. "Unless you conscript literally every citizen of Tirulia, you will be dealing with a civil uprising long before then. Sir."

Eric blinked. Grimsby's cold blue eyes and stalwart face gave no indication if he was being serious or flip. The man never offered his uninvited opinion on affairs of the kingdom, much less made jokes about it.

"I came out to say that I had lunch delivered to your study since you and the princess left before you had finished, Master Eric," he added after a moment, finally putting the pipe away in his pocket. "So you may take it in private while you work on your music after your walk, as you are accustomed."

"Lunch? Compose? *Walk?*" Eric looked at him, aghast. "There's too much to do to have time to eat or . . . play around with music! I don't know where to start! Bring me the decree I signed for the warships, and the original order for dynamite, and *any* official correspondence with Ibria! At once!"

Grimsby's face broke out into a warm smile, like a beach that mostly sees cold rain and the pummel of waves but wants to prove it is entirely possible for it to enjoy the sun, if only given a chance. "I . . . *felt* there was something different about you today.

"Welcome back, Master Eric."

Ursula

After attending to her maquillage, Ursula put her muffler back into place and nodded approvingly at her "public" face in the mirror.

"Everything is arranged with the guards, Mistress," Flotsam hissed.

"Excellent. Now all I need to do is figure out *this* mess." She pointed at her throat, not bothering to whisper. No one was around who mattered. With a wave, she dismissed Vareet. The little maid scampered off, hopefully to make sure the rest of the royal apartments were being cleaned properly. That stupid dog's hair got *everywhere*.

"Perhaps a new voice would help? A new . . . *donor*?" Jetsam suggested.

"That's not a bad idea," Ursula said thoughtfully. "Not a bad idea at all. I'll get right on that, later. So much to do . . . throwing the little redheaded twit off the trail of finding her father . . . cementing our relationship with Ibria so I can proceed with our military plans. . . . But right now I have to deal with a *petitioner*. Ridiculous, really."

Her receiving room was little more than a large study with a few bookshelves and a partially hidden door in the back that led to the library proper. Taking up most of the space was a large naval-style desk strewn with the books she was currently reading, sheaves of notes, a log for meetings, and a small burner for the teas and tisanes she told people she enjoyed for their . . . *medicinal properties*.

Which was not entirely a lie. While being princess gave her a different kind of power than she was used to—power over *people* rather than mystical forces—well, call her old-fashioned, but magic was still magic. Its potential for destruction surpassed everything else.

And she had none in the Dry World.

So she set to work researching magic of the *land*. Among the many occult trinkets she kept hidden were bloodstained crystals; the tongues of several extinct beasts; a curvy, evil-looking knife with a shiny black blade—and several books bound in strange leather that did not smell very good. They explained many things, from the proper sacrifice of small children to the use of certain herbs.

In one of these she ran across a particularly interesting spell known as a *circuex* that could potentially and permanently imbue her with magic that she could wield in the Dry World. Unfortunately it was a bit messy and bloody, involving lots of sacrificial victims, and it required one very rare component. *Fortunately* this component was something she just happened to have—because, as said, she was a bit of a hoarder.

She played with the new golden chain around her neck and considered.

No, not yet. Casting the circuex required an awful lot of work and commitment. And an end to her fun with Tirulia! She had such plans for the little nation. . . . Maybe she would pursue the matter later. For now she would work with her rather prodigious *non*-magical powers: manipulation, deception, and all the gold in the coffers of the kingdom.

And as for the kingdom, right then she had to deal with more pressing princess duties. She settled herself primly into a tiny, very ornate golden chair with delicate curled legs that ended in the sweetest little tentacles.

Flotsam took a polished brass urn from a shelf and carefully tapped out leaves that resembled ashes more than tea. Jetsam decanted water from a crystal jug into a tiny copper kettle and set it on the burner. How he lit it would have been unclear to any human watching the scene.

One never knew when a tea like this would be needed. . . .

"You may let in the first," Ursula announced grandly—only remembering to whisper at the end.

"Lucio Aron, of the St. George Fishermen's Cooperative," Flotsam said snidely. Ursula tried to not roll her eyes. She was a *princess*. She did not have time for fools such as this.

A small man with clothes noticeably shabbier than the metalworkers' came in, bowing as he went. He clutched his cap and seemed generally uncomfortable.

"Thank you for seeing me, Your Highness." One hand went from his cap to his mustache, a plain, albeit thick, salt-and-pepper affair. His brown eyes were almost fully shaded by woolly eyebrows. "I wish my daughter could have come. She loves all the . . . royal things, you know. Princess things. Gowns, teacups, golden spoons. She's even mooning over several of the Drefui boys—sons of the duke, you know. I told her, 'You'll always be *my* princess, but don't set your sights above your station.' "

"What is it you want?" Ursula whispered, barely able to contain her irritability.

"Beg pardon?" he asked, leaning forward.

"What," she whispered as loudly as she dared. "Do. You. Want."

"Oh." He blinked, surprised at what he saw as an odd change in the conversation. He took his cap off and twisted it in his hands, dark skin cracking into white lines around his knuckles and wrists and palms and scars. "It's just . . . we need a new fishing trawler, Your Highness. I mean, I would like *us* to get it, of course, but one of the other companies would be better than nothing. We've been short one since the *Chanderra* sank."

"We're in the middle of a number of military campaigns," Ursula whispered haughtily. "I can't be throwing money around willy-nilly."

Lucio leaned forward, nodding as if he understood.

Everyone was silent.

He obviously hadn't heard a word she said.

"She said she's not going to buy you a new ship *because the funds are being spent on war,"* Jetsam hissed impatiently.

Lucio blinked first at him in confusion, then at Vanessa.

"No, no, you misunderstand, Your Highness. We have the funds. It's just that the shipyard is busy working on your warships full time. We were wondering if maybe . . . you could take a break . . . or . . . maybe establish another shipyard. . . . Yes! Another shipyard. That would be good. For everyone."

Ursula's eyebrows shot toward the ceiling.

"You want me to *what?*" she whispered. "Waste time with another building project for—*what?* So you can *fish?*"

"Yes, Your Highness. So we can fish. That is what we do."

He was obviously terrified . . . but it was also obvious that he had a cause and a belief he was committed to, and he wouldn't back down.

Ursula hated people like that.

"I think. As a princess. I know. What is best. For my people," she whispered, slowly and clearly.

"But . . ."

"Your audience is over," Flotsam added swiftly.

Ursula whispered something that none of the three men could understand. All leaned forward in confusion.

"Your *daughter*," she said, letting a little of her real voice come through.

The fisherman looked understandably startled.

"Yes?"

"What is her *name*?" she said.

"Julia," he said, first seeming confused, then saying her name again with pride. *"Julia.* A beautiful, but sometimes naïve, girl."

Good.

Ursula *loved* people like that.

Flotsam took the fisherman by the elbow and steered him out.

The sea witch wondered for a moment how, with all their fables, stories, and morality plays, humans still fell into the same old traps. It was kind of amazing. With their pathetically short lives they repeated the same mistakes of previous generations, almost as if they were all one endless being. Why tell a stranger the real name of someone you love? Why brag to a person in power about the beauty or skills of your son or daughter? Why offer up any information, or any need, when it could be used against you?

"Send in the next," Ursula said with a chuckle. The meeting with the fisherman had put in her a surprisingly good mood after all.

"Iase Pendrahul of Ibria," Flotsam announced.

With rather more sureness than she liked, the ambassador—spy—sauntered calmly into the room. *Now that's a powerful gait,* the sea witch thought. His skin was clear and his cheekbones high, his hazel eyes lit from within like an ember you thought you had put out. Thick, curly brown hair attacked the air around his head, barely contained in a riotous ponytail.

"My dear Iase," Ursula whispered indicating the only other chair—a stool, really, with no back, set there for the express purpose of making the other person feel lesser. Yet the representative from Ibria took it and sat arrogantly at ease.

"I've heard you have a cold. A thousand blessings on your health," he said, touching his heart.

"Forget about it, it's nothing," she whispered. "Let's talk about our alliance."

"We can talk—or at least *I* can," he said with a smile that didn't reach his eyes, "but I do not see any advantage to our siding with you. Your fleet is still short three of the warships you swore to provide—six, I believe, was the original promise. Your land skirmishes have been of questionable success at best. Burning down defenseless villages isn't really much of an accomplishment—I'm fairly certain Gaius Octavius would agree with me on that one. Ibria is wealthy enough. We have no reason to spend resources on a war that doesn't directly lead to our advantage."

"Oh, but it will," Ursula whispered, putting a hand on his arm.

Iase stared at her fingers with distaste.

"I'm sorry, what?" he asked.

"*It will,*" she hissed louder.

"You'll forgive me, Your Highness, but you have given me no proof of that. I see no reason to make deals with a princess who dresses prettily but lacks any strategic ability."

"You refuse to deal because I am a *woman*?" Ursula growled, perhaps a little loudly, in her own voice.

"On the contrary," Iase said, patting her hand and then removing it from his arm. "I have had many dealings with fine women I respect. Including at least one pirate captain. It is *you*, personally, Princess Vanessa, whom I am hesitant to entrust the resources or future of my country with."

The two were silent for a moment, looking into each other's eyes. His were steady and dark; hers glittered strangely.

Ursula wished she were underwater. She wished she had her tentacles. She wished she had her *old* necklace. She wished she had anything she could smite him with— frankly, a large piece of coral would have done nicely.

First she lost her stolen voice, and with it the charm and *forget* spells that made dealing with the humans around her easier. *Now* it looked like she was losing a potential—and very powerful—ally. Not only would this be a severe setback for her war plans, but her failure would be the talk of the court. She would look weak and pathetic and incapable of mustering the help they needed to conquer their neighbors. And the weak were devoured. It was the way of the world.

"Thank you for your honesty," she finally whispered.

"I beg your pardon?"

"Oh, never mind. I need some tea for my throat. Join me?" She indicated the bubbling teapot: this gesture was perfectly clear, even if what she said was not. Flotsam was suddenly at the desk, laying out a pair of beautiful Bretlandian teacups, golden spoons, a fat little jar of honey, and some lemon slices.

"Don't mind if I do," Iase said carelessly. "Feel a tickle in my throat myself."

She put the pretty gold strainer—not silver, no no, never silver; when prepared properly the metal had the power to negate certain desired effects of a potion—over his cup and poured, and over her cup, and poured. Strangely grey liquid came out, neither opaque nor completely translucent. It was precisely the same color at different depths.

Each person doctored the drink the way he or she liked: lemon, two lumps . . . Ursula put a candied violet in hers—one that had a silver dragée as its center.

"Good for the throat, eh?" he asked, holding the cup up to toast her. "To life!"

"To friends," Ursula whispered over the rim of her teacup.

He raised his cup again before bringing it to his mouth—but waited until she sipped before taking a draught himself.

She watched him, the grey liquid pouring over his lips and into his mouth . . . and he swallowed. . . .

Ariel

On the fourth tide she was back at her lagoon as promised.

Flounder leapt into the air, flipping himself like he hadn't since he was small.

"Ariel!! *Talk! SAY SOMETHING!*" he cried.

She smiled, feeling her cheek tug to one side the way it used to when she was indulging her best friend. She closed her eyes and put her hands in a student-y clasp, reciting:

"There was a young guppy from Thebes, whose fins would often grow—"

"Ha-*HA!*"

Flounder leapt into the air again.

She laughed, too, and ran into the water to hug him, unconcerned about her clothes. They were uncomfortable and hangy and close anyway, much heavier than what mer chose to wear. Flounder cuddled and leapt and nuzzled her like a puppy before recovering himself.

"Tell me all about it!"

So she did. And it was strange, telling a story with her mouth. She let her hands do some signing. It would have been uncomfortable keeping them still.

"Wow," Flounder said when she was done. "That's all . . . crazy."

Jona dropped silently from the skies and landed on a nearby rock with the delicacy of something that wasn't a seagull. "What did you learn in town?"

Ariel sighed and sat down in the shallow water. A warm breeze picked up the tendrils of her hair that were sticking out of the head cloth. She wrapped her arms around her knees, feeling young and exposed.

"I learned it is the wrong season for calçots. I learned about tattoos.

"I learned that Ursula is using Tirulia as the jumping-off point for her private empire, seizing land from neighbors who probably aren't strong enough for reprisals, and that she is antagonizing other, larger powers. I learned that the town is full of soldiers. I learned that twenty-three of them have died in her crusade and yet dozens more boys go to join up because of the promise of gold for their families and the gold buttons on their uniforms."

Flounder gulped. Jona let out an avian hiss.

"And all I can think of are these two things. One, I am in some ways responsible for those twenty-three who will swim no more."

Flounder started to open his mouth; by long habit Ariel just held up a finger to silence him.

"Two, I think about what *I* would do as ruler of Tirulia. If I were Eric, thrown into this mess now. Human politics and life seem far more dynamic than mer. I've never had to deal with anything like it in my time as queen. Nor has my father. Nor my father's father."

"Oh, but what about the Great Kelp Wars?" Flounder asked with a shiver.

"That was over an eon ago," Ariel pointed out gently. "There have been no wars, no battles, no . . . large *disagreements* since then. We've lost touch with the Hyperboreans and haven't heard from the Tsangalu in decades. We exchange Great Tide gifts with the Fejhwa but little else. We have had naught but silence and peace for decades."

"Sounds like a utopia," Jona said. "Especially if no one is grappling over the last tasty morsel."

Ariel smiled. "Yes. Nothing but arts and leisure, beauty and philosophy. . . . But it's all the same, and no one has had a desire to go *find out* what happened to the Hyperboreans or Tsangalu, or acquire anything from them besides presents. Surely their art and philosophy would be interesting, and might invigorate our own . . . somewhat static culture? The humans, on the other hand, are still exploring their world, every crevice and cranny."

"But . . ." Flounder made a face. "But we were here to get your father back. Not to get involved in human things."

"Yes, but the two are intertwined," Ariel said, though she was impressed with his desire to stick to the point. The old Flounder would have let her talk indefinitely and hung on her every word. This was better. She *needed* friends like him right now. "I had to find out what the consequences of my actions were, and unfortunately, I have satisfied that. I have a duty to make things right for the Tirulians, in addition to—*after*—saving my father. He can help us defeat Ursula once he's back in his original form and king again.

"Unfortunately, it's also going to be much harder to find him now, because as I said before, she has been alerted to my presence. I made the first move, I had the element of surprise, and I blew it."

"Stop beating yourself up, Ariel," Flounder said sternly. "There's no guarantee you would have found him the first time you looked, anyway. Ursula isn't *stupid*. She's not going to leave the king around in a vase labeled *Ariel's Father, Don't Touch*. Just because you made the first move doesn't mean you would have been successful. Games take a long time, and a lot of moves, before someone wins."

"But I don't know how much time we have now. I don't even understand why Ursula kept my father around *this* long. Yes, she likes an audience and probably loves bragging about her triumphs to him . . . but even she must get bored of that eventually. What if she's keeping him around for some other reason? Which I have . . . interrupted?"

She squeezed her hands in sudden panic, pulled at her braids since she couldn't run her fingers through her hair.

"Now that you've found him, you're terrified of losing him again," Jona said quietly.

Ariel nodded, too full of emotion to trust her words. That was exactly it. What if she had set something in motion by trying to find him? What if something happened? It would be her fault, all over again. And she would never get him back.

"I have to go back to the castle," she said, fighting down the childish surge of panic. She stood up and tried to give her friends a reassuring smile. "Even though it's a risk. At least I have a better understanding of the situation now. I'd better disguise my voice, huh? Since up until now everyone has only heard Vanessa using it. *Mebbe I shood tahhk liiike this.*"

She deepened her voice and put her hands on her hips, made a frowny face.

Flounder couldn't help laughing. Jona leapt into the air for a moment, letting out a squawk.

She wrung the water out of her skirts and prepared for the walk back to face a castle full of sea witches and soldiers who were probably waiting to grab her.

"Hey, Ariel," Flounder called shyly. "Before you go . . . could you . . . could you sing that lullaby? The one you used to sing to me after I lost my mother?"

Her eyes widened. "Flounder, you haven't asked me that in *years* . . . even before I lost my voice."

"And I won't ask again! It's just that"—he looked around. Jona politely pretended to watch something out in the sea, over by the far rocks—"we're alone here. No one from Atlantica is going to hear us. I don't know when you're going to have another chance."

And Ariel, who lost her voice for years and had mixed feelings about singing for others, sang more sweetly than she ever had before, or ever would again. And no one heard but one fish, one seagull, the sand and the water and the evening breeze coming over the waves, and the rising moon.

Sebastian (and Flounder)

"I have been waiting over a week now for an answer!"

A barracuda towered over the throne in a way Sebastian was pretty sure he wouldn't have if Ariel had been sitting there, voice or no. The little crab glanced nervously at the guards: one a mer, one a surprisingly large weever fish with venomous spines. The two exchanged a look that was certainly not respectful, but nevertheless leaned in protectively, the tips of their spears coming close enough to touch above his head.

The barracuda scooted backward—but recovered himself quickly.

Fortunately there weren't many there to observe the scene; it was late in the tide and even the most dogged petitioners had gone home to wait until the next day. Or have dinner.

Or do something civilized, because they are civilized *people, unlike this shiny-scaled bully.*

Threll and Klios, the dolphin amanuensis, floated on the dais, but otherwise the throne area was empty except for a few cleaning sardines and some planktonic jellyfish that couldn't fight against the current enough to leave. Dark water curved overhead in a deep turquoise dome, full and empty as the sea always was before a storm. Despite the guards, Sebastian felt very, very alone.

"My boys took care of the wreck," the barracuda said defensively. "We cleaned up everything real good. Now it's time for you guys to hold up your end of the deal."

"Royalty doesn't 'hold up' 'ends of deals,'" Sebastian said haughtily, emboldened by the sharp spears overhead.

"Especially when the vendor is asking for far more than what was originally agreed," the amanuensis muttered, looking over a row of figures on his tablet.

"If Ariel was here, she would deal with me fairly." The barracuda opened his mouth a crack, a move that usually foretold a strike.

"Oh, she would deal with you fairly, all right," Sebastian said menacingly, snapping a claw at the fish. "Be glad it is *me* and not *her* dealing with you. Now go away,

PART OF YOUR WORLD

and maybe if you're lucky I'll see you another week."

The barracuda gnashed his teeth, and with a last warning flip of his tail, angrily swam off.

The moment he was gone Sebastian collapsed on the armrest, a little *tickticktick* pile of exoskeleton and claws and sad eyes.

"What are we going to *do*?" he moaned. "If Ariel doesn't return soon the whole kingdom is going to collapse."

"One annoyed barracuda does not a collapsed kingdom make," Threll said with a sniff.

The amanuensis saluted them and swam off into the depths, done for the evening. The little seahorse followed suit. Sebastian raised a weary claw in goodbye.

"What's with everyone being so mopey-looking?" Flounder asked, scooting in from the side.

"*FLOUNDER!*" Sebastian leapt up in excitement. He looked behind the fish, back and forth, eagerly scanning the sea. "How is she? *Where* is she? Does she have King Triton?"

Flounder stopped where he was in the water, hovering there. "Uh . . . no. She hasn't found him yet. And she's not with me. She's . . . um . . . made progress, but still has . . . some work to do. . . ."

Sebastian frowned at the large, brightly colored fish.

"Flounder. You are lying to me about something."

"Me? No. Nope."

Sebastian clicked slowly, sideways, up to the fish. Hunting.

"Is she . . . *really* all right? Did you lose her? Has something happened?"

At *has something happened*, Flounder's face began to swell. He felt all the blood rush to his front and swished his tail to try to stay calm. He *wouldn't* betray her. He *wouldn't*.

"I didn't lose her," he said tightly. *That* was true, at least.

"Yet you are not *with* her. You are supposed to be *with* her. If she is not here, *you* should not be here, either. You should be *there*. With her. Protecting her."

"I don't know how much good I could do protecting the Queen of the Sea," Flounder said, a little archly. "She sent me back to give you an update, Sebastian. Scuttle and his, uh, great-grandgull are keeping an eye on her on the land."

"YOU LEFT HER FATE TO A PAIR OF SEAGULLS?"

"Settle down, Sebastian. She's fine. More than fine. And she's not a helpless little mer anymore—even you should see that. These things just take time."

"Well, I hope they don't take *too* much more time," came a voice from behind them.

Attina hovered in the water, arms crossed. The look on her face was as spiky as the decorations that stuck out from her thick auburn hair.

"I want Daddy back," she announced grimly. "And

failing that, I want someone ruling the kingdom who can actually command a little respect around here."

At this Sebastian looked utterly defeated. Flounder saw his friend shrink into himself and frowned.

"Princess Attina, perhaps what is needed is an actual member of royalty ruling the kingdom in their absence," he suggested coldly.

Sebastian gawked at Flounder. It was so . . . not . . . Flounder.

Well, old Flounder, anyway.

The mermaid glared at him.

"Nice try, Flipper," she said with a sniff. "But you know that being queen was part of Ariel's punishment for losing our father. She can't escape it by turning into a human and running away to the Dry World forever."

And for the second time that evening, a tailfin was flipped and someone swam angrily off.

Sebastian and Flounder exchanged weary looks.

"This is all . . . very *hard*," Sebastian said, without his usual loquaciousness.

"I know," Flounder said with a sigh. "But the moon is waning and we're approaching the neap tide—when the ocean is pulled farthest back from the shores."

"Flounder, I know what a *neap tide* is."

"My point is that the trident's power will also be at its

lowest, so she *has* to come back soon! With or without her father. Or she'll suddenly turn into a mermaid, flopping around on the land."

"That would be a sight," Sebastian said thoughtfully. "A very, very bad sight."

And for once, the fish didn't disagree with the crab.

Ariel

The first part, at least, was easy. There was no issue trailing along with the other servant girls and boys as they finished up their errands and returned to the castle; many were already gossiping and flirting, done with work whether or not they were officially done. A couple of young men were definitely looking at her. She tried not to smile.

But then . . . several girls were looking at her, and whispering to each other. And they didn't look appreciative *or* jealous.

Ariel began to feel uneasy.

She had filled her apron with pretty shells, thinking her excuse could be that Vanessa wanted them to decorate her bath. She had thought that she fit right in with the other servants carrying piles of wood, bins of garbage, baskets of eggs . . . But maybe not?

There were *four* guards flanking the servants' entrance this time. Had they been there previously? She couldn't remember. They definitely looked more alert than when she had snuck in earlier—these scanned each and every person who passed, sometimes directly in the eye. Ariel hesitated.

One of the guards spotted her and frowned.

As casually as she could, Ariel turned around and walked back against the flow, peeling off to the strip of beach right in front of the castle in case she had to make a quick getaway into the waves.

What she saw there stopped her dead in her tracks.

At first glance, it seemed silly—no, *insane.* Royal guards were using long poles to draw things in the sand, over and over again, like children punished by a teacher for spelling something wrong.

Why would Ursula do this to them? Had she gone completely off the deep end? Was it some sort of weird disciplinary thing? But then Ariel stood on her tiptoes and saw *what* they were drawing: *runes.*

Atlantica runes.

Upside-down from her perspective, because they were facing the sea.

THE MOMENT YOU ARE SPOTTED ON THESE GROUNDS
YOUR FATHER DIES

Ariel backed away slowly as the letters burned themselves into her eyes.

Then she turned and ran—

—and slammed chest-first into Carlotta, who grabbed her by the arm and pulled her into the shadow of a pine.

"I saw you try to get in just now . . . *What are you doing here?*" she hissed. "We're on high alert because of what you've done. I assume it was you who took the necklace? Vanessa is in a murderous snit! Surprised she hasn't locked up poor little Vareet . . . She's rampaging around, doubling the guards, offering rewards for information . . . and doing strange witchcraft. Those symbols of hers . . ."

Ariel shook her head. "That is a message for me. She is threatening to kill my father if I come looking for him . . . which I have."

The maid blinked at her.

"Oh, yes, I can talk now," the mermaid added.

"Does this have something to do with the . . ." Carlotta said, indicating her neck. The nautilus. Or possibly a voice.

Ariel nodded and held up her wrist so the maid could see the leather band, the broken bit of shell attached to the golden bail. "I smashed it, breaking the spell, and now I have my voice back again—and she has none. Or her own, rather."

"That *would* explain the whispering and the muffler

and the talk of colds," Carlotta said, a little desperately, as if that one bit of logic were her lifeline.

Ariel felt bad for the woman, who was obviously having a hard time dealing with it all, directly confronted with the truth of magic.

"Everything's clearer now, you know," Carlotta said, falling heavily onto a tree stump. She waved her hand around. "That day. The cake I helped make. The lightning. I may . . . have even . . . *seen* you . . . your tail."

She looked Ariel up and down, as if for the first time. Then her eyes rested on the apron full of shells.

"What in the name of all that is good and holy is *that?* Something for a spell? More magic? More . . . sea stuff?"

"No, it's part of my disguise," Ariel said. "If anyone asked me what I was doing I would say it was for Vanessa."

"*Shells?*" Carlotta asked, starting to laugh. Ariel recognized that laugh. It was the beginning of hysteria. "From the beach? And *driftwood?*"

"They're beautiful," Ariel protested.

"Oh, oh, I know," Carlotta said, laughing and wheezing. "I'm sure you think so. But nobody wants those. Not a princess—not even a fake one, like Vanessa. There *was* a fad for a bit where fancy girls with nothing better to do would glue lots of tiny shells to boxes or frames like mosaics . . . hideous, really . . . but those were *tiny* shells. Dear, you wouldn't have lasted a moment even if you'd made it inside the castle. Oh, what are we to do?"

"I have to find my father," Ariel said firmly. "He is the King of the Sea and Ursula's prisoner. She turned him into a polyp. She has him hidden here somewhere. I need to find him and free him. Then, together, we can defeat the sea witch and free Tirulia from her rule forever."

Carlotta just stared at her as she said all that.

Then the maid shook her head vigorously, as if she could physically thrust away all the crazy things she had just heard.

"Whatever else, you can't set four steps inside that door without someone stopping you. You sound exactly like Vanessa! And believe me, everyone knows what she sounds like. Even if you disguise your voice, you still don't sound like a servant girl. I need to think about what to do. Who could help us? Who could be clever and figure out a plan? You need someone on the inside, more connected than me. Someone like . . ."

She looked up, her eyes suddenly set and certain.

"Grimsby."

Carlotta led Ariel by the hand into the castle, screaming nonsense at her and waving a hand in her face at just the right time when people looked too closely—especially the guards. The Queen of the Sea just let herself be dragged along; she was too terrified just being in the castle to do much else. Ursula could always be counted on to make good with her threats; Triton's life was definitely being put in danger by this. And Carlotta had only slightly eased her fears, bragging about the number of secret lovers' trysts she had covered for.

Ariel was also strangely embarrassed—and it wasn't just because she was being pulled along by the housemaid like a girl in trouble. They were going to see *Grimsby*. Although the butler bore no real resemblance to her father (and was, moreover, a servant) he nevertheless possessed an air of ancient patriarchal wisdom. His was the final and correct word in the castle. Sometimes more so than his master's.

The butler was downstairs in his tiny "office," little more than an upright desk in an oversized closet. He was admonishing a footman for some indiscretion. The young man was handsome, olive-cheeked and blushing fiercely. While Grimsby spoke mildly, his eyes were ironic and cold.

But when he saw the look on Carlotta's face he changed his tone, hurrying the whole thing along.

"Yes, well, don't do it again. Am I clear? You're dismissed."

"Yes, Mr. Grimsby, thank you. Thank you, Mr. Grimsby. . . ."

The youth, overwhelmed at the shortening of the lecture and cancellation of whatever punishment he had assumed he would get, practically fell over himself to get out of the room. In doing so he tangled with Carlotta and caught sight of Ariel, who was hiding behind the maid. She smiled at him. A dazed expression came over his face: one of utter rapture. It was a full moment before he recovered himself and ran down the hallway.

"Carlotta, what is the matter?" Grimsby demanded.

She didn't say a word, just stepped aside to reveal Ariel.

Ariel found herself shy, unqueenly, overcome with the urge to look down at the ground. But she didn't.

Grimsby's eyes, sunk deep behind veils of skin like parchment, widened like a child's. There was recognition, and for the most painful fraction of a moment, *delight*.

Then all too swiftly his face hardened and his eyebrows set like thunderheads over a cliff. The change was like a spear of ice thrust into Ariel's heart. She hadn't realized how much she had looked forward to seeing the old man again.

"Ariel, you look well," he said coldly.

"And you look as dapper as ever," she responded.

The thunderheads shot up, high into the sky of his brow in surprise.

"Yes, I can talk, and please"—she stepped forward and

took his hand in both of her own—"I know things are . . . confusing, and they ended poorly, and involved me, but I'm here to try to make it right."

"You have Princess Vanessa's voice," he said, seizing the one thing that he could comment objectively on.

"She's not a princess, she's not Vanessa, and it's *my* voice. That *she* stole. If you allow me, I'll fill in all the details of the story that both of you are probably just remembering."

Grimsby shook his head, obviously unhappy with the untidiness of it all. "Well, come in, shut the door, and tell me."

It was more than a little cramped in his tiny space; Carlotta's breathing seemed to take up most of the room. Ariel told her story as quickly and succinctly as she could.

When she was done there was silence but for the forlorn calls of a gull outside somewhere.

I've got to make myself seen through a door or window before they get too worried, she thought, imagining an all-out gull attack on the castle.

"You see?" Carlotta said. "That's why I figured she had to talk to you. It's all . . . very complicated."

"So—Ariel. You fell in love with Eric and became a human, and this . . . sea witch also became human, probably to make sure you failed in your quest," he recited the facts in his clipped Bretlandian accent, as calmly as a teacher lecturing history.

"Yes," Ariel said.

"But the sea witch never returned to the sea. She . . . stayed. And became our princess. And now rules Tirulia. With an iron fist."

"Yes," Ariel said, a little less certainly.

"And you're here to find your father, restore him to his rightful throne, and depose the sea witch."

When you couldn't speak, you couldn't say *ummmm* or *errr* or use any space-filling noises to indicate thinking or forestall potential embarrassment. *All of which would be very nice right now. But queens don't do that, either.*

"I came to find my father," she answered as truthfully as she could. "Everything else depends on that. We will do all we can to free you from the sea witch, afterward."

"Yes . . . about this 'sea witch.' Do we have proof that she is indeed a . . . cecaelia?"

"Cecaelia?" Carlotta interrupted.

"Half human, half octopus," Grimsby explained. "Like a mermaid, but with tentacles."

"Half in the form of the *gods*," Ariel corrected gently. "We are not humans who are half fish, the way you people always say. We are children of Neptune and are not like you—even half you—at all."

Both Carlotta and Grimsby looked surprised and a little confused. *All right, maybe not the time to get into ancient prejudices,* Ariel decided. Someday if she stuck around in the Dry World she would set it straight.

"Very well," Grimsby said carefully, clearing his throat. From the new look in his eye it was obvious he was reevaluating her. She wasn't the playful, simple girl who couldn't speak she had been before. She was someone who had things to say, who had goals, plans, *opinions.*

A woman, perhaps.

"There is little I can do myself, besides, er, keeping an eye out for something that looks like a . . . polyp in captivity. Which I will absolutely do, of course. But it seems now that spells have been broken, certain truths are becoming apparent, and our kingdom is driven even deeper into war with our enemies, well, something else must be done about this whole matter *immediately.* And I do not have the authority to decide that. Neither does Carlotta. Ariel, I think you know what you must do.

"You must go talk to Eric."

Ariel felt her cheeks flame and she looked at the floor—not moving her head, just her eyes. But only for a moment. She quickly regained herself and forced herself to look at the old man. His expression had softened.

"I'm a trifle surprised you didn't seek him out earlier, on your own," he said softly. "I don't know much about magic and undersea kings, but I'm fairly certain the two of you felt something strong for each other. . . . Isn't that *part* of the reason you came back? To see him?"

She opened her mouth to disagree . . . but stopped. The old human was right.

He put a hand on her shoulder, like he might a soldier's. "You two . . . began a series of events which wound up involving all of us up in this mess. And I think maybe the two of you can get us out of it. It's fate, or some such. It feels rather right. Rather Greek. Don't you think, Carlotta?"

"It's fated," the maid agreed. "I don't know about the Greeks."

"Anyway, Carlotta was right to bring you to me and I am right in sending you on. Whatever veil has clouded Eric's thoughts is gone now, and I think he would receive you in the right frame of mind."

"But how can I see him without Ursula finding out? She has guards and soldiers everywhere!" Ariel spoke the words clearly while her head was muzzy with possibility. "I won't endanger my father!"

"Eric goes for a walk after dinner," Grimsby said, straightening himself up. "Along the beach—a long way, north beyond the castle. He walks when he's not . . . *allowed* to get on a boat."

"I can provide a distraction for the princess," Carlotta said. "There's a hatmaker been *begging* for an audience.

Vanessa loves posing and preening. . . . We'll keep her tied up in bows and feathers for at least a watch."

"Excellent. It's a plan," the butler said, clasping his hands together.

"Thank you, Grimsby," Ariel said, kissing him on the cheek. "This is all a little . . . difficult for me. It must be impossible for you."

"Oh, no, not at all, dear child," he said, blushing a little. "And think, when this is all over, I shall be able to publish my memoirs about how I helped a mermaid!"

Ariel

She stood behind an old wreck, the hull of a fishing vessel that had been lost decades before and was then swept far up the marsh during a particularly stormy high tide. Blasted by sand and wind and sea, it now looked like the bones of a whale, its chest facing the sky.

When Ariel and Grimsby were trying to figure out the best place for her to meet Eric, Carlotta mentioned that the boat was a place where many couples, wishing to . . . speak in private . . . betook themselves. The thought should have given the mermaid a smile, but now she was overcome by the mood of the place.

The wind picked up and blew tiny whitecaps across tide pools like minnows jumping. Ariel put her hand up, feeling the breeze in her fingers. Things changed *much faster* up here than they did under the sea.

And yet change came nonetheless; it had been several days now since the height of the spring tide, when the full moon worked with the sun to grant the sea her greatest reach over the land. Now tides were lower and weaker, and would become lower still in the coming week. So too the power of the trident dipped.

Soon she would have to return to the sea.

A movement at the edge of the marsh caught her eye. Eric emerged from behind the stand of trees that blocked the view of the castle—and the view of anyone watching *from* the castle. His stride was sure and he looked around boldly, but it was with just a frisson of confusion; he had not been told whom he was meeting, only that it was important. He wore his old boots and beige pants, and one of the thick-woven tunics sailors in Tirulia wore on wet and chilly days. A faded blue cap was pulled firmly down on his hair. His ponytail escaped out the back, curling around his left shoulder.

Ariel grasped the bleached wood of the boat at the sight of him. He seemed . . . so much *realer.* All those times she had dozed off with visions of the young, handsome prince in her head . . . and here he was actually coming to meet her. Life was far more detailed than dreams. His neck bent into his collar, his hands were shoved deep into his pockets like he was cold. Something unimaginable in a fantasy.

Ariel looked down at the outfit she wore, just a dress and apron. How cold *was* it? For humans? Was she dressed inappropriately?

Eric continued to look around for whomever he was supposed to meet. He put a hand to the back of his head and scratched there, pushing up the edge of his cap.

It was this gesture, this boyish, unprincely, unrehearsed gesture, that made Ariel step out from behind the boat.

"Eric?" she called.

The reaction that overcame him was not the one that she expected: his face fell into a snarl of impatience, exhaustion, and disgust.

"*Vanessa*, how many times have I told you that I *need* these walks—"

But when he turned and saw her, *really* saw her, he fell silent.

Ariel smiled. Then she carefully took off her headscarf so he could better see her hair.

"You . . . It's *you* . . ." he whispered.

"It's me."

He started to open his mouth, but she interrupted.

"Before you say anything else, this is *my* voice. Vanessa stole it. Which you should know . . . I hear you wrote an opera about it. . . ."

Eric's hands fell to his sides, useless. His fingers fluttered as if there were something he wanted to do with them, some sign, some gesture, but he couldn't think of what.

That's oddly familiar, Ariel thought.

"It's all true . . . the opera . . ." He didn't blink as he stared at her. She could almost feel his gaze on her hair, the braids, her eyes, her dress, her feet, her arms.

He rushed forward—then stopped. His eyes were as clear and blue as the hot summer sky. His skin was not as peachy-dewy as when they first met; it was tauter, drawn more over his cheekbones, his brow, his nose. It was darker and drier, too, but no less handsome. Just different. She lifted a finger, overcome with the urge to feel it.

Eric caught her hand in his before she could finish the motion, and took her other hand in it as well.

"You're a . . . mermaid?"

"Yes."

"And you can talk now?"

"Yes."

"And you came back for me?"

His eyes shone with open emotion: hope and wonder after a long period of darkness, the beautiful look of a child who, having passed through the gloom of puberty, is suddenly shown that unicorns and fairies are real after all.

Ariel was taken aback. She hadn't expected this, not exactly. She hoped for his joy, she expected his confusion.

But this was . . . too much. She wanted to disappoint him about as much as she wanted to put a spike into her own heart.

"I came back for my father," she made herself say. The Queen of the Sea had little difficulty stating the truth out loud; a younger Ariel would have stuttered. "I received word he might still be alive, as a prisoner of Ursula."

"Oh," Eric blinked. "Your father. Of course."

"That's the main reason I have returned. We had thought he was dead all these years. I'm here to rescue him."

"I just thought . . . I mean . . . I had hoped . . . you came back to take me away from all of this. To go live happily ever after somewhere. Under the sea, maybe."

"You would drown under the sea."

"I'm drowning up here. I've *been* drowning. For years. Under water, it felt like. Now that I'm waking up, of course it makes sense that you would come. And . . . end it."

Ariel had a brief flash of where some of his thoughts were heading: to sirens who sang their lovers to their deaths, the human men and women still ecstatic even as their lungs filled with salt water.

"Ah, no," she said. "That's a little . . . morbid. I'm not—it's not like that."

They were both silent for a moment.

Suddenly Eric was touching the back of his head again

in awkwardness and embarrassment. But there was a lightness to his movements now, an energy that seemed new. A youthfulness.

"I'm sorry, yes, that was Mad Prince Eric speaking," he said with a laugh. "The Melancholy Prince. It's a bit of a role, I'm afraid. To keep me as sane as I am. This is all very strange. I can't believe it's real. That my opera was real . . . but I *knew* it was real, somehow. But . . . was it exactly like I recalled? Did it all really . . . happen exactly that way?"

"I didn't actually see the performance myself. I heard about it secondhand, from a seagull who saw it."

"A seagull?" Eric asked, startled. "Like—a seagull. Like one of those birds flying around up above us right now? One of those . . . many . . . birds . . ."

He frowned. There were at least a half dozen of them circling silently directly overhead. Eerily.

"They're keeping an eye on me," Ariel explained. "Making sure I'm all right."

"Of course they are," Eric said, nodding absently. "Protective seagulls. Why not. So—wait." He turned back to her. "Is this the story? Because this is how it goes in my opera: You really are a mermaid. You really did trade your voice to come up on land. And it was because you had . . . you had fallen in love with me?"

He said the words carefully, trying to sound like an

adult while sounding more like a child terrified of being disappointed.

Ariel closed her eyes. When put that way, it sounded really epic, the stuff of legends—or painfully stupid. Not just the folly of youth.

"I . . . always wanted to go on land, to see what it was like to be human." She reached out and touched the Dry World planks of the wrecked boat, the whispery traces left by human hands on its shape, the nails made of iron forged in fires that glowed without the help of undersea lava. "I collected things that I found, that had fallen to the bottom of the sea from ships. I really . . . I really had quite the collection. I was fascinated with all these things—some of which I still have no name for, the things you people make. And then, one day, I found you.

"There was a storm, and a ship. I think most of the crew died. But I managed to save you and take you to shore. You were so . . . handsome and strange."

"Strange?" he asked in surprise.

She laughed softly. "You had two legs, silly. And no fins. *Strange*."

"Right. Of course. Strange from a mermaid's perspective," he said quickly.

" 'From a mermaid's perspective . . . ' Yes. Anyway, I'll skip the more complicated parts, about my father, and other things that happened. Suffice it to say I made a bargain with Ursula the sea witch that if I couldn't make you fall in love with me in three days, she would keep my voice forever—and me, as her prisoner."

"Three days? That seems rather short. To make someone fall in love with you, I mean."

"I'm a *mermaid*," Ariel reminded him. "For thousands of years you people have been falling in love with us at first sight, immediately and forever upon hearing our songs. I didn't think it would be a problem."

"But you weren't a mermaid. You were a human."

"Yes, and I had no voice, which made things even harder than I imagined," she said bitterly. "But, I suppose, *just as hard* as Ursula hoped. I also suspect she had her hand in little incidents that went wrong along the way."

"So I was looking for the beautiful mermaid who sang me awake," Eric mused, thinking back on the time. "And all the while she was right there before me."

"*YES.*"

Ariel said it a little louder, a little more fiercely than she had meant. Her eyes blazed.

Eric looked at her, surprised.

"You had legs," he pointed out.

"I had the same face and hair, Eric," she said, using his name for the first time.

"But you couldn't sing. You couldn't even talk. I remembered that better than how you looked. It stayed with me. I was coming out of unconsciousness, Ariel. Please have a little pity. I had swallowed copious amounts of seawater—I was coughing it up for the rest of the day, and lay in bed with a fever for three nights. I narrowly avoided pneumonia and there's still a little bit of a twinge in my lungs on certain days if I cough too hard."

"Oh," Ariel said, taken aback. She hadn't thought it was like that at all. From her perspective she had saved him, fought with her dad, and returned triumphantly as a human to woo him. She hadn't given a moment's thought to what had happened to *him* in the meantime.

Same old Ariel, she thought with a mental sigh. *Impulsive—and a little thoughtless.*

"Would you have stayed? A human?" he asked curiously. "If I *had* fallen in love with you, and you got your voice back, and could stay on land?"

"I . . . suppose so . . . ?"

It was a question she had thought about many times over the past few years. The answer had changed with time. Back then, she absolutely would have stayed, and lived happily ever after as the human princess married to her true love in the Dry World.

But now . . . as someone who had been Queen of the

Sea . . . and, perhaps, had more time to think . . . Who knew? There were so many details to the world that she hadn't understood back then, when her vision was colored in bright primary hues and the borders between truth and fiction were defined in bold black lines. Would she have aged and died as a human? Would it have been worth it? Would she miss her friends, her family? Could she wake up every morning and not choke on the dry air?

". . . on the other hand, it's also possible my father, the King of the Sea, would have stormed your castle, drowned all the inhabitants, and dragged me back home. He's a bit controlling that way."

"*Drowned?* Everyone?"

"I mean stormed quite literally," Ariel said with a tight smile. It was a power she now controlled, by means of the trident disguised as a beautiful and ostensibly harmless hair comb.

Eric took a moment to digest this.

"I guess falling in love with mermaids is pretty dangerous," he finally said.

"Did you?" Ariel asked in a small voice. "Fall for me? At all?"

Eric gave her a measured look, treating the question seriously as she had his. "I *did* fall for you, just not in the way I expected it would happen. And maybe not in the way you hoped. It wasn't a lightning bolt. As I got to know you, I realized you were the most . . . energetic, fun, enthusiastic . . . *alive* girl I had ever met." He smiled at the memory—and Ariel felt her breath catch. "You know, for a boy who's all about sailing and running around with his dog and exploring, you were just about as perfect a companion as he could ever want. *And* beautiful, to boot. I would have been very lucky."

He said this wistfully.

Ariel wasn't sure when she was going to start breathing again.

What if, what ifs . . .

". . . So yes. I think I did," he said, taking her hands and squeezing them. "No, I *know* I did. You were one in a million. Even an idiot like me saw that. But then . . . Vanessa came along. . . ."

He looked confused.

"She had my voice," Ariel supplied. "And you remembered the song."

"Yes! But . . . it was more than that. Somewhere between *Wait, that's the girl who saved me!* and the next moment, everything went . . . fuzzy."

"Ah. Well. She cast a spell on you. On all of you, I think, somehow. But primarily you," Ariel said bleakly. "I think she knew her stolen looks and voice wouldn't be enough when coupled with her, um, *very original* personality. So she . . ."

"Stolen looks?"

"That's not what she looks like. At all. Even as a cecaelia. She's much older. And shaped differently. Her arms are shorter."

"She's . . . half . . . octopus?"

"No, she's half god," Ariel said impatiently. "And what's wrong with octopuses? You don't seem to mind girls who are 'half fish,' as you say. What's the difference?"

"There *is* a difference," Eric said, looking a little sick. "It might not be logical, at all, but for some reason, there's a difference."

"Well, you're married to a person who is old enough to be your grandmother—at least," Ariel said with a smirk. "With or without tentacles."

He looked sicker.

"Besides," Ariel said. "Octopuses are some of the smartest creatures in the sea—only dolphins and whales and seals surpass them. And dolphins have frightfully short attention spans. Octopuses are creatures of great wisdom, and ancient secrets."

"All right, all right. Octopuses are great. I'm a bigot with tentacle issues." He leaned against the boat for support, resting his head on his arm. "I knew my marriage was a sham, but this . . . surpasses all of my nightmares. I guess in my clearer moments I just figured she was a pretty and somewhat vicious enchantress."

"She is a witch. She is incredibly vicious. I can't speak to her looks objectively . . ." Ariel replied crisply.

"Oh, you're much more beautiful than Vanessa."

Eric probably really meant it. But he was still breathing funny and his eyes were turned inward. *Contemplating marriage and tentacles, no doubt.* He ran a hand through his hair and looked like a wild creature for a moment, trapped and ready to bolt. To go mad and die quietly in the wilderness.

Ariel felt a wave of sympathy for the anguished man. If her life had been hell, at least she had been aware of what was going on. He was just now dealing with truths that were even uglier than he expected, and that had been his life for the past few years.

She put a hand on his shoulder. He immediately took it, like a lifeline. He didn't look at her yet, though, still staring into space.

"Octopodes," he finally said.

"I . . . beg your pardon?"

"Oc-to-poh-dehs." Eric took a deep breath and finally looked up. "The real plural of octopus. Because it's third declension in Latin, not second. *Pus, podis,* podes."

"All right," Ariel said uncertainly.

"There was a thing going around last year. Everyone was—well, all my old university mates were—talking about it. Hard to explain. Latin jokes. *Volo, vis, vulture,* and so on . . . oh, never mind."

"*Romanorum linguam scio,*" Ariel said mildly. The look on Eric's face was very, very satisfying. "They were known to us—at least in the very earliest days, before the Republic."

"Of course they were," Eric said, rubbing his brow with his palms. "You know what? This would make a real amazing opera on its own. This marriage of mine. A *horror* opera. A new genre. A man wakes up one day to find he's been spending his whole happily married life with an evil octopus witch."

"Were you happily married?" she asked, curious despite her other concerns. *I sound like Jona.*

"Mother of God, *no,*" Eric swore. "Actually, it's like many state marriages, I suppose. It could have been worse. We show up for formal functions together, pose for portraits, and spend most of our days and . . . private time . . . apart. You know—she runs the kingdom and plans our next military venture, and I write operas everyone loves," he finished disgustedly. He reached into the deep pocket on his jacket, pulled out his ocarina, and glared at the instrument like it had been the sole cause of all his problems.

"*You* love music," Ariel pointed out. "It's sort of what brought us together. Almost."

"Ariel, I'm a *prince*. I should be ruling. It's my responsibility. If I had been more . . . awake over the last few years, or less of an idiot, I could have prevented the mess we're in now. You wouldn't understand," he sighed. "I have *responsibilities*."

Ariel regarded him with steely amusement.

"*Prince Eric*, since my father went missing and presumed dead, I have taken his place as high ruler of Atlantica. I am its queen. Informally known as Queen of the Sea. *All* of the sea. This one, at least. *Queen*."

Eric looked, quite understandably, dumbfounded. She felt his gaze change, felt him searching for—and finding— signs of a queen where his playful little redheaded girl had been. She drew herself up taller and pointed her chin, not quite unconsciously.

"Oh," Eric said. "Oh. Right. Oh. I should be—I should kneel to you then, shouldn't I? Foreign royalty of a higher station?"

Ariel laughed. The second real laugh since getting her voice back, and this one was far more burbling and not brittle at all.

"Oh, Eric, it's a little late for that," she sighed. "But . . . you do love music. Of all the things that should upset you about this situation, getting to do what you love shouldn't be one of them. *I* love music, too. I love singing. Taking that away from me was the cruelest form of torture Ursula could have devised—well, next to making me think I was responsible for my father's death."

Eric smiled bitterly. "She should have taken this away, then," he said, shaking the ocarina. "*That* would have shown me. She should have *kept* me from composing and performing and spending all my time with real musicians, and made me rule. That really would have been torture."

"I don't think she was looking to punish or torture *you*, specifically," Ariel said delicately. "I think you were just a pawn in her plans."

"Great. Not even a threat. That's me," Eric said with a sigh. "You know, speaking of our joint love of music— remember that song you sang? When you rescued me? I never put it into the opera. I could never get the ending right. I think I must have drifted into unconsciousness before hearing you finish it."

Eric moved the ocarina slowly to his lips, looking at her for permission. She nodded, and he played.

It was just like when he had played it in the boat, when she had watched him, unobserved. And just like then, the melody trailed off into silence.

But this time she could finish it.

Even if it wasn't Eric, even if it was Ursula herself playing the piece, Ariel would have continued the tune. The last note had hung there so invitingly, so *unfinished*, it was a blasphemy against nature to let it drop.

Ariel didn't so much sing as allow the song to come up from her chest, from her heart, from her soul, and let it merely pass through her lips.

Eric grinned in pure delight.

When she came to the end of the refrain she took another Dry World breath, to sing it properly from the beginning. Eric hurriedly put the ocarina back in his mouth and played along. This time he didn't play the tune—out of respect for the original artist, he let her sing that alone. Instead he improvised a harmony that was just a touch minor. The main melody still sounded bold and cheerful, enthusiastically describing the world as young Ariel had seen it. But Eric's part added an element of complexity: things weren't as simple as they seemed; details and nuances convoluted a bold declaration. It was no less beautiful, in fact, probably *more* so. Age and wisdom, life and the outside world, observations hitherto unseen.

They finished almost together, Eric cutting off his last note before she was done.

A nod to his mortality? Ariel wondered.

"That was beautiful," she breathed aloud. Of course

she had sung duets with the greatest mer singers, male and female, ones who were hundreds of years older than she with voices trained for as long. Somehow what she had just done with Eric was far more powerful and beautiful. All with no audience except for the sea grass, the water, and the wind.

And the one seagull who landed ever so delicately on the boat behind them.

"Sorry to interrupt," Jona said. "The skinny grumpy old man at the castle is acting fidgety and skittish—I think about Eric's absence."

"Thank you, Jona," Ariel said with a sad smile. "Eric, she says that Grimsby is getting nervous about you being out here."

"You can talk to seagulls?" Eric asked, eyes widening. He looked over her shoulder at Jona. "Seagulls can *talk*?"

"Life outside the human realm of understanding is complicated," Queen Ariel said gently. "For you, seagulls will never talk."

"I disagree," Jona said, a little waspishly. *"HEY, FEED ME SOME OF THAT BREAD."*

Eric jumped at the demandy squawk.

"See?" the gull asked triumphantly.

Ariel laughed. "Excellent point, Jona. She's right, though. I have to go. Maintaining this form is beginning to be a little bit of a strain—I have to return to the sea."

"Oh, you can do that. Turn back and forth," Eric said quickly. "But you couldn't before. But you can do it now. Because you're queen?"

"Something like that," she said, self-consciously pushing a piece of hair back behind the comb that was the trident in disguise.

"Right," Eric said, looking into her eyes like he was memorizing her, like he could make her stay.

"I have to get my father back," she whispered quickly before she could say anything else. "And then we can work on . . . you, and Ursula."

"Of course, of course," Eric said, nodding, looking back at the castle. "Of course. Please, let me help you. I'll find him *for* you. It's the least I can do."

"He would be in a jar," she said, wincing at the words as she said them. They sounded ridiculous. "Or a tank. And would look like a slimy, weird piece of seaweed or a tube worm."

"Just like in my opera," Eric said, nodding, but he looked a little queasy again.

There was a moment of silence between them, each fishing for something to say, to make the moment linger.

"Of course! All right, well, let's make a plan to meet again. Hopefully so I can bring you your father, and if not, at least so I can update you on my progress." Eric said it brightly and seriously, like it was a meeting between him and a shipbuilder, or between her and the tax fish.

"When the tide changes back, and the moon is full," Ariel suggested. "Right back here, by this boat."

"Agreed!"

Eric started to put out his hand to clasp hers, then started to pull it away, then shrugged, then put it back to rest at his side.

Did he want to kiss her, instead?

Ariel wanted to kiss him.

But the mood was wrong, weird. It was upbeat and positive: she had a direction and an ally. He had a quest. Two members of royalty had agreed to right past wrongs.

None of this was romantic.

None of this fell in line with the smell of the briny wind, or the tumult of the clouds, or the breathy, eternal sound of the waves coming in against solid ground.

She took his hand in hers and squeezed.

"Agreed," she said gently.

Hopefully, there would be time for other things later.

Eric

How epic! He was going to help rescue the King of the Sea!

His heart exploded a little each time his thoughts came close to the idea. All his life he wanted to set sail for adventure, and here it was—*right here*! And it was greater than anything he could dream of, greater than discovering a golden city in the deepest jungles of the lands in the west. The king of the merfolk, cousin to gods, in *Eric's castle* . . . hidden as a polyp in jar.

All right, that part was a little strange.

But mysterious!

And then of course there was the king's daughter, Ariel.

Who, now that she could speak, said things Eric could not have imagined the old Ariel would have. Yet at the same time she was far more reserved now than she had been on those happy days long ago. She held herself in: proud, stoic, still. There was something both wonderful and sad about that—not unlike the reduced state of the sea king. And . . .

She was *beautiful.*

Before, she had been pretty and gorgeous, lively and smiley, all red hair and perfect skin and quick movements. Now her eyes were deeper. He could fall into her face forever and happily drown there, pulled into her depths. There were worlds in her mind that were only just forming before.

"What a damn fool I was," he muttered, entering the castle. All of this . . . *all of this* . . . could have been averted if he had just gone with his heart instead of his—what? Ears? *Ironic, really, when you think about it.* A good composer could summon human emotions and transform them into music. A true love would have been able to resist the witch's spell somehow. He hadn't listened—to his heart—at all.

"Good evening, My Lord. A perfect night for a walk. One couldn't ask for better. Can I . . ." A footman approached him, hands out to take the prince's jacket.

Eric pushed past him. The smarmy young man wasn't one of Vanessa's two despicable manservants, but he wasn't one of the original staff, either. The prince had no idea when he had turned up. Depressing, since he used to pride himself on personally knowing all the people who worked for him—how their parents were doing, how many children they had . . . Even if he didn't know their name days, he made sure that *someone* did and passed along a little present or extra silver in their wages.

Grimsby appeared like a shadow at his side.

"Yes, we met, we'll talk later—" Eric began.

"It's not that," Grimsby said, keeping pace and not looking at the prince, as if the two were just speaking casually. "The emissary from Ibria was found while you were out . . . dead. On the unused balcony on the third floor. Causes unclear."

Eric cursed under his breath.

"Poor fellow. Not the worst sort, for a known spy."

"Absolutely regrettable. But it's a dangerous occupation, sir."

Then the prince considered the situation more deeply, and the possibilities it presented him.

"Er, it's in rather poor taste, I know, but I could use the distraction right now to follow up on something . . . privately. If you would make sure Princess Vanessa directs the inquiry until I officially take part, that would be extremely helpful."

"Princess *Vanessa* direct . . . ?" Grimsby said, eyes widening.

"I need her attention elsewhere," Eric said, giving him a look.

"Ah. Very good, sir. At once."

Like a well-trained military horse, Grimsby peeled away, intent upon his mission.

Eric felt his shoulders relax. He could depend on the butler with his life. And now he could devote himself to his own task without worry. For tonight, at least.

Now, where would Vanessa hide the King of the Sea?

Eric wondered for a crazy moment if he could somehow get Max to help him, to sniff out the merman. Or if he could convince one of Ariel's seagull friends to help. He glanced out a window, but there were far fewer birds in the sky now that it was dark, and those gliding were utterly uninterested in the castle and its inhabitants. He redoubled his steps to Vanessa's room, urged to speed by the ending of the day.

He did pause for a moment at her doorway, readying himself as if for a plunge into cold water.

Dear God, what a tacky mess.

First he went to her shelf of trinkets, picking up goblets and statues and what looked very much like reliquaries but really couldn't be, *because that would be too much, even for her, right?* In his zeal he forgot to be careful; suddenly he realized in a panic that he hadn't remembered exactly where each thing sat or how it was turned. He was behaving like a reckless idiot.

He made himself stop, took a deep breath, and began again. If worst came to worst, he could claim he lost a medal or recognized one of her treasures from a book and wanted to see it close up. It never even occurred to him to blame his mess on a maid.

But he found nothing.

"Gewgaws and gimmicks aplenty," he swore. "Devices and doodads galore—what the heck is she *doing* with all this?"

The shelf of terrifying, unknowable black instruments and dangerous-looking things made *some* sort of sense, at least. She was an enchantress. Or witch. Or something. The rest of her collection could only be explained by a child-like, endless need to find, keep, and store any sparkly—or horrifying—thing she saw.

He pushed aside books, clawed through chests, even looked under her bed and pillows. He went through the walk-in closet that led to the baths, shaking out each dress and squatting on the floor to look in the back corners, under petticoats. He tried not to think about the rumors that would result if he were caught doing that. *Mad Prince Eric indeed.*

Exhausted, with maybe only a few minutes before Vanessa returned to dress for the evening, he threw himself disconsolately into the poufy chair in front of her vanity. The top of the dressing table was covered with strange little bottles and jars and vessels and containers of every unguent known to man. Another ridiculous symptom of her never-ending collecting of garbage.

He looked at himself in the mirror. When they were first married—and he actually paid some attention to his beautiful, mysterious wife—the prince would watch her apply all these oils and astringents while she talked to herself, posing, primping, and making moues for her reflection.

(As time with her passed he chose instead to lie on his own bed in his own room with the pillow over his head, wishing she would shut up so he could sleep and escape his nightmarish existence for a few hours.)

The way she behaved would be pathetic—if she weren't actually evil. She *always* needed an audience. In public she surrounded herself with nobles and hangers-on. In private it was extremely rare that she was without her two slimy servants, or her little maid, Vareet. And when she was utterly alone, her other self was always here, listening to her boasts from the other side of the mirror.

Wait—

Eric frowned.

Was she talking to herself?

Wouldn't a jar labeled something else be the *perfect* place to hide a polyp? He grabbed one and opened it up. Nothing—just some rose-scented powder.

He picked up another one.

Vanilla oil.

He picked up a third . . . and it didn't feel right in his hands at all.

It *sloshed*. Despite its very clear label—BRETLANDIAN
SMELLING SALTS WITH BRETLAND-GROWN LAVENDER FROM
BRETLANDIAN FIELDS MADE AT THE REQUEST OF HIS MAJESTY
KING OF BRETLAND, complete with a little Bretlandian flag—
the contents flowed back and forth nauseatingly like a
half-filled bottle of navy grog.

Eric's first instinct was to shake it, but he caught himself
just in time.

The tin had a pry-off cap, but as he looked around for
something to wedge it off with—a knife or a makeup spade—
suddenly it *changed*. When he tried to focus on the box,
however, it was just itself again, silver, red, white, and blue.

He pretended to slowly turn away, but kept his eyes
fixed on the label.

The outline blurred, as if it knew it wasn't needed
anymore.

"AHA!"

The prince couldn't help calling out in triumph when
he whipped his head back, "catching" it.

What was once a tin of stupid Bretlandian cosmetics
was now a glass bottle with a cork stuck in the top. There
was a little gravel in the bottom and it was filled the rest of
the way with cloudy seawater. Sucking at the sides was a
hideous thing: oozing and pulpy, with what looked like soft
claws *and human eyeballs*. Yellow, but sentient. Barely.

It blinked at him forlornly.

Eric resisted the urge to throw the thing away from him.

He looked beyond it, back at the vanity. As if the spell had given up entirely, at least half of the cosmetic jars were now similar bottles full of similar slimy things. Emptied of beer or rum or wine, full of seawater and sadness. No two were alike: they were all shades of black and green with four, three, or no appendages. Some had suckers; some had horrid tendrils that they couldn't seem to control. All had eyes. Some had heads so heavy even the buoyancy of the salt water they were in wasn't enough to support them, and their faces looked up awkwardly at the prince from their prone positions.

Eric swallowed the bile rising in his stomach.

There were at least a dozen . . . all prisoners? Transformed merfolk?

It was like her own personal prison. Or a medieval torture chamber.

The prince crouched down to get a better look at the feeble creatures. They turned to follow him with their eyes.

"All right," he said, clearing his throat. Whatever they looked like, whatever they were, now or before, they were prisoners of an evil witch and he was a good prince. There was protocol. "I promise you, each and every one of you, I will help free you. I'm not sure how to go about doing that right now, I admit. I don't suppose I could just put you all back . . . in the ocean?"

There was a flurry of slow but desperate head shakes that was sickening to watch. Some let off little clouds of what he hoped was like squid ink, darkening the water around them.

"All right, all right. Find the king, set him free, defeat the sea witch, *then* turn you back. Nothing until then," Eric said with a sigh. "So which one of you is King Triton?"

The large eyes looked at him unblinkingly.

"Any of you? Raise a . . . flap? A fin? Anyone?" Eric asked.

The one he had first picked up shook its head dolefully and made what looked very much like a shrugging motion with its appendages.

Slowly the rest copied it, shrugging and shaking.

"Oh, boy," Eric said with a grimace. "This is going to be harder than I thought."

Ariel

If a person had been watching, she wouldn't have seen the obvious transformation of a human to a mermaid. She wouldn't have been able to believe her eyes, or explain what had happened so quickly in the dusky half light of early evening. It could have been a trick of the light, a curious seal, a strangely shaped piece of driftwood; anything but what it actually was.

Ariel did a couple of rolls and then floated on her back, looking up at the mixed sky of clouds and stars. Everything was quiet. She felt her hair loosen from its braids, yearning to float free in the water as it once did. She took the comb out, and it was a trident once again in her hand—but the braids remained firmly wound.

Half in and half out, she thought, then rolled and

PART OF YOUR WORLD

submerged herself into the depths. It was slightly slower going this time, what with the burlap sack of apples she dragged along.

Flounder appeared surprisingly quickly; he must have had every undersea eye and electroreceptor keeping watch for her.

"*Ariel!* You're back! Do you have him? Is that him—uh, in the sack?""

"No, I failed. Those are apples. But I am back, for a little while."

Flounder bumped his head against her hand—a safe gesture because no one was around. He didn't need the world to see that he still enjoyed being petted.

But he wasn't young anymore, and didn't miss the meaning below her words.

"You're going back with the full moon, aren't you? When the trident is back at its peak power?" he asked, full of disappointment.

"Flounder, I didn't find him. I *need* to go back," she said gently. "But I have a clear path now."

"*Clear path?*" he said with a snort. "I can't *wait* to hear you say that to Sebastian."

Ariel smiled. Flounder was one of the very few people who could use that tone with her. He was dead right. Now that she could speak again, she was already using words like a trickster. *Clear path.* What did that even mean? She had allies, she had a goal. That was all. It wasn't like a parrot-fish had just chomped through a snarled lump of dead coral, revealing a beautiful cave of treasure beyond.

She needed a plan, a *direction*, in case Eric failed.

She ran a hand along the base of Flounder's dorsal fin. "Nothing is easy. I can't go back to the castle at all now, although Eric is looking, for me. And I assume Ursula knows I'm back, and has hidden my father someplace better."

"All those things sound like the exact opposite of easy."

"I *know*. Also, *why* is she keeping my father around at all? You'd think she'd at least want to use him as leverage for bargaining. . . . Like, she would give him to me in return for our never bothering her and Tirulia again."

"Would you take that trade?" Flounder asked curiously. "And abandon Eric?"

"Well . . . I think I've learned the hard way that there is no fair bargaining with a sea witch. Also, I wouldn't just be abandoning Eric. I'd be leaving his kingdom to a terrible fate as well. Our worlds should never have collided, and the people of Tirulia are dealing with the results of . . ."— *a rash decision by a lovesick mermaid*—"choices I myself made years ago."

"Fine, but," her friend said with wry smile, "you still have to come down and check in with His Crustaceanness. And explain all of this to him, too."

"Fine. Race you?" she asked, darting ahead.

"Hey, wait, no fair!" Flounder squealed, shaking his tail as fast as he could.

"OH, ARIEL, THANK THE THOUSAND SEAS OF THE WORLD YOU ARE BACK. IT HAS BEEN A TERRIBLE NIGHTMARE OF BUREARCRACY SINCE YOU LEFT!"

Ariel, Sebastian, and Flounder were alone in the deserted throne room. Ariel had her audience very much to herself.

She opened her mouth.

"YOU HAVE NO IDEA THE THINGS I HAVE HAD TO BEAR." Sebastian clacked a claw against his foreshell dramatically, turning away from her. His eight walking feet clicked tinnily on the armrest of the throne.

Ariel took a breath and opened her mouth again.

"The constant fighting," Sebastian continued, "the interminable discussion of *rituals. Taxes.* The stupid sharks and their stupid sea-grabs. Distributing parts for the Severene Rites. And no one knows where the Horn of the Hyperboreans went!"

The little crab collapsed in a heap, more like a molt than a living creature, burying his eyes under his claws.

Ariel and Flounder exchanged an exasperated look.

"Not a moment for *me.* Not a moment for my *music.* Not a moment to compose, or prepare a chorus for the Rites," Sebastian continued feebly. He poked his eyes piteously up through the crack in his claw. "What is a musician to do?"

"Maybe stop whining and be grateful for a chance to serve his kingdom," Ariel suggested dryly.

Sebastian's eyes twitched in a crab version of blinking.

"ARIEL! You can TALK!"

Using quick scooting motions, Sebastian swam sideways to plant himself on her chest, pressing his face against her skin. A crab hug.

"Oh, my dear, dear girl. I am so happy for you. I want to shed!"

"Ugh. Please don't," Flounder said.

Ariel picked the little crab off her and held him, cupped in her hands, before her face.

"But how did this happen?" he asked, looking around. "And where is your father?"

"It's . . . complicated," Ariel said.

"Ariel!"

Attina was frozen in surprise behind them, staring at her sister. Then with a snap of her tail she was next to and around her, holding her shoulders and looking her all over, as if she would be able to see a physical reason for her change.

"Ariel! I'm so happy for you! How did you . . . ? Where's Daddy? Is everything back to normal now?"

"Not . . . precisely." Ariel wished she could stay there, basking in her big sister's good humor and attention. But there were truths to be told.

"Oh," Attina said, her facing falling. "So . . . does this means you're back to assume your responsibilities again? For good this time?"

Ariel thought about the twin meanings of that word: *good.*

"Why don't you listen?" she suggested, making her voice lilting, not quite begging, but the sort of *come on* sound a younger sister would use to wheedle sense out of an older sibling. "I was just about to tell the story."

"I'm all ears." Attina crossed her arms and drifted away from her.

Ariel decided to ignore her sister's tone and just leapt into the tale, starting with Jona and Scuttle's furious attack on the guards and ending with a slightly censored and greatly abbreviated retelling of the conversation she had with Eric.

It was hard to tell that part. Her lips moved as she recounted their official discussion, but her heart wandered away from the conversation. She could still hear echoes of their duet lingering in her mind.

"*Help* from the human prince," Attina drawled. "I'm so surprised."

"All right," Ariel said mildly. "Do you have a better idea to get our father back? Because if you do, *I'm all ears.*"

"Now, girls," Sebastian said, holding up his claws. "It's good that he's searching the castle, but . . . Ariel . . . he's the reason you lost your head to begin with."

"I'm not going to lose my head again," the queen said with a steely look. *No, really.* Despite the flutters her heart felt when she thought of him. "I'm older and wiser, and I have a mission. I'm not going to be distracted from rescuing my father by a human boy. Even Eric."

"*Even Eric,*" Attina said with a sigh, throwing her hands up. "There are *millions* of 'human boys' up there. You're the *queen of the merfolk.* Don't you ever think about that? Are *any* of them worth *one* of you?"

For a dizzying moment Ariel saw things from her sister's—and her father's—perspective: countless humans swarming everywhere on the Dry World; only a tiny kingdom of mer below in the World Under the Sea. Losing a daughter to a human wasn't just tragic on a personal level; it also meant the loss of one of the dwindling mer to the ever-growing mass of humans. Triton had already lost a wife to them—and Ariel, a mother.

"Just . . . forget about Eric for a moment," she finally said. "You'll just have to take my word that my father and my kingdom come first. That's all I have to offer."

"I guess," Attina said uncomfortably. "It's strange to hear you talking like this, now that you can talk. 'Take my word' and everything. Like a queen."

"I was talking like that before I could *speak* again," Ariel reminded her sharply, signing the words as she spoke. "Were you listening?"

"Oh, yeah, of course," Attina said, unsettled and chastised. "I just meant, in general. The last time you could speak—aloud—you were all . . . 'Guess what I found, Attina!' And 'Listen to this song, Attina' . . . and all those silly stories about what you saw or thought you saw."

"And then I lost my father, and my voice, and the boy I loved, and then you made me queen. I guess that will change a person."

"Yes, I guess so."

The two sisters regarded each other silently. Ariel had no idea what was going on in Attina's head, and that was strange. Some secret part of her hoped it was jealousy, that Attina was regretting her decision to make her littlest sister the queen, that she felt she should have taken the crown herself. Jealousy would have been simple—though sad—and easily dealt with.

Not so this quiet reassessment, this weighing and evaluating from her oldest and closest sister.

Ariel swished her tail.

I'm going to rest for a bit and then give an update to the council before I have to leave again. Sebastian, Flounder, I hope you join me. Her hands wanted to sign these things.

"I brought you these apples," she said aloud, holding out the bag.

Attina's eyes widened as she peeped inside.

"When did you . . . how did you . . . ?"

The king's daughter greedily grabbed one in both her hands, holding it before her face like she was afraid it would disappear.

"There's enough for all of you. *Us*," Ariel corrected quickly.

Attina shot her a look, but it softened almost immediately. "Thanks. This is—thanks."

"I'm going to rest for a bit and then update the Queen's Council on what has happened before I have to leave again. Besides the usual agenda, I plan on opening discussion to possible strategies for rescuing our father, since currently I am at a bit of a loss—maybe heads older and wiser than mine can think of something. Sebastian, Flounder, please work with Klios and Threll to come up with an official announcement about the return of my voice. It's best if everyone else learns it at the same time. Cuts down on gossip and chatter. After it has gone out, join me in the council."

She swam away, trailed by her friends, resisting the urge to look back at her sister.

I guess that will change a person.

Something inside of her tore a little.

But there were sharks to manage and taxes to go over.

Carlotta and Grimsby

Grimsby and Carlotta sat in the butler's private office having tea together. Carlotta was wedged in; it would have been even harder for her to fit if the door hadn't been left open "for modesty and propriety." Carlotta had tried not to laugh at that; the dear old Bretlandian gent was never going to change his ways, not at this age.

As chiefs of their respective staffs they often worked late together, revising lists for parties, making sure the right number of footmen were there to serve, and coordinating what they needed to order. The chef usually came as well.

But this time it was just the two of them, and instead of beer or soup or tankards of wine—what most of the lower staff drank—they were having tea. Grimsby had invited her *specifically* for tea, prepared the Bretland way: in a proper tiny cup, with no more than two lumps of sugar for ladies.

Carlotta sipped it as slowly as she could, since there was actually very little of the hot beverage in its adorably minuscule vessel. Not her thing, really, but as far as tea went it wasn't bitter and even a little floral. *Delicate*, like the rose-patterned teacup. Funny how formal and fussy the old gent was!

But once the ceremony of pouring and serving was over, they sat in awkward silence.

"A bit . . . a bit surprising, isn't it," Grimsby eventually ventured.

"With the . . ." Carlotta moved her hand like a mermaid, back and forth through the water.

"Yes—precisely—"

"And the . . ." She waved her hand, indicating everything else.

"Yes, quite." Grimsby leaned forward eagerly.

"Yes, it is," Carlotta agreed.

They lapsed into silence again, falling back disappointedly into their seats.

"What do we do about it, Mr. Grimsby?" the maid finally asked.

"I really don't have the foggiest idea. It's not our place. I have sworn to protect and serve the royal couple; it is an oath I cannot break. . . ."

"Yes, yes, yes." Carlotta almost used the cup to gesture

with, scattering scalding hot tea everywhere. The fine bone china weighed so little in her hand that she had almost forgotten it was there. "But I never signed on to serve an undersea hag, if that's what, you know . . ."

Grimsby turned white at the term *hag*, as if she had mentioned something as terrible as her own unmentionables.

"No, neither did I," he haltingly allowed. "And she's certainly not acting like a proper princess. . . ."

"Oh, hush on that. There's been plenty of warrior princesses in both of our lands, Mr. Grimsby. But she's not even acting like a proper warrior—or *any* sort of normal human being—because she *isn't* one. She's like a rabid dog—er, shark—biting everyone and everywhere. Mr. Grimsby, we—all of Tirulia—are in thrall to an evil supernatural being, oaths or no!"

"I think I could forgive whatever she was, if Eric truly loved her."

Carlotta almost dropped her teacup at this heartfelt admission from the old gentleman's gentleman. It was only shocking because the very Bretlandian Grimsby was usually as sealed up as a clam when it came to what he felt or believed.

"You've been with the prince a long time, haven't you?" she said softly.

"Well . . . you know, our careers don't often give one

much time for things like family," the old butler said mildly. "I care for him very deeply. Like a son."

Carlotta looked stern. "Then we should let our hearts and souls dictate our actions, Mr. Grimsby, not contracts. There are others who can judge us, maybe, for what we swore and didn't swear. But they aren't on Earth, if you see what I'm saying, Mr. Grimsby."

"I don't like talk of mutiny, Miss Carlotta—it's not our place—"

"Oh, heavens forfend, Mr. Grimsby. But if you meant what you said about Eric, I believe there is *another* . . . girl . . . thing . . . whom the prince might indeed have feelings for."

"I always thought he did, I always wished that he had . . ." Grimsby trailed off wistfully, thinking back to earlier times. Then he redirected his attention on the maid. "All right, then. Perhaps if you have something in mind for an . . . acceptably subtle and appropriate course of action that might benefit our original employer, given the circumstances, well, I might be persuaded to go along."

"First thing we do is find all the downstairs folks we can trust and put them to work looking for the sea king. As for other ideas . . . I'm sure an opportunity will present itself, Mr. Grimsby," Carlotta said, eyes twinkling over her teacup. "It is a very *small* castle, after all."

Eric

In the world of operas, when a hero is searching for something, be it the identity of a woman who rescued him or the letter that will free his daughter from being unjustly imprisoned, the tenor sings heartbreakingly about his quest, wanders around on stage, picks up a few props, and looks under them. He finds the thing! Voilà. Done.

Real life was a lot more tense and a lot less satisfying.

And, unlike in opera, Eric's search for the King of the Sea was often interrupted by real-life stuff: sudden appearances of Vanessa or her manservants, meetings, rehearsals for the opera's end-of-summer encore, formal events he had to attend, or princely duties—such as hearing a coroner's report on the death of the Ibrian.

(No foul play discovered, although why such a healthy youngish man had keeled over would remain a mystery for the ages. Vanessa had no trouble getting along with his replacement, who was much more amenable to collusion anyway.)

Often when interrupted Eric would forget which was the last object he had looked at and have to start a room from the beginning.

Then he hit upon a brilliant idea to keep track, inspired by his life as a musician. He would carefully mark the first thing that he looked at in a room, observing its precise placement, and the last thing he looked at before leaving— and then *he would write it all down in his musical notebook.* The altitude of the item was indicated by a note: high G over C, for instance, for the top shelf of a bookcase, middle C for the floor. A portion of a room was a measure of music; each room was a refrain. He filled in the details with what could very easily have been mistaken for lyrics.

Some parts were harder to put into code than others; the library, for instance. He pulled out *every book* because Vanessa was known to spend entire afternoons there, espe- cially in the sections on history, folklore, and magic. An hour going through all the floor-level shelves resulted in a whole page of middle C notes. Very suspicious, even to someone who didn't know much about music. In a burst of inspiration Eric labeled the sheet *Part for Upright Bass, Picked: Anticipating the Coming Storm*. It was a bit more experimental than the sort of music he normally composed, but these were modern times, and the Mad Prince was nothing if not eager to try new things.

Progress was slow but steady. He had no doubt that soon he would find the king.

And then something so unimaginably horrific occurred that Eric couldn't even gather his wits enough to escape it.

Chef Louis said to him:

"Eet has been a long time since the royal couple has dined *en privé*. Maybe a special dinner is required?"

The entire staff was in on this decision, reacting exactly like an extended family scared that Mom and Dad were drifting apart—what could they do to keep them together?

Grimsby and Carlotta, bless them, did their best to quell the whole thing. The maid yelled, the butler made Bretland-accented speeches of disapproval.

It didn't matter. The dinner would be happening.

Part of Eric thought he deserved this. He had been avoiding Vanessa like a coward and not behaving like a true, brave prince. It was only a matter of time before he was forced to face the villain—he just hadn't expected it to be at opposite ends of a long dining table with a white linen tablecloth and golden candelabra; a multicourse feast for two lonely people in a giant empty room that overlooked the sunset sea.

When Vanessa came into the dining room Eric stood up, as was only right. He looked at her—*really* tried to look at her. But whatever spell kept her appearing human was different from whatever hid the polyps. Her form remained. And it was a beautiful form; very curvy in the right places, maybe a little too skinny and waspish in the waist. *Implausible.* Her hair was radiant and her face was symmetrical and prettily composed. But what looked out of her eyes and tugged the corners of her lips wasn't married to the flesh it wore and seemed hampered by its limitations.

Tonight, as befitted the "romantic" occasion, she wore a bloodred velvet gown and matching bolero to cover her shoulders. A fox was draped around her neck, behind which sparkled the chain of a golden necklace Eric didn't remember seeing before. But besides the fur there was no other nod to the sickness she kept pretending to have. The weather was far too warm for velvet, really, but Vanessa never seemed to get hot or cold. And she never pretended to feel faint like other ladies.

That, at least, Eric could appreciate.

He wore a military-style dress jacket, royal blue, with a sash across the front indicating his brief service in the army that was required of all royal sons.

"Good evening, My Prince," Vanessa whispered. They air-kissed, like cousins. He pulled her seat out for her. "Thank you," she simpered, oozing down into it.

Chef Louis himself came out to present the first course, small golden cups of perfectly clear consommé.

"It should be good for your throat, eh, Princess?" he said before bowing out.

Eric was feeling annoyed and reckless. He gazed at the woman opposite him daintily sipping from a tiny mother-of-pearl spoon.

"I don't think I've ever seen you sick," he observed. "Not the entire time we've been married."

"Oh, it's this ghastly summer weather. Cold one moment, hot the next. Plays havoc with the . . . nerves . . . oh, I don't know, whatever it is the silly little things say about the weather," Vanessa finished, too bored to bother completing the thought.

She pulled the fur from her neck and let it drop to the floor. Eric flinched when its taxidermied nose made a soft *clack* against the tiles. There was no reason to disrespect an animal you killed. It wasn't a *thing*; once it had been a living being.

"You haven't been . . . yourself lately, either," she said, somewhere between a purr and a growl, letting the whispering part of her act die off as well. "It seems like you've been acting different since . . . well, almost exactly since the time I lost my voice."

"Perhaps so. I *do* feel pretty good these days, actually," Eric responded airily.

They finished their soup in silence, looking into each other's eyes—but not like lovers.

Not at all.

Eventually a serving boy came in and cleared the bowls; they clattered against each other loudly in the vast room.

The next course was a magnificent chilled seafood salad on three tiers of silver dishes mounded with ice. Glittering diamonds of aspic decorated the rims.

Eric picked up a tiny three-pronged golden seafood fork, thinking about the trident in Ariel's hair. She hadn't worn it years ago, when they had first met. Maybe it was a sign of royalty.

"Don't suppose your feeling good has anything to do with a pretty little mermaid, does it?" Vanessa asked casually.

Eric froze.

Vanessa smiled coyly down at her plate.

"Why, yes, as a matter of fact, it does," he said as he speared a tiny pickled minnow and delicately eased it into his mouth.

It was extremely gratifying to see Vanessa's eyes grow huge in childlike surprise.

"Yes, I definitely started feeling good when I managed to get Sarai to hit the high F over C in her final aria, 'The Goodbye.' Like this."

And then the Mad Prince sang in a terrible falsetto.

Vanessa just sat and watched, unblinking. Through all seven minutes. No doubt people in the kitchens were listening in fascinated horror as well.

When he finished, Eric took a few pickled bladderwracks in his fingers and popped their air bladders thoughtfully. "It was a real triumph. Now I just need to get her to do it onstage."

Vanessa narrowed her eyes.

He tried not to grin as he ate the seaweed. The princess slowly pulled out a piece of fish and cut it, thoroughly and assiduously.

A different serving boy came out with a basket of steaming hot bread and, in the Gaulic fashion, little tubs of sweet butter. Eric preferred olive oil, but along with all the other terrible things going on in the castle, Vanessa had embraced Gaulic culture with the tacky enthusiasm of a true nouveau riche.

"I do so love baguettes, my dear, sweet, *Mad* Prince. Don't you?" she said with a sigh, picking up a piece and buttering it carefully. "You know, we don't have them where I come from."

"Really? *Where you come from?* What country on Earth

doesn't have some form of bread? Tell me. Please, I'd like to know."

"Well, we don't have a grand tradition of baking, in general," she said, opening her mouth wider and wider. Then, all the while looking directly at Eric, she carefully pushed the entire slice in. She chewed, forcefully, largely, and expressively. He could see whole lumps of bread being pushed around her mouth and up against her cheeks.

The prince threw his own baguette back down on the plate in disgust.

She grinned, mouth still working.

"Your appetite is healthy, despite your cold," he growled. "Healthy for a longshoreman. Where *do* you put it all? You never—seem—to—gain—a—*pound*."

"Running the castle keeps one trim," she answered modestly. "Military planning, offensive strategies, tactics, giving orders, keeping our little kingdom safe, you know. We could be attacked any time. From the land . . . from the sea . . ."

"Actually, Tirulia's biggest problems are with those who *leave* the sea and come *here* to live. . . . Hey, maybe I should write an opera about that."

He gave her a bright smile.

"You're so very clever," Vanessa said softly. "Such a *clever* little musician. With your *clever* little operas. You're giving everyone a free show at the end of the month, aren't you? One wonders if you would even have time to devote yourself to the kingdom or anything military—even if you had an interest in it."

"No interest whatsoever. I'm just the Mad Prince, that's all. Don't mind me," Eric said, saluting her with the butter knife. "Carry on with your little war games. It does seem to keep you occupied."

"I will, then, thank you," the princess said primly. "By the way, I have orders out to kill Ariel on sight if she shows up on castle grounds again, you know. Not just her father."

Eric choked.

When he recovered Vanessa was smiling at him venomously.

Eric worked his jaw, trying to quell the rage that would have him across the room and throttling her if he didn't stop it.

When the immediate anger subsided he felt a terrible emptiness, a sick, sinking feeling that drained his whole body. He sat back in his chair, feeling defeated.

"Do you really have tentacles?" he asked flatly.

"Yes," she said wistfully, through her full mouth. "Really nice ones, too. Long and black. I miss them."

The serving boy came in and pretended not to notice the exasperated, obviously *not* eating prince, and the princess who had to keep chewing ponderously because of the amount of food she still had in her cheek pockets. Off a silver platter the boy took two paper cones—*Bretland* style, of course—filled with perfectly deep-fried baby squid gleaming in a crispy golden batter. After carefully setting one down in front of each of them, the boy immediately withdrew, trying not to look over his shoulder. The mood in the room was palpably icy.

Vanessa looked at the cone with delight, and the moment she swallowed the bread—another large, loud, disgusting gesture that showed the bolus going down her throat in an Adam's apple-y lump—she picked up a squid with her fingers and popped it into her mouth.

"How can you do that?" Eric burst out, unable to contain himself.

"Do what?" Vanessa asked innocently.

"Eat . . . something that looks like you. Something out of the sea. Can't you *talk* to sea creatures?"

"Well," Vanessa said thoughtfully. "There are seas, and there are *seas*. There are the seas that you know and fish out and dump your garbage into and generally destroy in your careless human way, and the seas you *don't* know. Seas that hide secret treasures and kingdoms of merfolk and portals to the Old Gods. And there are seas beyond that . . . between the waves, between the stars . . . where some of the truly Elder Gods come from. What I'm trying to say is"—she leaned forward and popped another squid into her mouth—"these are *very* delicious."

"Disgusting," he muttered.

"Like you humans care," she said, rolling her eyes. "Have you ever tasted latium shark?"

"No. Is it good?"

"No idea, because you idiots ate it into extinction. Along with several kinds of sea anemone—such beautiful fronds!—sweet-hake, and other fish whose names were literally also the names of food. We could have quite a long discussion about tuna and lobster and cod and shrimp if you cared. I don't. But then again, I'm what all of *you* call an evil witch. 'Evil' indeed. Meanwhile you humans scuttle across the sea and land literally devouring everything even remotely edible. If only you knew—you're not that different from the more apocalyptic Elder Gods. Not really."

Eric slumped, all the fear, anxiety, anger, and energy draining out of him.

"What do you want?" he asked wearily.

"What?" Vanessa asked, surprised. A squid was poised halfway to her mouth.

"What. Do you *want*," he repeated. "Why are you still here? If my . . . memory . . . and legend has it right, you really are a powerful witch under the sea. What do you want to be *here* for?"

"Hmmm," Vanessa said thoughtfully, chewing on the squid. "*Powerful witch under the sea.* My, I *do* like the sound of that. I suppose I was. But . . . does *legend* have it? Or did a certain little ridiculous mermaid tell you?"

"You got all the revenge on her you wanted!" Eric said, smashing his fist down on the table. "You got rid of the King of the Sea, you stole his daughter's voice, you kept her from getting the prince . . . me. Why stay here? Why not return to the ocean, where you're a powerful witch? Why do you *linger*? Why stay married to . . . me?"

His last words sort of trailed off, like a weak wave returning from the shore to a vast sea, disappearing in the limitless water.

Vanessa laughed throatily and deeply. If Eric didn't look directly at her he could easily imagine a much older, much larger woman, voice husky from years of cigars or hard living. But he did look at her, and the dissonance he experienced while viewing the weirdly innocent face was too much like a fever dream.

"Oh, dear, no," she said, moving her face in a way that implied she was wiping tears of laughter, but her hands moved differently, still breaking the legs off baby squid. "I will say you have a certain . . . charm. And youth is always attractive. But, my love, you're short at least eight tentacles. Maybe six, if I were generous and counted your legs. Also, I like my partners with a bit more . . . heft to their physiques."

Eric was unsure if he was more horrified or relieved.

"It's always the case, isn't it? Men are pretty much the same the world around, regardless of their race," Vanessa said, exasperated. "They always assume they have the complete, undivided attention of whatever female creature happens to be in the room."

"All right, yes, I get it, this is a marriage of convenience, thank you. But *why*? *Why are you here?* If you don't even like me? What is there keeping you here? You're not even doing magic anymore, are you? I haven't seen you conjure any spells or do any magic since we've been together, since the initial one you cast over me and my kingdom."

Vanessa looked up at him sharply.

Huh, Eric thought, noticing her reaction. *She hasn't because she* can't. Maybe in human form she couldn't do magic. He decided to file that thought away for later.

"Well," she said. "You're not quite the dumb, handsome prince you look like. Here's the truth, then, if we are speaking plainly. I find I rather *like* you humans—I didn't expect that at all! You're so venal and shortsighted and power hungry and imaginative and . . . such a mess of wants and desires. And so short-lived! Hardly any of you has the wisdom that a century or two of living endows one with. Such fun to play with . . . And there's so many *more* of you than merfolk. The possibilities are endless."

She gave him a winning smile.

Doctor Faustus's Mephistopheles has nothing on Vanessa,

Eric thought. *Toying with souls and bodies like it's all a child's game for her.*

"And here's the thing," she said, changing her tone. She stabbed five mussels in a row with her knife and shoveled them into her mouth but continued to talk. Like the hungriest, most brutish old sailor in a pub after months at sea. "True, I was a powerful sea witch. But can anyone really have *enough* power? Even with Triton gone there are seven sisters defending his crown, and a mer army, and countless other soldiers, guardians, priests, and allies who would effectively keep me from running the show. Here? I *am* running the show. And all it took was a marriage! Not a drop of blood spilled. Or a person transmogrified."

"Not a drop of blood spilled?" Eric demanded, leaning forward. "We lost twenty at the Siege of Arlendad and three in the attack north of the Veralean Mountains when you were trying to 'send a message' to Alamber. That's twenty-three young men who will never give their mothers a grandchild, who will never see another spring, who will turn into dirt before they reach twenty!"

"My, you really are quite the poet," Vanessa said, perhaps really impressed. "But those were the result of empire expansion. My ascension to power, in itself, was bloodless. Also, I don't remember your being quite so eloquent on behalf of Tirulia's young male population at the time I first proposed these ventures. . . ."

"I was under your bloody *spell!*" Eric shouted, standing up.

"Dear, the staff," Vanessa said primly. "Let's not let the help know about our marital issues. They're all terrible gossips."

Eric made a strangled cry and pounded his fists on the table.

"Just be a good boy and let mummy Vanessa run things. Soon Tirulia will be a power among powers, to rival Druvest or Etrulio. Then you'll be grateful for what I've done. And what will *you* have had to do, to get all these new lands and resources? Nothing. It's just me, sweetie. You go and write your plays and operas and let the people love you.

"Actually, we make quite a good team together, when you think about it. You're the spiritual side of the operation. I'm the tactics. And the . . . *body*."

Eric looked at her blackly.

And that was when the chef chose to come back in.

"How waz everything?" he asked, clasping his hands together.

Vanessa hurried to pick up her fox and wrap it around her neck. *"Quite good,"* she whispered.

"Oh! Zat is wonderful. I will attend to ze palate cleanser now. . . ."

The idea of spending another half hour, another ten minutes, another *course* with Vanessa, made Eric sick.

As soon as the chef was gone Vanessa gave him a nastily patronizing smile. "Don't fret, darling. I really do have Tirulia's best interests at heart."

"I highly doubt that you have Tirulia's *best interests* anywhere near what passes for a heart on you."

"Well, I suppose hearts are a mostly human condition, aren't they? Especially *yours*. You're so full of *love* and *feeling* for everyone around you. Your country, your little mermaid, your dumb dog, your butler. . . . Say, speaking of hearts, his is rather *old*, isn't it?"

Her words chilled Eric to his bones.

"Hate for anything to happen to it. A man at his age probably wouldn't recover from an attack," she said thoughtfully.

"I . . . I'm not sure how you could arrange that," the prince stuttered. "Since we just established you don't perform your witchery anymore."

"Oh, there are other magics, my dear," she said coyly. "And things besides magic when one must make do."

Eric fumed, unable to think of a snappy retort. The dead Ibrian lay like an unspoken nightmare in the middle of their table.

"So while you're keeping everyone's best interests *at heart*," she continued through clenched teeth, "perhaps it's best if you stay out of my way. If I so much as *suspect* you're helping the little redhead, Grimsby will be dead before the day is out. And if anything should suddenly happen to *me*, he is also dead. Along with a few others I have my eye on. Am I clear?"

"As seawater," Eric said, through equally clenched teeth.

And that was how the chef found them, glaring silently at each other, when he came back in with the sorbet. He shifted from foot to foot for a full minute before fleeing back into the kitchens.

Ursula

Of *course* her spells didn't work on land.

Idiot.

She was a *sea witch.*

The cantrip she had cast over the prince remained because she had begun it in the sea, just like the one for her new body. So too the mass hypnosis she had blown across the sleeping citizens of the land like an ill fog—it had been created while she was in the ocean. Flotsam and Jetsam were transformed while they were still in the shallows. Ursula had also disguised her favorite polyps on her last trip down to the bottom of the ocean when she realized her future lay on land. She had waved a cheery goodbye to the prisoners who remained in her "garden," selected a few to keep Triton company, cast a quick perceptual slanter on the rest, and never looked back.

Mostly she viewed her current situation as a minor inconvenience that could be handled, like all things and people. It didn't bother her. Systems where there were prices and balances and choices were the world where she lived, and lived very nicely. It was never a question of what was fair; it was a question of how far you could push the rules.

Of course, then she had found that black-bound book from Carcosa, the one with the complicated circuex that would give her powers she could use on land. While this was still an option, it was a difficult and dangerous undertaking. Only the greatest magics could break the rules of the Dry World and the World Under the Sea.

Only the sacrifice of many, many people would be enough to propitiate the Elder Gods.

And only one very, *very* rare ingredient could complete the spell: blood that contained within it the might and heritage of an Old God.

Like the body she currently wore, she had kept Triton around for just such an unexpected emergency.

She played with the heavy golden chain she wore under her dress, thinking. Things were in fact getting a tiny bit out of hand in Tirulia. Although the stubborn Iase had been taken care of, his otherwise agreeable replacement wasn't taken seriously by the king of Ibria. She was still three warships short of the fleet she had promised potential allies. The number of soldier recruits were down this week— the townspeople were growing uneasy about her military maneuvers. There was a mermaid amok in Tirulia, and Ursula's power over Eric was effectively gone. All she had left were threats and promises.

Every piece of this mess could easily be cleared up with a bit of magic.

But things would be very different after the circuex. There would probably be a larger mess. There might not be much of Tirulia remaining afterward. And it would certainly mean an end to her current experiment with humans.

Plus she would lose Triton, whom she so loved to hold over Ariel. Actually, she loved just holding him in general: *I have a king! Ursula the exiled has a* king *for a prisoner!*

Bah. Speaking of Triton, if she was going to keep him around for much longer she would have to throw the dumb little redhead off the trail. Maybe she could kill two polyps with one hook: repair her relationship with the king of Ibria *and* get the King of the Sea someplace safe, far away from the ocean and meddling princesses. *And maybe have some fun while I'm doing all this . . .*

"She'sss here, Princess," Flotsam whispered.

"Do send her in," Ursula said, remembering to whisper at the last moment. She would wait a little longer for the big spell. Preparations had to be made, times and places—and sacrifices—prepared. In the meantime there was a country to lead into war and an empire to carve, for which she needed a voice.

A young woman stepped tentatively into the room. Yet it was obvious that this was a girl utterly unused to being tentative—or shy, or cowed. The strain on her face showed as she tried to wrest her feelings under control: excitement, eagerness, fear, a trace of anger that she felt any fear. All on a proud, beautiful countenance with clear sand-colored skin, bright brown eyes, and dark rosy lips. *Put a few pounds on her,* Ursula thought, *and she'd be a very pretty mouthful indeed.*

"Julia, is it?" she said in a kindly whisper.

"Yes, Princess." The girl dropped an elegant, if last-minute, curtsy. Her dress was tacky, all flounces and far too many underskirts and weird pastel colors that didn't go with her complexion. Her hair was so brushed and oiled and coiled it shone more like eelskin than anything human. She was so *not* noble it was painful.

But her voice . . .

Ah, her voice. Real potential there. Musical and lilting but with far more substance than the dumb little mermaid's. *Now* that's *a voice I could work with!*

"I have heard so much about you," Ursula whispered, ". . . in that I have heard anything at all, which is, you understand, unusual for someone in my position. And yours."

"Yes, My Princess," the girl breathed, not even reacting to what was probably an insult, too anxious to hear what was next.

"I hear you like a boy," Ursula purred, giving her a twinkly, knowing look.

Julia gasped.

Ursula tried very hard not to roll her eyes. Even if the girl's father hadn't told her, the sea witch would of course have guessed. Silly girls were the same wherever they lived—the Dry World or the World Under the Sea. It didn't matter. There was always a boy. Or a girl.

"Or, should I say, a *family* of boys," she went on. "Handsome, adventurous, *good* boys from a good family."

"Yes, My Princess," the girl said, eyes wide with shock. "But how—"

Ursula shushed her, tsking. "You think I don't understand? Of course I do. I of *all* people. You think I don't hear the rumors—however faint—about *my* lineage? 'Where did that girl come from' and 'Who is her family' and 'Is she truly a princess?'"

Julia said nothing but began to look thoughtful.

Not stupid, Ursula thought. Sometimes that made things harder, sometimes it made things easier. Intelligent people who knew what they wanted and *thought* they understood the consequences were the most fun. They were also the most impatient: they saw her shiny, barbed hook, and often grabbed it voluntarily, swallowing it themselves. No force or trickery needed.

"Look at me," Ursula said, twisting her body, showing off her jewels and the room. "No one dares says those things aloud. I know what it's like, girl. I utterly sympathize."

"I'm sorry?" Julia said, terrified of saying it too loudly, leaning forward. "I didn't quite hear you. . . . Your throat . . ."

Ursula closed her eyes, beating back fury. Pretended she was *working up her strength.*

"I can help you."

"I-I am grateful," Julia stammered. "Your attention and hospitality are already more than I could ever imagine. But why . . . ? Why me?"

"But my dear, sweet child, that's what I do! It's what I live for. To help unfortunate mer—uh, *towns*folk like yourself: poor unfortunate souls with no one else to turn to."

Ursula could see hope and doubt fighting one another in the girl's eyes. True, when it came to charity, Vanessa hadn't exactly been the poster queen. Or princess.

"I would be eternally thankful for any advice or aid you would give," Julia said softly. She was as beautiful as a medieval maiden, chaste and penitent, praying on the beach.

Ursula had seen a number of those in her time.

"Of course, my dear," Vanessa whispered. "Of course. But we must keep it our little secret for it to work properly. You need my help, I need a little help from you. Meet me at the Grey Lagoon at midnight and we will discuss matters further. Trust me, and all shall be yours. I *promise*."

And so that night Ursula struck a bargain with the beautiful, desperate girl: her voice in return for a title for her father, invitations to all the right social events, some wardrobe adjustments, three days to win a noble son, etc., etc. The usual terms. Ursula would have a new voice, a new polyp in her little collection, and she would go on ruling properly, and live happily ever after in her new kingdom *by* the sea, if not under it.

Only . . . not quite.

This is what actually happened.

The Grey Lagoon was an artificial folly on the north side of the castle, fed by the tides. Originally it was protected by a cavern wall decorated with shells and fake stalactites in the fashion of Etrulian bathing grottos. Over the years it had fallen out of use and now slowly decayed into that shabby grandeur Bretlandian tourists so liked to sketch. Locals avoided the place because it had become more or less a swamp, overgrown with tall grass, clinging vines, and sharp, scrubby trees. It fairly screamed *cholera* and *malaria*. Also *haunted*.

So it was deserted, this weird landscape feature shielded from the castle by drippy, unhealthy trees, and most importantly: *it was fed salt water by the sea.*

Ursula arrived at ten to make preparations, and it was a bit of a pain because taking Flotsam and Jetsam along would have rendered the whole undertaking too obvious. That was the worst thing about the Dry World: how hard it was to lug things around. Things *fell.* Heavy things fell *harder.* Feet *hurt.* Sometimes after a day in the stacked-heel booties she wore it felt like knives were impaling her through her soles, like obscene torture out of some fairy tale.

She had to manhandle a smaller-than-she-liked cauldron out to the middle of the shallow water all by herself, along with all the other things necessary for the spell: ingredients and mordants that she managed to keep away from prying eyes.

Getting a little sweaty and trying to keep her tentacles under control—they burst free of their own volition upon touching the salt water—Ursula was ankle-deep in muck and agitated when Julia showed up. The girl was like a picture: her hooded, innocent-yet-arrogant face lit by the small lantern she held before her. She stepped carefully around the bracken, not wanting to snag her precious clothes on the sharp twigs.

"You came," Ursula said, accidentally in her own voice.

The girl, already nervous, jumped at that.

"I don't understand what we are doing, My Princess," she admitted, trying to remain calm.

"My dear, we need to just alter a few things about you," Vanessa said with a smile. "Not just your clothes and introductions. Fortunately, I know a little magic. . . ."

"Magic? Like the devil?" Julia stepped back, pulling her cloak tighter.

"Not at all," Vanessa said with a smile. "Like the kind you use to make love philters and predict who you will marry with the blow of a dandelion."

It probably would have sounded a lot more carefree and girlish in the dumb mermaid's voice. . . .

Julia looked uncertain.

"Just step forward into the water," Vanessa urged. "Not all the way, just your feet."

"Into the water?"

"Yes, dear, like for . . . a baptism. Nothing more. A blessing of magic."

Julia looked skeptical.

"And this will turn me into a princess, like you?"

"It will not turn you *immediately* into a princess, but remember, dear, I didn't 'become' a princess until I married Eric. Everyone just went along with my insistence that I was a princess, to keep up appearances and the family line. I'm going to help you get to that point, too. Now, into the water, dear."

"And you ask nothing in return?" Julia asked.

Ursula sighed. *Clever girl.* For a moment she regretted that she had neither time nor inclination to take on an apprentice, or daughter, or whatever you called a young version of what you were. Julia had flexible morals and a quick wit that was lacking in so many of the young mer the witch had often dealt with. It was a shame she had to simply eat her up and use her, rather than take her time. . . .

"Yes, child, there is always a price. But it is not for *me*, it is for . . . the universe. You can't get something without giving something. That would be unnatural, and against the good order of things."

She almost couldn't believe how easily this garbage came out of her mouth. Once she had a decent voice again, Vanessa would be unstoppable.

"What do you . . . I mean, the universe . . . want?"

"Nothing much, really . . ."

"My immortal soul?"

"No, no, child!" Ursula didn't have to pretend too hard to be shocked. She was continually surprised by humans' single-mindedness when it came to religion. "Nothing so precious. Just your voice."

"My voice?" Julia touched her throat. Such an obvious

gesture, so predictable. Once again Ursula had to work not to roll her eyes.

"Yes. But you get it back once you achieve your wishes, in three days."

"Is three days how long I have to seduce and marry one of the lords?"

Damn, this girl catches on fast.

"Yes. And time is wasting. . . . The . . . ah . . . clock is about to strike the quarter hour, and we must proceed before . . . the halfway point. . . ."

Julia looked at Vanessa, standing in the water: the princess with the wet skirts, in the deserted lagoon filled with black flies and the smell of rot.

"I do not like the feel of this, My Princess."

"Don't be silly, dear girl," Vanessa spoke softly, wheedling. "It will be no problem for you. Three days is nothing. You will come to the banquet tomorrow night and sit by me, as my special guest. They *have* to pay attention to you then. Lords will be falling over themselves for you."

"But why does the universe need my *voice*?" Julia demanded. "What am I getting in return that you couldn't give me for free, without magic? The invites and the dresses and the introductions?"

"*Oh, all right,*" Ursula swore, giving up. "The universe doesn't need your voice. *I* do. I want a young pretty voice to match my young pretty body. And if you don't pay up, you will be nothing, nothing at all, for the rest of your life. Just a stupid, worthless, want-to-be member of the nouveau riche, never quite making it into the exclusive club of nobility. So make your decision, girl. Are you going to stay Julia, the gold-digging flirt whose father builds ships with callused hands, or become Princess Julia?"

"I am going to keep my voice," Julia said, backing away.

"Come *here!*" Ursula ordered, wading through the water toward her.

Julia turned and fled.

Ursula lunged.

She missed entirely, flopping forward into the fetid, murky water. Slime ran down her borrowed, beautiful hair. Tentacles scrumped and played in the mud, happy to be free for a moment.

Julia didn't even have the decency to drop the lantern and cause a big, gothic fire on the marsh. She just ran on, the lantern bouncing and growing smaller like the glow from a fading anglerfish.

Eric

The King of the Sea remained stubbornly hidden.

So the prince continued to stubbornly look for him.

Sometimes Eric wondered if he was still under a spell or suffering dementia. If the Mad Prince was rummaging around the castle in the middle of the night and stolen hours for imaginary friends and other things he had made up.

Well, if so, it was a pleasant way to devolve into insanity.

"Prince Eric, I'm afraid it's time for the memorial service with the families of the deceased soldiers."

Eric was just jotting down a tune for the knickknacks and bric-a-brac that decorated the public drawing room when Grimsby caught him. The prince was especially diligent around the orchids and assorted tropical plants in glass jars—they seemed like the perfect sneaky place to camouflage a polyped king.

"O-oh, yes. Of course. Immediately. I'll go change," he stuttered. "I'm just looking for . . . I just . . . misplaced . . . my . . . composition book. Again." It was hard to lie to his old friend.

"Surely not the one you're holding," the old butler said dryly.

"What? This? Oh, no. This is . . . uh . . . *another* composition book . . . that I need. I'm redoing a bit for the encore performance of *La Sirenetta*. Fixing some things . . . can't remember which page, you know? 'Mad Prince Eric' and all that. Maybe I've an early form of dementia."

Grimsby sighed.

"Eric, you trust me with your clothes, your thoughts, your ideas, your *Max*. . . . Perhaps you would be willing to trust me on other things as well."

The prince looked at him for a long moment, weighing his old friend's words. How much did he really know?

No, he couldn't risk it. Vanessa had been quite clear with her threat.

"Grims, you can't help me here. I won't let you," he finally said, putting a hand on the butler's shoulder. "The best thing you can do right now is *be* there for me. A lot of this mess is my fault, and I don't want anyone in the cross fire while I clean it up."

He winced: terrible metaphor. Embarrassing for a poet. Mixed and meaningless.

"I understand, Eric. But sometimes . . . helping people isn't about you at all. Or even the help. Sometimes it's about the people who *want* to help."

"Grimsby, I . . ." Eric wilted. He hated how this hurt his old friend. He hated how he couldn't say what he wanted to say.

What he actually said was, "Just don't ever find yourself alone in the castle. And don't hang out near balconies. And don't eat anything I don't send to your study myself."

"I am currently subsisting on a diet of biscuits directly from the homeland, thank you. In sealed tins. They are a tad dry but nutritionally sufficient. Here." The butler pointedly handed him a folded piece of paper. "A receipt for the postage on a private package to be delivered to Ibria. Very expensive—I believe you stated a desire to approve all unusual expenditures above a certain amount?"

And with that he spun on his heel and clicked out of the room.

Eric sighed. It broke his heart to treat Grimsby this way. *But I would feel even worse if something happened to him.*

He opened the paper, wondering why the butler thought it was worth his time. It wasn't even that high an amount—although ludicrous, really, for the shipping of a single package. There were international carriages for that sort of thing now. And all the instructions that were tacked on were absurd:

KEEP IN THE SHADE AT ALL TIMES; DO NOT ALLOW
TO GET TOO HOT; ENSURE THE HOLES IN THE BOX AREN'T
BLOCKED SO AIR CAN CIRCULATE; HANDLE CAREFULLY,
LIQUID AND GLASS WITHIN . . .

Eric blinked.

He reread the instructions:

TO BE DELIVERED DIRECTLY TO THE HANDS OF
KING OVREL III OF IBRIA, AND NOT A SERVANT OR FOOTMAN.
ALSO CONDOLENCES ON THE LOSS OF YOUR EMISSARY,
FROM PRINCESS VANESSA.

Glass . . . liquid . . . holes so air could circulate . . .
*Vanessa was shipping the King of the Sea out of the castle
right under Eric's nose!*

Grimsby *knew.* He knew what Eric was looking for—
and had found it.

Good old Grimsby!

Eric's first instinct was to call out a princely order to
stop the whole thing. He would head to the Office of the
Treasurer immediately to do so.

Then he stopped.

Vanessa had the whole castle on alert, spying for her. If
he did anything and was caught—a very likely possibility—
Vanessa would punish Grimsby. *Or Max.*

What should he do?

Ariel

When the time came she changed in the deep channel between thickets of razor-sharp grass on the northern side of the marsh, farthest from the castle—and its guards. The tide was still coming in, so the water hadn't been sitting in the muddy marsh for hours, growing still and stinky.

On cue Jona dropped down from the heavens and settled on the top of a sturdy tuffet.

Moments later Eric came striding on the path through the grass. He looked lost when he didn't see her by the boat as he expected.

"Eric!" she called out quietly.

"Ariel!" His face broke into a wide smile that warmed her from the inside. "I was afraid you wouldn't be here!"

"Have you found him?" she asked eagerly.

The prince took a deep breath and gripped her shoulders.

"I did find some polyps—but not your father. Some other prisoners of Vanessa's. Horrible things, disguised in her cosmetics."

Ariel felt the sea inside her retreat into the depths of her soul.

What a happy ending it *could* have been—Eric bringing her father; freeing Triton right there, on the marshes . . .

But life was complicated.

Eric saw her wilt and he held her steady.

"I'm so sorry, Ariel," he said. "Also . . . Vanessa knows I know about her."

Ariel shook her head at the multiplicity of bad news. "But how did that . . . ?"

"Long story. Terrible dinner. Actually, *great* dinner. Just terribly awkward. But there *is* a little bit of good news."

He showed her the receipt.

"I believe Ursula is trying to sneak your father out of the castle right under my nose . . . and impress a potential ally at the same time. She's giving Triton to the king of Ibria as a specimen for his zoo."

Ariel looked at the paper, the edge of her lip rising in disgust.

"A specimen for his *zoo*?"

"Yes, and according to a little prying I've done on my own, she even told him directly that it was the King of the Sea, transformed. I doubt he believes it, but still. A lovely story for his noble guests."

"Can't you stop this? Grab the, uh, *package* from her?"

"Ah . . . yes . . . well . . . Besides knowing that I know who she is, Vanesa also knows I'm helping you. She has threatened to kill Grimsby if she finds evidence of it."

"Grimsby?" Ariel cried. "He's harmless! That *monster. . . .*"

"She knows how much he means to me," Eric said darkly. "*That's* her magic. Not real magic. She's brilliant at finding the thing you love most and threatening to destroy it."

Ariel groaned. "I wish I had that insight before I visited her the first time."

"Age brings wisdom," the prince said with a dry smile. "But look, it's not actually such a bad thing. If I act like normal Eric, like I don't even know what's happening with the gift or the mail at all, that makes it far more unlikely that she will suspect anything, or try to stop us."

"Good point. So what do we do?"

It didn't even cross her mind for a moment to trade Grimsby for her father. Throwing an innocent under Ursula's chariot for her own gain would make her no better than the sea witch herself.

"Well, when I said 'we,' I really meant 'you.' The carriage leaves for Ibria tomorrow. It will stop in the market to pick up other packages for delivery beyond the kingdom at midday and leave from the tavern at one o'clock. You could waylay it with your storm powers and grab your father, and no one would be the wiser! At worst they might think it was the work of a highwayman looking for gold."

"I can't," Ariel said gently, although she was amused by the image: Queen of the Sea and Highway Robber. "My powers don't work on land. Only water. Just like hers."

"Oh." Eric's face fell. His lower lip was stuck out a little. It was a tiny bit childish but terribly endearing. She almost felt bad that her godlike powers had presented this limitation to him.

"Couldn't you . . . stay in the sea . . . and direct a single, tiny wave or wind to hit it?"

"It's not that precise. And it's less like shooting out a bolt with my trident than encouraging the powers of nature to do something of their own accord. It's not . . . neat. But if it's just one or two men in the carriage, I think I can manage, with some help from my friends."

"The seagulls?"

"Also my . . . mermaid charms." She smiled. *Too bad Sebastian won't be there to hear me, singing like a siren.* "Trust me, we can do it."

"Perfect! By this time tomorrow it will all be over."

"And I will have my father back!" Her heart leapt. There was still going to be a happy ending after all.

"And then we can get rid of Vanessa," Eric said. "The sooner, the better. She's far more dangerous than I ever realized."

"It's a plan," said Ariel. "All we need to do now is carry it through!"

"Absolutely!"

"Great!"

"Good!"

"Excellent!"

A moment passed as they smiled at each other.

Another moment passed, somewhat awkwardly.

And then a third.

". . . All right, then! Good luck! Hopefully when we next meet you'll have your father back!" Eric blurted out.

"Yes! That will be great!" Ariel replied enthusiastically.

They shook hands and parted.

I hope Eric feels as stupid as I do, Ariel thought grumpily.

Ariel

She entered the town late the next morning, and kept her headscarf close around her.

The market was different today—different vendors selling entirely different wares. In Atlantica it was always the same people selling the same things to the same people, only a slight variation with the seasons. *It's Red Kelp Festival Day! Oh, it's the Incredibly Rare and Beautiful Blue-Tipped Anemone Spawning Day! Oh! It's that guy who makes those little wood carvings of the gods out of shipwreck material!*

Actually, those were pretty great, Ariel allowed. She owned at least a dozen of them.

Jona flew above her, occasionally landing on a roof when it was convenient. Several dozen gulls circled close by. Ariel hoped they wouldn't be necessary; she didn't want to draw attention to the situation. With any luck she could just distract the coachman, maybe sing a sireny tune or two to mesmerize him, then grab the package. And then she could return to her kingdom triumphantly, her father in hand, and it would all be over.

The carriage pulled up behind the tavern precisely at ten. There was only one driver.

Easy, the Queen of the Sea told herself.

But the driver was staring at her.

Leering at her.

In a strangely familiar way.

Ariel fell back, suddenly realizing who it was.

Run! she told herself.

Somehow she didn't.

The door to the carriage creaked open, pushed from inside by the footman—who was the driver's twin.

Out stepped Vanessa.

For just a moment, Ariel saw Ursula. Grinning and sharp-toothed, surrounded by her waving black tentacles. All predator, all evil. Sharks killed to eat. Ursula *enjoyed* the pain she caused.

Then the moment was over and the princess of Tirulia stood there, "disguised," wrapped in a long, flowing shift that made her look like an actor playing a foreign priestess in one of those operas Sebastian conducted from time to time. Her eyes were large and doe-like, but her smile was vicious and exactly the same as the sea witch's.

Ariel felt a cold rage settle on her shoulders, and the world narrowed down until it was just the two of them.

"Were you expecting something from the postman, maybe?" Vanessa purred, in Ursula's voice. "A package, perhaps?"

"Very amusing, Ursula. You're so . . . *funny*," Ariel said, trying not to let her anger show.

"Thank you. Nice legs, by the way."

"Thank you," Ariel said. "I made them myself."

"Oh, yes . . . you're 'Queen of the Sea' now. With all the powers and privileges thereof. *And the trident.*" Her eyes flicked greedily over Ariel, looking for some sign of the weapon. "Isn't it funny . . . ? Your father could have turned you into a human any time he wanted to. But he didn't. Withholding his abilities so selfishly . . . trying to keep you locked up at home. . . ."

"He was trying to protect me," Ariel said flatly. "It's not the choice I would have made in his position, but he thought he was doing best."

"But you *are* in his position now," Vanessa said, eyes wide and innocent. "Are you telling me that if you had a daughter, you would just—let her go?"

"If I had a daughter I would make sure she had every opportunity to do what she wanted to enrich her life. Sometimes being a good parent means knowing *when* to let go."

"Well, well, isn't *that* a thoughtful and mature philosophy," Vanessa said, looking at her nails. "Never really had the inclination for children myself—except as dessert."

Ariel just gave her a look, and it wasn't one of horror. One of the most tiring aspects of Ursula wasn't even her villainy; it was her constant bid for attention, for shock value, for turning the conversation back to herself.

"I believe you took something of mine," Ursula said.

"I believe you took something of *mine*," Ariel retorted.

"I believe I traded that from you fairly, in return for something of *mine*. My magic to help you win your man."

"It wasn't a fair trade. You were preying on my desperation and knew that I would fail."

"I believe you were, as they say, of sound mind and body when we made the deal. No one forced you into it and you knew exactly what you were doing."

"I was a dumb, innocent girl!" Ariel snapped, disappointing herself.

You're a queen now, not that innocent girl. Do not sink to her level. She is beneath you.

"And it's been—what? Five or six years since then?" Vanessa asked innocently. "*Nothing* in the span of a mermaid's life. The tiniest fraction of a percentage. But I suppose you're all grown up now?"

"I have grown," Ariel said frostily. "And I am queen.

And I suspect that if we were to go back and reexamine those three days from all sides, like a god, we would see that you had cheated somehow. Even before you used my own voice and someone else's body and your magic to steal Eric from me!"

"There was no noncompete clause," Vanessa said, almost reasonably. "I never said I couldn't go after the same lovely human. He *is* lovely, by the way."

Ariel knew the witch was trying to get a rise out of her.

. . . and she was succeeding; the mermaid could feel warmth rising to her cheeks.

"*Please.* He has no tail or tentacles. I doubt you find him attractive at all. He's just a pawn in an elaborate game to punish me and my father."

"You got me there," Vanessa sighed dramatically.

"Thank you. Now give me my father."

"He's not in the carriage, sweetest. He's not anywhere you can get him. I have *other* plans for the King of the Sea—none of which involve you or the zoo of the king of Ibria. Both of you fooled . . . It's quite delicious, really. The king *is* getting a gift, a lesser member of my pretty polyps. Not that the stupid human could tell the difference."

"Very cleverly done," Ariel said coldly. "I suppose you have to resort to plain trickery since your powers don't work on land."

"Well, perhaps my *magic* doesn't. Not *yet*," Vanessa

allowed—but a quick twist of fury that came and went like lightning across her face spoke of something that irked her deeply. *That definitely merits further investigation later.* "But I have other powers, you know. Power over the infinite corruptibility of humans. Power over absolute *sacks* of gold—which you and I couldn't care less about, but these people worship more than their gods. Power over life and death in that castle where your darling prince lives."

"Ursula. I know Father exiled you from the kingdom, and you wanted revenge on him. But why involve me?"

"Well, you were a pawn, dear, of course. Another *lovely* pawn," Vanessa said with a sensual shrug. "The best way to get at Triton was through his favorite daughter."

"I'm not—"

"*Please*," Vanessa interrupted sharply. "The *youngest*. The *prettiest*. The one with the *beautiful voice*. The one who looked the most like his own dead wife. Everybody knows it. Humans do the same thing—have children who are their favorites—but *they* constantly rail against the habit in their religions and laws. They try so hard to defeat their own base natures. It's one of many things I find rather attractive about them."

Ariel didn't answer immediately, processing this. She almost wished she still had no voice so she could vamp for time while coming up with the right signs.

"Is that why you're still here, causing trouble?" she finally asked. "Because you like the humans you live among?"

"Well, yes." Vanessa put a finger to her lips, seriously considering the idea. "They are so rash and easily manipulated and full of *feelings* and quick to agree to anything—more like a race of children than a real race, if you ask me. You know, I almost understand your fascination with them now. Before, I thought it was because you were just a dumb bored teenager looking for a way to shock your father."

Ariel opened her mouth to respond but Vanessa cut her off, coming near. She lowered her head and hunched her shoulders, like Ursula preparing to attack, and Ariel was pretty sure that if there had been shadows in the alley, the one behind her would have shown tentacles waving high, poised to strike.

"You will never, *ever* get your father back. You, the merfolk, everyone under the sea—you have all lost the great King Triton *forever*. And you will lose so much more. . . . That is what you get for exiling Ursula. *That* is what happens to everyone who crosses her!"

Ariel said nothing—she just raised an eyebrow, as if to say, *Are you done now?*

"And you can just forget about ever getting Eric back, too," the sea witch added snidely. "Whether or not he remains devoted to *me*, he is oddly devoted to his people."

"It's not odd," Ariel responded, a little sadly. "A good

ruler—a successful ruler—loves her people and governs at their will. She doesn't use them up for her own selfish purposes. Someday you might actually learn that, even if you triumph against me now. The humans will not put up with you forever."

Vanessa's face dissolved into another Ursula-style snarl.

"If I catch Eric helping you in any way, Grimsby will die."

Ariel *almost* said, *I know this already*, but stopped herself just in time.

She wasn't a great actress and couldn't feign last-minute surprise. So she spoke the truth.

"You're a monster."

Vanessa crossed her arms. "You're up to something. I can tell. You're trying to cheat, somehow."

"How does that feel?" Ariel asked innocently.

"If you're going to play a game of knives, you had better prepare to *win*," Vanessa growled. "All you have ever done so far is lose. Lose your voice, lose your prince, lose your father. . . . Don't for a moment think you have gained the upper hand just because you have a crown now. Content yourself with ruling the merfolk; they are about all you can handle.

"Go back to the sea, little mermaid. Go back and leave the human world forever. Leave them . . . to me."

Ursula

She made a suitably dramatic exit, stepping languidly up into her carriage and having Jetsam slam the door and Flotsam whip the horses to move off.

It was a *little* bit uncomfortable in the carriage, it being a mail coach and not made for the transporting of royal princesses. Also, there was indeed a large wooden crate for eventual delivery to Ibria, random and delicate polyp within.

But at least it was dark and cool inside. She pulled down the isinglass shade, which cut the glare further and also amused her: its translucent material was made from the swim bladders of fish. As she ran a finger down its textured surface she grinned at the number of lives given just so she could avoid a headache.

The coach slowly began to roll off—and Ursula's smile faded. She had come out on top in their verbal spar . . . she should have been exultant. She should have celebrated the fact that the stupid mermaid princess—*excuse me,* queen— had appeared just as she predicted. And did the sea witch ever show *her*! She had all the cards, all the leverage, and the mermaid had none. Ursula was at the top of her game. There was *nothing* Ariel could do but swim back to her little home under the waves forever.

"Stupid minnow," she said aloud.

"Ridiculous *hussy*," she added a moment later.

But she was uneasy.

It wasn't a feeling she liked.

She looked out the window at the passing scenes: gigantic ancient trees with their hard stems and their weeping branches, a group of soldiers sharing a flask, a school of little brats chasing each other around in the dirt. *Almost* in the way of the carriage. Tempting.

Being among the humans for all these years had been fun. There was a learning curve, of course, but that was fine: up till then it had been literally decades since the witch had been forced to learn anything new. Her mind had relished the opportunity and the chance to start again. In the Dry World she had remade herself into a ruler. In the Dry World she had no magic powers—yet—but something almost better: power over people. In the Dry World, blood flowed down, in a stream, to the ground, and pooled and dried there.

But . . . that stupid little mermaid. Just when Ursula was about to launch her wars and move up the ladder to queen, or empress, Ariel came back. *To take it all away.* Just like Triton had taken it all away from Ursula: the kingdom, her title, her entourage, her *life*.

What was wrong with the two of them? Why couldn't they just leave her alone?

Ursula twisted in her seat, really thinking about the sea for the first time in years. The place where she once had power, and where the stupid mermaid should have stayed. All of Atlantica just sat there, smugly, under the water, not caring if the sea witch was exiled to a nearby cave or the Dry World or the moon. She didn't matter to any of the merfolk at all anymore, except for Ariel and her father. It was like her revenge counted for nothing.

She began to drum her fingers on the ledge of the window. Thoughts ponderously swirled in her mind, like the slow circling current that foretold an eventual whirlpool.

Real revenge would be wiping the mer off the face of the planet. All of them.

Even if the humans never found out or understood what she had done, *she* would know. Anyone who survived would know. The fish would know. They would all know about an ancient, mysterious civilization that had just . . . vaporized one day, leaving relics and mysteries behind them.

And . . . if Ariel were on land when it happened, trying to find her father, and escaped the destruction of her people . . . She would also know. And so would her father. They would have to live with that for the rest of their lives.

And merfolk—even as polyps—lived for a very, very long time.

But if Ariel were in the sea and died with her people, well, that would mean a tidy end to all of Ursula's problems. She would be free to play with her humans, unimpeded, until the end of time. Or until she grew bored. And bonus: Triton would be extra miserable.

A hideous grin began to spread across Vanessa's features, far wider than should have been possible with the lips she had.

How perfect! No matter what happened—she won! Those were the sea witch's favorite odds. And no messy spells involving the Elder Gods were needed.

"Flotsam!" she shouted, knocking on the window. "We're making one stop before the castle. Take me to . . . the shipyards."

Flotsam touched his hat.

Ursula began to laugh, feeling like her old self again.

Ariel

She lay in the warm sand, exhausted and not a little stunned. Clean, fresh seawater lapped at her feet.

Flounder turned sad circles just off the shore. Jona stood close by Ariel's head, obviously resisting the urge to comfort-groom her.

"What now?" Flounder eventually asked.

"I thought this would be it this time, I really did," Ariel said, a little hollowly. "Once again, I thought I would rescue Dad and he would forgive me and we would return home and everyone would be happy. Am I *stupid*?"

"No, you're not stupid, Ariel!" Flounder said, worried at her tone.

"I believe your sea witch has been practicing evil and

trickery for centuries," Jona pointed out reasonably. "You haven't even practiced evil once. She's much better at it than you."

Ariel smiled tiredly. "Thanks, Jona."

She sat up and hugged her knees, looking at her toes, the sand, the water beyond.

Ursula isn't sitting around gloating—or maybe she is, but she's also planning her next move. Get up, girl! No time for self-pity.

She stretched the kinks out of her body and stood, ready to make the sad walk back into the sea.

"What about Eric?" Flounder asked. "Are you going to let him know what happened? So he can go back to searching?"

Oops. Of course she had to let Eric know what had happened. She was so consumed with her own failure she had entirely forgotten the prince—who had a whole kingdom resting on the fate of Ursula. *Thoughtless, Ariel.*

"Oh, yes . . . But I don't know *how* to let him know. I can't get near the castle."

"I can," Jona volunteered.

"That's right, you can! Hmm . . ." She took off the leather strap she had been wearing on her wrist, the one with the little golden bail that once held the nautilus. Then she tossed it into the air and touched her comb, using the power of the trident to summon and affix something to the end.

"Here." She threw the necklace to Jona. "Give this to him. He'll understand. And now . . . I have to return to Atlantica and face everyone."

"You won't do it alone," Flounder promised, patting her with a fin.

Eric

He paced the castle anxiously, waiting for—*something*.
Some kind of word. Everything, the last few years of his
tortured life, could be resolved in the next few hours if she
succeeded! And if not . . .

. . . *Well, if not, we'll deal with it.*

He was so deep in his thoughts he slammed, head-on,
into Carlotta.

"Egads! Sorry!" Eric extricated himself from the folds
of cloth and aprons and clothes she was carrying.

"It's all right," Carlotta said, patting herself down as
best she could with one hand and fixing her little hat. "I
was just coming to do the princess's linens."

"*You?* Isn't that one of the younger maids' jobs? Maria,
or Lalia, or one of those younger girls?"

"Well"—Carlotta bit her lip—"it takes a special touch to, er, tuck in the edges properly and . . . *poke around a bit*, you know. . . ."

Eric gave her a severe look. "Carlotta, is the entire downstairs staff in league together on something?"

"No," she answered primly, refolding a pillowcase expertly over her arm. "That's why *I'm* the one fussing about the princess's room, and not someone as can't be trusted."

The prince sighed. "I don't know whether to be relieved or annoyed that you're involved. I suppose I'll tell you as straight as I can: Grimsby will get into serious trouble if he's caught helping out, er, *foreign* powers. So far I've heard nothing about you."

Carlotta growled and put her hands on her hips, pushing her chest into the prince's. "Why, that low-down, dirty . . . *so-and-so*! She threatened Mr. Grimsby? How much more can she get away with? Prince Eric, it's not my place, but Tirulia is a *modern country*. We will not be subject to the policies and habits of such arcane despots! *You must reveal her to the public as the beast she is!*"

"Er . . ." He looked side to side desperately for an escape. She had him pressed practically against the wall.

"*And* also *that she is a murderer,*" Carlotta whispered, raising her eyebrows suggestively.

"Carlotta, hush, you're talking about Princess Vanessa. That's treason. And besides, she couldn't have done it. Her powers don't work—uh, I mean, the Ibrian just seemed to have *died*."

"She's a clever little sea princess," the maid said. "Do you think she might not be working on ways around her . . . limitations? That she hasn't found some? Perhaps, Your Highness, you haven't been following her latest hobbies." She gestured with her chin out the window. "Although many noble ladies do garden, I suppose—there's nothing unusual in that. And now, I really must make the lady's bed before the lady threatens *me* with something or other." And with that she flounced off.

Eric looked out the window she had indicated, at the neat rows of flowers before the willow grove. Everything looked normal, if a little dull since his grandmother had grown too frail to keep taking a personal hand in her seaside garden.

Then, squinting, he saw a patch that looked different from the rest. Freshly turned, and irregularly planted.

He leapt downstairs as fast as he could and ran outside.

The fact that there was an entirely new, if tiny, garden on castle grounds that Eric hadn't heard anything about was . . . disheartening. It was just one more detail that cemented Eric's flailing, ignorant, and useless place in his own castle. His grandmother would have known about it immediately. Would have been told the moment the gardeners started spending their time on anything besides her heirloom roses and exotic perennials.

The plants growing in this new patch were not roses—though they did more or less fall into the category of *exotic perennial*. Eric studied the leaves and little identifying tags.

Artemisia. Okay, that was like wormwood, what they made absinthe out of. His grandmother had always liked their pretty woolly silver leaves.

Belladonna. Clary sage, henbane. Old-fashioned herbs. *Mandrake.*

He recognized the last because a sailor had once shown him a particularly fine specimen of the root; it looked like a little person. "There's folks in Bretland will pay a king's ransom for this. I just have to tell them it screamed when the farmer pulled it out of the soil."

Eric shook his head in wonder. Even to someone more skilled in the arts of the sea and music than farming, it was obvious Vanessa was trying her hand at a witch's garden.

Her magic didn't work on land. So she was trying to learn new magic. *Land* magic.

Was that . . . a thing?

Was witchcraft real?

If it was, could Vanessa harness its powers? Would she

be able to summon undead armies to do her bidding, call down storms and plagues on countries they were at war with?

Would she be able to cast new charms? Would Eric once again find himself foggy and forgetting, hypnotized and half-awake? Would he do everything his terrible wife said?

He swallowed, trying to control the panic that was coming on.

Boneset. Some said it was good for aches and pains. Modern doctors disagreed.

Wolfsbane.

Foxglove. A pretty flower, and dangerous to animals. It was also known as *digitalis* and contained a substance that destroyed the heart—literally. Eric remembered his father telling him not to let Max anywhere near it if they found some in the woods.

Whether or not witchcraft was real, poison certainly was.

No one really believed the Ibrian had died of natural causes. And here, more or less, was the proof: holes in the ground where some of the flowers had been pulled out. *Used.* The plant could be put into anything: tea, soup, tobacco mix for a pipe . . . Vanessa could make good on her threat at any time. Grimsby would keel over from a heart attack and no one would suspect anything—it would be sad, but an entirely natural, predictable death.

Nothing Eric could ever do would convince the butler to abandon his post, short of tying him up and putting him on a boat to the lands in the west against his will. Eric ran his hands through his hair, frustrated and at wit's end.

A large bird landed on a statue behind him, casting a cold black shadow. The prince turned, fully expecting a crow or raven, as befitted the mood of the garden.

But it was a seagull. With something stringy and brown in its mouth.

"Hello," Eric said politely. "Did Ariel send you?"

The bird answered by dropping the thing it held onto the ground. It squawked.

"Thank you . . . ?" He picked up the leather cord; it was the one Ariel wore around her wrist. Now, letting it flow through his fingers, he realized it was the strap from the necklace that Vanessa used to wear, the one with the nautilus on it.

(Now the princess wore a gold chain that dipped down under her bodice. He had no idea what sort of pendant was on it—probably something unsettling and hideous.)

A white scroll was tied to one end of the strap; it unfurled of its own accord into his hand. On it, sketched in gold, was a carriage with a half-octopus, half-woman thing emerging through the door. There was also a drawing of a crown with what looked like a slash or a tear through it.

Eric swore when he realized what it meant. "It was a trap. The king wasn't even there!" The little scroll faded into glitter, disappearing entirely even as he tried to grasp at the bits.

But if Ariel had cast this pretty little spell, he realized, it meant that she had to be in the water. Which meant she was safe. Just . . . disappointed, and probably grieving. His heart went out to the poor queen of the merfolk. They had both been so sure their respective ordeals were almost over. . . .

"Is it back to searching the castle again, then?" Eric asked aloud, partially to the seagull. "Well, if that's what we have to do, that's what we *will* do. Guess I'd better expand the search to the rest of the grounds, too, huh? I wish *you* could help. I could use another set of eyes. Ones that aren't easily fooled by magic. I wish I had an animal friend who could watch Grimsby for me. I'm afraid Max isn't much up to the task."

The bird squawked again and shook its tail. Almost like it was saying, *Yes, but what can you do?* Then it settled down to preen itself.

Eric laughed and reached out to scratch it on its neck, like he would have Max. The bird seemed to enjoy it immensely.

Ariel

I deserve this, Ariel thought as she delivered the news of her failure again and again and again. Of course the general populace was disappointed. She expected the frowns and the occasional dramatic tears.

Telling her sisters was extremely unpleasant. They wept *real* tears and swished their tails back and forth in dismay. And then they swam off, all but Attina, who gave her a quick hug before leaving.

The Queen's Council was also disappointed—though not terribly surprised, and quick to talk about the future, and Ariel's loyalty to her people, and how maybe further rescue attempts should be turned over to those who weren't the acting queen.

"We should send an army of merfolk—with legs—up through the castle, and seize it," the captain of the merguards suggested. Her eyes shone and her partner, a giant bluefish, nodded eagerly. "It will be like battles of old, sword against sword! We will retrieve the king triumphantly and remind humans of our might!"

"And while you are waving your shiny swords, the humans will be shooting at you with their guns," Ariel said wearily. "That's why I wanted to do this alone—and stealthily. To limit the loss of life."

"Forget the army. Use the power of the sea," a merman senator suggested. "Use your trident and teach the humans a lesson!"

"Yes," Ariel said, leaning back on her throne. "I've actually thought of that. I could destroy the castle and everyone in it with one mighty wave. The advantage of killing Ursula this way is that my father and *all* of her prisoners would be transformed immediately upon her death and released directly into the sea."

Flounder and Sebastian exchanged surprised—and shocked—looks. Had she really considered this?

Ariel turned her eyes to the glowing dome of the surface to avoid seeing their faces. Yes, she *had* thought about it.

If her goal was truly just to get her father back and wreak revenge on Ursula, it was probably the most direct and efficient route. A giant tsunami wiping out a kingdom's castle and all within . . . Some would call it a natural disaster, but others would suspect the truth and tell stories. Maybe people would start respecting the sea again, properly. Maybe they would stop fishing it out and dumping their garbage into it.

And, from an artistic perspective, how utterly apocalyptic and perfect: destroying her enemy and possibly her lover at the same time. *Very* Old God. They'd be singing about her for centuries.

One side of her mouth tugged into a wry smile. The old Ariel wouldn't have even had these thoughts; she would have dismissed them immediately as horrific and unthinkable.

Now she could think them. She just couldn't *do* them.

"No, guys," she said aloud. "I'm not actually killing everyone in the castle in a tidal wave of utter destruction."

Sebastian and Flounder looked chagrined that she had read their minds—but also relieved.

"Your Majesty, I must attend the Planktonic Life Interior Committee meeting," Klios the dolphin said apologetically, with a bow. "I will continue to ponder our problem of rescuing the king. But for now, other duties call."

"Yes, go. We could all use a break anyway," Ariel said, rubbing her head for the second time that week. "We'll reconvene on the next tide to discuss further."

As most of the council swam off, Sebastian approached her, sideways and slowly. "Well, then, while we are taking a break thinking about all *this* . . . maybe we can talk about something *else?* My next masterpiece, maybe? A celebration of the tides. A celebration of the sea. A celebration celebrating the return of your voice, starring . . ."

Ariel narrowed her eyes at him.

". . . well, your voice?" He gave her a winning crabby grin.

"Queens. Do not. *Sing.* Sebastian."

"But Ariel, now that you *can* sing again . . ."

"My father did not put on pantomimes or act in farces. My mother did not perform burlesque. My station does not allow for such gross frippery. No one would take me seriously again."

"Your mother's voice was terrible."

"Sebastian!"

"Sorry, but it's the truth. And you are not your father. . . ."

"No, but would you suggest this if I were a *prince?* Somehow I think not."

"But Ariel! Think of your people! They have lived without hearing your voice for so long! Don't they deserve to hear your singing?"

"My singing is *my singing*," she said, bending down to

put her eyes on level with the little crab. "My voice is *my* voice. I gave it away myself and I got it back again myself. It is not for anyone else's enjoyment or amusement. If I want to sing, I will sing. Right now I use my voice to give orders and run a kingdom. Someday, if our situation changes, perhaps I will consider your idea. Until that time, however, I ask that you not speak to me of it again."

Sebastian clicked his claws together in the crab equivalent of fists and ground his mandibles, trying to keep from saying anything. Flounder put a steadying fin on his back.

"Let it go," he whispered, pulling the little crab away.

As the two left together, Sebastian might have been heard to mutter something about her being *exactly like her father*. . . .

Ariel gloomily looked over the piles of paperwork that were her "reward" after the meeting.

She sighed and tapped on her desk with a pen—a sharp-tipped whelk—and rested her chin on her hand.

It was no use. She couldn't concentrate. All she could think about was her father . . . and losing her temper at Sebastian.

She would have to make it up to the little crab somehow. Maybe she would commission him to write and prepare a celebratory chorus for *something*. Maybe that would assuage his wounded ego.

She thought about her duet with Eric. It was almost uncanny how the boy she had fallen in love with once had managed to enrapture her again as his current older self. He was sadder, captive to a strange fate, but still possessed the heart of the old prince and his love for music. After all this, even if they were confined to their own worlds forever, she would love the chance to sing with him once last time.

. . . nope. Actually, she didn't want that. She was going to be honest; that's what queens did.

She wanted to kiss him.

She wanted to embrace him. She wanted to try spending time with him somewhere—his world or hers, it didn't matter. One more duet was meaningless. She wanted to own his heart.

That hadn't changed.

"Working hard?"

Ariel jumped. Attina had swum up in her usual sneaky, silent way.

"I just . . . There's so much here. Got lost for a second."

"Is life down here getting boring?"

"Attina, just—all right," Ariel said, throwing her pen down. It bounced slowly in the water, raising up a little bit of settled coral dust on the edge of her perfect marble desk before eventually skittering off the side and over to the sea-floor. The two mermaids watched it in surprise.

"A little defensive, aren't we?"

"You're picking at me. Please just admit it."

"Settle down, little sister. I know that you're upset about not getting our father back—*again*." But before Ariel could open her mouth to yell at her, Attina continued, louder. *"And I know you are taking it much harder than the rest of us.* Please."

She added, more softly:

"I know how hard you're trying. But you may, at some point, have to admit to yourself that it might not be enough. That it's too hard a task even for the great Ariel, Queen of the Sea and Walker on Land."

Ariel opened her mouth to say something, but couldn't find the right words, overcome with what her sister had said. It was so understanding, so deep, so . . .

"*Also,* you are completely bored under the sea. It's totally obvious."

Ariel snapped her mouth shut. Attina was looking at knickknacks on her desk, specifically not at *her*, but there was a twinkle in her eye.

The Queen of the Sea managed a little smile.

"Well . . . to be honest, it *is* boring. But I have a thousand other, more important things on my mind! Why *has* Ursula continued to let our father live despite my repeated rescue attempts, and yet refused to use him as a bargaining chip? It's unsettling, and it's probably for very bad reasons. Where is he right now? What is she doing to him?

"I'm worried about the fate of two kingdoms and one old butler. I'm worried about time passing . . . and meanwhile, I have to go over some bizarre ancient contract specifying which member of the lineage of Kravi gets to perform which Rite of Proserpine in the Equinocturnal Celebrations. Like it matters?"

Attina looked over her shoulder at the paper. "Give the lead to Sumurasa. Her brother would just flub it up."

"I mean, I know, but he was born first. There's no way around that."

"Well . . . find something else for him to do that sounds good but doesn't have any real responsibilities. A nice title he can brag about."

Ariel raised an eyebrow in surprise.

"That's not a bad idea. Maybe you should start coming to the council meetings, too. . . ."

"Nahh, not really my thing. Boring, like you said." But Attina again avoided her gaze, drifting over to a golden bowl of bright sea leaves. She examined them closely: exotic oranges, reds and yellows, a single slender purple . . . and finally just plucked out the biggest one and began to munch on it. "Bah, not like an apple. How's your little, uh, human toy doing up there?"

"Hopefully he's looking for Father. Since *I* failed to find him."

"You still love him?"

"Irrelevant to the matters at hand," Ariel said primly.

"You are *so strange*," Attina whispered with something like awe.

"I'm not—"

"You *are*. Don't you get that? You always have been. As a girl you never liked *anything* the rest of us liked. We looked for shells, you looked for ship garbage. We swooned over mermen, you lusted after statues of creepy two-legged Dry Worlders. You had this beautiful voice that everyone envied—and you *gave it away*. You don't like being queen, but you do it willingly and honestly as some sort of penance for what happened to our father. You've never tried to abdicate, though it's *pretty obvious* you hate it.

"You don't want to be here. You *never* wanted to be here."

Ariel raised an eyebrow at her thoughtfully. "Mostly true. Nice use of the word 'abdicate,' by the way."

"What I'm trying to say is . . . your stupid desires and wishes got us into this terrible mess and got our father taken away, and I'm still mad at you for that. But—if you do get our father back—you should . . . you know . . . go after that dumb mortal."

The Queen of the Sea looked at her sister in shock.

"We'll miss you if you go, of course. But I'd understand. Well, I mean, I don't understand," she added, twitching her tail. "Humans are ugly and dumb and evil and short-lived. But all that aside, there's something a little Old God about you, Ariel. . . . There's something epic about loving a mortal and wanting to leave your eternal, paradisiacal world. Something the rest of us will never understand, but people write sagas about. Even your failure and sadness are the stuff of poetry."

"Um. Thanks?"

Attina sighed. "You know, in your own way, you were once a super girly, carefree, bubbly, beautiful little girl. I still don't understand how you got to be so strange underneath it all."

Ariel was about to answer that very older-sister, not-really-a-compliment remark when Threll appeared.

"My Queen, Princess-Doyenne Farishal and her consort are waiting to speak to you about their children's official Coming of Age?"

"Oh, joy," Ariel said grimly. "Excuse me, sister; duty calls."

"Of course it does," Attina said with a sigh, still chewing on a leaf. "*Hey!* If you *do* see Eric again, have him grab us some more apples, will you?"

Ursula and Eric

"But when will my ships be done and ready *to launch*?"

It was getting harder and harder to pretend that the summer cold that had taken her voice was still hanging on, especially since she didn't act like the rest of the ridiculous, simpering ladies of the court did when they had ague or anxieties or chills or whatever else they complained of. Ursula continued to stomp up and down the castle corridors, and she ate like a champion.

But right then she didn't even care about her voice; she slammed her fists down on the table and bared her teeth at the broad-chested older man standing before her.

The fleet admiral regarded her with icy black eyes.

"We have employed every qualified shipwright in the

kingdom, My Princess—and quite a few unskilled manual laborers. The shipyards are at capacity. If we had scaled this up properly, we would have built a second shipyard before-hand. You're asking for a battle-ready fleet to be amassed in almost no time, out of thin air. Give us more space and another month and you will have one of the finest armadas on the continent."

"In a *week*, if I wanted to, I could . . . set certain *things* in motion that would allow me to no longer require a month, or your pesky ships, or even *you*," Ursula growled. "A month is too late. For your own health, if nothing else, get those ships on the sea and loaded with explosives, *now*."

Anyone else would have looked uncomfortable at the order, but rarely did any emotion pass over the dark skin stretched tightly over the bones in the admiral's face.

"I don't care if you're actually a witch," he finally said. "I don't care if you believe the moon gives you special pow-ers or if you can control the seas. But neither spiritualism nor cetaceamancy nor threats to my person will make these ships ready any faster, unless you have the power to con-jure a hundred more men and another dock. If all goes well we will launch and begin our assault on the Verdant Coast by the end of the summer."

"Who said anything about attacking the *coast*?" Ursula demanded. "Forget about the stupid forts and towns for now. You have new orders, drawn out here. And you will get those ships done in two weeks, because I am your princess and that is your job."

"Then it is *not* my job any longer," the admiral said crisply, undoing the medal at his chest. He neatly—not viciously—threw it on her desk, where it landed with a *thwap*. Then he took off his blue tricorn hat and put it under his arm. "Good luck, Princess."

He spun on his heel and marched off, every inch the military man.

Bother.

She had been really looking forward to wiping out the mer as soon as possible. It was like the best treat ever. It would still happen, of course—just later than she wanted. But she hated waiting around for things. Was it time to try the circuex?

No ... things weren't that bad. Yet. Just mildly annoying.

But ah, there is that other idea I had for getting to Ariel. It's not as grand, but would keep me amused for a while, and give those pesky townsfolk something to think about besides their own worthless opinions on my military expeditions.

Eric came striding into the room a moment later. "Why is Admiral Tarbish in such a huff? I've never seen him like that!"

"He quit," Vanessa said mildly, picking up the medal

and examining it. The admiral's move was unexpected, but not necessarily unwelcome. It was a definite opportunity, and surprisingly, conveniently done.

"*QUIT?*" Eric exploded. "Our fleet admiral just *quit?*"

"Yes, I'm afraid he lacks the confidence to amass our *fleet* of ships in a timely fashion. Never mind, I have the perfect replacement. Lord Savho very much likes the sea and has been looking for some way of . . . contributing . . . to our current military endeavors."

"Savho has never captained a ship, much less led an invasion! Or an exploration! Or a trading mission! I doubt he's ever been beyond the bay!" Eric swore, taking his cap off and throwing it on the ground in the most unprincely display of humors Ursula had seen yet. It was almost amusing.

"But he does have a lot of money, and he would be extremely loyal," Vanessa said with a shrug. "I'm sure the first mate or whatever can bring him up to speed."

Eric felt his anger collapse under exhaustion and the weight of it all. How did you get rid of a woman who, with no magic powers to speak of, managed to manipulate and twist the whole world around her finger?

Or tentacle, really.

"Listen to me," he said wearily. "I don't like you. I don't love you. But I'm married to you, and you are, currently, the princess of Tirulia. And you are tearing Tirulia apart. I'm not going to let that happen. For now we are still Prince Eric and Princess Vanessa, and you have to stop communicating with my generals and admirals without me. Starting now."

"Careful, *Prince Eric*," she said, trying to sound calm—but a quaver crept into her voice. "What might have been yours at one time is now shared by us. Should anything happen to you—"

"Should anything happen to me?" Eric laughed dismissively. "I'm not Grimsby. I'm hearty as a horse and everyone loves me. There are many who do not love you. Including my parents, who are king and queen—or had you forgotten that? You've been lucky so far: they don't like to get involved in the territories their children control. They believe we should be able to rule independently. But if something 'unusual' happened to me, you would be out in less than a day, possibly tarred and feathered, and my sister Divinia would take the castle. She never liked you anyway."

Vanessa turned pale.

Interesting, Eric thought. *Had she not considered the possibilities before?*

. . . or no, she just hadn't thought *Eric* would think of the possibility. She was counting on his still being hazy from her spell—and perhaps not that clever to begin with. The princess was a haughty egotist who thought that everyone around her was dumber and less capable than she. *Just all-around generally unpleasant, besides being a tentacled sea*

witch, Eric thought. How did any of the nobles and commoners she manipulated put up with it? Couldn't they see
through to her hateful, egomaniacal self?

Well, maybe humans were, as a race, just fallible. . . .
Everybody wanted something. Maybe it was as banal and
"evil" as gold, but maybe it was as sweet and basic as true
love. Maybe it was a baby you couldn't have, or some way to
keep your family from starving. Maybe you needed a friend.
Maybe you just *wanted* to believe that all these things could
be received as gifts, from the universe or God or the spirits.

*And here is an evil, comely witch who promises it all. It
would be so easy to overlook her shortcomings with your wish
so close to being granted. . . . Maybe only luck saved humans
from having to deal with terrible creatures like Vanessa on a
regular basis, who make people sign away their—oh! Wait a
moment . . . !*

"Vanessa, you *cannot* hurt me," Eric said aloud, feeling a very Mad Prince smile forming on his lips. He loomed
over her.

"You . . . signed . . . a *contract.*"

"I didn't! I never!"

"A *marriage* contract."

The shocked look on her face was infinitely pleasing.

"Princess Vanessa, you signed a *legally binding* docu-
ment in which you promised to have and to hold, to support,
to act as a partner in, our royal marriage."

She looked sick. Actually sick. Green and yellow, mouth hanging open like a dog's. She swallowed dryly once or twice. Her eyes glazed over as she stared at something that wasn't there, between the floor and his face.

Maybe she was remembering their wedding day. It all happened very fast, thanks to her overwhelming need to win against Ariel. There was a thrown-together cake, a hastily fitted white dress, and a piece of parchment quickly scrawled out by the one counsel who stayed in the seaside palace of Tirulia.

(Who, it's only fair to say, never thought he would have to do anything so crucial and important; his job was mostly a sinecure, reading through various real estate documents and decrees while lounging by the beach.)

He had pleaded with Eric not to marry at least until the king and queen had been informed and Vanessa's family had been checked out. Under the spell, Eric had shaken his head and shoved the paper under the poor man's pen.

Still, even under pressure, the lawyer had managed to turn out a fairly solid little marriage contract that referred to previous contracts with a lot of *ibids*, *see-above*s, and *refer-to*s.

With a flourish and a smirk, Vanessa had deftly signed her name, adding what looked like a cute little octopus as a heraldic crest. The sun set, they kissed, and it was over for Ariel and her father.

Eric smiled indulgently. "As I understand you immortal creatures—and I do, because I'm a Mad Prince, and also because I'm married to one immortal creature and friends with another—contracts are even more important to you people than they are to us. You have signed with your soul."

"Not legal. Not binding," Vanessa wheezed, trying to catch her breath and stave off what looked like a panic attack. "Signed . . . as Vanessa . . . not me . . ."

"Well, the thing is, you kind of look exactly like Vanessa," Eric said, cocking his head and pretending to look her over. "I think even someone as unschooled in legalese as I could probably make the case that as long as you look like Vanessa, live on land like Vanessa, and have no tentacles—like Vanessa—well, you are pretty much one hundred percent Vanessa. Although Vanessa, it's true, might actually be a girl prone to fits of dementia who believes herself to be a half-octopus undersea witch. Oh, and by the way: there's always a line in royal marriage contracts that deals with demented spouses, especially wives. I don't think you'll like what it spells out."

Although she still wasn't looking at him, Ursula's eyes widened as she realized the implications of what he was saying.

"And speaking of *wives*, I should also add that there are other, *nastier* little clauses in typical royal contracts. Ancient stuff, like what happens if you fail to produce a male heir, most of which would be dismissible in court today. But even in our modern era of astronomy and steam engines, well, I'm afraid Tirulia is still a bit backward. Anything you own is technically mine, any inheritance you receive is mine, any property you manage is mine, any decision involving purchases or transference of goods, schooling of children, firing or hiring of domestic help . . . it's all. Ultimately. Mine."

He took a step closer with each final word and grinned down at her.

Vanessa's eyes finally cleared; she looked at him with raw hate. Eric repulsed the look with a sunny smile.

"You see," he added almost apologetically, "you immortal creatures have your powers, your promises, your wish fulfillments, and your contracts, it's true.

"But we humans have *lawyers*."

Vanessa's face stretched into a rictus of a smile. She slowly straightened herself up and adjusted her dress.

"You're not quite the dummy everyone thinks you are," she finally said.

"Just you," Eric pointed out. "Everyone else thinks I'm distracted and creative. Only you think I'm actually stupid."

"Fair enough," Vanessa conceded. "I always knew playing with humans would be fun. You're all a lot more—*fun*—than I imagined. It's really astounding, the propensity for evil the least of you have. Here I was thinking that *I* was the master of tricky and binding agreements. Apparently

I have a lot to learn. What's that saying? 'The devil is in the details'? You make me think that humans *invented* the devil."

Eric said nothing. He wasn't, as she said, stupid. And he was a little wiser than the first time around. There was no celebrating his victory over her yet. Something as horrible and ancient as Ursula no doubt had another shoe to drop—possibly seven shoes.

She shook her shoulders and settled back into a proper Vanessa pose, prim and pretty.

"All right, then, Prince Eric, a *partnership*. 'For Tirulia.' At least until one of us figures out how to . . . *dissolve* it."

"All I care about is my country," Eric said with feeling. *Don't think of her. Don't think of Ariel. Don't think of how you're continuing to help her, looking for her father.* While he was unsure if the witch could read minds, it was clear that Vanessa could read faces—and would. "And its people. As long as they are safe and happy and prosperous, I don't care what mad little witcheries or whatever it is you do on the side."

"What a generous offer. *Thank you*, My Prince," she said, giving a very ornate bow—not a curtsy. "*Mad little witcheries*, indeed. Time was I would turn you into a barnacle for such language."

"Those times are over, Princess," Eric said with a thin smile. "Welcome to the human race."

The Good Folk of Tirulia/Rumors

AT THE ABSINTHE HOUSE:

"I don't know, Lord Francese. Do we even wish the good prince to return to his senses? At this stage? It seems that all is going along rather splendidly. . . . I've already received several nice . . . shall we say . . . *returns* on my investment in the clearing of the Devil's Pass. A pair of vineyards, in fact. Let the lad write his songs and the lady lead us into wealth!"

"I don't object to the general idea of expansion, Lord Savho. And I've made quite a bit myself on the shipment of munitions from Druvest. But I think it's rather ridiculous to consider us Druvest's *equal*, or Gaulica's. The world is changing, and I am not convinced Tirulia is ready to be the world power our dear princess wishes it were."

"Oh, I agree, darling. And I feel nothing but empathy

for that lovely prince of ours. He's so haunted—such a hand-some young man."

"He is indeed, Lady Francese. I was just having tea with the princess, and upon leaving I saw him cutting such a lovely, gothic figure kneeling in an overgrown garden."

"Whatever was he doing there, Emelita? Practicing his poetry?"

"Honestly . . . it rather looked like he was talking to a seagull. . . ."

AT THE MARKET:

"Mad he might be, but I don't think he wants us to be all over the place starting wars with which and who. And I agree."

"Don't you say that! Florin came back from the assault in the mountains with a necklace for me. There's opportuni-ties in the army for the youngest son of seven that don't exist elsewhere."

"He could get a place on a ship like everyone else, Lalia."

"Yes, and come back with stinky fish. Not necklaces."

"Well, *I* don't like it. None of you are old enough to remember the troubles of Thirty-Five—"

"When none of the boys in your village came back alive, yes, yes, we've heard it before. This is different. Vanessa is clever! She has all these modern weapons, *explosives*, and tactics . . . our boys don't even need to risk themselves."

"Really? Dead times twenty isn't a *risk*?"

"I may hire on to a fishing boat myself. There's enough work to go around, though not enough boats. . . ."

"Plus there's that contest! A chest of treasure for finding a magic fish! That could buy you a *thousand* necklaces, Lalia. . . ."

AT THE DOCKS:

"I think our prince has taken for the worse—have you heard? He's started talking to seagulls!"

"So? He's an artist. That last opera of his was supposed to be mighty fine. I can't wait to finally see it when they put it on again. But maybe all this music work took something out of him, something vital."

"You ask me about taking something vital out of him, I'd say you're looking in the wrong place. It's that princess of his. . . ."

"Keep your voice down, Julio! Or we'll be next to the front lines, feeding crows with our bones and not seagulls with our fish."

Eric

After Ursula made her (predictably) dramatic exit from her study, Eric stayed, pulling out his composition book and turning to the piece called "Interlude for a Villain's Lair." Since the sending Triton to Ibria thing had all been a ruse, Vanessa was probably still keeping the king as close to her as possible. If she had just killed him, she wouldn't have hidden the fact; she would have bragged about it. The sea witch wasn't terribly complicated once you got to know her. Almost predictable in her less dangerous habits.

He carefully checked off everything that was the same as the last time he searched the room: creepy, evil dagger? Check. Teapot and tea accessories? *Check*. It all looked pretty much the same. . . . In fact, the only really new item was an untidy pile of maps and charts on the table. Eric riffled through them. Some were immediately obvious and discouraging: troop numbers, approximate locations of enemy forts and towers, friendly towns. There were atlases with arrows drawn on them in pencil, where future land grabs might be made. There was a list of world leaders, mostly minor, with notes next to each name: *Friendly! Neutral. Mad? Aggressive.*

Her plans were like a little girl's fantasy, all sketched out in a book titled something like *Princess Vanessa's Plan to Conquer the Known World*, in curlicue letters, with hearts dotting the Is.

Eric shook his head and pushed the papers aside. Beneath were the plans for the new warships and marine cartographic charts, with coasts, depths, and dangerous reefs sketched in, channels described, destinations plotted. . . .

He frowned at the coordinates.

She wasn't sending the fleet up the Verdant Coast to harass and intimidate their neighbors like she had threatened—and as would be logical, were one beginning to conquer the continent.

It looked like . . .

It looks like she's sending them out to sea? Deep *sea?*

Along with the charts was a map, mostly blank and unlabeled. There was no key, no compass rose, no marks around the outside to indicate latitude or size. The background was plain as if it were just open sea or field, but with no decorative patterns to indicate either. On this was drawn what appeared to be islands, sketched by an unskilled hand, but ringed as if the topography were known. One large bean-shaped mass had a few details to differentiate it from the others: a scalloped edge on one side, and what looked like a tiny crown in the middle of the right half of the bean.

Eric stared at it, puzzled. It didn't look like any part of the world he knew, or even illustrations of New South Wharen. He looked around on her desk to see if there was anything else that might give a hint as to what it was, but only found different versions of the strange map, smaller and even more crudely drawn. First drafts. Some of these had arrows on them in the same way the war maps did, but they floated over the open spaces and had no troop numbers or anything indicating enemy defenses.

Mysterious. Was it a map to invisible sources of power? Were the arrows ley lines, flows of magic or power that were all the rage among modern seers and bored gentlefolk?

He took the smallest, crudest map and folded it into his pocket.

Maybe Ariel would know. They would meet again at the next tide, in nine hours. In the meantime, he would go through atlases and research it as best he could until that time. Her father might have to wait a bit while he did.

On his way to the library he passed through the drawing

room, where serious visitors were entertained with brandy and harpsichord music and interesting books and globes. Vareet was sitting at the fancy mahogany desk, drawing.

Eric walked by her—and then stopped.

He had *never* seen the little maid entertaining herself with her own pursuits in public. He rarely saw her smiling. Once in a great while he saw her skipping through the halls, overcome by some fancy, or grinning as she exited the kitchen, special gifted treat in her hands. But whatever she did when she was given her—*precious little*—time off, she did it on her own, someplace hidden.

"What are you doing, pretty lass?" he asked, kneeling down. It was a little awkward. He had no trouble throwing balls to children who were chasing each other outside, or getting into mock fencing bouts with young footmen. But he had no clue how to approach a quiet little girl.

Vareet's face was carefully neutral. She showed him her pictures: standard five-legged horses, unrecognizable human-monster things, squiggly grass—all the sorts of figures children normally drew.

What she was drawing *on* was remarkable, however: strange vellum, whose tactile surface was almost unpleasant to touch. As Eric looked at the pictures and tried to figure out what to say, Vareet impatiently turned them over so he could see the back.

On that side were runes—but not by a child's hand, as outlandish as they were. It was definitely some sort of written language.

"Oh . . . are these Vanessa's?" Eric whispered. "Are you trying to tell me something?"

The little girl said nothing, just quickly gathered up the rest of her drawings and prepared to go.

"I'm just going to hold on to this for a while," the prince said of the one he still held. He would show it to Ariel, to see if she could make head or tail of the writing. "I really like the way you made the horse's neck. It almost looks like it's . . . really . . . moving."

"It's a *bunny*," Vareet snapped. Then she skipped off, exasperated.

The prince gave a wry laugh. Mad Prince Eric, indeed, who had secret friends in butlers and maids—but also in seagulls and little girls, and who could understand neither.

Ariel

As the tide turned she surfaced on the north side of town, on an isolated beach. Sheltered from the sea by grass and the mainland by sand dunes fringed with scrub, it wasn't only perfectly hidden from the castle and its spies; it was *also* the perfect place to raise baby seagulls, and to tend to older ones.

She hadn't seen Scuttle in a while.

But as soon as the mermaid emerged from the water she saw something strange was up. The gulls were screeching even more loudly than usual, wheeling and crying and diving so furiously she couldn't understand what they were saying. She shaded her eyes against the sky and scanned the bright edge of the dune for her friend.

"Scuttle?" she called.

"*Ariel!* Look, everyone, it's my friend Ariel!"

An inelegant but enthusiastic tumbling mess of a bird thrust his body over the edge of the dune, letting gravity drag him toward her, opening and closing his wings in more of a controlled fall than an actual flight. The sand was soft and Scuttle wasn't going that fast; Ariel wasn't too concerned. When he finally came to a stop, she knelt down to stroke his head—pulling her hand back at the last moment when she saw several fish tails sticking out of his beak.

"Sorry," he said, smacking them back in and down his gullet. "Sorry, Ariel. But they were already dead. But I don't like you seeing that."

"Uh, thanks."

"Jona—she's a first-rate great-grandgull, that one. She's been bringing me a *feast*. Everyone else was just stuffing their own gullets. Not her. She thought of her great-grandfather first." He preened his chest feathers and wings to remove any lingering fishy oil. "What's up? You got a lead you need me to check out, or something?"

"No, I just came here to see how you were doing." She scratched him under his chin, but was distracted by his words.

"Awww, that's great, Ariel. That's really nice. I appreciate that."

"Scuttle, what 'feast'? What are the gulls 'stuffing their gullets' *with*? What's going on?"

"Oh, you don't know? All the fishing humans are going *crazy*! Worse than us, if you can believe it! At least that's what they say. Piles of fish for the taking."

Ariel took this in, trying to figure out what it meant. *Piles* of dead fish? That seemed unusual, even for humans. Surely with everything else going on with Ursula, it wasn't a coincidence.

"What are they—I mean, the humans—doing with the piles?"

"I dunno. Not guarding them very well, I gotta say. You getting any closer to finding your dad? Jona told me all about the carriage and Ursula and everything."

"Nothing yet," Ariel said slowly. "I think I want to go see what's going on before I meet Eric. Where *is* Jona? I'd like to get her help."

Scuttle turned over his shoulder and squawked. Someone else squawked back.

"My boy here says he saw her out over the water—away from the docks. I'll bet she was looking for you."

"All right—if I miss her and she comes back here, tell her to meet me back in town."

"Will do, Ariel," Scuttle said, giving her a salute. She turned to go. "And . . . Ariel? Thanks for . . . thanks for just coming to visit. Not just 'cause you're the Queen of the

Sea and all important and everything. I *missed* you, Ariel. It was hard . . . those years . . . when you didn't come to the surface anymore. I mean, I completely understand why. You had every reason. But . . . I still missed you."

"Oh, Scuttle, I'm so sorry. . . ." She nuzzled his beak with her nose, closing her eyes. "As soon as I get my father back on his throne, I'll have way more time to visit."

Scuttle looked delighted—and a little surprised. "So you're just gonna . . . come up now? To the Dry World? To stay? Or visit a lot? I mean, after whatever happens with your dad?"

Ariel paused. Once it was all over, of *course* she would go back to hanging out with her friends, old and new, in the world beyond the sea. But . . . how would she do it without the trident? Would her father help her? Even if she successfully rescued him, his views on the matter certainly wouldn't have improved by years of imprisonment. What if he refused? What if he didn't let her go?

I'll just have to find a way on my own.

But . . . another part of her pointed out, *that was how this whole thing started in the first place.* Her father had refused to let her go, so she found another way, and it led to him being captured and her losing her voice and Tirulia gaining a tyrant. She squinched her face up at the conflicting thoughts.

Deal with it later, Ariel, she ordered all the voices,

wrapping her headscarf tightly around her face and neck once again. She would get the job done first—find her father, defeat Ursula, set everything right. *Then* she could work on the happily ever afters.

She had just reached the edge of town when Jona wheeled down out of the sky to perch on a rock nearby.

"I was looking for you," the gull said. "Be careful. There are a lot of shiny buttons walking around. I think you're a *persona non grata* here."

She tried not to look proud of the words she used, but failed badly.

"Shiny button—oh. *Soldiers.* Yes. That's why I . . . Wait, how did *you* recognize me?"

She had to push the headscarf fully out of her face to see the gull clearly at all.

"I can spot half a sardine carcass sticking out of a flower-pot a quarter mile away," Jona answered. "I'm a *gull.*"

Ariel smiled.

She carefully clambered up the rock next to the bird. Climbing things was still a tricky proposition; you *hurt* if you fell in this world, where everything was heavy and hard and inclined to falling. A very light breeze tickled her forehead as she stood on her tiptoes get a good view of the town. . . .

. . . which brought with it one of the most revolting odors

she had ever smelled. Bodies, rotting flesh. Death and decay in staggering amounts.

She almost fell off the rock.

"Are you all right?" Jona asked politely.

"What is that . . . horrible . . . stink . . . ?"

"You mean the gigantic piles of dead fish the humans are leaving on the wharf."

She had, at least, the good taste to avoid smacking her beak as she spoke.

"Scuttle said . . . I didn't think . . . Why aren't they being . . ."—she tried to swallow her nausea; she had to know—"*eaten* by the humans?"

"Don't know," Jona said with a wingy shrug. "But it's been a very popular development among us and the rats and cats."

Ariel couldn't see anything from her higher position, and the wind was terrible, so she slipped back down from the rock, stomach still a little rocky itself. *You're a queen.* She pulled herself upright as best she could.

"I'm . . . going to go look into this," she said, trying not to breathe through her nose. Eric, even her father could wait. She had to find out what was going on to leave her subjects dead and rotting in piles. Jona nodded and launched herself into the air above her.

As she approached the main street Ariel noticed that

even the humans who regularly ate fish were covering their faces and noses with cloth; she didn't stand out in the crowd wearing her headscarf. The stench was overwhelming. Some people looked sour and complained bitterly. Others looked excited and rushed to and fro, mending nets, grabbing friends, chatting and shrieking in glee.

And there, on the docks, just as the gulls had said, *every kind of fish* was rotting in piles. From the species that humans loved to hunt and eat to the ones that were deadly poisonous. Squid, octopodes, eels, sharks, branzinos, rays, hake, oarfish, at least one small dolphin . . . they were all represented among the dead, baking and decaying in the sun.

The Queen of the Sea just stood there staring, overwhelmed by horror and sadness.

Finally she began to do the only thing she could for all of them now: she whispered a prayer. Again and again, willing their spirits to find the eternal ocean of heroes, where they could be happy and free forever.

Ariel had repeated it twelve times—with no intention of stopping—when she was interrupted by a familiar voice.

"I'm so sorry, my lady."

Ariel looked up. Argent the Inker stood there, a disgusted look on her face. She put a hand on the mermaid's shoulder.

"I wanted to see you again to thank you for the extra coins and gems you gave me, but this isn't the way I'd hoped we would meet."

"What goes on here?" Ariel demanded.

The old woman made a face, the divots and wrinkles in her skin pulling into a rictus of contempt. "The castle is offering a reward for the capture of a 'magical fish.' A trunk of gold and an estate and a title to whichever fisherman brings it in."

"Magical fish?" Ariel repeated slowly, hoping she had heard it wrong.

"Princess Vanessa has finally lost her mind—at least, that's what some people are saying," the woman said with a snort. "Maybe she never had one to begin with. Maybe she kept that hidden until now. But people don't care—who would? A trunk of gold and a title for one fish. Whether it's actually magical or not. But I assume, with you here, of course, there's a chance it actually is. . . ."

"What is this magical fish supposed to do? What does it look like?"

"No idea what it's *supposed* to do. I guess that if it grants wishes, it's probably not going to get turned over to the princess, if you know what I mean. They say it doesn't look like the normal fish we catch around here. It's slow-moving, and fat, with yellow and blue stripes."

For the second time that day Ariel felt a wave of nausea pass over her.

Of course. Of course. She should have guessed.

Flounder.

Ursula had set a reward out for the capture of her best friend.

Something changed in Ariel.

Over the span of a single breath, the nausea subsided, along with the sadness and sickness and helplessness. Something far more solid—and terrible—took its place.

"I would suggest you and whomever you love stay off the ocean for the next tide," she said as calmly as she could.

"What . . . ?"

Argent searched Ariel's eyes, huge and aquamarine, clear as the seas in Hyperborea. She must have found something there. Blue anger? Or perhaps it was just Ariel's confidence: the calm assumption that she could back up insane statements with an even more insane reality.

The eyes of a queen.

"Yes, thank you. Of course, I'll tell them," the old woman said quickly. "Thank you, my lady." She practically bowed. Her earrings jingled as she ran away on her long, rangy legs.

Ariel spun around and regarded the piles of fish, the laughing and angry men and women, the boats out at sea, one last time.

Not caring who saw, she took off down the dock and dove into the water, her tail beating the water into foam before she was even submerged.

Ariel surfaced just beyond the bay. She was consumed by fury over so many things: the piles of dead fish, Ursula tricking her with the carriage, her own inability to find her father, the loss of her voice, the loss of who she was when she first had a voice.

A wave formed, swelling around Ariel's body. It lifted her up higher and higher—or maybe she herself was growing; it was hard to tell. She held the trident aloft. Storm clouds raced to her from all directions like a lost school of cichlid babies flicking to their father's mouth for protection. Lightning coursed through the sky and danced between the trident's tines.

Ariel sang a song of rage.

Notes rose and fell discordantly, her voice screeching at times like a banshee from the far north.

She sang, and the wind sang with her. It whipped her hair out of its braids and pulled tresses into tentacles that billowed around her head. She sang of the unfairness of Eric's fate and her own, of her father's torture as a polyp, even of Scuttle's mortal life, slowly but visibly slipping away.

Mostly she sang about Ursula.

She sang about everyone whose lives had been touched

and destroyed by evil like coral being killed and bleached, like dead spots in the ocean from algae blooms, like scale rot. She sang about what she would do to *anyone* who threatened those she loved and protected.

And then, with her final note, she made a quick thrust as if to throw the trident toward the boats in the bay, pulling it back at the last moment.

A clap louder than thunder echoed across the ocean. A wave even larger than the one she rode roared up from the depths of the open sea. It smashed through and around her, leaving her hair and body white with foam. She grinned fiercely at the power of the moment. The tsunami continued on, making straight for Tirulia.

But . . . despite her rage . . . underneath it all the queen was still Ariel. Her momentary urge to destroy everything came and went like a single flash of summer lightning.

She pulled the trident back.

As the wave traveled through the bay it grew weaker.

Not so weak, however, that it didn't smash Vanessa's anchored fleet with a satisfying, wood-cracking explosion against the wharves.

The other boats, the fishing vessels that were out in open water, were tossed like toys or bits of flotsam and jetsam.

The ocean rose and flooded the docks, taking the dead fish back to their home, allowing the few living ones left to escape.

Eventually the water calmed. The wave Ariel rode slowly diminished, and she returned to the relatively tranquil surface of the sea. Dark clouds lingered but lightened their load by letting out a soft rain. The storm was over.

Ariel dove into the depths, exhausted. Hopefully Eric would have the sense to realize their meeting would be delayed for at least a tide.

She would send some dolphins up to rescue the drowning.

Ursula

She stood in the hall, one hand on Vareet's head, a distant look on her face. Someone passing by might have taken the scene for that of a distracted member of royalty lecturing the lesser staff with a patronizing if affectionate air. But she was thinking about her three destroyed warships. She had been close . . . so close . . . to absolute victory over Atlantica.

And now the explosive cannonballs from Druvest lay somewhere on the bottom of the bay, undetonated, *useless*.

In a month, if she was *lucky,* she would have three new ships—and three was not enough. She wanted to make sure she had enough cannons and firepower to defeat whatever the mer tried to throw at her, and enough munitions to obliterate everything down there. Not to mention her failing alliance with Ibria. Once again she would be short three ships. . . .

As for the cannonballs and explosives themselves— well, it was hard enough wheedling them out of Druvest, and getting Eric to pay for another batch seemed unlikely.

Ariel had ruined her whole plan.

Again.

Vareet squirmed under her touch as Vanessa's nails dug deep into the roots of her hair and twisted them in anger. But the little maid had sense not to cry out. Or try to escape.

Ursula wished it was Ariel's hair she had her tentacles sunk into. Pulling and tearing those stupid red locks, rip- ping them from her flesh . . . Oh, how she would love to drag the mermaid through the water as she struggled and screamed, forced to watch as everyone she loved died. . . .

Unable to hold back any longer, Vareet let out a single whimper.

Ursula looked at her maid with vague surprise, as if she had forgotten the little girl was even there. Vareet paled, plainly expecting punishment.

But something else was occurring to the sea witch. A calm detachment settled over her like a warm current from a sea vent. Her rage dissipated as her next, her *only* action became clear.

If Ariel would wield the power of the gods in this battle, then so would she.

All she needed now was a time and place.

Eric strode by, stuffing his hat on his head and buttoning his cloak.

"Going off on your . . . post-prandial constitutional?" she asked hollowly.

"Oh, yes, yes, walking does wonders for the stomach," Eric said, patting his and trying to keep moving.

"Tell me . . . Are you still planning the big performance? The free one, for everyone in town? That everyone will come to?"

"Of *La Sirenetta*? Yes, of course. Why?" He looked unsettled, nervous.

"I was just wondering. You heard the news about the fleet." It was more a statement than a question.

"Er, yes. Terrible," Eric said. "I'm very glad no one was hurt."

"I think there's something you should know," she said, finally turning and looking at him directly.

"Yes? What?" the prince asked impatiently.

"As a result of this . . . incident . . . with the fleet, I find I have time now to devote to another project of mine." She spoke almost lightheartedly. "Something big. Something terrible. Something your puny little human mind could not possibly comprehend. Far beyond my usual *mad little witcheries*. And when I am done, Ariel will wish she had taken my advice and fled back to the sea, far, far away from me."

She enjoyed seeing Eric's face go pale. It was the only fun she had all day.

"Pass the info on, if you happen to see the mermaid," she added, walking away, pulling Vareet with her.

The girl, resigned to her fate, didn't even look back at Eric.

Ariel and Eric

Eric was already at their meeting place, looking nervous and fidgety in the moonlight. He tapped his lips with a piece of paper clutched in his hands. His eyes looked positively ghostly in the moonlight.

"Eric?" She spoke softly. Despite being less deft on her feet than anyone naturally born to the Dry World, she moved silently, as all magical creatures did. And from the way he jumped, it was obvious he hadn't heard her at all.

"Ariel!"

He put out his arms, then stopped.

"What did you do to my ships—to *all* of our ships?" he cried.

Her eyes widened. *Not* what she expected him to say.

"Sorry, sorry." Eric ran a hand through his hair. "No one was killed. A couple people were hurt. Weirdly, those at risk of drowning were rescued by a couple of friendly dolphins, and, if I am to believe what the cabin boy said, one particularly old and giant terrapin."

"Eric," Ariel firmly interrupted. "I am the Queen of the Sea. I protect my people. There are rules in place to allow us and you to live side by side. But if something threatens my realm beyond the scope of those rules, I will respond with all the force in my power. We must put up with your fishing to some degree. But if I hear *anything* else about some sort of reward for the capture of my friend Flounder the 'magical fish' and it involves killing hundreds of other perfectly innocent fish for no reason, I will destroy every boat within my demesne—as well as the towns they launched from. Understood?"

"Oh, the devil," Eric swore. "I thought I caught wind of some foolishness like that. Now it all makes sense. Fishermen pulling in great piles of fish, looking for something. . . . I heard the stink was unbelievable. Flounder is . . . a . . . friend of yours?"

"Since he was a fry."

"I'll put a stop to it at once," Eric promised. "For now and forever. Believe it or not, things like this have happened before. There was a rumor once that the Narvani, to the east, believed that the poisonous spine of the chimaera fish would help with . . . Uh . . . Let's just say it would help them have babies. It's a deepwater fish, ocean floor, but that didn't stop every idiot from just netting up every fish around and picking through them like an old woman through spoiled lentils."

"The greed of Dry Worlders continues to shock me," Ariel admitted.

"Yes, well, the greed of some tentacled sea-dwellers continues to shock me, too."

"Good point. I don't know where the mer fall in that. I think their sin is complacency, not greed."

Eric sighed. "I wish I could see them. It sounds like a paradise. *My* kind of paradise. Here, on earth, in the sea. Maybe . . . someday . . . you could take me there?"

He asked so innocently, so plainly, she was taken aback. He sounded like a little boy.

Or a little mergirl, dreaming of the warm sand.

"I'd love to," she whispered.

He took her hand and squeezed it. She held her breath, waiting for whatever was going to come next. He started to open his mouth. . . .

"But speaking of tentacled sea-dwellers . . ." the prince said reluctantly, instead of kissing her. "Vanessa has threatened something . . . well, large and unspeakable and terrible. Magic, I think. She seemed quite serious. She said you'll wish you had taken her advice and returned to the sea. And she told me to pass it along to you."

Ariel swore and tried to lash her tail. Instead, she made a funny kick-kick move, which was far less satisfying.

"*Everything.* Everything she does. Every time I think I have her beat, or at least in a corner, she figures out something to do! I get my voice back; she keeps me from going back to the castle by threatening my father. You help me; she threatens Grimsby. I think she's sending my father away—and it turns out it's all a trick, a trap. Now she threatens something vague and terrible. Is it true? Isn't it? Who knows? She knows my weaknesses and yours. So we all wind up just like we're children rearranging pieces on the board of a game of koralli."

"I guess that's like chess?" Eric asked.

"I guess."

They fell into a somber silence. The air felt chill and alive against her skin. The sky was almost starless because of the moisture in the air; not quite clouds, and not quite clear, the ether was veiled. The moon had set. Tendrils of breeze picked up the edge of her skirt. She sighed again and hugged herself, something she would never have done while she was underwater, queen. She constantly felt if she did anything that was even a little less than regal, she would be ignored even more than she already was when she was mute.

"I'm sorry," Eric said again. "I wish I had better news

to bring you, but I'm still having no luck finding your father. Believe me, I'm trying. But I *did* find these things. This first drawing was among the military papers she still tries to keep away from me. The places on it make no sense to me at all—they are of nowhere I know. It's where she was intending to send the fleet before you destroyed it. It's not of any of our neighboring countries. Maybe somewhere near the western lands? Some uncharted islands off Vespucci? Or hidden in Arawakania? Or nearby, in the Ruskal Sea? Do you recognize them?"

Ariel took the paper and carefully unrolled it. There were indeed blobs that could have been islands, surrounded by multiple outlines, like mountains that had been cut into slices and redrawn. She turned the map this way and that, trying to make sense of it.

And then it suddenly clicked into place—like when the water is foggy with plankton and a current comes and sweeps it clear so you can see the reef on the other side, or when the sand stirred up by a blenny finally settles.

"This isn't a map of Dry World islands," she said slowly. "This is a map of my home.

"Ursula means to destroy Atlantica."

Ariel and Eric

"Atlantica?" Eric asked. "You mean . . . your kingdom?"

"Yes, look." Ariel tapped at the parchment. "This is the Canyon of Dendros. This is the Field of Akeyareh, where ancient mer warriors fell in the battles against the Titans. Their bodies drifted to the seafloor and their bones turned the sand white. This is the Cleft of Neptune's . . . uh . . . 'Back,' a valley with hot geysers and occasional magma flows. This is the Mound of Sartops, where our priests and artisans tend to live; it looks out into the great depths of the ocean—some say to infinity. I know this map like the ribs in my tailfin."

If she *had* her tail right now, it would be tipping and thwapping the water in consternation. Kicking her foot didn't seem the same somehow.

"The munitions Ursula ordered . . ." Eric said, thinking. "They're not to wage war on our neighbors—or even Ibria, as I thought she might eventually do. It all makes perfect sense now! Tarbish's reluctance, all the explosives, the dynamite. She's going to drop depth charges—they'll detonate gunpowder-filled mines down on your city."

Death from above.

Ariel looked at the map. She had no idea what those extra words meant. She understood *explosive* and *your city*. Ursula could direct her ships exactly where she wanted them, and then, thanks to the cursed gravity that made life so hard for Ariel on land, the witch could simply *drop the weapons* on Atlantica and obliterate it. Eric talked about *gunpowder* and *die-namite* with the same trepidation he did her own powers.

"By destroying her fleet you might have saved your kingdom," Eric said softly.

Ariel was seized by a strange fit of panic. What if she *hadn't*? What if she hadn't lost her temper and impulsively done that?

"*Why?*" she finally asked, voice cracking. "She's got my dad, she's got your kingdom, she's got me beat no matter what I do! What more does she want? Why does she need to destroy *everything*?"

"She's not a rational being, Ariel. She's like . . . a walking mouth that's hungry all the time. She sees something and she wants it. So she does everything she can to get it. She wanted revenge on your father and you. She *thought* she got it, and was content, and moved on to the next thing—ruling Tirulia. But then you showed up again. To stop her. You're like an annoying gnat she can't slap away."

"I don't know what a 'gnat' is."

"Um . . . kind of like a remora? Tiny thing that bites you and sucks your blood and irritates you?"

"I'm a parasitic fish that has latched on to her and won't let go," Ariel said flatly, trying not to imagine what the words looked like.

"No, that's not—look, forget the gnat. And the remora. She *hates* you, maybe just because you remind her of your dad. Weirdly, I don't think she's just jealous of your beauty or youth, which is how it would go in a traditional fairy tale," he added, looking thoughtful. "That's sort of how I made it in my opera, and it's a motive that most people understand. Audiences *love* that kind of thing; jealousy is simple, it makes sense. But I don't think that's all of what's going on here."

Ariel mentally replayed the scene of going to talk to Ursula about giving her legs, but from a different perspective—Ursula's. There she was, a pretty, talented mermaid princess with a voice people would kill for, not a care in the world, and a future paved in pearls. And she had basically told the sea witch she was utterly discontented with her lot and wanted to be someone—and somewhere— else entirely.

And there was Ursula, perhaps *rightfully* exiled from the kingdom, but exiled nonetheless. Aged. Forced to deal with her fate alone. Bitter and resentful. In swims this pretty mermaid . . .

"Oh, my *cod*," Ariel said, putting a hand to her head. "What an *idiot* I was. I didn't even stop to think. . . . She's a *witch*. 'Hello, could you give me a pair of legs? For close to free? Even though you don't like my father?'"

"Exactly. Then she wins the bet, you lose your voice, she gets your dad, she becomes princess, you swim sadly back down to the bottom of the sea . . . But then you resurface in her life, and you're *Queen of the Sea*. You manage to get your voice back. You control storms and the heart of the man *she* is married to. . . ."

"I do?" Ariel asked with delight.

"*I'm just telling a story here*. But yes, obviously. You've become a queen, a woman with a complicated personality. You have hidden depths and a wisdom and intelligence that all went unnoticed before by an idiot prince whose heart couldn't listen to anything his ears couldn't hear."

Ariel felt a little giddy. "I control storms and the heart of a prince. I like that." If she were in the sea she would have been swooning, thrashing her tail and spinning in circles until she was dizzy.

Well, as a girl. Not as queen, not where anyone could have seen her.

Eric smiled. "I think my character would have a song about how he's been caught by a siren and is under her spell."

Ariel made a face. "I'm not a siren. Trust me. I have cousins . . . distant cousins . . . We don't get along. But what were you saying? About Ursula?"

"Just that everything she did to you and your father didn't keep you down. You popped up, older, stronger, more powerful than ever. She realizes she didn't beat you *enough* last time. Now she wants complete victory, which involves wiping out your home."

"If she wants complete victory, why not kill my father outright?"

"Well, that's the thousand-gold-piece question, isn't it?" Eric said with a frown. "Why bother pretending to ship him off to Ibria—why bother keeping him here at all?"

"She's up to something," Ariel agreed. "Something involving him. I feel like I started some sort of chain of events in her mind when I reminded her of my existence."

"Well, maybe this has something to do with it," the

prince said, pulling out the piece of vellum Vareet had drawn on.

"Oh," Ariel said, taking it. "What a cute . . . um . . . walrus."

"It's a *bunny*," Eric corrected with great dignity. "You've never seen one. Anyway, it's what's on the back that's important. Ursula's maid risked a lot by letting me 'discover' this. . . ."

Ursula's maid again. Ariel's heart broke a little when she thought of the girl, remaining silent so the mermaid could sneak out with the necklace unseen. Despite her life being in danger now, she still chose to help Ariel.

The pictures on the back of the strange-feeling vellum were far more disturbing than the weird Dry World creature on the front. There were lines and shapes that looked like they could be runes but shuddered when she tried to look at them too closely. Curves somehow didn't bend properly on the paper, and constellations of dots made her sick when she studied them, suggesting terrible things.

Ariel shook her head at the blasphemous sigils. "I don't know what these say for certain. They aren't mer runes; they're like a twisted, upside-down version of them. If I had to guess I would say they're black runes of the Deep Ones. Forbidden, evil . . . the whole deal."

"Can you read them at all?"

"This is just a noise, I think," she said, pointing. "Like

äi äi. No idea what 'phtaqn' means. This here I think refers to a circuex, a powerful spell that is capable of disrupting— or joining—worlds. This looks like the mer word for 'blood,' and that looks like a determinative for 'god.' Or possibly 'great' or 'lots.' "

"So . . ."

"So she needs blood, the blood of a god." Ariel bit her lip, seeing where it was all leading. "Ancient blood flows through my father's veins. . . . That would explain why she's keeping him around. She needs him for something, something involving magic. But for what exactly I can't tell."

Ariel felt sick as she said the words. She pushed the paper back at him.

"Here, please take this. I don't enjoy the feel of dead human skin."

"Dead . . . ? Human . . . ?" Eric took it back, aghast.

Ariel closed her eyes and rubbed her knuckles into her forehead. "This is all . . . so . . . *frustrating*! We do one thing, and she does another to block it. We think we know what her plans are; it turns out she has something even bigger and sicker in mind. She always has an answer, always has a countermove. And she *knows* what my weaknesses are—and yours, too. If I didn't care about my father, if you didn't care about Grimsby or your people, this would all be over in a flash."

"Back to your old 'children playing a game of koralli,'" Eric said with a wry smile. "But if we were human kids playing chess, at least, an adult could come over and put an end to everything eventually."

An interesting point, but how relevant? If it were her and Eric against Ursula, who was the adult in the scenario? Her father? An Elder God? Or . . .

Something was just at the edge of her mind, like a playful eel nosing in and out of the sunlight at the edge of the shore. Slippery, sparkling, and just out of her grasp.

"I think if adults—if *everyone* just knew what she was really like," she said slowly, "who she really was, they would do something. But how do we convince anyone she's an evil tentacled sea witch?"

"I don't know. Even if you just managed to show one person . . . there's no way to prove it to anyone else, much less *everyone* else. Enough people to do something about it," Eric said.

Ariel thought of poor terrified Vareet, who had seen her mistress change in the tub. She was the only one in the entire castle who knew the truth of the matter—very viscerally—besides Grimsby and Carlotta.

"But don't worry, we'll figure it out," he added, seeing the look on her face. He took her hand and squeezed it. "We have to, and soon. So she doesn't have a chance to do that ritual or whatever."

But Ariel didn't feel as much faith in them as Eric did. Somehow, despite being a rapidly aging human, he had managed to keep some of his youthful optimism, while she had lost some of hers. It was kind of adorable.

She leaned forward and kissed him on the cheek.

He smiled in surprise. He put his hand up to touch her face, perhaps brush away a stray hair . . . before his fingers did what they really wanted and pulled her chin closer to him.

He kissed her on the lips.

It was brief, but in the moment their skin touched she closed her eyes and consumed him: his smell, his warmth, the movement of his mouth against hers.

It was like . . .

A good-night kiss.

Over too quickly, but every moment of it meant a universe.

All those years before, and all those years in between . . . She had dreamed so many different scenarios of this moment! Ariel as a human, Ariel as a mer. *Eric* as a mer! Eric opening his eyes right when she rescued him and kissing her, falling in love with her on the spot. Eric kissing her in the boat, when she really, *really* thought he was going to, and the night was so romantic. . . . Kissing her on any of the three mornings, or realizing at the last minute Vanessa was a fake and kissing Ariel instead, and the wedding would have been for them. . . .

And here it finally was. She was a human—temporarily—and he was a human, and it was night, and they were getting ready to leave, and it was cold, and she had barnacle-bumps on her skin, and her feet hurt, and . . .

She found herself laughing, albeit a little breathlessly.

"That wasn't the way I imagined it would be. . . ."

"'Imagined it would be'?" Eric asked with a smile. "You've been thinking about me? Does that mean I have indeed caught the heart of a mermaid?"

"You did years ago when she was an idiot minnow, and look where it got us," she said, pushing his chest. "Where it got *me*."

"I know, I was just—" He sighed. "I know."

She kissed him again on the cheek.

"Let's . . . just . . . see how it goes," she said, heading off to the water.

He watched her walk straight into the waves, no hesitation, no floating, until it was up to her neck.

"Hey—aren't you going to ruin your clothes?" he called.

She rolled her eyes and dove, letting her tail hit the surface like a whale's, slapping a spray in his direction.

Eric

He watched Ariel's head disappear under the waves and a fin appear in its place. He couldn't help smiling.

He had just witnessed the transformation of a girl into a mermaid. Back *into a mermaid,* he corrected himself. Despite the terrible things they had endured—and probably more before it was all over—despite the years he had lost in a haze to Vanessa's spell, he felt like a delirious little kid who had seen his first firefly, or bioluminescent jellyfish, or shooting star. Everything was beautiful and anything was possible: the world was an amazing place just waiting to be explored.

He laughed and picked up a handful of sand and pebbles, throwing it into the ocean.

Though her whole walking straight into the water without floating or swimming thing *was* more than a little creepy. Almost like a lead soldier.

Eric took off his shoes to walk his way back home barefoot; despite how cold it was he wanted to feel the sand on his feet. It was part of the sea, part of her home.

When he entered the castle with his hair askew and trailing beach detritus, no one was much shocked. It was just Mad Prince Eric, out on one of his walks again.

He thought about Ursula. Sometimes winning wasn't just about playing fair, but knowing the rules so well that you could exploit discrepancies. That was the sea witch's whole method of operation.

He puzzled over ways to expose her true identity to the people who fawned on her and protected her. But as a musician and a prince his ideas were mostly dramatic, elaborate, and complicated. Like throwing a magnificent masked ball, for instance, and installing a hall of mirrors like at Versailles, and then having a bathtub full of salt water there somehow as a prop for Ursula to fall into, causing her to revert to her cecaelian state. Then her image would be reflected a thousand times, and everyone would see. . . .

He scribbled that down as an idea for a later opera. Rather unwieldy in real life.

The prince felt bad about the opera he was *supposed* to

be working on—he hadn't been to a rehearsal in days. Still, kings of the sea, mermaids, and evil sea hags came first. The real ones, that was.

(Eric did, however, make time to occasionally visit the poor polyps still trapped on Vanessa's vanity. He gave them little updates on things and told them to buck up. He had no idea if they understood, but it seemed like the right thing to do.)

He found it easiest to think logically when he worked at the puzzle the way an artist or musician would: by sketching out a stage direction plot, with Ursula in the middle and, around her, all the people she had vowed to kill if she was ever threatened in any way. He almost felt like his old self, sitting at his desk under the window and scribbling away— but this time clearheaded and glamour-free.

"Prince Eric," Grimsby greeted him, a trifle coldly, bringing in hot tea. It was served the traditional Tirulian way, with lots of sugar and cinnamon and cardamom.

Eric sighed. The other man had still been distant and, well, grim, since the prince had ordered him to stop helping.

"Grimsby old boy, *someday* you're going to have to forgive me for trying to protect your life. It's what princes do. Well, good ones, anyway."

"Of course, sir," Grimsby said crisply. He put down a napkin and the saucer and eyed Eric's drawing. "Oh, you're still working on the opera. I daresay you have a lot else on your mind right now. . . ."

"No kidding. And no, this isn't for the opera. I should really just put that on hold for a while, until other things . . . clear up."

"I wouldn't necessarily do that, Your Highness. Everyone is looking forward to the show. Now may not be the best time to ostracize your subjects. And it's a convenient way to keep certain people thinking you're, well, thinking about *other* things. Distracted, you know, when your keen mind is focused elsewhere . . ."

"That's not a bad point, Grims. All right, then! The show must go on!"

"Good for you, sir. You know . . . I must really get the carpenters and seamstresses to redo the royal box at the amphitheatre. Apparently, it's been quite . . . decorated by seagulls and the like. We don't want to upset the . . . er . . . *refined* sensibilities of Princess Vanessa. You know how she likes everything around her to look perfect when she's the center of attention. Probably have to add some gold flourishes or something, too . . ."

"Yes, she . . . wait . . . *What?*" Eric suddenly looked up at his butler. "What did you just say? What did you *really* just say? About Vanessa?"

"The princess enjoys flaunting her questionable taste and wealth?" Grimsby stammered.

"Grimsby, old man, you're a *genius*!" Eric kissed the confused butler on both cheeks, the Tirulian way, and ran out of the room.

"Thank you?" the Bretlandian said, dabbing at his cheek with the napkin.

"Whuff?" Max asked, watching the prince go.

"No idea," Grimsby said with a sigh.

Flotsam and Jetsam

"Sssso, which one did she wind up choosing to send to Ibria, in Triton's place?"

The two eels-become-men were walking side by side, shoulders touching, making their rounds of the castle. Paying out the spies, threatening servants who wouldn't snitch, stealing bits in the kitchen in front of everyone and snickering about it. . . . the usual afternoon's work.

"Garahiel," Jetsam answered, thin lips pulled back over a toothy grin. Neither one of them opened their mouths very far when they spoke; they were all teeth and tongue.

Flotsam laughed a long, hissing strain of laughter. "Excellent choice! I always hated him. Of course, I always hated all of them."

"Oh, but he was a pretty one. He is ssso fit to be in the zoo of a king!"

"Well, he *was* a pretty one," Flotsam amended. "And lucky fellow, too, escaping what Ursula has planned."

"He'll be the only one!"

They both laughed and laughed, and when a maid looked at them in disgust, they couldn't *quite* hold back from snapping their necks and jaws at her like the predators they were.

Transformations only went so far. . . .

Ariel

It was a puzzle.

Not unlike the puzzle of finding the right member of the Kravi to sing the story of Proserpine in the Equinocturnal Celebrations, but far more important.

(She decided, as Attina had suggested, to have the younger sister sing it, and make the older brother Director of the Celebrations. It was an honor in name only. Everyone already knew what to do and where to stand; they had been performing the Rites for thousands of years.)

How could they expose Ursula's true nature to as many humans as possible?

She signed bills, listened to complaints, chose chariots, finally worked out an equitable payment plan with the pesky barracuda, and considered the possibilities.

Ursula could . . . review all the troops. She could give a speech about the prowess of Tirulia as a military force while striding up and down in front of the rank and file of soldiers. But . . . by the sea! And then a giant wave could come and splash her. . . . And her tentacles and true form would be revealed!

Ursula could . . . have a new warship built and take it out to christen it! Didn't humans do that silly thing where they wasted a bottle of wine, breaking it over the prow of the ship? And while Vanessa was there, surrounded by her crew, a wave could lap over the side and . . .

What if Ursula had a birthday party, and the chef baked a giant three-tiered cake, and Ariel was hiding inside, and when the sea witch went to taste it, the mermaid burst out with a bucket of salt water, utterly dousing the birthday girl?

Ariel laughed quietly to herself. It was a pleasant and deeply satisfying fantasy.

"What's with you, giggle-puss?"

Attina had been slinking around the public work rooms of the palace more and more often lately. A less forgiving sister might have thought she was hoping for apples, like a semi-feral seahorse—or that she found she liked the taste of power after all.

But maybe she just wanted to hang out and be near her little sister, offering what little support she could.

Whatever the truth of the matter was, Ariel was relieved at this new development and always happy to see her.

"You're all smiley-faced and, well, not broody," Attina pressed. "What's going on?"

It was true—since Ariel got back she had been more lighthearted, smiling and flipping her tail more. But when Flounder and Sebastian asked her why, she felt like she had to keep it a secret.

Isn't that what sisters are for?

She put down her whelk pen, deliberating. Attina looked like she was going to explode.

Finally the queen spoke.

"I kissed a boy."

"WHAT?"

With two quick lashes of her tail, the auburn-haired older mermaid was over by Ariel, eyes wide.

"Eric. I kissed Eric. We kissed. Eric and I kissed each other."

"When? How? What? Why? I mean, what took so long?" she added, trying to sound casual.

"Didn't seem appropriate before," Ariel said, shrugging. "There were too many other things to talk about, to plan. . . ."

"You are so weird!" Attina practically shrieked. "And so is he. Who ever heard of a human *waiting* to kiss a mer? He must be weird, too. What was it like?"

"Not the stuff of a teen's fantasy," Ariel said with a rueful smile. "But it was genuine, and it was . . . nice."

"Well. The sea be praised," Attina muttered. "*Something* is moving ahead. What's going on with our father?"

"I'm working on that. I think we're going to have to get the Tirulians—uh, humans—to take care of Ursula for us. It's tricky. Maybe you can help—come up with an idea, like you did with the Celebrations?"

"Sure. Just tell the humans she tastes like candy," Attina said dryly. "Or that a mouthful of her flesh can cure their diseases."

"*Thanks.* I'll give your suggestion the thoughtful consideration it's due."

"Any time, little sister."

Sebastian scuttled on the floor toward them, seeming very pleased with himself. Threll swam above, looking likewise.

"*Don't talk about this!*" Ariel whispered.

"Talk about what?" Attina asked innocently.

Ariel made a desperate *hush* motion with her finger to her lips, minutely tipping her chin at her friends.

"What are you doing? I don't think I learned that sign . . ." Attina said, looking very puzzled.

Ariel glowered at her.

"Oh! But wait, don't you think your *friends* should know as well?" her sister pressed.

"Know what?" Sebastian asked curiously when he reached them.

Ariel floated upright off her stool, fists clenched at her sides, wishing she could pummel her sister like in the old days.

"Oh, that this whole thing with the Equinocturnal Celebrations and the Rites of Proserpine is over. She figured it out," Attina said with a sweet smile, batting her lashes at the queen.

"But we already know that," Sebastian said, confused. "You have the sister singing it. What other news is there? Oh . . . ARE YOU GOING TO SING?" His eyes twitched in the crab equivalent of widening; he tiptoed forward, claws delicately tapping each other's tips, as if afraid to scare away the idea.

Attina guffawed silently and swam off.

Ariel looked at the little crab and felt bad. She had felt bad ever since the stern talking-to she had given him about how she would never, ever sing while she was queen. She hadn't changed her mind about that. But how could she make it up to him?

She thought about the other musician in her life, Eric. In his own way he loved an audience as much as the little crab did; he relished the goodwill of the townspeople and was very much looking forward to the encore of *La*

Sirenetta, performed for all who had missed it the first time. Composing was one thing, but both of them felt the most fulfilled when they could directly gauge the reactions of their listeners.

That's an idea. . . .

"Sebastian, I was serious. I will never sing for an audience while I am queen. However, *that being said*," she continued quickly as the crab looked like he was about to explode, "two things. One, I want you to devote a portion of your spare time to writing me an aria—a really amazing aria—that I will sing, triumphantly, when my father is returned as king and I can go back to being a mostly private citizen. It should be a celebration of his return. This has to be epic, Sebastian. Things like the capture and return of the King of the Sea do not happen but maybe once in a thousand years."

Sebastian was torn, she could tell. His little black crabby eyes twitched desperately. Everything about this idea appealed to every part of him, from the artist given a truly special challenge all the way to the egomaniac whose work would be performed and remembered forever.

But it still wasn't the same thing as having her sing *now*.

He was trying very, *very* hard not to say that. She could see it in the way his antennules clicked silently against each other.

"And for the Equinocturnal Celebrations, I plan to give a speech to all the participants about my promise not to sing until Father is returned, and what we are doing to facilitate his return." *Did I just say "facilitate his return"? Next I'm going to start saying things like "leveraging the synergy . . ."* "And then I will talk about the Return Aria and turn the floor over to you, so you may talk about your composition and your vision."

"That sounds highly acceptable," Threll said with an eyecrest raised at Ariel—the closest thing he had to a wink.

"Don't think I don't know what you're trying to do, young lady," Sebastian growled. But then his voice got dreamy. "Still . . . I can just see it now . . . 'The Return'! Everyone is seated in the Grand Amphitheatre . . . No! We will do something unique! We'll build an *all new* amphitheatre!"

"Uh, Sebastian, I didn't say anything about approving funds for—"

"We'll have an *upside-down* amphitheatre! Starting at the top very big, then rows and rows getting smaller down until it's just you, on the seafloor—*No!* On the Mound of Sartops, so everyone will be looking at us . . . I mean, you . . . And then I will raise my claw, so, and I will give a little speech of thanks for this opportunity and Triton's triumphant return. . . ."

Ariel blinked.

"Everyone will be there because it's a performance," she said slowly. "And they will all be looking at you. . . ."

"Yes, of course, yes," Sebastian said impatiently. "But also you. And then I will raise my claw, *so* . . ."

It hit the Queen of the Sea like an orca slamming into a plate of ice.

"I have it!" she cried. "I know what to do! Somebody, go find me Jona . . . Sebastian, you have the helm. I'm surfacing, but just for tonight!"

"But my aria . . ." Sebastian called out sadly.

She was already gone.

Ariel and Eric

Eric had trouble falling asleep. He had the beginnings of a brilliant idea for a plan, and no way to contact Ariel!

It was late when his dreams finally overcame him, and it seemed like only a few moments later when he was woken up by Max.

"Mmm, what's up, boy . . . ?" Eric murmured, turning over.

Then his eyes shot open.

The old dog slept a lot now, and always through the night. He *never* begged for walkies when it was dark.

The prince pushed himself up on his elbows. Max had risen on his hind legs with one front paw on the wall for balance. He was staring out the window, gesturing at it with his lolling tongue and interested muzzle. Outside was a gull, its white wings flapping as delicately as a moth as it hovered there.

"You?" Eric whispered. "From . . . Ariel?"

The seagull bobbed as best it could. Then it peeled away from the castle. Eric watched it descend and then look back at him and give a quiet cry.

It wanted the prince to follow it.

Eric didn't bother putting on shoes; he hastily pulled on a pair of trousers and tiptoed out of the room and down the stairs. His bare feet made no noise on the floor and for a moment he reveled in that; it was like being a young prince again, sneaking out to see the full moon.

Outside, the gull, glowing a pale unlikely white in the night, waited patiently drifting through the air.

He followed it south, past the castle beach and into the stony area with the basalt cliffs. When sand gave way he had to clamber on the rocks; the waves broke over seaweed-covered boulders and got deep very quickly.

Holding on to one of those boulders was Ariel, strangely placid in the turbulent water. Her tail snaked sinuously out behind her, keeping her level and on the surface of the water like a kraken.

"This is *amazing*!" he said, as delighted as a child. "This is how you really are."

"This is how I really am," she agreed, touched that he had phrased it that way. She was no longer a human girl who became a mermaid to him; she was a mermaid first and foremost, and a human occasionally by choice. "But listen, we need to talk."

"I know, I know!" Eric said excitedly. "I had an idea!"

"So did I! I was thinking of some sort of performance, which Ursula would attend, giving a speech or something pompous that would put her in front of a huge crowd."

"Exactly! Something where, for a moment at least, she is the absolute center of attention—"

"Something that really tickles her vanity, so she absolutely agrees to go—"

"Like the encore performance of *La Sirenetta*," Eric finished.

"Your opera!" Ariel said with a gasp. "It's perfect!"

"It's *so perfect*. Everyone will be watching. The only problem is that I just don't know how to turn her back. Maybe the altos can bring in a giant tub of salt water on their heads and splash it on her? I don't know, though, some of them are surprisingly dainty and delicate. Maybe they could each carry a *small* tub of salt water on their heads. . . ."

"Or . . . since it's a concert for the people, you could have it outside in the town square, right next to Neptune's Fountain. And we could just knock her in," Ariel suggested lightly. Sebastian and Eric were more similar than she had even guessed. Always leaping to the most complex and fussy ideas when a simple one would do.

"Oh, right." Eric grinned sheepishly. "I hadn't thought of that. You're sure it will work?"

"Absolutely, and it's foolproof, because the water comes straight from the sea. So you need to make that fountain part of your opera, or at least stage it around it."

"Easily done. This is *great*." He laughed and punched the air. "I can practically *feel* the happily ever afters coming for us!"

"Slow down there," Ariel said cautiously. "This is Ursula. Nothing is over until it's actually over."

"I know, I know, but it seems so . . . perfect! Artistically, too," he added thoughtfully. "You know, ending it with an opera that's actually about the two of you, and there's singing, so it's all about your voice, and that's what does her in. . . ."

"Yes, yes, very clever and semiotic. But I should go—I don't know if this counts as 'castle grounds' or not, but you are definitely helping me. It would be stupid to risk Grimsby when we're so close."

"Agreed. And I should get back and . . . I don't know, walk around the beach talking to myself and Jona or something. Maybe sing. Keep up the whole Mad Prince thing a bit longer."

"Oh, I hope you don't ever give it up entirely! I rather like it."

"For you, it will come out of the closet occasionally." He leaned over into the water. Ariel kicked her tail and rose up just long enough for a quick kiss—cold, wet, salty, and slapped by the sea at just the wrong moment.

Heaven.

Eric good-naturedly laughed at himself as he brushed the foam and seawater out of his now-limp forelock.

"You have to make sure she attends," Ariel warned.

"Oh, leave that to me," Eric promised. "I know exactly what to say. I'll also work hard to keep the original performance date—on St. Madalberta's feast day. Two weeks from now."

"I hope that's soon enough—that it's before the circuex or whatever she's planning."

"Nothing in the castle has seemed out of the ordinary so far. No weird things ordered, no giant cauldrons procured—in fact, Vanessa has been rather quieter than usual since her big threat. I wouldn't worry too much yet. You'll be there, right?"

"I wouldn't miss it for the world," the mermaid said dryly, and dove back down into the depths.

Eric wandered back to the castle, zigzagging to pick up shells and a stray feather, sticking the latter in his cap. Just in case anyone caught him.

He saluted the gull above him and could have sworn it did a victory roll in response.

Ursula

"Come again?"

She was seated on her poufy chair, Vareet perched uncomfortably on a stool at her feet. Sometimes Ursula ran her fingers through the girl's hair, which, while certainly not as pleasant as stroking an eel, was at least a *little* satisfactory.

The prince stood before her with a strange look on his face, somewhere between timid, ironically amused, and chagrined. It was impossible to predict what was going to come out of his mouth, and what finally did was mind-boggling.

"I am here to offer a détente, and a bit of an apology for our . . . argument in your study."

She raised a very skeptical eyebrow.

Eric sighed.

"It was *very* rude of me to point out the technicalities of our marriage contract the way I did. *While it is all still true,* it was very bully-ish of me and highly unmanly. Threatening a woman is the basest of sins." He bowed, but the edge of his mouth twitched in a smile.

"Please leave gender out of this," Ursula said without thinking. *But really.* Even if he meant it as a joke. "Also, apology formally accepted—although I don't believe it for a moment."

"Believe what you will, I have no power over that. The fact is I am genuinely embarrassed by the way I acted. At the very least we can be civil while we're together."

"Hmm," she sniffed. She couldn't detect any obvious falsehood, but since he was turning out to be smarter than she thought, nothing he said or did could be taken at face value anymore.

"Here is part one of my peace offering," he said, and gave her the brooch he had been holding.

Ursula looked at it with surprise. She knew about his secret meeting with the head of the metalworkers guild, and had assumed it was to re-explain what she had already said, the way men boorishly did—or to outright contradict her. But apparently *this* was the true purpose of the meeting: a tiny metal octopus, its tentacles all akimbo and curled, detailed down to its little suckers. The eyes looked suspicious and were rubies. It was made from . . .

"Bronze," she said with a chuckle. Eric gave a little bow.

It was really quite delightful. Normally she didn't care about jewelry beyond what was considered trendy and appropriate for princesses to wear, but this . . . this was an adorable little trinket. No one had given her anything like it . . . any gift at all, really . . . in years. . . .

She fastened it onto her collar and tried not to admire it there, sparkling temptingly.

"Part two is that the encore—and farewell—performance of *La Sirenetta*, I am dedicating to you."

"Why?" She didn't even pretend to be touched. There was a reason behind this that had nothing to do with kindness—she could *feel* it.

"We need to present a united front. As is obvious from that horrible dinner, the staff and probably the townspeople think we're—on the rocks, as it were."

"I don't see why what they think is important. *Riffraff.*"

"Then apparently you don't understand humans as much as you claim to. At some point one of your friends or enemies is going to use our inimical relationship to drive a wedge through the kingdom. Many countries are already getting rid of their kings and queens and princes and princesses—or at least taking away their power while letting them keep their pretty crowns. Royalty that actually rules is a dying breed. Do we really want to give anyone the opportunity to speed it along here in Tirulia?"

Ursula had never thought of it that way before. It was

true—a lot of nasty populist places were having revolutions and becoming republics and democracies, patting their royalty on the head and pushing them on their way.

(If the royalty was lucky, that was *all* that happened to their heads.)

The fact that Eric was concerned about this was a novelty; she had always thought he was just a happy-go-lucky, entitled prince who, yes, cared for his people—but in his own privileged way. She never thought that he actually valued his *princehood*, or keeping it.

"You may have a point," she allowed.

"Thank you. Thus, ostensibly I am dedicating the opera to you as a promise to spend more time on our . . . ah . . . marriage, and to me being a good prince. We have moved the venue to the town square so everyone can come and we're constructing a raised dais just for you. I'm having this chair made, sort of muse-of-the-arts-y. . . ."

He unfurled a scroll of paper and showed her the plans: where the performers would stand, where the orchestra would sit, and where there was a beautiful velvet-canopied pavilion with an ornate chair that was basically a throne.

She would look like a real queen sitting there.

Not some dumb princess.

The royal purple fabric . . . the gilt chair . . . the way it was angled so both the audience and the performers could both see her. She would be queen in all but name.

All would be watching her as she brought down destruction on them, like a true Old God tyrant.

"I . . . don't . . . trust you," she said.

"I don't expect you to. I don't trust you, either. But once in a while we may need to actually work together for survival. And as I said, I am, if nothing else, genuinely regretful for the way I spoke to you."

He's a regular Prince Charming, Ursula snorted to herself. If nothing else, it was amusing to see him spend all this effort trying to get her to go to a performance she never had any intention of missing. If he had a trick or two up his sleeve, well, it was nothing compared to what *she* had planned.

Performing the opera outside, in the square, was better than she could have ever dreamed. *All* the people of the little seaside town would be there. A thousand victims to sacrifice, a thousand hearts bleeding together with the King of the Sea.

Thanks to Eric and his *generous* apology dedication of the performance, there was no way the spell could fail. The powers released by all that death would grant her true magical mastery over the Dry World and the World Under the Sea. She would be unstoppable. Atlantica would fall. All would bow to her or fall to her wrath.

Ursula realized she was absently stroking the little bronze octopus and stopped it immediately.

Ariel

When the day of the opera came she wished she had better clothes; it seemed a shame to attend Eric's opera in the rags of a maid. But she changed into what she had, slipped the trident into her hair, and looked for Scuttle.

"Right here, Ariel! Just a moment!" the old gull called. He was standing at the shoreline gazing into a very calm tide pool at his feet, adjusting his chest feathers and preening his wings. "All set!" he finally declared and glided haphazardly over to her. "Wanted to look my spiffiest for everyone's big day."

Ariel smiled warmly and stroked him on his head. There was a bit of slick black seaweed around his neck, arranged to look a little like a cravat.

"Got me a nooserton," he said proudly. "Just like the fancy human birds."

"You look wonderful." She kissed him on the beak, then offered her arm. "Care for a ride? Just so you don't get tired too early."

"It would be my honor to escort you, my lady," he said with a bow, then hopped lightly up.

Well, not that lightly. Ariel had to grind her teeth to stop from reacting. She had forgotten how heavy things were in the Dry World, even supposedly light things, like birds.

They probably made for a very odd sight, strolling from the beach into town: a robed and mostly hooded maid with a seagull balanced on her arm. But there was no one around to see. The houses, churches, markets, and shops were mostly abandoned; everyone had gone early to get a good place to sit or stand for the free show. Ariel walked between the empty buildings, regarding them with mixed feelings.

If they failed, there was a chance she would be dead—or at the very least, a polyp—and never again free to go where she wished, either land *or* sea.

There was also a chance, if they *succeeded*, that her father, once returned to full power, would never allow her to come onto land again. He could make it so that *no one* could become human. Of course, she could always search for another way. But last time that had led to Ursula, and . . .

Her thoughts spun. There were objects in the window of a shop that she couldn't quite fathom: possibly candy, possibly gems and crystals. There were so many alien things about this world she still didn't know. There were so many more things in the *rest* of the world, both above and below the sea, that were yet to be discovered. . . .

"You okay, Ariel? You seem a little, I dunno, worried or spacey or something," Scuttle said.

"I just . . . I was just thinking about past choices and future possibilities."

"Huh. Deep stuff. Well, the world's your oyster after today. I can't wait to see Triton again! You think he'll give me a medal or something? For helping? For starting this whole thing?"

"I'm sure he will," she said with a smile. It wasn't quite a lie. Despite her father's distaste for all air breathers, she would make sure her friends were properly rewarded.

They caught up with a few stragglers: families gathering small children onto their shoulders, limping soldiers, farmers from holds farther out. Scuttle took off. Ariel hoped he would find and stay close to Jona—who was, somewhat ironically, keeping an eye on Eric and developments at the castle end of things. And to think she was originally supposed to protect the Queen of the Sea!

"My lady!"

Ariel turned to see Argent hurrying down the avenue to catch up with her. Despite her old age it was easy with her long legs. She swung a heavy walking stick in the air enthusiastically—with little need for it, apparently.

"You're here to see the show?" the apple seller asked with a smile.

"Oh, yes. I promise you, it will be a . . . *show* that everyone will remember for years to come."

"I sense there's something beneath those words."

"Today it will be revealed who your princess really is," Ariel said, feeling mysterious and queenly. "You shall be witness to something amazing. Watch closely, and be ready to tell the story of what you saw."

"Oh, I can do better than that," the woman said with a wink. "I'll *ink* it, if asked."

"Yes, I think you'll find it very inspirational," Ariel said, thinking about the other sea-themed pictures on the woman's arms. She was pretty sure there wasn't an octopus . . . not yet, anyway.

"Well, I'd better get a front-row seat," the old woman declared, striding forward. "*EXCUSE ME!* Old lady coming through! *Make way for a grannie.*" She handily pushed people aside, forcing her way to the front.

No frail biddy, she.

Ariel also wanted a close view, though not so close that

Ursula could pick her out of the crowd. She smiled and slipped sideways and murmured apologies and, yes, flashed a beautiful mermaid smile at large in-the-way boys when she needed to. She succeeded in getting halfway into the main square, about a third of the way back from the stage. A low platform had been erected behind Neptune's Fountain for the singers to stand on, and stand only. It would be a far less dramatic performance than in the amphitheatre—not much moving around. Ariel felt a little disappointed despite knowing just how ridiculous she was being. But from the way Jona had described the original show, it had sounded like a lot of fun—and she was curious to see how Eric and the humans had re-created her ancient underwater world.

The orchestra was grouped against the wall of the indoor market; their music would echo off its stones and back to the audience. *There's a pun in there somewhere about songs and dolphins and their singing-sight. . . .* But she was too excited to think it through.

On the side of the fountain closest to her and the audience, raised just a *smidge* higher than the impromptu stage, was a jewel of a box seat, canopied in cloth of gold and purple velvet. A banner even flew from the top. Ariel's eyes narrowed when she saw the sigil of the black octopus on it.

The sky was blue, the crowd was happy, the air was crisp and fresh. Everything was bright and pretty and happy, and she was caught up in the mood despite the dire reasons for her being there.

It was like attending the markets and fairs when she was a child, when it was all new and everything seemed exciting. Back then she darted everywhere and begged for treats and admired strange merfolk she didn't know. She missed that and it was nice to recapture it again.

The royal carriage pulled up, the crowd breaking into cheers when Eric stepped out. Ariel hoped they would react poorly when Vanessa emerged, but she was disappointed. The false princess looked stunning. She wore a very modern, highly corseted ocean-blue dress with a half dozen underskirts, and she had jewels and shells intertwined with her hair that looked . . . almost . . . tentacle-y. She flashed a sly, toothy smile and the crowd ate it up. No one believed the truth of the opera, but they all loved the *idea* of a villain modeled on their princess. An antihero.

Flotsam and Jetsam oozed to the sides of the box seat, flanking it.

Vareet was right behind them. She wore a simple, pretty frock and her hair was arranged like her mistress's, her naturally curly tresses tightly wound around her head with ocean-blue ribbons. But she was very pale. The little girl could tell something was up, or she knew something was about to happen.

Grimsby made his way to the royal seats from a different carriage, gradually and strangely carefully—and then Ariel saw that he was leading Max, who was nearly blind but still wagged his tail, excited to be there.

She thought her heart would break. He had been there when it all started, and Eric obviously wanted to make sure his friend was there when it all ended—no matter how it ended. She felt tears bead up and her heart continued to flutter.

And flutter.

A *lot.* Scritchily.

Panicked, Ariel put her hand to her chest.

"HEY, WATCH THE FINGERS!" a voice snapped as she touched a strange, hard lump below her clavicle.

"Sebastian?"

The little crab scuttled up so his eyestalks popped up above her neckline. It itched and tickled mightily but the queen restrained herself.

"What . . . What are you . . . *What* . . . ?"

"I couldn't let you do this all alone," Sebastian said matter-of-factly. "I have done nothing all this time but rule the sea in your place and worry. I had to do *something.*"

She carefully reached down her front and unhooked him from the rough wool, then held him up to her face.

"Sebastian . . ." she said, trying not to smile. Trying to look frowny and fierce.

The crab put a claw over his antennule. "Can't talk. No oxygen out of the water. I have less than a day before I need to go back. Have to conserve."

"Well, thank the sea for *something*," she said, then kissed him on his carapace and carefully placed him on her shoulder. *First a seagull, then I'm hosting a crab. Am I the Queen of the Sea or of random sea creatures?*

Back on the dais, Eric was gracefully making sure Vanessa was on his right side, closer to the saltwater fountain. They stood together, every inch a mighty power couple.

"Good people of Tirulia," he cried. "Thank you for joining me this afternoon. That I could give you this performance fills my heart with no end of gladness. . . . I only wish I could do more for the greatest people in the world!"

The crowd went wild, stamping and hollering.

"No artist can create without an inspiration; no man can work so without a muse. So it is with your prince. Everything I've ever done, every piece you've ever heard, every tune I've ever scribbled in the wee hours as a Mad Prince does, they are all because of one woman, who owns me heart and soul."

This was met with *awwws* and cries about the power of love.

Eric looked out at the crowd, but his eyes didn't find hers. It didn't matter. Ariel knew he was speaking to her, and she felt her eyes moisten.

He let the moment drag out and then turned dramatically to Vanessa, making a very distinct break between what he had said before and now—but only to those who knew.

"I hereby dedicate *La Sirenetta* to the most unforgettable princess in the world. For Vanessa, and for Tirulia!"

He took out his ocarina, toasted her with it, and then hurled it into the crowd.

There was a little bit of a scuffle, but it wound up in the chubby hands of a toddler on someone's shoulder. Everyone cheered madly when she raised it above her head in triumph.

Eric laughed. He bowed and kissed the princess's hand.

Ariel felt her stomach turn. Despite his vow of silence, Sebastian muttered and clicked angrily.

Vanessa curtsied low, then sashayed forward.

Flotsam and Jetsam were suddenly behind her. They held a chest between them.

"Thank you, Prince Eric," Vanessa said sweetly—or as sweetly as she could, shouting in Ursula's voice. More than a few people looked confused. "And thank you, good citizens of Tirulia. Bear with me while I hack and cough through this . . . the summer cold I had destroyed my lungs."

Did anyone really buy that?

Sneaking a glance at the people around her, Ariel saw a mix of reactions: surprise, skepticism, and horribly enough, *pity.*

"Could a princess be any luckier to have found such a prince? Truly, I am honored to be the . . . *inspiration* for his art. I have just a couple of words to say before we begin."

Ariel tensed—the sea witch had to be pushed into the fountain *soon*. But Vanessa was sort of in front of Eric now, moving diagonally away from where she needed to be. With Flotsam and Jetsam up on the stage with her, it might become even more difficult. Could Eric handle them if they saw their mistress was in trouble?

"First, I would like to thank Lord and Lady Savho, who have generously loaned the government of Tirulia two of their heaviest cargo vessels to fill in while we rebuild our fleet. They are on maneuvers right now, even as we speak, heading toward the open waters. . . . Testing powerful new munitions we plan to use against enemies of the state."

Ariel felt her heart stop. Ursula's eyes glittered and she looked carefully out over the crowd—hoping to see a reaction, hoping to catch out the mermaid, hoping to gloat.

"What does she mean? So what? I don't . . ." Sebastian whispered.

"She means to blow up Atlantica. She means to do it *now*, while everyone is at the opera—including me!"

The Queen of the Sea thought quickly. If she ran, she could dive into the water, summon a storm, and possibly stop them in time. But the moon wasn't in the best phase; it was already taking most of her effort to remain human.

And this might be the only chance they ever had to stop the sea witch. Ariel needed to be there in case something went wrong. Vanessa said *heading* to open waters. They still had a little time.

Her heart pounding, she decided to stay. For at least a few more minutes.

"Secondly," Ursula said, looking disappointed as she failed to spot Ariel, "I wish to announce the winners of our special fishing contest—to find the magic blue-and-yellow fish. Unfortunately, and somewhat embarrassingly, the prize goes to my own servants, *Flotsam and Jetsam.*"

They knelt forward and threw open the top of the chest they held, sickly grins on their faces.

Flounder tried to leap out.

"But that's—" Sebastian started to cry.

Ariel squeezed his mouth shut with her hand and tried not to cry out herself.

Eric's eyes practically popped out of his skull. He shook his head desperately, looking for Ariel in the crowd. He had managed to stop the contest, but not Ursula.

The crowd booed. Cries of *"Cheaters!"* and *"It was rigged!"* were hurled at the dais. Vanessa deflected them with a cool grin.

"Of course this looks bad. My servants are highly skilled hunters—I mean, fishers. Fishermen. Best of their people."

As she said this she came forward and seized Flounder violently but securely around his waist. He threw himself back and forth, but behind Vanessa's weak and skinny little arms was the might of the cecaelia, and she didn't even flinch.

He screamed silently—his words killed by the atmosphere of the Dry World.

"Flounder," Ariel whispered. She put her hand to her hair, feeling the trident. If only . . .

The moment dragged out. The crowd grew impatient and grumbly, but not prone to violence—yet. And Vanessa just stood there calmly, not so much gazing at them as *scanning* them. Looking for the mermaid.

She was doing all of this just to lure Ariel out into the open.

As much as she hated it, Ariel had to resist her instinct to jump up and rescue him. She would wait.

"My servants are a generous pair of boys," Vanessa finally continued, sashaying closer to the fountain. With a nonchalance that disgusted Ariel to her core, the sea witch tossed the fish into the fountain, then clapped her hands to clean them of water and scales. Flounder dove deep for a breath then leapt out of the water a few times like an upset goldfish, confused and terrified and trying to figure out where he was.

Ariel breathed a deep sigh of relief. Ursula was keeping him alive for now—probably to use as leverage later.

The crowd was still agitating. The sea witch seemed to gauge them for a moment before coming to a decision.

"My servants have decided to give up the prize to the good people of Tirulia!" she cried.

With skeletal leers, the two eel brothers reached into the bottom of the chest that had held Flounder and pulled up dripping handfuls of gold coins. They flung them into the crowd.

There were immediate cheers—and a few shrieks as the heavy coins struck some in the head and face.

Ariel frowned. That was an unexpected move. The sea witch never cared about the feelings of the commoners, even when she was under the sea. She generally referred to them as *riffraff.* Her goal had always been to rise far above the masses, as princess, queen, or god. Why did she care what they thought of her now? Why was she trying to buy them off?

Unless it was just to keep the crowd calm and happy for some *other* reason. . . .

Eric moved toward Vanessa, slipping in between her manservants while she was distracted, enjoying the cheers.

Flotsam and Jetsam were *not* distracted; they immediately pulled out daggers with their free hands, crossing them in front of the prince.

Most of the crowd didn't notice this; they were too busy looking for missed coins, arguing with their neighbors, cheering, or watching Vanessa.

Grimsby noticed.

"Prince Eric!" he cried, his thin voice barely carrying over the crowd. He thrust Max's leash into Vareet's hands and tried to push his way to the stage. Max howled and barked and lunged forward, also trying to get to the prince.

Ariel put a hand up to cover and protect Sebastian and also started to move forward.

A gull called from overhead. Suddenly, Jona dove like a porpoise right into Flotsam's face. (Or maybe it was Jetsam. Honestly, Ariel could never tell them apart.) She stabbed her beak into his face like she was spearing an especially truculent fish.

Flotsam (or Jetsam) eerily did *not* scream—he merely put one hand up to protect his face and very methodically tried to pick the bird off with the other.

Scuttle followed close behind, ripping at Jetsam's (or Flotsam's) nose. That eel also didn't scream; he just knocked the old gull aside with the back of his hand.

Eric threw himself forward, trying to push through.

One of the eels sucker-punched him in the stomach.

The prince doubled over, falling to the floor.

"No!" Ariel cried.

Vanessa was watching all this . . . and laughing . . . and then . . .

Slowly, like a giant ship sinking, she fell over into the fountain.

The splash was enormous.

There were shouts of confusion from the crowd.

"What happened? What happened?" Sebastian demanded from underneath Ariel's hand.

The mermaid stood on the tips of her toes, trying to get a look.

There, standing at the edge of the platform, panting and exhausted, was Max. Also Vareet, with the empty leash in her hand and a look of triumph on her face.

The dog growled once at the princess he had knocked into the fountain, then wagged his tail and barked happily back at Eric, who was just getting to his knees.

"By the sea," Ariel whispered, grinning.

"He did it!" Sebastian cried, thrusting a claw into the air. "That little girl and the terrible shaggy dogfish *did* it!"

Someone screamed.

The crowd grew silent. The Tirulians watched in horror as Ursula emerged from underneath the water, pulling herself up over the side of the fountain with slick black tentacles that glittered in the sun.

Eric

"Max!" he gasped. *"Good boy."*

Breathing was hard. Jetsam had got him good, up and under his rib. Moving was also hard. The prince gritted his teeth and forced himself upright anyway, leaning hard on his left leg with both his arms. The despicable henchmen had abandoned him to aid their mistress.

Eric gestured Vareet over and used her shoulder to help him the rest of the way up.

He took a deep, painful breath and addressed the crowd.

"Look!" he shouted. "Look at what your *princess* truly is. Lord Francese, do you see? Savho? Señor Aron? Do you *see* the creature before you? The one you gave promises to, and gold, and your loyalty? *Look, people of Tirulia.* Behold not Vanessa, but *Ursula*, witch of the sea!"

"It's real?"

"She's really the sea witch?"

"The opera—it's all true?"

The opera singers and orchestra members drew back in horror. The crowd closest to the stage pushed and shuffled, some surging forward to see and others trying to get away. But except for confused murmurs, everyone was silent, as silent as a beach before a tsunami.

And yet . . . Ursula didn't seem nonplussed. She sort of floated in the water, her forearms resting on the marble rim of the fountain like a child at a pool. Her tentacles danced in a ring around her, splashing in the water as if they had minds of their own and were deliriously happy. She smiled and grimaced and leered at the people as Eric spoke. Vanessa's jacket hung in rags around her shoulders.

"Kill it!" someone in the crowd shouted in disgust.

"She's the spawn of the devil!"

"She *is* the devil!"

"Oh, you humans. *So predictable,*" Ursula purred loudly. Her voice resonated across the square in a way it never had in her tenure as a princess. "You know, not *everything* is about you and your Dry World gods."

Her tentacles grabbed at the sides of the fountain harder, and looking neither fully octopus nor fully human, she pulled herself over the side, flowing like foul black ichor onto the dais.

Flotsam and Jetsam, bloody but uncowed, grinned to see their mistress in her original form. They immediately put themselves between her and Eric, giving him venomous, threatening glares.

The castle guards and soldiers looked unsure of themselves. They kept their muskets trained on the crowd, which was roiling and growing unpredictable. There, at least, was a threat they understood and could stop. . . . Yet some of them separated from their comrades, turning weapons on— well, it was hard to tell whom. Surely it wasn't the other soldiers? Or the prince himself?

Ursula cleared her throat. "Tell me, is there a . . . is there a *mermaid* in the audience? I have something to say to her. Come forward, darling."

Ariel looked around nervously. Everyone else looked around as well, confused. For a brief moment there was a space between the bodies and her eyes met those of the apple seller. Argent shook her head: *don't do it.*

"Well, no matter, I know you're shy," Ursula continued, drawling. "Sometimes it seems like you're so timid you can't speak at *all*. Heh-heh. All that is required from you is to *watch*. And *listen*. And do *nothing* as your entire world is destroyed."

"Silence, Vanessa!" Eric cried. "It's over. Give up. I'll try to keep the guards and the people from killing you."

"Very generous," she said, laughing throatily. "Here,

let me make myself a little more comfortable, before we get around to all that. . . ."

With a sneer that was pure evil, she ripped off what remained of Vanessa's jacket. On top of her black camisole she wore a heavy golden chain. And hanging from that chain was . . .

Triton.

Ariel

Father!

She began to cry the word aloud, but pushed a fist into her mouth at the last second. The people she was standing next to looked at her in confusion, but it hardly mattered.

The large pendant Ursula wore was a glass ampoule with a bronze and wax top. Inside this floated a sad, disgusting little polyp whose tendrils still resembled the beard and mustache of the ancient sea king.

"Oh, come *on*." Ursula swore in disgust, looking out over the crowd. Her hands were on her hips. "I've got your *father*, dear! I *know* you're out there *somewhere*! I know you two were planning something big for me today. Although," she added, looking at Eric, "I rather expected something more than *being pushed into a fountain*. Disappointing."

Ariel took a tentative step forward.

Sebastian pinched her hard, on her shoulder.

"Don't you dare, young lady," he hissed. "You're jumping in too early, like you always did with your solos. For once in your life stop being so impulsive and *think*!"

Ariel winced from the pain of his words. Was he right? But . . . that was her *father*! The whole reason she was there! He was maybe a goby's leap from her!

"Guards, seize the creature who pretended to be Vanessa," Eric commanded. "She is a dangerous enemy of the state."

The captain of the guards and his top men jerked into action, finally with a clear path: their prince had given an order.

Yet still—some of them did not.

"Guards, stand down." Ursula waved at them, almost lazily. "Or my boys will kill your prince."

In a wink Flotsam and Jetsam had their daggers pressed against Eric's neck.

Once again the captain faltered, as did the men closest to him.

"All right, I was hoping to draw out the little mermaid queen, but I guess the show must go on without her," Ursula said with a sigh. "In case she *is* here, somewhere, hiding, let me make this very clear to her. And to all of you. My reign as Princess Vanessa of Tirulia is over."

"No kidding," Eric growled.

"It's been fun, and I have so loved ruling you all," she said, blowing a kiss to the crowd. "I'm going to miss you terribly. Well, probably not. But it was a nice growth experience. Just understand that what is about to happen is all *because of* 'la sirenetta.'

"I was perfectly happy being your princess—and then *she* showed up. So I told her to go away. Very clearly. To leave *us all* alone. She ignored me, and came back, infiltrating the castle with her spies and henchmen."

She paused and added, sotto voce:

"I have that dumb broad Carlotta strung up in the basement, and I am *not* feeding her. She could stand to lose some . . . *attitude*. . . ."

Ariel choked. *Carlotta, too? Was no one safe?*

"And then—just as a side project, to shut up the dumb mermaid and her idiot people forever—I had planned to destroy her kingdom. Oh, yes, there's an underwater kingdom of peaceful happy mermaids out there—but the point is, it had nothing to do with *you* all. Tirulians. I would have wiped the mer off the face of the planet and none of you would have been the wiser."

The crowd began to mutter, puzzled by this. *Ursula*

really doesn't understand humans at all if she thinks they wouldn't care. In one sentence the sea witch had admitted to the existence of a kingdom of mythical creatures—and how she now wanted to exterminate them.

"But she foiled that plan by destroying my fleet . . . and a number of your own fishing vessels as well. Remember that great storm? Yes, that was her. Every time I've tried to take care of her quietly, she comes back, ruining everything. If she had just *stayed away* none of this would have happened."

It's my *fault that Ursula has my father? I* made *her try to bomb Atlantica?* Ursula was twisting everything around so much—did she even believe her own rhetoric? Or did she just say whatever made her look good, knowing even while she said it that it was false information?

"Some of you who actually saw the opera might already know a bit of my past," Ursula continued casually, regarding the tips of some of her tentacles. "I was a . . . *powerful witch under the sea.* But really, how much power is enough? So I became a powerful ruler on the land. And that was fun. But then I thought . . . *why choose?*"

Time stopped for Ariel. Blood filled her ears as the strangely banal question rang loud and ominous.

What did she mean?

"So," Ursula sighed, taking the necklace off and holding

the glass ampoule in her hands, "I won't. Thanks to the ancient blood running in this little guy here, and . . . well, a lot *more* blood—your blood, in fact—I will soon be what you little folk would refer to as a *god* of both the Dry World *and* the World Under the Sea.

"Hold still now, won't you? This won't hurt a bit. . . ."

Ursula

Iä! Iä! Egrsi phtaqn! Bh'n'e vh ssrbykl Y'ryel varrotel phtaqn!

The ancient words flowed like black music through her body. No one had recited them in over three thousand years, and the culture that had spawned that priestess had disappeared into a howling vortex of chaos and agony.

Soon these Elder Gods would come and take the people of Tirulia as her offering and feed upon the soul of Triton. In return they would grant Ursula the unthinkable: power over two demesnes, two worlds that had always been separated under ancient, inviolate law. She would be the mightiest creature Gaia had ever seen—or bowed down to.

Hideous shrieks from beyond the stars rent the atmosphere, preparing the way for their singers to come through.

The crowd went deliciously mad. Like a mermaid's song turned inside out, the verses ripped into their skulls through their ears. People screamed, trying to block out the sound with their hands. They sank down to the ground, and Ursula saw precious, bright-red drops of blood start to seep between their fingers.

Well, all right, she conceded. *It* might *hurt. A little . . .*

Ariel

"No!"

She cried out before she had a plan.

Sebastian didn't even chastise her, too busy staring in horror at the groaning and screaming people around them.

Ursula looked up. It was easy to find Ariel now; she was the only one still standing. The terrible chant in the forbidden language didn't affect her the same way it did the humans, perhaps because she understood some of its foul purpose and its origin. It wasn't meant for her, only the poor humans.

Ariel pushed her way to the front. *Think like it's a game of koralli,* she told herself. *What do I have that Ursula doesn't expect? What is Ursula's weakness?*

"*URSULA!*" she cried again. "*Stop this!* I surrender!"

A slow, ugly smile grew from one side of the sea witch's mouth to the other. Something like relief and pleasure mixed disgustingly on her face: she really had been afraid Ariel wouldn't show. That she wouldn't witness Ursula's triumph.

The hideous wailing from the blackness beyond the stars wavered and slowly died off.

The groans of the Tirulians could be heard now as they recovered, weeping and bleeding.

"And why do I need you to surrender?" the cecaelia asked languidly. "I have everything I want now. Land, sea, power, a bit of a show, *blood* . . . What could I possibly want *you* for?"

"Please," Ariel begged. "I know you want revenge on me and my father. But leave the humans out of it. They have never done anything to you."

"*La sirenetta?*" someone whispered in wonder.

"Is she a mermaid?" another Tirulian asked, slowly straightening herself out, wiping the blood off her face.

"Wait, is the octopus-woman a mermaid, too?"

"Is that the mermaid from the opera?"

"She's beautiful. . . ."

"Ursula, I know this isn't what you really want," Ariel hazarded. "What you *really* want is to rule Atlantica, to show all the merfolk what you do to those who treat you badly. You want to to reign over and enslave the people who know who you really are. These humans have no idea!" She waved her arms at the crowd. "They have no concept of what happened to you a hundred years ago. Your triumph over the Dry World is meaningless, because they don't even know who Ursula is. Everyone under the sea *does*."

"*Don't tell me what I want!*" Ursula snapped.

But she looked uncertain.

"Don't tell me you actually like it here," Ariel pressed. "It's so *dry* and everything is so *heavy* and things *fall* and people live such short, ugly lives. . . ."

"My feet were killing me," Ursula admitted.

"*Think* about what you're doing. Think about the forces you are calling on. Do you really want to summon the Elder Gods if you don't have to? You know as well as I do that they don't always follow mortal rules or deals," Ariel said.

The sea witch was definitely looking unsure now. Ariel had to reel her in and finish it quickly.

"All right, so maybe *just* ruling Atlantica isn't really what you wanted," she said while she still had the moment. "But here."

She took the comb out of her hair. It sparkled in the sunlight, far more clear and detailed than something that small should have appeared. It shimmered and melted and transformed into a mighty golden trident, flashing brilliantly.

The crowd gasped; even Eric caught his breath at the magic and beauty.

Ursula's eyes grew big at the sight, utterly entranced.

"Just . . . let the people of Tirulia go. You can have Atlantica, and me. . . ."

"And your father?" Ursula demanded.

Ariel swallowed.

The whole reason for her being here . . . Her one constant desire for the last five years . . .

Would she trade his ancient life for a town of humans? Some of whom killed her fish . . . and one of whom loved her?

Ariel nodded. Once.

"Ariel, *no*!" Sebastian howled.

Ursula cackled with glee.

"All right, then! I can always try the circuex another time. I'll still have Triton! Come on down, pretty little mermaid! You've got yourself a deal!"

The Tirulians stumbled out of Ariel's way as she approached the dais and climbed up onto it.

"Ariel," Eric whispered. "Thank you. For my people. I am . . . so sorry."

She didn't say anything.

Flounder leapt up onto the rim of the fountain.

"Goodbye, old friend," she murmured, going over to give him a kiss.

"Ariel, don't," he begged.

"I'm sorry, Flounder." She stroked his fin. "But one thing you learn as a queen is . . . *to never trust the word of a sea witch!*"

And with that she let her hand fall into the salty water of the fountain . . .

. . . and with her other hand, she shot a bolt at Ursula's heart.

Eric

It took a moment for him to grasp what happened.

Just a moment before, the love of his life had surrendered herself, her kingdom, and her father to the evil sea witch to save *his* people, and was saying a sad goodbye to her fish friend.

Then, suddenly, her eyes were blazing as she hurled bolts of magic at Ursula.

The sea witch reacted surprisingly quickly; her tentacles shot up all around her torso, protecting it. Ariel's aim might not have been perfect, but it was enough to singe the side of Ursula's face and char a streak across two of her appendages.

"*Ha!* Ariel!" Eric shouted in joy. Was there *anything* she couldn't do?

Flotsam and Jetsam watched, dumfounded, for only a second before leaping to defend their mistress, throwing themselves in front of her. Eric grabbed one of them by the arm as he passed, yanking him back around and then smashing him in the face with his fist.

It felt really, really good.

"Father!" he heard Ariel cry.

The little mermaid threw herself at Ursula, grabbing at the ampoule.

The other manservant backhanded her away, a terrible, fleshy-sounding blow that sent Ariel reeling.

Eric launched himself at him, with no real plan besides wanting to feel the thug's neck being squeezed in his hands. Jetsam (or Flotsam) brought his dagger up to stop him and Eric smashed it aside with his forearm.

Shots rang out from somewhere behind him. Were the guards firing at the crowd? Above the crowd? Were they warning shots? Was there another threat he couldn't see?

Someone was firing back. *Who?*

Eric delivered a good blow—considering it was his left hand—into his opponent's side, but the man was strangely slippery, wiggling and twisting despite his apparent pain, away from Eric's reach. Out of the corner of his eye the prince could see Flotsam slowly pulling himself up, crawling over to help his brother.

Ariel was rushing the sea witch, trying to grab her father.

"I'll kill you all!" Ursula screamed. *"ALL OF YOU.* Humans, mer . . ."

She smashed the mermaid aside with some of her tentacles.

Others snaked themselves around Eric's throat.

He flailed his arms, trying to grasp at her face, her neck, anything he could reach—but his arms were too short.

He started to get dizzy as the air was cut off, and the world began to go dark.

Ariel

She fell to her knees, invisible bells ringing and tolling around her. She had never felt such pain, except when her voice was ripped from her body—and when it was returned. No one had ever dealt a physical blow to her before. She could hear nothing outside the beats of her own heart.

But her father needed her.

Staggering back to her feet, she refused to let the world swim away from her. Chaos was on all sides: people with mouths open like they were screaming, Flounder with his mouth open like he was suffocating. Eric was struggling. Ursula was wounded and looking around anxiously, trying to decide what to do or where to flee. She didn't move very well in the Dry World, on her own tentacles.

One of which waved slowly in the air and still held her father.

With a scream she could only feel, not hear, Ariel threw herself at Ursula. The ampoule slipped surprisingly easily into the mermaid's hands—suckers didn't work very well on dry land. Ariel tumbled to the ground, rolling, her father cradled in her arms.

More shots were fired over her head. Max whimpered and growled; her hearing was slowly returning.

People screamed. Some tried to run away, some huddled, some rushed the soldiers, some rushed the dais. In the back of her distracted mind Ariel noticed that there were some soldiers who didn't side with the palace guards—they were challenging them and trying to get to Ursula's side.

"*The sea witch!*" a familiar old woman's voice roared. "*Get her!* She's got Prince Eric!"

A mad scramble ensued as people rushed the dais. Some soldiers seemed to align themselves *against* the would-be saviors, aiming their muskets at them. Ariel curled up on the ground, protecting the delicate housing her father was in, like a shell wrapped around a nautilus. *Spirals and spirals . . .*

Max and Vareet came to her side and tried to defend her against the chaotic stampede.

"I'm fine! Go help Eric!" Ariel begged. "Where is—*oh!*"

The prince was struggling, Ursula's tentacles around his neck. Flotsam was sneaking up behind him, dagger raised.

Suddenly, with a final bit of strength, Eric hurled himself to the side, trying to smash Ursula's head into the base of the fountain.

Flotsam threw himself into the melee, dagger still at the ready.

"Don't let her touch the water!" Ariel screamed.

But it was too late. Grabbing the stone basin with her tentacles, Ursula dragged all three of them into the water, where they sank to the bottom.

Ariel leapt up and ran over . . . but all was still.

A single bubble rose to the surface and then popped.

And then a cloud of blood swirled up through the water, dark and ugly.

Ariel

"No . . ." she sobbed.

Flounder leapt up out of the water, which flew from his body in viscous, sparkling red and black drops.

"Eric is all right! Help him out—he's all tangled and trapped under her body!"

Ariel stumbled over to the fountain, her father still clutched in her arms. In the blurry depths she could see Ursula's massive body . . . and Flotsam's dagger somehow buried in her chest. The witch's face was growing pale, and her mouth hung open slackly. Her servant was stunned, entangled around her in eel form. Underneath the two of them Eric struggled weakly.

"Here!" she commanded, thrusting her father into Vareet's hands. "Guard him with your life!"

Trying not to choke on water polluted with the sea witch's foul ichor, Ariel dove in, reverting to her real body immediately. Tentacles and arms and legs were everywhere. She wrestled with the slick cecaelia body, heaving it aside. Grabbing the front of Eric's shirt, she pulled him away from Ursula, wedging her tail against the dead woman's midriff.

All the years she had thought about what she would do when she finally defeated Ursula, what she would say or experience . . . and now the sea witch was just an object, a blunt obstacle that was keeping her from saving Eric.

With a mighty heave Ariel managed to fling Eric out onto the side of the fountain, his chest cracking against the marble. He coughed and water came streaming out of his mouth.

"She did it! She defeated the terrible sea monster!" the apple seller cried.

The crowd screamed and cheered and clapped and went berserk.

Eric was a *mess*, all broken and bloody and barely upright, legs still dragging under the water. But he was alive. Flounder kept his distance, not wanting to breathe in any more blood.

Everything around them was bruised and broken but the confusion seemed to be slowly clearing up. There was a pile of mostly unconscious soldier bodies on the dais—ones with tiny black octopus insignia on their sleeves. A triumphant ragtag crew stood above them: Argent with her stained and cracked walking stick, which she now held like a club; Grimsby, who had somehow managed to acquire a musket and was holding it quite steadily; two seagulls; several loyal soldiers and their captain; a soprano and two bass clarinetists.

Vareet stood by the fountain, Triton cradled safely in her small arms.

"So this is what winning feels like," Ariel said. "I think I like it."

Eric groaned and would have slipped back underwater if she hadn't grabbed him.

Eric

If it had been up to the prince, there would have been happily ever afters right then. The bad guy had been defeated, the love of his life was holding him, she had just said something funny, the crowd was cheering—the perfect place for an opera to end.

Alas, real life was a little more complicated than that.

And real blood, not stage blood, was continuing to leak out his nose.

The captain and the remaining loyal guards—who would all be rewarded richly later—scanned the situation and reacted appropriately, placing themselves between the prince and the confused, curious, adoring crowd. "You, Decard," he said weakly. "Send two men to go find Carlotta in the castle. . . . In the basement . . ."

"Yes, Your Highness, immediately." The captain saluted and spun off.

With that last order given, Eric succumbed to a wave of weakness and began to slip back into the water.

"Nope—no, you don't," Ariel said, hoisting him back up and all the way out of the fountain. Grimsby was there instantly, offering his shoulder to lean on. Even in his current state Eric couldn't help watching the mermaid with her glorious tail thrown out for balance, sparkling in the sunlight. Behind them he could hear oohs and gasps as the townspeople saw her clearly for the first time.

He couldn't blame them. She was magnificent.

He tried not to put all his weight on the old butler. Things shifted perspective and swam before him—unsurprisingly, there was water in his ears.

"Well done, Prince Eric!" Grimsby said, voice shaking with excitement. "Good show!"

"It was you and Vareet and Max who really got the ball rolling," he said with a grin. Then he put his arm around the other man and gave him a good squeeze. "You mean so much to me, Grims. Have I ever said that before? I was so worried about you."

"O-oh, well—there, there," Grimsby stuttered, smiling but looking around with embarrassment. "You're a bit out of your head. Shhh."

Ariel was saying something to the fish in the fountain. Eric felt a strange sense of loss. The fish was truly incredible, unusual by any account. But all he saw was a glaze-eyed animal who apparently was saying something in its silent fishy language, and it made Ariel throw back her head and laugh like a girl. She kissed it on its head and then slipped off the fountain, legs forming as she did.

"I'm getting better at this," she said, turning to face her human friends and twirling the trident.

"I think this is yours," Vareet said, handing her the glass ampoule and curtsying. "What is it?"

"This, brave girl, is my father," Ariel said, kissing her on the forehead. She carefully set the jar down on the ground— then shot a bolt at it.

Smoke—no, water vapor—swirled up and up and up into the sky. On the ground, the polyp grew and lengthened and stretched and hardened into a man.

A man that Eric now remembered: he must have been seven or eight feet tall, broad, and somehow lit from within. He seemed more real than the petty humans around him, the cobbled streets, the fountain; as though they were all a child's drawings while he was the original, badly copied. His beard was white and flowed down over him, looking the way Eric had always imagined the patriarchs in the Old Testament. His skin was a coppery shade, more precious metal than flesh. His eyes were almost hidden beneath a bushy brow, but sparks shone there.

When Eric saw him last, that fateful wedding day, Triton had the tail of a fish. Now he had two broad, strong legs.

"Father," Ariel said, and a thousand meanings were in that word: apology, sorrow, joy, love.

"Ariel," her father breathed, choking on the first word he had said in years. Then without a moment's hesitation he wrapped his arms around her and began to cry.

All the humans around them felt similarly to Eric, he could tell: amazed but vaguely uncomfortable, wanting to leave the two alone. Even in his emotions, the king of the merfolk was mightier than mortals.

"I am so sorry," Ariel whispered. She, oddly, was *not* crying, though she hugged her father back firmly. "For everything."

"You are forgiven. For everything," he said, stroking her hair.

"How?" she asked in wonder.

"Someday, you will understand," Triton said with a smile. "Perhaps when you are a mother."

Then he looked around and seemed to notice the small crowd of mortals.

"Father, this is Prince Eric," Ariel said smoothly, taking Triton's hand and indicating Eric with her other. "He has been a great help in your rescue and defeating Ursula."

"Eric," Triton said neutrally, "I thank you for all the service you have rendered to my royal self and the mer of the sea."

"King Triton," Eric said, bowing his head. "It is an honor to meet you."

"All of these people, all of these *humans*, helped save you," Ariel said. "This is Grimsby, Eric's right-hand man. This is Vareet, who, despite her age and size, risked her life to get us valuable information. This is Argent, who knew about mermaids and can apparently wield a shillelagh with no small skill. Sebastian and Flounder you already know. Jona the seagull and Max the dog were both instrumental in defeating Ursula. Scuttle is the reason we are all here today, and why you are now free!"

"I did what I could," Sebastian said modestly from her pocket.

"I thank you all," Triton said with a bow. "Would that I could stay and reward you as you so honorably deserve right now—but I miss my home, and must needs return to the sea at once. Ariel, my trident."

She handed it over gracefully and formally, but might have been gritting her back teeth.

"You will be recipients of my gratitude shortly," the king added, addressing the townspeople in front of him. "The sea does not forget."

He put his arm out and Ariel took it. But not until after she gave Eric a quick kiss on the cheek. It was so familiar, so *Honey, I'm going out for a few minutes, back soon*, that Triton—and not a few other people—gasped. Grimsby looked as delighted as a gossipy old hen. Vareet looked embarrassed, disgusted, and vaguely amused. Max barked.

"See you in a few tides," she whispered.

Eric grinned and then kissed her back firmly on her lips, tipping her head back so he wouldn't accidentally bleed onto it.

The townsfolk cheered.

When they were done, Ariel scooped Flounder out of the fountain, holding him under her arm. She and her father walked through the crowds—which parted, almost everyone bowing to the mer couple. They went straight to the docks and leapt off together, tails slapping the water as they dove down.

"*HA!*" shouted the old woman with the club. "I got to see *two*! *TWO* mermaids!"

Jona

This was the second time in a month that she had been conscripted by a foreign entity to carry a message of grave importance. The gull winged her way out over the sea laden with a sense of historic gravity, the special roll of paper tied to her leg and tucked up into her feathers. She was probably the only bird in the world who carried regular communiqués between two of the major—though somewhat self-important—civilized races of the world. It was something to think about.

Crazy joy overtook her, and she allowed herself exactly one loop-de-loop and a single long *whoop!* before returning to her original heading and task.

She was, after all, her great-grandfather's great-grandgull.

Sometimes the crazy was hard to keep in.

Eric

There were terrible, terrible messes to clean up afterward.

For the first and perhaps only time in history, a seagull was used to deliver a message to the ships sent out to sea—to prevent them from bombing Atlantica. While the prince was fairly certain Ariel and her dad would stop it in time, it didn't hurt to offer an official order to prevent them before another deadly storm was unleashed.

Carlotta was rescued and royally thanked. She was given a vacation (which she didn't take), a snug country house (which she did), and a significant raise.

Eric had his men chain Flotsam and Jetsam together and toss them into the ocean. Either they would be found and treated appropriately by the mer, or . . . not. Not really his problem.

Then he oversaw a careful scripting of the official record of events of the day, to be read, announced, distributed, shared, and generally understood by all the good citizens of Tirulia who had borne witness to the events. There was no mass hypnosis spell to make everyone forget the existence of mermaids this time. Now everyone knew. It was important that they all knew the *same* thing, and didn't concoct potentially dangerous fake news about what happened.

Except that he *did* have to draft a fake formal announcement for the death of Princess Vanessa. Tirulians would understand what really happened; the rest of the continent would only know the faintest details: she died. Possibly drowned.

Troops from everywhere had to be recalled immediately.

Ambassadors and emissaries had to be thoroughly debriefed, and in some cases exiled.

It was endless and exhausting work. Eric stayed up until the wee hours of the night trying to get everything done. Sometimes, given a spare moment, he would glance ironically at the moon and think about how he used to compose music at that time. But that was all right. He had a duty to his kingdom. Being prince wasn't just fun and games.

There *were* a few bright moments—like when he summoned Vareet into his office.

The little maid had passed out from exhaustion the afternoon after everything happened, and slept for over a day. Eric couldn't imagine what was going on in the poor girl's head, in thrall to a witch-princess for years and then saved by a mermaid girl.

She came in wide-eyed and understandably suspicious when the prince smiled at her and shook her hand. "Nice to meet you, formally."

She continued to look confused, but her eyes widened in interest.

"Vareet, you have borne more than any of us, in some ways, and come through it all bravely, helping us out in our darkest hour. Of course you shall have whatever you like— *fresh*, ahem, drawing paper, toy soldiers, a pony—you have but to name it.

"But also: I have hired a tutor from the Academia to come live at the castle. She will teach you how to read and write and do maths. And probably Latin. Sorry about that, but it's part of the package. Then you can make a choice, when you are caught up: either stay here as my personal secretary, or go to university and attain whatever else you wish to do with your life."

Vareet remained silent.

The prince suddenly felt awkward, something he had rarely experienced. He had no idea what the little girl was thinking. Should he repeat what he had said, slower? Would that be insulting?

Then suddenly she flung her arms around his neck and buried her head in his chest.

Eric laughed and hugged her back. *That* was the happily-ever-after moment he had been waiting for, and it wasn't even his.

Ariel

Triton's arrival was epic, although a *truly* epic official parade was planned for the next day. Flounder, once returned to the sea, shot ahead and told every fish he met. By the time Ariel and her father got close to Atlantica, a massive crowd had already formed: most of the mer, and many, many other people of the sea. Whales and sharks and minnows and sardines and tuna and cod and octopodes . . . Even all the little corals, anemone, and barnacles came out to wave their fronds.

"FATHER!"

Five slippery, sparkling mergirls shot out of the crowd and wrapped themselves around him like the fat tentacles of a kraken. Attina hugged Ariel.

"You did it," she whispered, pressing her forehead to

her sister's like they used to when sharing secrets. "You actually did it."

"I did," Ariel said with a smile.

"You really are something." The oldest mer princess smiled and shook her head. When the others regretfully disengaged, she, too, went to greet her father, with a solid—if slightly more formal—embrace.

"Good people of Atlantica," Triton said, holding his trident aloft, *"I have returned!"*

His voice boomed out through the water, far more commanding even than Ariel's newly regained voice. The crowd went wild: cheering, flapping their tails, slapping, bubbling, gurgling, swimming in circles.

The king himself was only too happy to retire quietly that first night, drink goldenwine with his closest friends, swim lustily through the kingdom, and generally stretch his tail, arms, and fins the way he hadn't in years. When his daughters finally forced him into his coral bed, he only resisted a little.

The celebrations, feasting, and partying the next day were like nothing mortal eyes had ever witnessed. Old rivalries were forgotten; the barracuda even brought gifts of apology. Ariel surprised everyone by singing some of what Sebastian had composed so far for his "Tribute to the Return of the King."

And on the third day, everyone finally got back to work.

Triton sat at the throne, reviewing all the policies and paperwork Ariel had managed while he was gone. He did not use a desk, instead having people hold tablets, decrees, and documents *for* him while he read. The king frowned and muttered and said things like "Mmmh. Good point about the right-of-way" and "I would have told the rays to consider an alternate breeding ground" and "Bah, the Rites. I always hated dealing with those. Always made Threll and Sebastian do it."

At this Ariel raised her eyebrows at Sebastian. The little crab shrugged, chagrined. The seahorse coughed nervously.

"Overall, a very impressive job," Triton said, raising his eyebrows as he studied his youngest daughter. "Please don't take this the wrong way, Ariel, but I am pleasantly surprised by how you have matured. Your time ruling has shown wisdom, pragmatism, quick thinking, and unique solutions to difficult problems. You might even have surpassed your old man."

"Thank you, Father."

"You know," he added, speculatively, "I *could* use a hand with all of this. A right-fin man, or mer. I know you probably want to be off again with your sisters, or singing—"

"Nope. No," Ariel interrupted immediately.

"Well, then, it's settled," the old mer said with a grin. "Father-daughter day! Every day! What a team!"

Ariel cleared her throat. Her thumbs passed over her fingers and back, as if thinking of something to sign.

"Actually, Father, I had another idea. . . ."

"This isn't about you going to the surface again, is it? Because let me tell you—"

"Hang on," Ariel said, putting her hand up to stop him—something she never would have done before. She did it calmly, without anger or a sudden burst of temper at his attitude; also something new. "We'll get to my career options in a moment. Let me first make it absolutely clear, however, that I love Eric and want to be with him. And I can do that for at least one week a month, with your help."

"WITH MY HELP? IF YOU THINK FOR ONE SECOND I—"

Ariel fixed him with a cool eye. "Remember what happened last time I had to find an alternate solution for walking on land? I'm sure there are other ways out there, and I'm sure I could find them. Do you really want me doing that?"

"Are you threatening me?"

"I am merely stating what will inevitably happen if you resist this. I *will* see Eric. If you want to turn him into a mer for a week every month, I'm fine with that, too. However, currently he is a prince with actual duties, and I doubt he has the time for such things."

"And what about *you*? A *princess* with actual duties?"

"Father, I've ruled, and while I might be good at it, I don't like it. I want to do what I've *always* wanted to do." She pointed out at the dark ocean. "*Explore*. Meet new people. Learn new languages. Discover new *things* and the artists who make them. I want to find out what happened to the Hyperboreans. I want to reengage trade with the Tsangalu. I want to know if there's anyone else out there like Ursula. . . ."

Triton—and Sebastian, and Flounder—shuddered.

"Maybe they're not all *like* her," she said quickly. "Father, the world of the mer has been getting smaller and smaller, consumed with ourselves and our own arts, thoughts, and philosophies for far too long. Humans have conquered most of the Dry World—we need to unite the World Under the Sea, for survival if nothing else."

Triton frowned, but not skeptically. He scratched his left eyebrow.

"But this is the job for an ambassador or an emissary, not a princess. . . ."

"Who better? I have royal blood. I have interacted with humans. No one, *no* one of the mer is more qualified."

"But . . . you're my youngest daughter. . . ."

"Dad, let her go," Attina said softly. "She doesn't want to be here. If you want to keep her at all, this is the only way. Otherwise she will just leave. And not come back."

"It's true," Flounder agreed. "She's got itchy fins."

"As much as I'm probably gonna regret what I'm about to say," the eldest princess continued hesitantly, "what about this? I'm no Ariel, but if you need help now and then, and it needs to be from a royal princess, I'll swim up to the task."

"Really?" Ariel asked in surprise. "You mean it?"

Her father looked doubtful. "But—"

"Let Ariel start by being our official envoy to the idiot humans whom her idiot prince rules. That will give her time with him, and we can see how good her negotiating skills are—like keeping them out of our hair and the Great Tides that feed us."

Triton and Ariel both looked at her in surprise.

"Well, that's . . ." Triton said, scratching his beard. "That's . . ."

"A really good idea," Ariel finished, smiling. "An excellent compromise."

"Yeah, well, I'm second in line to rule, you know, so . . ." Attina said, stretching. "I'm sort of a natural at this." She winked at Flounder.

"I haven't agreed to anything yet," Triton growled.

"It's okay," Attina said, kissing him on the cheek. "*We* have. Say, do I get a necklace or day-crown or something for my new job? I need to look the part."

Triton looked at Sebastian helplessly. "I thought I was getting my kingdom back. I don't even have my *daughters* back listening to me."

"Ah, women. What can you do?" Sebastian said in displeasure.

"Listen to them," Flounder suggested. "Since they both outrank you."

Ariel laughed, and so did Attina.

And eventually even Triton joined in with a chuckle.

Ariel and Eric

A full moon gleamed over the bay. Eric leapt onto the banister of the long stairs that led to the beach and slid down it, balanced on his stocking feet with arms outstretched. Ariel, standing in the shallows, laughed softly.

"Aren't you getting a little old for that sort of thing?"

"I feel like a kid again," he said, scooping her up in his arms. He spun her around and she laughed again, drips of water flying off her toes like diamonds in the moonlight. Then he put her down and they kissed. Properly. For a long time. For the first time Ariel understood the human expression "making one's toes curl."

"So what's the story?" Eric asked when they finally parted.

Ariel shrugged and sighed. "I'm to negotiate a path for your ships to take when entering the open sea, past the coastal shelf—to not disturb us. Also to work out a schedule so humans avoid the beaches at turtle and plover nesting times. After this week is up, I then get to make an exploratory trip to the territory held by the Neraide. We never lost complete contact with them, but we haven't exchanged diplomatic pleasantries in a long time, or officially visited."

"Neraide . . . Greek? Are they like the ancient Greeks?"

"No, they are mer," she said with a smile.

"Of course." Eric bowed. "I should absolutely know better than to say things like that now. Forgive me!"

"Forgiven. And you? What have you been doing?"

"I'm trying to set things in order, too, so *I* can eventually make a trip . . . to the islands of Arawakania in the lands to the west. My father would prefer I go to Ranahatta, but I want to see what tropical waters are like. I hear there are reefs you can just walk out to, as colorful as a rainbow."

"You'll have to tell me all about it," Ariel said with a touch of jealousy.

"I thought you would come along and lead our ship into safe harbors," he said, tweaking her nose.

"Maybe. Mer move slower than human ships, and mer kings slowest of all."

"So is there a chance? That we could ever be together?

Forever?" Eric asked, trying not to sound childish. Trying not to sound desperate.

It was adorable.

"There is always a chance," Ariel said, kissing him on the cheek. "And each day, it looks better and better."

"I'd leave Tirulia to my sister in a heartbeat. Say the word and I'm mer forever."

"I'm . . . exploring that option as well. But what would your people think?"

"What, are you kidding me? They're already positively moony over the story of you and me, and the defeat of Ursula. . . . The only thing better than having an official mermaid ambassador would be having her marry their besotted Mad Prince and the two living happily ever after. Especially if I gave 'em an opera or two about it."

"I can see it now. Sebastian and Eric: *A Tale of Two Worlds*," Ariel said, putting her hand up as if reading a sign.

"I work alone."

"Yes, so does Sebastian. Ah well, another great idea tossed into the Great Tide . . ."

"*Hey*, check this out," Eric said, pulling up his sleeve and holding out his arm.

The name *Ariel* was written out—in mer runes! It circled his arm like the sort of band a warrior would wear, and glistened with oil he had rubbed into it.

"Eric! What did you *do*?"

"What? Don't you like it?"

"I love it, but . . ."

"Until we have wedding rings, I thought it was a nice permanent commitment. Argent did it! Sebastian helped me with the letters."

"It . . . must have hurt."

"You have *no* idea. That's how much I love you," he said, kissing her on the forehead.

They held hands and walked down the beach under the moon, talking about nothing important. Not mermaids, not armies, not sea witches, not fathers, not kingdoms, not distant lands to the west. What they *did* talk about, no one could much hear; there was a breeze, and the lapping of waves, and the cry of a strangely alert gull. And when they kissed in the light of the moon again, no one saw, and no one cared—except for themselves.

And they were very, very happy.

Vareet

The moon was just waning. Ariel had gone.

Vareet looked out her window grumpily. She knew the mermaid would be back soon, but it was still hard. Eric was nice—and awfully cute—but she didn't feel as close to him. Her tutor was endlessly patient. Carlotta was doting and Grimsby spoiled her rotten . . . but none of them was Ariel.

At least the seagulls were a constant presence. Scuttle had been moved to a comfy nook in a belfry near her, extremely happy with his glittering medal, luxurious retirement, and doting great-grandgull. Jona was made official bird emissary and messenger, keeping lines open between the mer and Eric until Ariel returned. And when Jona wasn't needed, she tended to stick around Vareet. They couldn't talk, but they did communicate in their own way. The gull even rode on her shoulder sometimes like a falcon.

Still, Vareet felt a little lonely.

She sighed and climbed into bed, wondering how she would ever get to sleep with all these thoughts in her head.

Then she noticed something on her pillow.

A beautiful, swirled brown and white shell like the one Ursula used to wear, but larger. A whelk, not a nautilus. Vareet picked it up in wonder, turning it over in her hands, admiring its gleam in the moonlight. On a whim she put it to her ear.

Her eyes widened.

In the depths of the shell, she could hear what must have been the echo of distant waves . . . and also the song of a mermaid.